COLLIDING WORLDS VOL. 2

A SCIENCE FICTION SHORT STORY SERIES

KRISTINE KATHRYN RUSCH AND DEAN WESLEY SMITH

PUBLISHING

CONTENTS

INTRODUCTION

MAYBE JUST A LITTLE BIT ALIEN

DEAN WESLEY SMITH

Sixty of my science fiction stories and sixty of Kristine Kathryn Rusch's science fiction stories combined in a six-volume set called Colliding Worlds. One hundred and twenty science fiction short stories from two major bestselling writers.

This is volume #2, although I must admit, the volumes do not have to be read in any order. You can start with volume #6 if you want.

In fact, each book stands alone as a great twenty-story collection. That's what we intended, but we also intended to do a major collection that in the old days, would have gotten us a lot of attention in the science fiction world. (Sadly, that world is now dead.)

But as you might imagine, there were a number of problems with the construction of this project. We both had far and away enough stories, so that wasn't a problem. But somehow Kris and I had to figure out how to organize these six volumes so that they made some sort of sense. Not so much to readers, but for ourselves.

Since we left the choices of which stories would be in each volume to ourselves, meaning I picked my ten and she picked her ten, we really needed a unifying theme of some sort per volume.

It was Kris finally came up with six general topic categories, which helped a lot. After editing so many issues of different magazines, she is a master at finding organizing themes for books or issues of a magazine. (I would say "Jedi Master" but not so sure of her swinging a light saber.)

This second volume in the six she just called "Aliens." That was nothing more than an organizing word, but wow did it help me decide which ten of my stories would fit in this book.

What I found interesting is that my ten alien stories are mostly light and goofy, while Kris treats aliens in a far more serious way. Nothing wrong with either direction. Just another example of how different we are as writers and our perspectives on the world.

TEN STORIES

BY

DEAN WESLEY SMITH

MY SOCKS ROLLED DOWN

DEAN WESLEY SMITH

MY SOCKS ROLLED DOWN

A person can only go so far in life with only one pair of magic socks. I know, I know, it's tough to imagine anyone only having one pair of magic socks, but you can come and search the three drawers in my small bedroom of my trailer, or look under my old second-hand green couch, or even check the coin-op laundry where I do my clothes. You won't find more than one pair. And I wear them every day and have for my entire life, all twenty-three years of it.

Sad, huh?

I've never had more than one pair. My mom gave them to me on her deathbed when I was born, rolling my little feet into the magic white cotton like putting little rubbers on two small penises. I don't remember the act, of course, but for some reason, that pair of magic socks are the only pair I have ever had.

As with all magic socks, they fit me perfectly and always have, growing perfectly with me right up until I stopped growing at five-four and a half.

And they never wear out. I wash them once a week, never leaving the washer or dryer while they are in there. I've heard of people stealing magic socks. It's bad enough only having one pair. I really can't imagine those few poor souls who have none.

What scares me is that I am only one pair of magic socks away from those poor, sockless souls. It would really be better if I could find a second pair. And three pair would be perfect. I might be able to do something with my life if I had three. That way I wouldn't have to do laundry so often.

Well, my dream to have enough money to buy more magic socks finally came true on January 13th at five in the evening. I was sitting there, watching my old television, hoping a truck didn't go by outside on the gravel road and shake the rabbit ears I had made of tin foil.

Every week I bought a lottery ticket, and every week I played the same numbers and watched the lottery drawing on television before turning the channel over to *Wheel*. Can't let a night go by without staring at Vanna's tits, you understand.

If I just had more than one pair of magic socks, she might talk to me.

I had my feet kicked up on the old pine coffee table while I sat on the couch drinking a Pabst, the best beer anywhere for the price. My boots were by the front door and my magic socks looked like it was time for another trip to the coin-op.

The first number was six, and the magic socks on my feet tingled a little. The last time they tingled like that I found a five-dollar bill on the sidewalk.

Six was the first number I always picked. It was how old I was when I shot my first rabbit with Grandad's twenty-two.

Next number was eight, and my old magic socks were giving me a real itchy feel. Last time they did that, when I was sixteen, I got laid for the first time by the mother of my best friend at the time.

Eight was the age I was when Dad brought home my new stepmother who stayed for two years before she disappeared one night and Dad came back kind of muddy and smiling.

I took a swallow of the Pabst and set it down on the coffee table as the next number came up.

Fourteen, and my magic socks were rubbing my feet so hard they were getting almost hot. In all my years I'd never had my magic socks get so excited.

"Down, boys, down," I said, reaching for the drawer and pulling out this week's ticket to make sure I had the numbers right. I did. The first three were six, eight, fourteen. Fourteen was when they arrested Dad for killing stepmom number three, or maybe it was number four, I wasn't sure.

The police talked to me for a while, then said that I was going to a foster home, but I ran off, got my clothes and hunting equipment and Dad's hidden rifle and ammunition and made it off into the mountains along the coast. I camped out until I turned eighteen, which was my next number.

The guy on the television watched the old ping-pong ball slide up the tube and he said, "Eighteen."

My magic socks felt like dancing, so that was what I did, got up and danced around the living room for a moment, letting them celebrate. I really liked how they were hugging my feet like a woman hugging a long lost lover. That felt great to be honest.

With four right numbers I had already won a few thousand. Just one more of the two and things would be really fine.

My next number was twenty. That's when I moved into this doublewide trailer up Jenson Creek.

The old guy that lived here before me is buried out back, and so far no one has missed him at all. I told two neighbors he got sick and moved into Portland and I was renting the trailer. That seemed to keep them happy, and I buried the old man deep enough no coyotes were going to dig him up. Now after three years, a tree was growing on his grave. Nice little thing, too.

The old guy had on his one pair of magic socks when I shot him, but weirdly enough, when I went to shoot him, my aim suddenly went bad and instead of hitting the old guy in the chest, I hit him in the foot, right through one magic sock, blowing it all apart.

As the old guy jumped backwards, screaming and swearing and holding his torn-up foot, I shot again.

And again the gun seemed to have a mind of its own and it shot the guy in the other foot. I gave up shooting him and tried to pound his head, but I just kept missing like he was moving around, even though he wasn't. The old guy bled out after a few minutes and died anyway, and his magic socks were worthless and dead as well. A real bummer and to this day I have no idea why I couldn't shoot straight that day.

The announcer said, "Twenty."

My magic socks sort of flipped my feet up in the air so hard I went over backwards, smashed into the wall and hit the floor hard.

Then, even though I was hurting something awful, the socks got me to my feet and ran around the small living room of the trailer, bouncing me off the walls like I was so much kindling.

"Slow down!" I shouted at the white socks on my feet, but they didn't.

I heard a thought clear as a bell in my mind. *You dumb idiot, don't you realize you've just won enough money to buy a dozen more magic socks and I won't have to put up with your smelly feet all the damned time.*

My magic socks could talk to me. Wow!

"How come you've never said anything before now?"

What for? Holding a conversation with you would be like talking to an outhouse wall, like you did for all those years we were camping.

"Hey, nothing wrong with—"

Shut the hell up and let's see if you've won the entire thing!

The announcer said, "Twenty-three."

My final number, because that's how old I am now.

An instant later my magic socks had me walking on the ceiling, then doing a moon-walk backwards across my ceiling and down the wall.

Now you can buy a thousand pairs of magic socks. And you can retire me.

"What happens if I don't want a thousand pair?"

The magic socks stopped me cold in the middle of the floor. *What did you mean by that?*

"I didn't know socks could talk. I'm not so sure I want all them living here and talking to me."

There was a nice silence in my mind, like normal, then my magic socks sort of growled low and deep, like a wild animal ready to attack.

Then I decided something real clear like. "You know, I could buy a huge house and have rooms full of magic socks and tell them that none of them could ever talk to me. Only to each other."

I smiled for a moment before I realized that my magic socks had made me say all that.

"I'm not going to do that and you can't make me," I said.

Again there was a low growl, then the socks said inside my head. *That's it. I'm still young, I have a life to live, other socks to meet, baby magic socks to create. I don't need to stay here with you anymore.*

"You're my socks and I'm not taking you off," I said.

You are such an idiot. You think you are in control. All of you humans believe that, letting us live off your energy, giving us special places in your life. But we control you, every last one of you. And idiot boy, it's time I moved on.

Now I was getting mad. "And just how do you think you're going to do that if I don't take you off?"

The voice of the socks sort of gave off a snorting sound, then I walked against my will over to the wall, up the wall, and out onto the middle of the ceiling, hanging upside down from my white socks.

Oops, the voice inside my head said, and suddenly I was hurtling toward the green shag carpet. I tried to get my arms up to break my fall, but I couldn't. I hit on the top of my head and flopped sideways.

"That hurt!" I shouted.

Damn it all, the voice said.

My magic socks were trying to kill me!

No, shit, Sherlock.

With that my magic socks walked me to my phone and made me pick it up and dial 911.

Then, when the operator asked what was my emergency, I said without wanting to, "I killed an old guy and he's buried out under a small tree in my backyard. I can't take the guilt. I'm going to kill myself."

Then I laid the phone down and walked down the hall to where I kept my rifles, all of them loaded.

My magic socks weren't allowing me to say anything, so instead I just thought at the socks really, really hard that they should stop.

Wow, a thought, the socks said. *From the idiot. Stunning.*

"Why are you doing this?" I asked as at the same time I dug into the guns and pulled out my favorite without wanting to.

Because I'm tired of your sweating feet, I want to meet other magic socks as you call them. Actually we are called Yekcoj, a race millions of years older than humans.

I just didn't believe that. My magic socks had lost it, gone off the deep end.

You want to know what we really look like?

Suddenly my white socks shifted around my feet and combined, with both of my legs fitting into the teeth-lined mouth of what looked like a nasty groundhog, only with scales and ten eyes and four arms.

To be honest, I'm tired of you standing and walking around in my mouth. Why my people thought this was a good idea is beyond me.

One long black eye blinked at me and then my magic socks were back, white as ever.

The socks walked me back out to the living room. The operator on the phone was saying, "Sir! Sir! Help is on the way."

I sat down on the couch against my will, put the gun in my mouth against my will, and put my finger on the trigger against my will.

Thanks for the worst twenty-three years any socks could ever dream of living. See ya.

I pulled the trigger.

The socks laughed and pulled themselves off of my body's feet.

I could see my body through the eyes of the magic socks, or weird groundhog or whatever it was. The gunshot had blown most of my brain against the front window and some part of my skull was hanging off the drapes.

Now you've done it, I thought at the socks.

What...? What...? What are you doing here? You can't still be here, in my mind, you're dead.

Never heard of the Four Laws of Magic Socks, have you?

I hadn't known them either until I died. Now I knew them and a lot more stuff I had never known when alive. Weird how dying made me a lot smarter.

What four laws? the magic socks asked.

It was part of the treaty with humans when they allowed your people to come here to live.

I hadn't known that either until that gun blew my brains out.

Law #1: You must always let humans wear you at any time.

Yeah, yeah, the magic socks said.

Law #2: You can't speak to any humans or let them know of your presence. Broke that one, didn't you?

Just go on, my magic socks said.

Law #3: You must always follow the orders of your human unless it conflicts with Law #4, which is that Magic Socks cannot allow harm to come to humans unless otherwise avoided.

Oh, my magic socks said softly.

Let's get back into place on my feet, I thought at my not-so-faithful magic sock companion, *so when the Magic Sock police get here, they'll know what to do with you and with me.*

Together we moved over to my body and formed clean white socks around my now very dead feet.

Outside, coming up the dirt road, the police sirens filled the narrow valley. Back when I was alive, that would have scared me enough to go get my gun. Now it just made me laugh.

Too bad I'm never going to get to collect the winnings on that ticket. I might have bought a big place and lots of your friends for you to play with.

Please, please, please would you just shut up for a few minutes? my magic socks said, clearly angry.

Nah, I thought at my magic socks as together we rested around the feet of my dead body. *I figure we can spend our last few hours together going over all the great years we had together.*

My magic socks made a groaning sound.

Remember that day when I was four and had to take a crap really bad, and didn't make it to the bathroom and crapped all over you? Wasn't that a great time? I think that pulled us closer together, don't you?

My magic socks said nothing, once again following the Second Law of Magic Socks.

The police knocked hard on the door, then shoved it open, covering their mouths when they saw the mess my brains left on the window and drapes.

"He's got magic socks on," one cop said, pointing to my feet and me and my magic sock companion.

"How could he do this, then? Magic socks won't let you hurt yourself."

Both cops looked at each other, then one of them said, "Rogue Socks."

"Call the Magic Sock Police representative," another cop said. "If his socks went rogue, it means this guy is still in there with the socks."

I made old magic socks move what used to be my big toe up and down like I was doing a mini-nod.

"Shit," one cop said and both backed up.

So they call you rogues, huh? I thought at my magic socks.

My socks said nothing.

Remember that time I was all out of toilet paper and needed to use you to wipe my ass? Great fun, huh?

Hey, idiot-boy, my magic socks thought at me, *with all your new knowledge you should know what's going to happen next, now that you told those cops I was a rogue and you were trapped in here with me.*

"We do it together," one cop said.

"Count of three," the other cop said as they stepped closer to me and my magic socks.

Suddenly I realized what the two cops planned to do. When magic socks went rogue and killed a human, they had to be killed at once, not only to stop the rogue socks, but to release the soul of the departed.

Hey! I thought at my magic socks, suddenly very panicked. *Get us out of here. Make a run for it!*

I'm not allowed to talk to you, remember?

But you're supposed to follow my instructions. Run!

The two cops got closer and both aimed their pistols, one at my right foot, one at my left.

I don't have to, my magic socks said. *I'm rogue, remember?*

"One," a cop said, pointing a big gun at my old right foot while the other cop pointed at my left foot.

Don't you want to live?

My magic socks laughed. *With you? Not any more. Twenty-three years was more than enough.*

"Two," the cop said.

I should have used you for toilet paper more often, I thought at my magic socks.

I should have killed you long before now, my magic socks thought back.

Screw you, I thought at my magic socks.

Another original thought, my magic socks thought back.

"Three," the cop said.

There was a huge explosion and I could feel myself slipping away, fading into the darkness.

And the last thing I heard before I vanished into the blackness was the last thought of my magic socks.

Oh, thank the Great Sock this is over!

THE GREAT ALIEN VIBRATION

DEAN WESLEY SMITH

THE GREAT ALIEN VIBRATION

As first dates go, it had been a failure for him, a total success for her.

As first alien contacts go, he would walk funny for a few days.

Jimmy Loche had first met Stephanie Peters at work. Actually, at first he only saw her from a distance. But he considered that meeting-without-talking sometimes a much safer form of interaction for him.

He found her amazingly attractive. Short brown hair, large oval glasses that accented her green eyes, and a figure not well hidden by her white lab coat she always wore while working.

She most likely stood about two inches taller than he did, but at five-foot-five, he had grown used to being around taller women and didn't much mind it at all. Especially if they talked to him. Always a key to his not minding the height difference.

She was a bio-tech chemist; he worked in the engineering side of the same company. The company they both worked for was cutting-edge development and research into devices that would be needed in space. The company had numbers of clients, including NASA and five different private firms.

On the third time that he noticed Stephanie, he smiled at her and she smiled back. That had made his day.

They kept smiling at each other at various points of the day over the next few weeks, usually around either arriving at work through the massive stone lobby or at lunch in the plant-filled white and tan company cafeteria.

At work he usually wore jeans, an open collared dress shirt, and tennis shoes. And they both always carried iPads. He started tipping his iPad to her to say hello across any distance and she would smile and nod back.

Starting the second week of tipping, she tipped her iPad back and things moved forward from there.

Two weeks later, they had talked a few times, she had seen he was shorter than her and hadn't seemed to mind or even notice. And they had discovered they were both major movie fans.

Through a friend of a friend in another cutting-edge company, Jimmy managed to score seats in a private first screening of a new and very secret feature film that used new technology in theaters.

His friend told him that he would be the only man in the small test theater, since the show was a test-run to see how women liked it.

Jimmy had no problem with that.

In hindsight, he should have had a problem with that. He should have just asked Stephanie to see the new Marvel movie. But no, he had to feel like someone special and get her into a first-run test of a brand new movie with brand new technology in the theater.

She had agreed to go with him, of course. It was special and very secret. They didn't even know the name of the movie.

But that evening, when they met in front of their company headquarters, it was the first time he had seen her without her lab coat. And she looked even better in jeans, a white blouse, and tennis shoes. They had decided to just go in their normal casual clothes so he remained in what he had worn to work that day, only with a clean shirt.

It seemed that casual to both of them was the Jimmy level, which boded well for the night ahead.

They walked, talking all the way to a local chain restaurant for a fun meal, then did the ten minute walk from there to the small theater in the back of a local university science building.

It seemed she liked to walk as much as he did, and considering he had an old Ford with far too many fast-food meal remains on the back-seat floor, it was good she liked to walk. He hated cleaning that car.

There was no popcorn or anything at the theater, and only a man taking their tickets and indicating where they should sit. From the looks of it, there sure wouldn't be trailers for new coming attractions either.

Over dinner, he and Stephanie had laughed and both figured that even if the movie was the worst thing ever, it was a fun first date. He had liked the sound of the word "first" being used in such a fashion to modify date.

Clearly she liked him. And he clearly liked her.

So they ended up in the back row of the theater. There were about thirty large chairs in all up a steep-stair-step theater, with only sixteen people spread out in the thirty chairs.

Almost everyone had come in pairs. He saw no woman sitting alone. And as he had been warned, he was the only man in the room.

"These are comfortable," Stephanie said, indicating the chair.

She was right, they were comfortable and very modern. The padding seemed to almost form around him like one of those expensive beds did around people on television. He only had an apartment near the company headquarters and he had bought his mattress used at a flea market. It was soft all right, but not in a good way.

The seats had wide armrests and when he sat back, his head was supported like a really fancy car seat.

Then, as the movie started, the lights went dim. But not dim enough that he couldn't see the others in the theater below him.

The title of the movie was "Alien Vibration" and it had nothing else after the title except the words "Test Number One."

And today's date.

Jimmy was amazed. His friend was right, this really was the very first showing of a new movie. This might turn out to be the best first date ever in his meager list of first dates.

At twenty-six, he just hadn't had that many first dates, and not for the lack of trying. Too much time instead working to get that doctorate in engineering to date. That was the excuse he gave himself.

"This is fun," Stephanie said, leaning over and whispering softly to him.

"It is," he whispered back.

That was a first. No woman on a date with him had ever told him something they were doing was fun.

Then the movie started and for Stephanie and the other women in the theater, the fun really started.

For him, not so much.

The movie began with three well-muscled men working out, talking in deep voices, and joking around to show they had a sense of humor. One was white, one black, the other some sort of Asian mix.

Then the movie followed them to the showers. That's when Jimmy started to get worried about this new movie.

Thankfully, it was nothing graphic, no actual body parts were shown, but camera angles allowed all of the audience to see a lot more of those three men than Jimmy wanted to see.

Especially their butts.

Jimmy hadn't seen another man's butt since gym class in freshman year in high school.

He wasn't happy about seeing them now.

He glanced at Stephanie. She didn't seem to be minding at all.

And it was at that point that Jimmy noticed the seats were moving slightly, sometimes in timing with one of the guy's on the screen hip movements.

As the men dressed in a very well-filmed fashion, and then left the gym, Jimmy was expecting them to become aliens or something, considering the title "Alien Vibrations."

But it didn't work that way.

The story-line jumped among the three men, one to the other, as they went through rather mundane days, then met again in a clean back room of some club.

The seat was getting annoying at that point with its movement, but Jimmy noticed that Stephanie was following the show with her mouth slightly open. And she was pressed back into the chair.

The three men went into a dressing room of the club and again stripped off their clothes, showing perfect bodies while not showing their more-than-likely important body part.

But close.

Very close at times.

One camera angle was so close to a body part reveal that a few of the women in the audience gasped and then sighed as it didn't happen.

Beside him, Stephanie just sat, focused completely on the movie.

Completely.

And one hand was between her legs as if it was cold, but Jimmy had a hunch that hand was far from cold.

And the damn seat just kept vibrating. As the three men finished dressing in skimpy underwear, then clearly rip-away costumes, Jimmy finally clued to what the job these men had entailed.

Then the camera angle went from the dressing room, following the first man out and onto a stage.

There was no one in the audience.

No one.

It was clear this guy was going to put on a show just for the women in this theater.

And when he looked into the camera as the music built and ripped off his pants, Stephanie let out a gasp and shuddered beside him.

He was about to ask her if she was all right, but then he realized he had a hunch what had just happened, since the cushion of the chair he was in was moving in motion with the guy's hips on the screen.

Perfectly timed motion, actually.

It wasn't doing anything for him, but it was clearly doing something really great for Stephanie.

And from the sounds of the gasps and sobs and sighs in the small theater, it was having an effect on the other women in the place as well.

And then the guy on the screen was down to his tiny, tiny shorts that showed nothing tiny underneath the shorts.

The guy's hips and the chairs kept moving in exactly the same pattern and then, as the music built and built and the guy's hips and the chair under Jimmy moved faster and faster, the guy suddenly stopped and thrust his slightly-hidden part right into the camera.

And as he did, something in the seat poked upward, making Jimmy jump.

It made Stephanie grunt and then pant, "Yes! Yes! Yes!"

And then the next guy came out onto the stage as the camera left the first guy. The second guy was fully dressed and he started the old hip movement and the chair picked up on the hip movement.

And the entire music started to build again, this time a little faster than the first guy.

More urgent.

Pounding music with a vibration that also carried into the chair under Jimmy.

And again the part of the dances ended with the mostly-naked guy on the screen thrusting his far-too-large and barely-covered private part at the camera as something in the seat again poked upward.

The guy thrust again.

The seat hit Jimmy in the butt again.

But this time Jimmy had been ready and had lifted his butt off the chair enough to not get the brunt of it right in his ass.

Beside him Stephanie was just panting "Yes! Yes! Yes!"

Over and over and over like the worst corporate flunky in existence.

Jimmy glanced at his watch.

This had been going on now for almost forty minutes, and now the third guy's movement on the screen was controlling the seats and the music was building faster and faster.

And the seats went faster and faster.

And the vibrations intensified.

And the camera panned over the man's huge, but covered, part more and more times and each time something under Jimmy poked upward.

Finally, the camera went in tight on the guy's body part, something in the seat poked up even more, and all hell broke loose in the theater.

More than likely it wasn't hell for anyone but him. But women were panting, crying, sobbing.

Beside him Stephanie was just shuddering and not even trying to control the fact that she had the hiccups. Her head was down, her eyes closed, and she was sweating.

In fact, her entire blouse was wet from sweat and he could see her white bra through it.

The film had stopped, but the lights had not come back up yet, which allowed all the women in the place to slowly pull themselves back together.

Jimmy sat there watching it all, shocked.

This had all been alien to him completely. He had never even gotten to first base with a woman and was scared to death to click on any porn sight on the internet for fear of viruses in his computers and someone finding out.

Yet he was fairly certain he had just watched an entire theater of women have multiple orgasms.

After two minutes, the lights came up slightly.

Stephanie had managed to pull herself back together with one final sigh.

No one had really moved or stood up yet.

Finally, on the screen, words appeared.

"Thanks for Coming."

The lights came up farther and the women snickered and laughed and that broke the tension.

"Well, that was fun," Stephanie said, turning to him. "You up for a pizza?"

"I would love one," he said.

They were the first out of the small theater and neither of them talked at all about what had happened, or why her blouse was soaked through, or anything. But they had great conversations about a lot of other stuff.

Then, when he walked her back to her car at the office, she beamed at him.

"That had to be the best first date a girl could ever ask for," she said.

She kissed him on the forehead, thanked him again, and turned for her car.

He knew right then and there that there would never be a second date.

And he was relieved.

No chance in the world could he measure up to those three men on the screen. Not in height, not in strength, and certainly not in the hidden-body-part area of things.

That theater had been state-of-the-art, cutting-edge technology that seemed to work just fine for everyone but him.

For him, it had been alien contact completely, especially with whatever was under that seat.

He had no doubt his ass was going to be sore for days.

SIGHED THE SNAKE

A POKER BOY STORY

DEAN WESLEY SMITH

ONE

"Poker Boy, the aliens are back."

Stan, the God of Poker, said those exact words to me as I sat in his office next to my sidekick and girlfriend, Patty, aka Front Desk Girl.

His office, glass-walled and floating invisible somewhere high above the Las Vegas strip, had felt cool and comfortable when we had entered from a hidden door at the MGM Grand Casino. The view just took your breath away as Las Vegas stretched out below, surrounded by desert and then mountains in the distance. The walls were invisible, so it felt as if Stan had put office furniture on a floating carpet. Only pictures of great poker players on the walls lined out where the room started and the air outside ended.

As we got seated, a United Airlines jet passed silently to our west, just below us, headed for the airport. I could only imagine what the passengers I could see through the window on that jet would have thought if suddenly Stan's office had become visible out their windows, with Patty and me sitting in front of his desk.

Sometimes Stan kept his office dark and dingy, like a back room at an old, downtown casino, straight out of the mob days. That was when he was in a bad mood or things were threatening. When he let it float above the city, as it was now, you knew Stan was feeling pretty darned good about life with the Gambling Gods.

But his casual statement about the aliens returning rocked me, and I studied his smiling face. Even with my black leather superhero jacket and Fedora-like superhero hat on, I didn't have the power to get a read on Stan. No one could get a read on the God of Poker, which was why he had the job. So I reverted to the most logical way to get an answer. I asked him.

"This makes you happy, the aliens being back?"

Patty had sat forward in her seat at the comment from Stan, her long brown hair flowing over her white blouse and dress slacks, her new uniform for work. She had just recently taken a job as customer relations at the MGM Grand Casino and Hotel, and we had been having lunch in the nifty little Greek place just off the downstairs promenade when Stan called us.

When I'm in Vegas, Patty and I not only work cases together, we are an item. Actually, she's my only item whether I'm in Vegas or not, but I haven't figured out a way to tell her that just yet. As Poker Boy, I'm not known for being a ladies' man, or for having just one woman in my life either. I wasn't sure how she would react, but knowing Patty, she probably already knew. She seemed to sense things about me before I did. I figured it was one of her many superpowers. Thank heavens she didn't play poker.

"Actually," Stan said, "not so much happy as satisfied. I won the pool."

"The pool?" Patty asked, glancing at me with those wonderful brown eyes of hers before looking back at Stan.

"We had a pool as to when they would return," Stan said, his smile getting bigger. "I got it to within a month. We started the pool the day after they left."

"They've been gone since the late 1950s," I said. "I'm impressed."

Stan smiled even larger. "Thanks."

"So, why are we here?" Patty asked, shaking her head and sitting back. She worked the hotel side of the gambling industry. And even though she was a superhero working under Laverne, Lady Luck herself, Patty sometimes just didn't understand the nature of a gambler's need to bet on things. The Gambling Gods had bets running all the time for one thing or another. It was what they did. The alien pool was no surprise to me.

"We need you two to make contact with their representative, find out what they are planning, that sort of thing. Right now he's sitting in a 2-4 no-limit game at the MGM Grand."

"Not over at the Bellagio, huh? I wonder why." I would have figured the aliens could afford the higher stakes.

"Not a clue," Stan said.

Now it was making sense to me. I hadn't been a superhero long enough to have met the aliens the last time they visited the planet, but from what I understood, they loved to gamble, which was why the Gambling Gods ended up being their major contact with the planet Earth. The world governments at the time had hated that, but in the end, had to live with it. I doubted anyone in the current world governments had even been briefed that aliens actually existed, let alone the Gambling Gods. The gods, and the superheroes like Patty and me, tended to stay under the radar as much as we could.

"Is the alien any good at poker?" I asked, smiling at Stan.

Stan laughed. "Not a clue. He's new. Go find out."

The wonderful view from Stan's office faded, and Patty and I moved from sitting in front of Stan's desk to walking down the hallway toward the MGM Grand's poker room. Always took a second for the mind to adjust when Stan did that.

TWO

The poker room at the MGM Grand had been remodeled a few years back, and now was in the shape of an hourglass. It usually had a good ten games going at any one time, and ran daily tournaments that were pretty popular around town. They catered mostly to tourists, with a few local pros working the room. The big money and high-stakes games had moved over to the Bellagio a number of years back, but the MGM still had a loyal following and they spread a good game and ran a tight room.

"So, what do we do now?" Patty asked, clearly worried about meeting a real-life alien.

"Stop at the counter and stay close until I figure out what the guy wants. I'm going to take us in as much undercover as I can manage."

I had no idea why I was taking those precautions. It just felt right, and as a superhero and a poker player, I had learned a long time ago to trust that feeling.

Patty reached over and squeezed my hand, then let go, which was a good thing. I always found it hard to concentrate when Patty was touching any part of me. Some parts more than others.

As we neared the room, I brought up my Don't-Pay-Attention-To-

Me superpower and covered both of us. Someday I was going to have to give that superpower a better name, but describing the effect it had seemed as good as any name for the moment.

I got a rack of five-dollar chips from the front counter and moved toward the 2-4 no-limit table against one drab-colored wall. Four men and two women sat around the table. The two women were clearly together, clearly from some Midwestern state, and pretending to be in over their heads. They didn't even notice me.

The guy in the number four chair was a local pro named Dan, and he managed to see through my cloak and nod as I sat down. Dan stood no more than five feet tall, and usually wore a dress shirt and tan jacket that made him look more like an accountant taking a break from the office than a professional poker player. But I knew he was as sharp and mean as they came and made good money every day at this table. I had no intention of tangling with him.

The other two men were tourists, both with drinks in front of them, and both more interested in the women than in playing poker. That left the guy wearing a snakeskin cowboy hat, sunglasses, and a western shirt, sitting in the seat to the right of the dealer. The weirdest thing about the guy was his tiny nose and almost complete lack of chin. It was as if his face just sort of blended down into his neck and into his black shirt collar.

I sat down in the chair directly across the table from him and slipped the five hundred in chips out of my rack, stacking them neatly as he watched.

He lowered his sunglasses just enough to show me his dark, black eyes, then grinned without showing any teeth. "Poker Boy, I presume."

Dan jerked at the mention of my name, then just stared at me. Clearly, my reputation had gotten ahead of me. I ignored Dan and focused on the alien.

I got nothing, no read, no sense of any emotion at all.

I dug deep and put my best superhero Poker Boy poker-read on him, getting almost nothing but a strange, dark feel. That was getting me nowhere.

"I don't think I have had the pleasure," I said in return.

"Just call me Snake," the alien said, his voice as close to a hiss as I could imagine a human voice sounding.

I hated snakes. I didn't mention that to him. More than likely, he knew. Instead, I just nodded.

I folded the first two cards the dealer fired my way without looking, then watched as Snake glanced at his and folded as well. He had very thin hair sticking out from under his hat that looked combed back over a dark scalp, and he also clearly had a dandruff problem, since flakes kept falling on his black shirt.

"It's been a long time," I said, aiming at him as much of my Make-Them-Relax superpower as I dared use. "At least fifty years."

"Nah, that wasn't my people," Snake said, again grinning under his sunglasses without really opening his mouth. His leather-like skin sort of moved in waves up his neck to his mouth and then back down and I thought for a moment I heard a faint rustling sound. "We haven't been here for a good ten centuries at least."

Oh, crap! Stan wasn't going to be happy with that information. More than likely it meant he hadn't won the pool after all. And he hadn't told me that there was more than one alien race out there.

I felt my stomach tighten into a tiny fist. I hoped like hell Stan and Lady Luck were listening in on this. And I hoped like hell I had managed to keep my best poker face on when Snake told me he was with a different alien race than we were expecting.

"So, what brings you to our little corner of the poker universe?" I asked, forcing myself to stay as calm as possible.

"Why does anyone come to Las Vegas?" Snake asked, glancing at the two women who were ignoring our conversation and flirting with the two men. One of the women had just pulled the last pot and both were laughing about their luck. I had a hunch they were better than just lucky and this flatlander hick routine was just a ruse to take money. And the two guys were going to be more than happy to give it to them.

Dan, the pro, was just shaking his head at their antics and mostly watching me and Snake. I would wager he wasn't real pleased at how his favorite table had shaped up today.

"So," I said, keeping my attention focused on the alien, "you came across vast distances in space to vacation, gamble, drink, and have sex?"

He nodded, glancing at the two cards the dealer had just given him. "That pretty much describes it."

He put a chip on his cards and again sort-of smiled at me, the rustling of his dry skin clearly loud enough to hear this time. It sent shivers down my back. Did I mention that I really, *really* hated snakes? Especially snakes with a bad dandruff problem.

He raised a smooth hundred and Dan folded at once.

"But mostly," Snake said, again pulling down his sunglasses just enough for me to see the pitch black eyes behind them, "I'm here to see if I can beat the best poker player in the game. You up for a little heads-up action, Poker Boy?"

Now, I had to admit that having the alien call me the best player in the game stroked my ego just a little. I knew I was good, but I didn't think of myself as the best by a long ways.

"What did you have in mind?" I asked as I glanced at my cards and flipped the low pair of fours back at the dealer. Any two cards that would cause that kind of raise from Snake had a small pair beat from the start.

"We each start with a million in chips," Snake said. "When one of us has them all, he wins. Blinds level at five hundred, one thousand."

Every sense in my body, and a couple of my superpowers as well, were screaming there was more to this than a simple game for a million bucks.

"So, what would you do with my million, assuming you won it?" Actually, it would be the Gambling Gods' money, not mine. I was fairly rich, but not rich enough to risk a million against some alien.

Snake smiled again without opening his mouth. Again his skin made that dry rustling sound and I tried not to show the shiver that was running up my back. This guy could really be helped by a little lotion.

The dealer flipped me a pair of tens this time around, and I folded them like they were a seven-deuce off. No point in actually playing at this point in the conversation. One of the women giggled and raised and both of the suckers staring at her chest called. Dan and Snake both folded.

Snake reached down under the table and pulled up a golden apple, placing it on the rail in front of him. "I assume you don't remember this."

I stared at the apple for a moment. The thing shone in the casino lights, begging for someone to take a bite out of it. My stomach clamped up so tight, I could hardly breathe. I was talking with a member of the alien race that had caused the legend of Adam and Eve. It sure had been a while since they had been here.

A very, very long time, actually.

"Plucked right from the Tree of Knowledge, I bet," I said, keeping my calm exterior as poker-faced as I could, pretending to not really care.

Snake's thin, eyebrows raised above the top edge of his sunglasses. I had surprised him, and for the first time, my poker sense told me this alien had a weakness.

"I am impressed," Snake said. "I was led to understand that your race in general had no long-term memory, that you destroyed your past, or worshipped it for monetary gain."

"For the most part you're right," I said. "But you still haven't told me what the real bet is."

Snake tapped the apple with a long finger. "Contained in the apple is the design and basics for a good dozen major inventions that would forward your race into the stars." He touched the thing again. "Anti-gravity, time control, teleportation. It's all in here."

I didn't mention to him that the Gambling Gods already had all of those things and humanity would discover them in their own sweet time. I wanted to see exactly what he was after in return.

"Nice," I said. "Worth a million I would say."

Snake shook his head, the rustling so loud this time that even one of the guys staring at the women's chest looked around.

"Your money means nothing to me," Snake said.

"I assumed as much," I said, glancing over at where Patty stood near the main desk. Her eyes were wide and now Stan and Laverne were standing beside her. Clearly they were listening.

I gave Snake the old poker stare. "So what do you want in return if you win?"

"Political sanctuary," Snake said. "And twenty of your acres of land with a privacy dome over it so I can build my own climate-controlled garden to live in."

"And if I win?" I asked.

"You get the information in the apple and I will leave the planet and never return."

I glanced at the poker front desk where Patty now stood alone. Clearly Stan and Lady Luck had heard and were off doing what they needed to do.

"Give me fifteen minutes to talk to my boss, and I'll see what I can do," I said, pushing my chair back and standing.

Snake put the apple away and nodded, glancing down at his new cards. "I'll be right here."

I motioned for the dealer to watch my chips and deal me out, pushed my current cards back at the dealer without looking at them, and headed toward Patty.

THREE

We were ten paces down the hall away from the poker room when we suddenly found ourselves in Lady Luck's big office. Stan was pacing in front of Laverne's desk, and she was tapping her fingers, staring at a blank screen on the wall beside her desk.

After a moment an alien that looked exactly like the guy sitting in the poker room came on the screen. Only this guy wasn't hiding his snake-like body with four arms and two legs. He was also golden colored, with streaks of red and blue and bright orange along two sides. I had no idea how large he was compared to the guy downstairs, but he seemed much, much larger on the screen.

Who knew that alien life in the universe would develop from snakes as well as monkeys?

"Laverne," the snake said in perfect British English. "It is always a great pleasure."

"The pleasure is all mine, Commander," Laverne said, bowing slightly.

I just stared, more than likely my mouth open. Not often you see Lady Luck herself bowing to anyone.

"I was expecting your call," Commander said. "I assume you have encountered the Lacit fugitive."

"He is sitting in one of our poker rooms as we speak," Laverne said. "He has challenged Poker Boy to a wager: an apple's-worth of knowledge against political sanctuary in a heads-up game of no-limit poker."

Commander shook his head. "They do love that old apple trick. Their entire race seems to never tire of it. They cause more damage to young cultures than any other race."

"I'll take your word for that," Lady Luck said.

Commander frowned and glanced around at something off screen before going on. "We are not scheduled to arrive for another seventeen of your hours. You would do us a great favor by stalling him without giving him political sanctuary. We have been chasing this fugitive for a great deal of your time."

"What will he do if we don't agree to his challenge?" Laverne asked.

"More than likely flee, *after* doing some very permanent damage to your culture. A couple of those apples in the wrong hands would have a very destructive result on your young culture I am afraid."

Laverne glanced around at me. "Can you keep him playing long enough, Poker Boy?"

I glanced at the golden snake on the screen, then at Lady Luck. "I can, with a little help."

"Come in undetected," Laverne said, turning back to Commander. "Your fugitive will be waiting for you at a poker table in Las Vegas."

"Thank you," the big golden snake said, and the screen went dark.

I sure hated snakes.

Lady Luck turned to me. "What kind of help do you need?"

I glanced at Patty, then back at Laverne. "Can you, without Snake noticing, slow down the time in the casino while we play? Make the seventeen hours actually seem more like four or five? I can hold an all-in player for that long, but not a lot longer I'm afraid."

Laverne and Stan both nodded, clearly understanding what I was asking for. Patty just looked puzzled, so to make sure we were all on the same page, I explained to her what I was thinking.

"The Snake has nothing really to lose, so in a no-limit game, he can just shove in all his chips at any given point. Without me facing him in a one-hand showdown, he can just whittle me down slowly as I keep folding. My problem is that I don't dare win or lose. My assignment isn't to beat Snake, it is to play him for a long time, to a draw. Much, much harder thing to do."

"I get it," Patty said, nodding.

"Let's just hope he came to play," Stan said. "I'll set it up in a private room at the MGM. Give me five minutes."

With that Stan vanished.

"Good luck," Laverne said, her face tight and not smiling.

The big office of the head of all the Gambling Gods faded and Patty and I were left standing in the hallway outside of the MGM Grand poker room.

"I really hate it when Lady Luck wishes me good luck," I said, shaking my head.

"Yeah," Patty said. "That's got to worry you. Means she can't really help you much."

"Great," I said, taking a deep breath. I was used to winning, not playing someone to a draw.

"Ready," Stan said, appearing beside us. He indicated a door off to one side of the poker room.

Patty leaned over and kissed me on the cheek, which for a quick second made me forget about how much I hated snakes and remember how much I really liked her. "Luck," she said.

"It will be interesting, if nothing else," I said, smiling at her. I glanced at Stan. "Think you can slow things down a little?"

"We'll see what we can do," Stan said. "But if he starts to notice, we'll back off and you'll be on your own."

"Just keep the snakebite kit handy," I said, then turned and walked toward the table where the alien sat.

FOUR

"Private room," I said as I got near the alien, indicating the door. "Chips are being set up. You have yourself a bet."

"Perfect," the alien said, smiling again, rustling his dry skin.

I indicated that the pit boss should cash in our real chips and bring them to us, then led the way into the private room.

A poker table filled the center of the meeting room, and an MGM Grand dealer was sitting ready. Two large stacks of chips of varied denominations were stacked in front of the third chair and the seventh chair, facing each other.

I indicated that Snake should pick and he took the three chair while I shut the door behind us.

I sat down and then pointed upward. "We're being recorded and watched by two casino employees to ensure no problems."

"Understandable," he said. Then he smiled again and even from the length of the table I saw dandruff float down onto his narrow shoulders.

As Stan said, luckily, Snake had come to actually play. So, for the first hour, we traded hands back and forth, pretty much ending up level. I would raise and he would fold, he would raise and I would fold.

We saw maybe a dozen flops total, with one or the other of us betting and the other folding. Not the kind of match the television folks would be happy with. In fact, on television, the first hour would mostly be edited right out.

I held a slight advantage of less than eighty thousand going into the second hour, not enough to count in this kind of game.

About ten minutes into the second hour, I caught a pair of kings on the button and raised it twenty thousand. Snake smiled and reraised another fifty. I smooth called and we went to the flop.

A third king hit the flop, but there was also an ace and ten, rainbow, meaning all suits.

Snake, with a rustling sound moved another fifty thousand into the pot.

A smallish bet, which might mean he wanted me to call. I didn't like the feel of it.

I sat back and stared at the board, trying my best to get a read on Snake's hand. More than likely he had aces and had me dead. I doubted he would have reraised with Jack/Queen to give him the straight. And if he had ace/king, I had him dead with two pair.

But the key was, I didn't want to win this pot. If I folded now, I would still be slightly ahead, but I had to fold perfectly, showing him I had a read on him, to keep him under control and playing light.

So, like any good poker player, I went into acting mode. I always figured there should be an Academy Award for poker table acting. Those of us who are pros can act with the best of them. It's also why some damn fine actors become good poker players. They already have part of the skill down solid.

"Let me see if I have this right," I said, smiling at Snake and leaning forward. "You reraised me before the flop, not large, but large enough. Now, with the ace on the board, you come out betting, again not huge, but strong enough to make it interesting. Why do I feel like I'm being suckered into this pot?"

He again lowered his sunglasses and I could see his dark eyes under the lip of his cowboy hat. "You trying to get a read on me, Poker Boy?"

I laughed. "Oh, I already have that," I lied. "You're sitting there with a pair of aces in your hand and trying to sucker me in like I'm one of those rank players out there. Maybe next time."

I flipped my pocket kings toward the dealer, face-up so he could see them.

He stared at my kings for a moment as the dealer scooped them up and then the sound of snakeskin rustling filled the room. Oh, oh, I had made him mad. That snakebite kit might not be such a bad idea after all. I had been right about his aces.

He flipped his two cards to the dealer without showing them to me and started stacking the chips from the pot as the rustling slowly faded.

Why couldn't the aliens have been badgers, or gophers, or even alligators? Anything but snakes.

FIVE

For the next half hour, Snake shed a lot of dandruff and folded almost everything, and I gained chips on him, slowly working it up so that I had a couple hundred thousand extra on him, enough to fold some hands without being in any danger. If I hadn't been playing an alien snake, I would have said that my play had Snake snake-bit.

But I said nothing. I just hoped time outside of this room was moving a lot faster than it was in this room.

Finally, around the beginning of the second hour, Snake seemed to shake himself, a rustling sound that sent dandruff flying everywhere. I had no idea how much dandruff would be covering the table, the chips, everything, if he hadn't been wearing that cowboy hat. I just hoped the snake he made the cowboy hat from hadn't been a relative.

Or another poker player.

Two hands later, he raised and I folded.

For the next fifteen hands straight, he raised and I folded. He clearly had changed strategy and I was looking tight and weak to him with my play now.

"What's wrong, Poker Boy?" Snake asked as I folded yet another hand. "Afraid to play?"

"No cards," I again lied. Poker players lie a lot to other poker play-ers. Actually, I had folded six perfectly playable hands to his raises. I just didn't see any point in mixing it up yet, since I was still a good hundred and fifty thousand ahead of him and was in no hurry at all.

Three more hands he raised and I folded, then with him raising ten thousand, I looked down and saw the worst hand in poker. Seven/deuce off-suit. So I reraised him fifty thousand.

He stared at me from behind those sunglasses, his face ringed with a coat of dandruff white, then finally folded.

I flipped my cards again face up so he could see my bluff. "Got tired of the bad cards. Decided to play a couple."

The rustling filled the room again and the dandruff flew as Snake shuddered and got even angrier. At this point, he had to know he was way outclassed in this game and that I had a complete read on him, even though I didn't really. One of two things would be his reaction. He would settle into slow, steady play, or he would get even more aggressive.

Luckily, after a small dandruff storm, he settled down and stopped raising every hand, and we went back to exchanging blinds with small raises as we had done the first hour.

In that style of play, with me not having any ability to sense him at all, or his hands, he was dangerous in the long run. But it would take a long time for him to wear me down, and that's what I needed to have happen.

Finally, just under four hours into the game, we had a hand that television announcers would love. I had ace/queen and raised thirty thousand.

He flat called and we went to the flop. I put him on a pair, or maybe a weak ace such as ace/nine. At that point I was fairly certain we were going in mostly even.

Flop came out ace and two eights. I had two pair, aces and eights, but I didn't much like that flop.

He bet out forty thousand and this time I called him.

The next card was a third eight, filling me up. But again, I hated that card more than I wanted to admit. We were either going to tie if he also had an ace, or I was beat with my full house against his quads if he had the forth ace.

He checked.

I checked right behind him.

Dandruff flew, telling me he wanted me to bet. It seemed his tell was his bad skin problem. He had the eights.

The last card was a worthless rag, and he bet out another forty grand, just enough to keep me in. I called him, since I would still be up slightly even losing the pot, and he rolled over ace eight.

I rolled over my ace/queen and Snake said "Nice hand," as the dealer shoved him the chips."

"Nice bet," I said.

So after four hours of play, we were still almost even. So far, I had managed to do what I needed to do.

SIX

By the end of hour five, I was a hundred grand behind, all from small pots, and Snake's shirt was almost pure white from the dandruff.

By the end of hour six, I was two hundred thousand behind, and Snake had settled into the pattern that I knew from the beginning would wear me down. In a game where winning and losing were an option, I would have ended this hours ago. It had already gone on a lot longer than I had thought possible.

And I thought the same thing by the end of hour seven. I had pressured him into folding a few hands, being clear that he was beaten, but he had gotten me to fold even more, and now my chips were just over six hundred thousand.

"Be nice to my chips," I said, smiling at him. "They are about to come back my way. I can feel the cards turning."

He just grinned and rustled his skin and shed even more dandruff. "We shall see, Poker Boy. We shall see."

My comment had the desired effect and he started raising regularly again, forcing his play, and for a good dozen hands, I folded everything, pretending to get angry at the cards for not turning, even though I was seeing some perfectly good playable hands.

Then, on the button, I looked down at pocket rockets. Two wonderful red aces.

"It's about damn time," I said, and raised a smooth forty thousand. My comment, of course, would tell any decent poker player I really *didn't* have a strong hand. He just called and sat back in his chair.

Not a good sign. He had a monster hand as well.

Flop came ace/queen/jack, rainbow. He bet out forty thousand, the same bet I had made and I flat called him with my three aces. And then I sat back.

"Interesting," Snake said, looking over the top of his sunglasses at me with his dark eyes.

I said nothing and the turn came a ten. If he had ace/king, he had just hit his straight and I was beat.

Before he could reach for his chips I said, "I wouldn't bet much on that straight until you see the river."

His hand froze over his chips, letting me know I had figured his hand perfectly. And by speaking up, I had told him exactly what I had as well. His straight was the best hand, but I had to get any one of one ace, three queens, three jacks, or three tens to win the hand and two kings to tie him with a straight of my own. Twelve outs were a lot of outs.

At that moment, a shimmering went through the air and I had the sense that a bunch of hours suddenly passed. The door to the room opened and two large, gold-colored, snake-like men walked through, followed by Laverne and Stan and Patty.

In a hissing language I had no desire to learn, the two golden-snake men moved over behind Snake and made him stand, sending dandruff everywhere like a faint snowstorm.

Snake glanced at the cards and then up at me. "Nicely played, Poker Boy. A match I will always remember."

"As will I," I said. But not because of the poker, but I didn't say that.

"Any chance we can see that river card?" Snake asked.

I nodded to the dealer and he flipped the last card over. Another ten.

I rolled over my aces full.

"I guess it wasn't meant to be," Snake said.

A moment later the three aliens vanished.

"Nice job, again, Poker Boy," Laverne said, smiling at me. Then she, too, vanished.

I can't begin to say, as a poker player, how much I liked having Lady Luck smile at me.

Stan smiled as well. "We owe you one for that." Then he was gone.

Patty kissed me, and for a second I forgot all about snakes, poker, and Lady Luck as I enjoyed the feel of Front Desk Girl welcoming me back to the real world.

"Have I ever told you," Patty said as we turned and headed for the door, "how much I hate snakes."

"Oh, after about five hours of playing poker with one, you get used to them."

She laughed. "You up for a wonderful dinner, on me?"

"I think I need a shower first," I said as we walked arm-in-arm down the hallway.

"Oh, I like that idea, too," Patty said, hugging me even closer. "I'll scrub."

"Only if you use a lot of shampoo," I said. "Dandruff shampoo."

A DEAL
AT THE END OF TIME

A SEEDERS UNIVERSE STORY

DEAN WESLEY SMITH

A DEAL AT THE END OF TIME

Monday morning at the End of Time Bar, Saloon, and Eatery started off just as every day started. A beautiful sunrise over the mountains to the east painted the sky in reds and pinks and blues that made it impossible to not stop and stare.

And Palmer did just that, holding the fresh eggs he had gathered from his chicken coop in one hand while enjoying the fantastic sky show.

The fresh mountain air around him had a sharp morning bite to it even though it was in the middle of the summer. And the smell of pine felt extra thick this morning. By the afternoon, the smell would be of hot pine, something he loved just as much.

In fact, if he admitted it to himself, he loved everything about living in the high mountains of central Idaho. The mornings were crisp and then the day would warm up nice, leaving enough heat in the evenings to make sitting on the big log porch looking out over the Payette River comfortable.

In the winter he thought of the snow as a protective blanket, white and beautiful and covering everything.

At one point, before the event that killed most everyone, the End of

Time Bar had been a beautiful log home perched on a bluff overlooking the river. Five bedrooms and a massive open area with a huge fireplace on the main floor. He had found it while trying to get away from the smell of all the people who had died suddenly in Boise.

And everywhere else in the world it seemed.

No one had been here in this cabin, but the pantry was stocked and the freezer was full and there was a generator and a back-up generator that worked fine after the power finally shut off three months later.

And he had little doubt the previous owners were dead somewhere. Most everyone was dead that he knew, including his wife, his parents, everyone at Boise State University where he had taught in the law school.

Everyone.

And after a few days of wandering around in a state of shock, he realized he needed to find a place away from all the rotting death.

He had headed north into the mountains, walking, following the two-lane road toward central Idaho.

He had seen the big log home on the bluff through the trees from the road. After he realized it would be perfect for him to get through the winter, he raided other nearby cabins and went into Cascade to get supplies and then just stayed put for the winter until the smell of millions of dead finally faded.

He still hadn't been back down to Boise in the last five years since everyone died. He had no desire to see his home in the north end of town, his wife's remains in their living room, his friends all dead. He had no idea why he had survived, but another survivor he had met said it was because he had been in a bank vault.

It seemed that everyone who had survived had been underground or in something like a vault.

Palmer had gone into the bank to put some papers in his safe deposit box and when he came out everyone was dead.

He didn't remember much about those first days other than not knowing what to do with his wife's body. He had finally covered her with her favorite blanket and just left.

By the time the first spring rolled around, he discovered that other survivors had come into the mountains for the same reason he had. They were in cabins all over the area.

So one day while sitting all alone in the big living room area, he decided all the survivors needed a place to gather and what better place than a bar.

So he opened up the End of Time. He put a sign down on the road pointing up the hill that said, "End of Time Bar, Saloon, and Eatery. Open every day from eleven until past dark."

He lived upstairs and for a long time no one showed up. Then a couple from a few miles away stopped by and that got the word spreading.

It took most of the next year for the word to spread through the entire area and up into the more remote mountains, but during the second summer more and more survivors came out of their hiding.

And now most afternoons and evenings a good twenty people would be in the place, talking, pretending that everyone they had loved wasn't dead, and just going on with life.

He didn't take money for drinks or food, just exchange. And that kept his pantry full, his freezers stocked with venison, fish, and other game, and his liquor shelves full.

And he often had help in the kitchen when someone came up with a nifty idea for a new dish. Or something they had learned from their mother.

Some days it was hard to remember the old world, the old life.

Most of the time he didn't want to remember.

Three years after the event he heard about how survivors from all over the country were starting up four major new cities and Portland, Oregon, was one of them. He thought about heading there, but finally decided to just stay and run his little bar and restaurant.

And most of the others who lived in the cabins up and down the valley along the river did the same.

Now, after two years, the road from Boise up through Idaho had been cleared by a crew from Portland and his bar and restaurant were major stops along the way for anyone traveling through. Instead of people walking up the road to his place, most everyone had a motorcycle or an ATV or a truck. He had to clear out some brush for a parking lot last summer.

It seems his place had a real reputation for good food, fun conversation, and strong drinks.

He kind of liked that.

More than he wanted to admit.

So Monday morning was going along great. He had the eggs from the chicken coop in the fridge and the bread was finished baking, filling the huge log home with a rich thick buttery smell that felt like it could make a person fat just by breathing in too much of it.

He had fried himself two eggs and cut some hot, fresh bread and had just turned to take his coffee and his breakfast out to the tables on the log porch when she appeared.

She didn't come through any door.

She just appeared.

In front of the river-rock fireplace, among the wooden tables and chairs that filled the large area.

She was smiling, but with a worried look in her large brown eyes.

He just shook his head and stared at her.

Not possible.

She had short brown hair, cut close. Her face was round, with wide brown eyes. She looked to be about five-six with a thin frame. She wore jeans, tennis shoes, and a summer blouse with a sports bra showing through the blouse.

She was the best-looking woman he had seen since the world ended. A lot of women had come through here over the last five years, sometimes with other women, sometimes with men, sometimes even alone.

None had taken his breath away like this one.

And he felt like he had met her before. Not possible. He was sure he would remember, but it felt like he had.

Or he had dreamed about her.

How in the hell had she done that magic appearing trick?

He glanced back at the heavy wood front door. Still closed solidly.

He hadn't opened the slider yet to the porch, and she sure as hell didn't look like Santa Claus coming down the big river-rock fireplace.

So that made her a magician or a ghost. He was hoping for a magician. He didn't want his wonderful home and business to be haunted.

He looked down at the eggs and bread on the plate in his hand, then back at her.

Her eyes were wide and she was clearly worried about his reaction to her suddenly just being there.

Damn she looked familiar.

But after seeing the entire world die around him, he was beyond most reactions.

"I suppose you came for some breakfast," he said. "I don't normally serve breakfast, but I'll be glad to make you some."

He was surprised his voice stayed level and calm.

She now looked surprised, which made her even more beautiful.

Amazing that since Cindie had died, he hadn't thought much about any other women. They had gotten married in his last year of law school and he had only been teaching for two years when she and everyone died.

He missed her, a great deal the first few years, but sadly he didn't think of her often these days. He had blocked off that living part of his life. He called it "before" when talking about it.

He turned and put his plate on the big island that divided the kitchen from the big room and went around.

"Eggs, bread, coffee?" he asked.

She still just stood there, but she nodded.

"If you are not a ghost, come and sit while I cook."

He pointed to one of the barstools at the counter facing the kitchen.

She nodded and moved toward the stool directly on the other side of the counter from him.

"Two eggs or three?" he asked, opening up the fridge.

"Just two, thank you, professor," she said.

Her voice was low and level, but he could still feel the nervousness in it. And then it dawned on him what she had said. Around here no one knew his history. He was just Palmer.

No last name, nothing.

Just Palmer.

But this woman who had appeared like a ghost out of nowhere clearly knew of his past.

What the hell was going on?

"Just Palmer," he said, turning back to get the eggs while he got his nerves under control.

"And what is your name? Or should I just call you Ghost?"

She laughed and he loved the sound of that. He loved how she looked, her wide brown eyes, and her smile. And he now was certain he knew her.

Or he had to be still in bed dreaming.

No other explanation that he could logically think of.

"Ghost would actually be nice," she said, "but my real name is Marissa Warren."

For some reason he wanted to put a "Doctor" in front of her name, but he didn't say anything. He had no idea where that came from either.

After five years, maybe he was losing his mind.

He started the eggs cooking, then without turning around asked how she wanted them.

"Over easy," she said.

He turned and slid his plate in front of her. "That's what those are. Eat those before they get cold while I fix these."

She nodded as he slid her silverware and turned back to the stove.

He couldn't let himself look too much at her or he would lose all sense of anything. And right now he needed to figure out just what in the world was going on.

He pretended to just focus on the cooking while he took deep, slow breaths to calm.

After a moment she said, "Wow, this bread is wonderful."

"Thank you," he said. "Taught to me by a fellow who lives up by the old stibnite mining town. He comes down a few times a year, camps out in the trees down the river. I built an outhouse down there for those who want to stay overnight."

"And the eggs are perfect," she said. "I didn't realize how hungry I was."

"Mountain air will do that to you," he said, finishing up the eggs he was cooking and then cutting off another piece of bread.

He put his plate on the counter directly across from her and started to eat, standing there, half watching her finish eating.

Where did he know her from? Had she been one of his students? Was that where?

But there was no doubt she was stunning, just flat stunning.

And he was attracted to her, more than he wanted to be.

A lot more than he wanted to be.

Finally she looked up at him and he felt like a deer under a spotlight, frozen by her wonderful brown eyes.

"You're not shocked at me just appearing?" she asked after a moment.

"I watched the entire world and everyone I knew and loved die five years ago," he said. "So I don't shock easily, but I am wondering how you got in here. Ghost or magician?"

She nodded and sat back, smiling. "Neither. You ever watch the old *Star Trek* television show?"

"Sure, all the time," he said, laughing. "So you are telling me you beamed in from a spaceship? I didn't hear the transporter music."

She laughed, but then nodded. "Seems we forgot to cue the music for me this morning."

He didn't know whether to laugh or to run screaming for the door. But something was triggering in his memory now. A dream he had had back right after everyone died, about being on a spaceship and then being put back.

He had assumed that dream was caused by the same thing that had killed everyone and had just put it out of his mind, even though it had been very, very vivid.

But now he remembered where he had met her. She had been on the spaceship in his dream.

Holy crap!

"So you one of the aliens who killed everyone?" he asked, keeping as calm as he could.

She seemed startled for a moment, then she laughed. "Nope, I'm as human as you are. And what killed everyone was an electromagnetic pulse that came in from space and just shorted out human brains and a lot of animal brains as well."

"The reason all survivors were in vaults or underground," Palmer said, nodding.

She nodded. "Over one million people around the world survived that first wave."

"So why did you take all of us to your spaceships and then put us back into the death?"

She nodded. "So you do remember? I figured because of your genes you would."

He nodded. He was remembering more and more by the minute. He could now see the large meeting room full of smelly survivors, all shocked, looking down at the planet below.

He remembered a man explaining that they were rescuing all the survivors off the entire planet because another electromagnetic wave was coming. That over a thousand ships would take the survivors out of harms way and then return them so they could start rebuilding their home.

And he remembered her, giving medical care to people in the room, working with a smile and wonderful manner.

He remembered watching her until she approached him and they had talked for a few minutes, then she had moved on.

"There are still four large ships in orbit over this planet trying to help in the recovery," she said. "All are human. Actually, a branch of humanity called Seeders. We all have a special gene. Most humans do not, but you do, which allows you to remember the time on the ship."

"So why did you come back?"

She actually blushed slightly and looked down at her empty plate.

Then she looked up. "I was on one of the ships that left after the rescue. I had a mission on another planet to complete that took me three years. Then I asked to come back here because I wanted to see how you were doing."

"Me?" he asked, shocked.

And now he felt embarrassed.

She nodded and the silence filled the space between them for a moment.

Finally she broke it.

"I really love the life you have built here," she said, "and when we met again I didn't want to lie to you and pretend to be a survivor. So I got permission after almost a year of asking to just transport in directly to see if you would remember me."

"You are very hard to forget," he said, smiling at her. "But I have to admit in all that trauma, I wrote off that short time on the ship and meeting you as a dream."

She nodded to that.

"Are you a doctor?"

"I am," she said. "At least what passes for one in the advanced Seeders worlds."

He shook his head. "You'll have to explain that to me later."

She smiled and her entire face lit up and the smile reached those fantastic eyes. "I would be glad to."

"So, Ghost, how about we take our coffee and go out on the porch and enjoy the morning," he said. "You can enjoy my world while telling me about yours."

Her smile got bigger, if that was possible.

"I would love that very much."

And three hours later, after telling him some pretty amazing stories, he asked her if she wanted to stay for lunch and she said she did.

And she said she would pay her way by helping him. Together they got things ready for lunch and then while he cooked she waited on the twelve people who showed up. He introduced her as Ghost from Portland and everyone liked her right off.

She fit in perfectly with her bright smile and wonderful laugh.

It was everything he could do to not stare at her instead of cooking.

And who knew a doctor from space could carry four plates of hot food at the same time.

He was going to have to ask her where exactly in space she learned that skill.

No doubt it had been a strange Monday. But when you serve food and drinks at the End of Time, things like today have to be expected.

ME AND BEANS
AND GREAT BIG MELONS

DEAN WESLEY SMITH

ME AND BEANS
AND GREAT BIG MELONS

I have never thought, wondered, or even pondered the idea of having a supermarket love affair. If I had, I certainly wouldn't have thought it would start and end in front of the green beans. I'm the kind of guy who really doesn't eat green beans, red beans, black beans, or any other color bean. I'm not prejudiced in my bean selection. I pretty much just hate them all equally.

And I flat don't understand how anyone could even eat the things.

I met my supermarket lover as I tried to figure out which Hamburger Helper would work for the night. I was an expert in Hamburger Helpers and all the different incarnations of the stuff. I could almost make it without looking at the box. Almost.

"Excuse me," a soft, husky voice said.

I jerked around, realizing that my cart and my body had made an effective roadblock in the aisle. And I hadn't even set up any detour signs.

A woman stood there with one of those yellow baskets for small amounts of stuff. Just like me, she was wearing jeans and a blue tee-shirt, but unlike me she also had a brown purse over her shoulder.

The purse, oddly enough, accented the wonderful color of her hair.

I wondered if she had bought the purse because of that, or changed the color of her hair to match the purse. It was a question I would never think to ask any woman, even a woman I didn't know.

But yet, for some reason, she had made me think of it. I made a note to myself mentally to write down the weird supermarket moment. I hoped to be a writer in the future, when I could find the time, and often made notes about things that might come in handy in a story some day.

I found myself attracted to this woman wanting to get past me, and I did an instant inventory of her appearance.

Before I was laid off down at Sears, I had done lots of inventories of the warehouse, and had become known as "Innis, the Inventory King." I had decided one day to practice the same craft on women I met, and grocery stores were great places, full of inventory.

Using my skills, I instantly looked her over while moving my cart out of her way. She wore a loose blue tee-shirt with nothing written on it, tight jeans, and expensive tennis shoes. Total inventory cost of two hundred bucks. She had on no jewelry at all, not even an earring. She was an easy inventory subject.

Miss Brown-Hair-Yellow-Basket: Two hundred bucks.

"Sorry," I said, as I finished my inventory and cart moving at the same time, leaving the cart in front of the green beans, never thinking that she might actually be trying to get to that area. If I didn't eat green beans, no one else did I was sure.

My first wife had called that self-centered-universe attitude my defining characteristic. I had considered that a compliment and still do.

"No problem," the brown-haired, two-hundred-dollar-woman said, giving me a wonderful, bright smile as she moved past me. The aroma of fresh soap caught me and I stared at her from behind for a moment, first watching her long hair move against her matching purse, then her ass under her tight jeans.

I had always been an ass man, staring at woman's asses before any other body part if the chance arose. This woman had a stareable ass, of that there was no doubt. Really tight.

A stareable tight ass wasn't worth anything on my inventory list, but it should be.

She walked a few steps and stopped, looking at the canned vegetables.

I went back to trying to decide which Hamburger Helper to pick to eat while the football game was on tonight. Packers against the Rams. Could be a real shouter.

"Sorry to bother you again," she said from behind me.

I turned around to look into the deepest green eyes I had seen in a long time. If all women had eyes like her, I would shift to being an eye-man instead of an ass-man.

She pointed at the bean section that my cart was blocking.

"Oh, sorry," I said, moving to pull the cart out of her way for the second time. "I didn't think anyone ate that stuff."

She laughed. "Usually I like my beans fresh. But when I can't get them fresh, I make do with canned."

Usually I'm not real honest with the women I meet, but this woman ate beans and had annoyed me by making me move my cart twice in the middle of my Hamburger Helper shopping. So I said the first thing that came to mind.

"I'm that way with women," I said. "When I can't find the fresh stuff, I resort to the canned as well."

She stared at me for a moment.

I returned her stare.

The faint store music went away; the sounds of the other shoppers went away. It was a movie moment.

Of course, I had no doubt this movie moment was going to end with the woman walking off in a huff. At least then I could watch her ass and get back to my shopping.

But she surprised me.

Suddenly her smile returned, followed by the richest, deepest laugh I had heard in a long time. It echoed off the cans of corn and surrounded me, pushing me back against the shelf of Hamburger Helper.

"Now that's an opening line I've never heard before," she said after she caught a breath from the laughter.

"Opening for what?" I asked.

She smiled. "My legs."

I looked her right in the eye. "Now tell me why I would want to get between the legs of a woman who eats beans?"

Again I was serious, and again she stared at me, stunned into a second movie moment right there on aisle four.

Then she damned near lost a lung laughing that wonderful laugh of hers. I guess to her I was a real laugh-a-minute kind of guy.

She finally caught her breath and stared at me, her bright smile lighting up everything.

"Well?" I asked. "I'm waiting for my reason."

"Because," she said, "beans go well with franks at a picnic."

She stepped forward and grabbed my crotch, never letting her green-eyed gaze drop from mine.

She rubbed me through my jeans a few times as again we were having a movie moment, only this time it was a sex scene right there in front of the Hamburger Helper. I doubted I was ever going to be able to eat Hamburger Helper without a hard-on again.

"I assume little Frank here wouldn't mind a picnic in the park."

"His name is Ben," I said as she kept rubbing. "Big Ben. And he likes melons on his picnics."

"I think that could be arranged," she said, rubbing one small, tight breast against my arm. Whatever she had thought, that wasn't a melon. More like an apple.

"Any other menu items?" she asked.

Any man with a woman rubbing his crotch on aisle four of a grocery store might have trouble answering a question like that. I didn't. "A television to watch the game while I eat."

Her hand came away from my crotch like Big Ben had lit a match and burnt her. She stared at me, then said, "My ex-husband would have rather watched television than make love to me."

"Did he like Hamburger Helper?" I asked, adjusting Ben a little to ease the tension of tight underwear.

"Yeah," she said, clearly upset at my request for a television at her picnic.

"Figures," I said.

Now she was starting to get angry. A moment ago she was offering me a picnic, basket, apples, and all. Now she was mad. I had never had a woman mad at me on aisle four in a grocery store before. Two things new in one day, both on the same aisle. I would really have to write this down for the story I would do some day.

"And why does it *figure?*" she demanded, as if I owed her an answer just because she had given Big Ben a quick rubbing.

I shrugged. "You eat beans."

She made a choking sound, grabbed two cans of green beans, held them up for me to see like she was giving me the finger, put them in her little yellow basket, and walked off.

I watched her ass until she turned the corner and disappeared toward aisle five. Because her ass was so nice and tight, and her hand had felt so good on Big Ben, I thought for a moment about following her. But I knew there was nothing I could say to her to calm her down.

Besides, she ate beans. I hated beans, and no amount of Big Ben rubbing was going to erase that difference.

Also, if I spent time dealing with her over on aisle five, it might carry on to aisle six, and then even into the frozen food section on aisle eight, and if that happened I might miss the opening kick-off.

No bean-eating woman with a nice ass was worth missing the kick-off to a Packers-Rams game. Even if she had offered Ben an offer he had trouble refusing.

It seemed that my supermarket love affair had started and ended on aisle four.

I went back to trying to figure out which Hamburger Helper to get, finally picked up just the standard, and headed for aisle two where the Pabst Blue-Ribbon Beer lived and breathed and waited for me. No Hamburger Helper football game dinner was complete without Pabst.

I turned the corner onto the aisle. There was a short woman with a nice ass and short red hair parked right in front of the Pabst. She was studying the beer on the other side of the aisle as if reading labels would make the stuff any better.

I knew right off she was an alien, off one of them big ships from some other planet that had landed a year or so ago. All the alien women that I had seen on Fox News had short, bright-red hair and great bodies.

There had been hundreds of thousands of them, and all the countries of the world welcomed them to live. After awhile, they weren't even headlines anymore unless one of them got drunk and punched a cop or something.

The aliens had said they had come in friendship and just wanted to learn about us, but I had read stuff, and I knew better. More than likely they were going to kidnap us all and take us away and make dinner out of us.

But still, alien or not, she was standing in front of the Pabst and I had a game to watch.

"Excuse me," I said.

She turned to look at me, a puzzled look on her very human but very alien face.

Her dark eyes were like magnets, swirling pink and orange and brown. They held me with some unseen force. She was dressed in jeans and a blue tee-shirt, just like I was. Just like Miss Brown Hair had been. Only instead of apples in the tee-shirt orchard, she sprouted the biggest melons I had ever seen, especially for an alien as short as she was.

I did a quick inventory. Same as Miss-Brown-Purse. Two hundred bucks. It seemed it was two-hundred-dollar-woman-day in the supermarket.

"Yes?" she asked. "Can I help you?"

Very formal, like the secretary at my doc's office. But oh, Miss-Alien-With-Melons' voice could melt grease in a cold frying pan.

I pointed to the beer. "Hamburger Helper and a hand job are never complete without Pabst."

For some reason it was my day to be honest with women. And

aliens it seemed. Maybe someone had put something in the grocery store air to make me do it. Or maybe it was the excitement of a good football game that was causing it. I would have to think about it later, after the game, if I could stay awake long enough to do so.

She kept staring at me, then slowly smiled as she moved aside. "Aren't you forgetting one thing?" she asked.

"What's that?" I asked, figuring an insult to be next out of her mouth. Something about the rudeness of humans in social situations and that we all needed alien training or something. I grabbed my half case of beer and placed it next to the Hamburger Helper.

"A good Packers-Rams game."

Now it was my turn to stare at her like she was a winning lotto ticket. I didn't know alien women watched American football. Fox News had never mentioned anything like that. Maybe there was hope for all of us after all.

So, with that encouragement, I went ahead and asked the all-important question.

"Do you eat beans?"

She made a face. "Are you kidding? No human or alien should eat those things."

"Good," I said. "How's your ass?"

She turned around to show me, then said, "Engineered to be as tight as they make them. How's your big fella?"

"Big," I said.

She smiled and I smiled back.

I loved those alien eyes.

Then after my third or fourth movie moment of the shopping trip, this time right there in front of the beer, I stuck out my hand. "I'm Innis. I count things and hope to write stories."

She took my hand, her smooth skin sending wonderful warm sensations through my body right there in the cold beer section.

"Here on your planet, in your language, I'm called Melody," she said. "I'm not from around here. I rub things and hope to paint things.

And if we don't hurry we're going to miss the kick-off. How big is your screen?"

Her eyes seemed to swirl and she smiled with that question.

"Sixty inches," I said, proud of the moment I could say that to an alien woman.

She smiled even wider and then reached down and touched Big Ben through my jeans. "Sixty inches, huh? Mind if I join you? I'll buy the hamburger."

"Deal," I said, enjoying the fact that Ben was getting a work-out right there in the supermarket.

She put a second half-case of Pabst in my cart, left her empty cart in front of the other beer, and helped me push mine to the meat section, letting one of her wonderful large melons rub firmly against my hand.

It pleased me that she hadn't intended on sharing my Pabst. I really had to know a woman, or an alien for that matter, before I let that happen. Even if she was sharing her melons.

On the way past aisle six, we passed Miss Brown-Hair-And-Matching-Purse, who gave me a very, very long and angry look.

"Wow, what is her problem?" Melody asked, turning with me to watch the angry woman walk away. "Besides the fact that she has a tight ass."

"Very tight," I said, agreeing. "But she hates football and eats beans."

"Oh, that explains it," Melody said, shaking her head. "One of my people's biggest puzzles about your planet is how anyone could eat beans. They are poison to us. It may be a mystery we will never solve."

I was starting to really like these aliens.

"Let me know if you do," I said.

"The moment we figure it out," she said, laughing a high laugh that sounded very off-worldish. With that, me and my first alien supermarket lover headed for the check-out counter and a Hamburger Helper football game.

WHO'S HOLDING DONNA NOW?

DEAN WESLEY SMITH

WHO'S HOLDING DONNA NOW?

It was an accident.

Nothing more. A simple accident. I saw the entire thing.

It was awful.

My name is Jacob O'Grady. I own Sandy's Restaurant and Lounge down on twelfth. It's a pretty good-sized place with low, wood-beamed ceilings and more beer signs on the walls than should be allowed in one place. No windows, and a constant smell of lingering smoke.

The polished oak bar had come out of an old saloon from downtown Boise I hear, but never took the time to trace it back. That bar was forty feet long and the center of the place.

I bought the bar six years ago from Sandy's wife after Sandy called some girl a whore. Turned out to be this big cowboy's special girl. The big guy didn't even waste time with Sandy.

Five shots. All hit Sandy.

That guy could shoot. Sort of impressive, actually.

Now I never insult no one. Main rule number one.

I have a lot of main rules. I got to just to stay alive.

Donna was like Sandy. She didn't learn so fast. Now it's too late. Or at least I think it's too late. I honestly don't know for sure.

Donna had long black hair, thick black eyebrows, and just a hint of a moustache along her upper lip. I thought she was good looking, with her long legs, model type figure, and real warm smile. I think the smile was why I hired her.

I suppose I should have warned her right off. But about the time I hired her, I still didn't really believe what was going on. And then after it got started, I was afraid to tell anyone.

Hell, who would have believed me if I would have said that aliens dropped by my bar every night. I'd have been laughed right out of the neighborhood, if not locked up in a funny white suit.

But I had aliens all right.

Three of them.

They looked human, at least on the surface. One seemed older than the other two, maybe in his fifties if he had been human. He had rough skin and dark, intense eyes.

The other two looked to be mid-thirties, also dressed in normal human clothes for men of this area. Jeans, work shirts, work boots. One had a thick, dark moustache and the other had blonde hair.

At first glance, a person couldn't tell they were any different than the other loggers or rock miners that came in here. They dressed the same, drank the same kind of booze, and stayed off to themselves. Damn normal-like. But I could tell they were aliens. I just knew.

I should have warned Donna.

Hell, I didn't know they were going to start playing poker. It fit right in, though, when I thought about it later.

Any night in Sandy's there's at least three poker games going. There's always the high stake in the back room, plus some pretty good smaller games going out in the main room.

The three aliens watched the games real close for about two weeks, drinking just enough to make sure I didn't toss them outside, but not drinking that much as to seem drunk. For all I knew, they couldn't get drunk.

Then one of them asked Donna for a deck.

Tell the truth, I didn't give it a second thought, even though by then

I was pretty convinced they really were aliens, but their money was good and they sure didn't cause any trouble.

Donna gave them the cards. I remember real clearly because it was her second night and I had to show her where the decks of cards were stashed in the second drawer to the right of the cash register on the back bar.

The aliens worked at learning poker for about the next four weeks, never letting anyone join in, just playing their own game over in a corner.

Again, I didn't much care since they paid for their drinks and tipped Donna well.

They didn't ask many questions, but they asked enough around the room that I could figure out they didn't know much to start. But let me tell you, those three aliens were damn fast learners.

Damn fast.

Looking back, it's funny how things just sort of build up. Even them aliens playing cards would have been fine if Donna hadn't taken up with Cutbank Jones.

Cutbank was an odd bird. Long, kind of wiry, and just mean as hell. His eyes were so cold black that it used to make people squirm when he looked across a poker table at them. What Donna saw in him, I don't know. But one night I actually saw her make him smile. Amazing things do happen in Sandy's.

After the first few days, Cutbank came to think he owned Donna. About the only time she got away from him was while she worked. And even then, more times than not, Cutbank would be sitting in on one of the poker games and keeping an eye on her. He never let her get far from sight.

I meant to ask her one night if she needed help avoiding him, but just never got around to it before the night of the big game. I should have, I really should have. Regrets now in hindsight.

The big game started at about nine. The older of the three aliens got up and moved over to a table where Slim, Raymond, Cutbank, and Freddy were playing and bold-like asked if he could sit in.

No one seemed to mind, so after a few hands the other two aliens came over and joined the table, making it seven players.

All of them had the buy-in plus a little, and all seemed to play well, if not mechanical.

Eventually, Jones and Steven joined in when the high stakes game in the backroom got a little slow.

The entire thing made me nervous, but what the hell could I do about it? They were just customers, so I kept my mouth shut and made sure everyone had a drink when they wanted one.

Donna did the serving and the aliens tipped her well.

Cutbank treated her like trash. That not only annoyed me, but most of the men in the game. Donna was well liked. She just had that kind of smile.

For the first few hours, the game went fine and I was beginning to think the evening might just end up being a good one.

Cutbank held his own at the table. He might have been a nasty ass to Donna, but he could play a mean game of seven-card stud.

Both Raymond and Freddy had tapped out and left, with most of their money sitting in front of the three aliens.

An hour later, Slim was gone and not long after that, both Jones and Steven.

That left only Cutbank on one side of the table and the three aliens on the other. Except for a few chips in front of Cutbank, the aliens had it all. And that galled the hell out of Cutbank. I could tell.

So could the few customers remaining in Sandy's.

The hand that started the problem was the hand that Cutbank drew into a straight, King high.

Two of the aliens folded right off, but the older one held on, betting twice what Cutbank had left in front of him, smiling all the time.

The rules in a game in Sandy's is that if you didn't have the money to cover the bet, you lost the hand.

At that point, I never saw a man get so red. For a minute I thought Cutbank was going to jump right across the table at the alien guy. But he didn't.

Being the good player that he was, he first studied his hand, then laid his cards face down in front of him, pushed what was left of his money into the center of the table, and then asked the alien if he could have a moment to cover the rest of his bet.

Standard game policy in Sandy's.

The alien nodded and laid his hand face down on the table in front of him and scooted his chair back.

Again standard action. I had to admit, the alien had learned all the rules.

Cutbank nodded, his face still red, and then turned and scanned the bar. Not a soul there that would loan him a penny, let along the amount needed to cover the alien's bet.

His gaze stopped on Donna. She was standing beside the bar in the waitress station and she squirmed like a worm pinned to a hook.

Cutbank's eyes sort of lit up and he stood quickly and moved over to her.

I knew before he got there that it wouldn't do no good. Donna had had a good night, tip wise and all, but she didn't have anywhere near enough to cover his bet.

And it didn't take Cutbank long to find out.

She said she didn't have enough, but he could have what she did have. He called her something crude and then told her to get out of his way. He grabbed her drink tray and ripped open her money carrier. Maybe twenty bucks in there, plus change. Then he grabbed her and searched her pockets quick-like.

She was smart enough at that moment not to fight him. I'm sure he'd have beat her something awful if she had. Of course, none of the rest of us in Sandy's would have allowed that to happen.

She didn't have the money. As soon as Cutbank realized that, he tossed her roughly against the bar and then slammed his hand against the wall, cussing up a blue streak.

Right at that point, I really didn't blame him for being angry. Hell, I would have been with a hand like his and no money. But then I would have calmed down enough to throw in my hand and walk away.

Most men would.

But not Cutbank.

He went to three of the men in the bar, threatening them if they didn't help him. None of them had enough. He even glanced my way once but then thought better of it. He knew that he might threaten me out of the money tonight, but if he did, he'd never be welcome back in here again.

In a place like Sandy's, there are unwritten rules of the house. Break a rule and every other customer turns into my enforcer.

Cutbank liked Sandy's too much to go doing that.

But it turned out he didn't like Donna that much. He was across the room threatening old man Craig when he turned and saw Donna and the rest of the bar watching him. It was right at that moment that I knew he came up with the idea.

Quickly, he stormed back across the bar and grabbed Donna by the arm and dragged her off into the alcove near the bathroom. From where I was behind the bar I could see Cutbank talking and Donna shaking her head no. Once she tried to pull away from him, but he held her tight.

At that point, if she'd started putting up a fuss, three or four of us would have jumped in. But she didn't.

After a long minute of Cutbank talking real soft but intense at her, Donna's shoulders slumped and she nodded. Then she kept right on nodding. Satisfied, Cutbank pulled her over to the table and sat back down in his chair, leaving her standing beside him.

He smiled real snakelike at the alien and then announced that the other half of his bet would be Donna.

One night with Donna.

Let me tell you that caused a stir in the bar.

I wanted to object, but then remembered Sandy and how he had ended up and my main rule of not getting in the middle of something not my business.

Donna might work for me, but she had made herself Cutbank's woman and anything she did on her own time was her business. If she wanted help, all she had to do was ask and everyone in the bar would jump to help.

But she was just standing there, so no one moved.

The alien was as surprised as the rest of the room. He glanced up at Donna and then back at Cutbank. Then he asked Cutbank to repeat what he had just said.

Cutbank did.

Then the alien did what any self-respecting man would do in that kind of poker game. He looked up at Donna and asked her if she agreed.

Right about then, I guess Donna had another chance to get out. If she'd have said no, not a person in the bar would have let her leave with Cutbank. She hesitated, but it wasn't a long hesitation before she said it was all right with her. Whatever Cutbank wanted.

The alien nodded and told Cutbank he accepted his call. Then the alien turned over his down cards.

Full house, queens over sevens.

Donna turned almost white as Cutbank slammed his cards into the pile of money and told the alien to deal the cards.

As the older alien pulled the money and the cards toward him, he asked just what Cutbank intended to wager.

Cutbank indicated Donna and again the alien looked up at Donna for her confirmation.

Donna nodded real slow.

Real slow.

All three aliens nodded in agreement and then they spent the next half minute or so discussing what a night with Donna was worth on the poker table.

I could tell that Cutbank was getting a little crazy right at that point. His voice was higher, his gestures quick and angry. I wanted to stop the game, close the bar and just go home and take a hot shower to wash off the stink of men like Cutbank and the women who let themselves be used. But another one of the unwritten rules of Sandy's was that no one ever interrupted a game. What went on in a game was between the men in the game and no one else.

So I stayed behind the bar and wiped out the same glass ten times.

The next hand was even sadder.

Cutbank again had a damn good hand. This time he had the full house, kings over sixes. Any respectable player would bet damn near the limit on that hand in seven-card stud.

Only this time, Donna was the limit.

The older alien that held the marker for one night with Donna dropped out early, but the other two stayed in. One of the aliens had four sevens.

Unbelievable hand.

Enough to make anyone crazy.

And that's what it did to Cutbank. Again he slammed his cards and his fist down on the table. Now his face was red and I could see clearly that he was sweating.

Donna looked as if she might faint.

But somehow Cutbank held his composure long enough to indicate another hand.

And once again Cutbank had a good hand. Three queens.

The two aliens who already owned nights with Donna dropped out when it came time to push forward their money. But the one with the moustache stayed in.

The alien had a straight, ten high.

That was all Cutbank could take.

He took one long look at the alien's cards, his face getting redder and redder, then slammed himself back and away from the table while reaching inside his coat. He yelled something about cheating and the next instant a forty-five was in his hand and swinging up at the aliens.

He never had a chance.

Quick as anything I have ever seen, all three aliens had small devices in their hands aimed at Cutbank.

The little guns (or whatever they were) looked like pocket calculators and made high-pitched whining sounds.

Cutbank staggered back under the blows of whatever the three aliens where aiming at him. His forty-five went off, the sound of the shot echoing around and around the room.

His shot, knocked off line by the aliens fire, hit Donna square in the chest sending her flying backwards into a table and then crashing sideways onto the wood floor.

Cutbank ended up slumped against the bathroom wall, very dead, but without a mark on him.

The alien with the moustache went quickly to inspect Cutbank while the other two and the rest of us gathered around Donna.

She too was obviously dead. Her pretty face was contorted into an expression of surprise. Blood formed a large pool under her, soaking her clothes, and giving the room a sick, copper smell that seemed to overwhelm the always-present smoke smell.

Quickly, the older alien said something in a language that sounded something like Spanish and Chinese rolled into one. The one with a moustache picked up Cutbank's forty-five and pocketed it while the blonde alien man attached a small box to Donna's arm.

I objected, telling them that they shouldn't touch anything until the police arrived. Murder was a serious thing, even if it was self-defense.

The older alien just shrugged.

He said that they had each won a night with Donna and they were going to take their winnings. I was going to object a little more strenuously, but suddenly I caught a glimpse of one of those little calculator guns they had used on Cutbank and I thought better of it.

I guess everyone in the place at that moment thought better of it, because no one jumped in and tried to stop them.

Donna's body just sort of floated up off the ground until it was about waist high and then hovered there until the older alien expertly used Donna's foot to push her ahead of him out the front door while the blonde alien held the door open.

The one with the moustache followed and then the blonde alien just sort of nodded to the room and pulled the door closed behind all four of them.

Right at that moment, you could have heard a baby cry clear across town.

There were nine of us left and not a one said anything.

Finally, after I turned around and saw the big red puddle of blood and Cutbank very dead against the wall, I broke the silence by telling someone to please call the police while I made myself, and whoever else wanted one, a drink.

Of course, the police didn't buy the fact that three men just sort of zapped Cutbank and then floated Donna out, even with all of us telling somewhat close to the same story.

They did an autopsy on Cutbank and ruled that he had died of a heart attack. Made sense to me since there wasn't a mark on him. They didn't know what to do about the blood on the floor, so they didn't do anything and I mopped it up.

That all happened three days ago and now it's time to head to work. Tonight will be the forth night since they took Donna.

I don't know what to expect when I open up Sandy's. Sometimes I think Donna is just going to come walking back in the door live as can be.

And then sometimes I think that they just might dump her three-day-rotted body off after doing what they pleased with her for three nights.

That thought makes me sick, but it could happen. Sometimes you just never know.

I don't like to think that, so that's one of the reasons I've been covering for Donna the last three nights and holding her job open.

I can always hope.

LOVE WITH THE
PROPER NAPKIN

DEAN WESLEY SMITH

LOVE WITH THE PROPER NAPKIN

Hello, serious and beautiful woman across the bar.

The drink is my treat and the bartender will point me out. Remember that old joke about an alien being a piece of paper and the paper is making love to your fingers? Well, it just came true for you. Honest.

Don't laugh.

The bar napkin that this message is written on is an alien called a Roggen. It snuck into the human area through the supply section of the hotel here on the station. It has the ability to split itself into thousands of little bar napkins as a disguise to watch and study humans. At this very moment it is making love to your fingers and I can tell from clear across the bar you are enjoying it.

Have fun,

Anna

ps...hope you enjoy the drink.

———

Dear Anna,

Thank you for the drink and introducing me to these great little aliens. What planet did you say they were from? I'd love to go there some day.

Enjoying the feel,
Carla

———

Dear Carla,

The alien this is written on says your name is beautiful.

The alien said the sun their planet circles is called BAC 151. Damned if I know where that is.

He said he revealed himself to only a few of us so as to not cause too much commotion around the human section of the hotel. He also likes the beautiful dress you are wearing and I agree with him.

Trying not to stare,
Anna

———

Dear Anna,

What do you suppose would happen to the poor alien if I stuck him down the front of my dress? Can he turn himself into anything???? Oh, the possibilities are endless.

Thank you for the nice compliment and I hope you enjoy the drink in return.

Staring back,
Carla

ps...don't you think the bartender is going to mind passing all these notes back and forth?

———

Dear Carla,

The bartender loves it. I'm giving the poor kid twenty hotel credits every time. He'll deliver notes until doomsday for that.

By the way, the alien says doomsday for this hotel isn't for a few thousand years. Good to know, huh?

Notice the guy next to me. He thinks I'm weird because I talk to bar napkins. He should talk. His cologne smells like it was scraped off a well-used saddle.

Holding my breath and trying not to laugh,
Anna
ps...is that an empty stool there beside you?

————

Dear Anna,

I don't think you're weird. In fact, I kind of like what the bar napkins are doing to my fingers. Would you call it "paper sex?" Just the thought has me hot.

I'm afraid the seat next to me is taken by my current date, who happens to be off talking to some friends about something boring like rebuilding a cargo ship or something stupid like that. At least he doesn't make me sit and listen to it.

Stroking the alien,
Carla

————

Dear Carla,

Did you see that guy who just asked me to dance? God, what are they letting into the hotel these days? Some of these humans belong over in the other sections, I am sure.

The alien told me the guy only wanted to chew on my panties. I guess the alien can read minds or something like that.

He told me the guy next to me wants to do something kinky with ropes. Can you believe that?

Ask your alien a question. Go ahead. He'll tell you inside your head. No one will hear.

Go ahead and try it,

Anna

————

Dear Anna,

My God, you were right. I damn near fell off my stool.

I asked the napkin what your last name was and this little voice inside my ear said "Hartzell." Is that right????

Then I got afraid to write on one of them and the napkin said to go ahead. He said he loved it. I thought I had seen everything the galaxy had to offer. I guess not.

Gone completely nuts,

Carla

————

Carla,

I was watching and laughing.

Yes, my last name is Hartzell. The alien says you want to know if I'm a lesbian. I'm bi, just like you. (The alien told me...no secrets with these little white things around, huh?) Is this place getting crowded and loud or what?

Is your boyfriend ever coming back? I want to see this guy.

Waiting and drooling,

Anna

————

Anna,

The napkin says the fool who is my date (or I am the fool for being his) is over at a table by the dance floor talking to a young woman named Brenda Dare. The napkin says this Brenda is totally drunk, has already spilled two drinks and my date is staring down her dress.

I think he deserves her.

What do you think?

Annoyed,

Carla

ps...this alien napkin says my now ex-date hopes to get both me and Brenda in bed together. Hah! What a joker he is.

———

Carla,

How about me? In bed, that is?

How's that for forward?

The alien said my skin temperature went up a half degree just writing that first line. See what you do to me from clear across the bar. Damn, I wish these napkins were bigger and this bar not so crowded.

Wondering what your voice sounds like,

Anna

ps...the alien said he would be happy to be any size I wanted. Too bad I can't find a man that flexible.

———

Anna,

Why don't you come on over? If that jerk of a date returns, I'll tell him to take a walk out an airlock without a suit.

And bring as many of those napkins as you can. This alien told me that with enough of his old self in one place, he could reform quickly into something that just might please both of us. He showed me an image of what he would look like and I agree.

Stuffing napkins in my purse and pockets,

Carla

———

Carla

On my way.

I tipped the bartender a hundred credits to deliver this last note and let us take as many napkins as we can carry. The alien showed me the same image and I damn near melted off my stool. What do you say we head for somewhere much quieter and far less crowded, such as my room?

Almost too excited to walk,

Anna

ps...the alien told me that the more napkins we take, the bigger he will be able to reform. I've got an armload. How about you?

DRIED UP

A POKER BOY STORY

DEAN WESLEY SMITH

ONE

I very seldom get the feeling that something is wrong while sleeping beside Patty Ledgerwood, aka Front Desk Girl. In fact, until that very moment, it had never happened. Nothing ever seemed to be wrong when I was with Patty and not on a mission.

I get the "something-is-wrong" feeling at poker tables all the time, usually when another professional player is attempting to bluff me out of my shoes and all my money. I have learned to pay attention to that feeling, almost as if it is one of my superpowers. By paying attention, I have saved myself a ton of money over the years.

Right now I was in Patty's apartment near the University of Nevada, Las Vegas campus. In her master bedroom, to be exact. I could hear her regular breathing beside me, which told me she was sound asleep. The wonderful smell of her rose perfume filled the air and the feel of her expensive, fine-cotton sheets against my mostly bare skin felt wonderful, just as they always did.

Patty had had the day off, and we had spent it together; first at a movie, then a nice dinner at the buffet at the MGM Grand, and then back to her apartment to cuddle on the couch and watch television before heading to bed.

It didn't get much better these days.

But now, even without opening my eyes, I knew something was wrong.

I eased one eye open without moving, and couldn't see a thing in the dark room. The only light came from a nightlight in the bathroom to the right of the room and an alarm clock on the nightstand beside me. There was no light coming under the heavy curtains over the patio door, so it was still dark outside as well.

I eased over to glance at the time, and a lightning storm went off in the sheets.

And that wasn't a metaphor for some sexual thing.

A real lightning storm erupted around me, as more static electricity than I could imagine let loose.

And each spark was like a kid pinching me. Let me tell you, the sparks hurt.

"Wow!" I said out loud as I sat up.

It was as if I had rubbed my entire body across a carpet and then was touching things.

My movement caused the sheets to explode with even more static electricity which woke Patty up, and she sat bolt upright in bed as well, causing even *more* sparks as she sat stunned at the light show going on around us.

And the tiny pinches of pain with every large spark.

Somehow, every bit of moisture had been sucked out of the room, and a very large, background, static electric charge had filled the air.

"Sit still," I said, as Patty moved slightly and the room lit up with a light show once again.

"Ouch!" Patty said, freezing in place. "That hurts."

I had heard of many reasons for friction in bed, but this was ridiculous.

But in the light caused by the sparks with Patty's last movement, I had seen the problem.

Two alien-looking creatures with large black eyes and oblong heads stood at the end of the bed, staring at us.

It was like a scene out of a bad alien-abduction movie.

The UFO conspiracy people called them "Grays," but I knew them to be members of a race native to Earth called the Silicon Suckers.

In fact, they had been around far, far longer than humans.

They hate water and could deal with very little if any of it. Clearly they took what water they needed right out of the air around them.

They lived in very dry caves in the desert. The caves were so dry, the air would kill a human after just a couple of days, even with enough drinking water, which wasn't allowed in the homes of the Silicon Suckers.

Their very presence in Patty's apartment had sucked all the moisture out of the room.

I had never heard of a Silicon Sucker being seen inside a human city. Something had to be very, very wrong.

I carefully motioned for Patty to look at the foot of the bed. The sparks from my slight movement bit into me again and lit up the room.

She saw them and her breath sucked in with surprise. She instinctively pulled the sheet up to her neck covering up her nightgown and causing a large electrical storm around her and me.

Damn those little sparks hurt. It was lucky we just didn't burst into flames right there.

"Sorry," she said, holding her breath against the pain.

I had dealt with the Silicon Suckers a number of times before, and been in their sacred caves they called "sand castles." I had always been welcomed in their world because of a couple of favors I had done for them over the last few years.

"Greetings, honored guests," I said, bowing my head slightly and hoping the movement wouldn't set the sheets on fire. "What do I owe this great honor?"

Both Silicon Suckers bowed in return. Both looked identical. The one on the right spoke.

"Poker Boy, Front Desk Girl, we ask for your assistance in a matter of importance to our people."

"Of course," I said.

Both Patty and I bowed slightly.

After the sparks stopped I said, "It will be a great honor to help our friends."

Both again bowed in acceptance. "Our leader will speak to you at sunrise."

"We will attend," I said, also bowing again and setting off even more sparks. This room was going to need a humidifier real quick or we would be calling for fire trucks.

Without another word, the two turned and went out through curtains covering the bedroom's patio door, setting off a huge wave of sparks. I knew for a fact that the door had been locked and secured when we had gone to bed.

I had no idea how they had gotten in, or how they would get from Patty's apartment near UNLV, across town, actually across the Strip, and back into the desert.

The moment the curtains dropped back into place in a shower of static electricity, I instantly transported us into the living room area of Patty's apartment. The air there felt dry, but nothing like the intense lack of moisture in the bedroom.

I loved my newly learned superpower of teleportation. I just never expected to use it teleporting out of Patty's bed.

Patty used a napkin to flip on a light, took one look at me and started to laugh.

Now trust me, a beautiful woman in a sheer blue nightgown laughing when she sees your almost-naked body does not do wonders for even my superhero ego.

But I had to admit she looked just as funny. Besides all the tiny red marks all over her arms and wonderful legs that showed under her nightgown, her long brown hair stuck out in all directions from her head like she had been attacked by a mad hairdresser. Her hair was spread so wide, I doubt she could even get through a door.

And her wonderful face looked like it had a bad case of measles.

I glanced down at my own legs and chest, also covered with hundreds and hundreds of small red marks, as if I had been attacked by a swarm of bed bugs. Then I felt my brown hair, which was also standing straight out in all directions. And I could also feel my face was covered in the tiny red bumps from the electrical shocks.

Thank heavens I had worn my boxers to bed. The thought of electronic shocks to certain parts of my body just made me shudder.

TWO

After we carefully opened the windows and doors to let in some of what now seemed like balmy and humid Las Vegas summer air, we both drank three large glasses of water.

Thirsty didn't begin to describe what I was feeling.

Then, when we both had extra-large glasses of water in our hands, I shouted at the ceiling. "Stan. Need help!"

I have no idea how he always heard me, but he always did. Stan was the God of Poker, and my immediate boss.

An instant later he appeared in Patty's living room in front of us, looking grumpy that I had disturbed him in the middle of the night. He normally wore brown slacks, a light sweater, and black shoes. He was a short man, not even close to my six-foot height, and I seldom saw him smile. His dark hair was cut very short all the time, and his eyes looked almost black.

But tonight he had on a white golf shirt and blue golf shorts and the shorts looked like they were on backwards. When the God of Poker can't even dress himself, he really was tired.

He started to say something, then took one look at us and started laughing. I had seen him laugh a few times, but when a god starts to laugh at you, it is always worrisome.

But I had to admit that we did look funny. There was no containing our hair and the red marks on our faces, arms, and legs were getting brighter by the second.

"You two go through a swarm of bees on a rollercoaster?"

"Nope," I said as he laughed. "Just an electrical storm in bed."

He started to make some joke, then looked at Patty, then back at me and couldn't say anything because he was laughing too hard.

"I'm not kidding," I said. "Two Silicon Suckers woke us up and asked for our help."

Stan's laughing instantly vanished and he went back to his normal poker face. His golf shirt and golf shorts instantly became his normal slacks and sweater and black shoes.

It seemed I now had his attention and he was very much awake.

"How in the world did they get here?" he asked, shaking his head. "And when are you supposed to meet them?"

"We are meeting their leader at sunrise."

"You are meeting the Great One?"

Now he was stunned and when he said it like that, it bothered me as well. Patty just looked worried under all the red marks and massive head of hair spread out three feet around her head. It was going to take her some real time once the static charge faded to untangle all that wonderful long hair.

"You ever heard of the Silicon Suckers coming into any human town?" I asked Stan. "Just to ask for human help?"

"Never," he said, shaking his head.

"Have you heard any rumors about anything going wrong in their caves? Or anyone having a run-in with them?"

"Nothing," he said, "but I might have missed something. Stay put, I'm going to go get Burt and maybe Laverne."

He vanished.

Laverne was Lady Luck herself, in charge of all of the gambling and gaming universe. Burt was her second in command. I'd been around Lady Luck a number of times now, and Patty and I and the team had actually saved her life once. But she still scared hell out of me.

If Stan thought this was worth waking up Burt and maybe even Laverne, then Patty and I really might be in over our heads. We were just lowly superheroes.

Really dry and marked-up superheroes.

I had just taken another drink of water and was about to suggest we get a little more dressed when Laverne and Stan appeared. Lady Luck had on a strict brown business suit with her brown hair pulled back tight in a bun. She did not look happy.

When she saw us she raised one eyebrow, but did not smile, even though we looked really, really silly. With a wave of her hand Patty and I were both dressed, the static gone from our hair and the red marks gone from our skin.

Patty in her normal black pants and white blouse. Laverne had put me in my normal jeans with dress shirt, black leather coat and Fedora-like black hat. That was my poker uniform.

"Thank you," Patty said.

I nodded agreement. "Yes, thank you. I feel much better."

I could also feel the extra power that my coat and hat brought to me from the nearby casinos.

"No idea at all what the Silicon Suckers want?" Lady Luck asked, all business.

"Not a clue," I said. "Has something like this ever happened before?"

"Never," she said. "I have only met The Great One once, a few thousand years ago. But I do know that he only concerns himself with matters of major importance."

"I wonder why he came to us instead of you?" Patty asked. "It makes no sense."

"He didn't want to bother you," I said to Lady Luck, knowing the answer to Patty's question. "This is something he feels Patty and I can accomplish."

Both Laverne and Stan nodded.

"That makes sense," Laverne said. "But it gets us no closer to what he might want. And we just don't have time to figure it out. You had better get going."

"We have one stop to make first," I said.

I turned to my direct boss. "Stan, could you get me six thermoses and two backpacks to carry them in, and meet me at The Diner?"

Stan nodded and vanished.

"Good luck," Laverne said. "If you need my help in any fashion, just call out. I will be standing by."

"Thank you," Patty said as Laverne vanished.

I glanced at Patty, who looked stunning, as always, in the dark slacks and white blouse that Laverne had dressed her in. Her brown hair was combed and under control. Only the worry showing in her dark-brown eyes flawed the picture.

"Ready for an adventure?" I asked.

"With you, always," she said, smiling.

I took her hand and jumped us to The Diner, our favorite restaurant and meeting place tucked off on a side street in downtown Las Vegas. It was a place decorated in a fake 1960s look and run by Madge, a superhero in the food service part of the world. Madge seemed to always be there and she made the best milkshakes on the planet.

Ten minutes later, Madge and Stan had us ready to go and we jumped to the outskirts of Las Vegas near a huge Las Vegas billboard.

THREE

The cool morning desert air hit my face and I was glad to have the leather jacket on.

Patty had over one shoulder a backpack with three thermoses of hot chocolate, and I had the other backpack on my back with the other three.

Hot chocolate was like an extreme drug to the Silicon Suckers. One single drop of the liquid would send a Sucker into a drug high that seemed to last for a long time.

I had learned a long time ago to never think of going into one of the Silicon Sucker cities without a gift of a thermos of hot chocolate. And since we were going to see the Great One, it made sense to carry even more of the gift.

We had arrived fifteen minutes ahead of our time to meet the Great One, but I had a hunch it would take us that long to get to where he was through the vastness of the underground city. The sun had already lit up the hills and desert with a golden glow and the air still had an early-morning chill to it that promised to be gone very shortly in the summer heat.

"You ready?" I asked.

Patty nodded, but looked very nervous. She had never been inside a Silicon Sucker "sand castle" as they liked to call their huge network of caves and tunnels in the sandstone and rock.

While the hot chocolate was being made, Stan had briefed Patty on all the rules of the Silicon Sucker city.

We could never touch a wall. We could never sit down unless invited. We had to always treat the Suckers with respect by bowing. We had to give our full and honest name before being allowed to enter. And so on and so on. They were a very rule-bound race.

I had us face directly east, then, to the seemingly open-air twenty paces from the big billboard, I said, "Poker Boy and Front Desk Girl ask for entrance into the great city of the Silicon Suckers."

The entrance of a large tunnel shimmered into existence in front of us. It seemed to go into the side of a hill that just didn't appear to be there. Very weird.

I slipped off my shoes, leaving them on the desert sand. Patty did the same, and we stepped forward into the tunnel that slanted down-ward gently.

About twenty paces inside we were met by a Silicon Sucker who bowed as we bowed and gave our full names.

"Welcome to our castle once again, Poker Boy," he said. "It is always an honor to have you as a guest."

He turned to Patty. "It is also an honor to have you visit our castle."

"The honor is all mine," Patty said, bowing slightly.

With all the greetings done, the Silicon Sucker turned and indi-cated we should follow him.

As I had guessed, it seemed to take a long time for us to reach the major cavern and work our way down one wall on sloping ramps. For a person afraid of heights, this path on the face of the wall would be pure hell. It was a long ways down and there were no guardrails and you weren't allowed to touch the wall on the inside.

The cavern seemed to stretch into the distance and the walls were riddled with paths and open tunnels. They seemed to be crawling with Silicon Suckers.

I had never seen so many out and moving at the same time before. I felt like I had been shrunk down and was walking in an anthill.

The floor of the huge cavern had hundreds and hundreds of buildings and I knew from earlier visits that the caverns and tunnels went deep under all the buildings as well.

Seeing so many Silicon Suckers moving at once, I suddenly wondered what all of them ate and how so many could be fed? No doubt I dare not ask such a question.

I glanced at Patty who was following me. She seemed to be doing fine on the wall face, even in the drying air. I could feel the moisture in my lips and skin drying up and the leather jacket I wore didn't feel so comfortable now in the growing heat. But I didn't dare take it off, not only because it would be an insult in the city, but it gave me extra power. And there was no telling what I might need to do in this situation.

The deeper we got into the city, the drier the air got. We could not bring any kind of water with us. Plain drinking water was forbidden in a Silicon Sucker castle.

These places were very, very dangerous to humans. I knew of one superhero who had managed three days in a Silicon Sucker castle negotiating with them on some land swap, but she had barely made it out alive.

We reached the cavern floor and headed toward the huge center building. There was nothing ornate about it and no windows at all. It seemed more like a giant mound of sand. But it was the largest building and it did seem to be in the center of the cavern, which I was sure had some significance.

We were led inside and into a large, domed room with no furniture of any kind. It seemed to be the very center of the large mound of sand that was this building.

The floor was nothing but hard sand, warm under my bare feet, and the walls were brown like everything else in these underground cities. It looked like the special rooms weren't any more decorated than any of the other rooms in this cavern.

The Silicon Sucker who led us into the room indicated we should stand and wait and then he left.

There was only one other door into the room, an archway on the other side. We both stood, facing that doorway, not talking.

I could feel beads of sweat forming on my face and then drying away almost instantly.

I always got scared inside these cities. After all, Silicon Suckers looked just like every alien I had seen in the movies. That fear was very deep in all humans, more than likely from centuries around this race.

Honestly, at the moment I was more scared than I had ever been before.

If Laverne had only met the Great One once in thousands of years, why were we standing here?

And how many ways could we make a mistake and never see the light of the desert above again?

Suddenly, in front of us, a Silicon Sucker entered the room completely alone. As with all of them, he wore nothing, but he moved slower than the rest, and as he got closer to us, I could see his bright red eyes. And his face looked longer than the rest. But otherwise, besides the red eyes, I would have never been able to tell the Great One from any other Silicon Sucker.

Patty and I both bowed to him and he returned the bow.

"I thank you for this audience," he said, his voice strong and commanding.

"It is an honor to be asked," I said.

Patty and I both bowed again slightly.

"We have brought gifts, if you would allow us."

He held up his hand for us to not move, and we both stood still.

"I thank you for the gifts," the Great One said, "but I must first talk to you about why I asked you here. My people find themselves in a problem of our own making."

Patty and I carefully said nothing.

"It seems that the gifts you have brought us in the past, and the

105

regular payment for the land we have exchanged, has brought us to a crisis point."

He paused and then looked down as if embarrassed.

I knew he was talking about hot chocolate. Over the last few years I had brought his people six thermoses full. And for a piece of land they were getting ten thermoses every month. I knew that hot chocolate was a very powerful drug to the Silicon Suckers, but I couldn't imagine it becoming a crisis.

Then it hit me. *A powerful drug!*

Could he be mad at me for getting his people hooked on hot chocolate? Had I created a drug problem in his perfectly ordered world? No wonder he wanted to only "talk" with me.

But why had he also asked Patty to come along? Was it because she was special to me and he needed to take something special of mine for what I had done to his people?

I would not allow that.

The Great One looked up at me, the large unblinking red eyes clear.

"Poker Boy," he said, "I do not think you understand the value of your gracious gifts to my people. Your precious gifts give us life and energy. It gives us an excitement that we have not felt in many, many centuries."

I somehow managed to keep my mouth shut and just let him continue. I needed to be ready, if this turned very ugly, to jump Patty and me out of here quickly, or call for Lady Luck to come to our rescue.

The Great One continued.

"Your gifts have allowed me to walk out here without being carried and to stand here as a leader once again."

Now I was staring at him and my eyes suddenly felt like they were as wide as his were.

"Our problem is that our numbers are increasing with the new vitality from your gifts and land payments. And each cycle the payment for the land is not enough to supply my people."

Suddenly the fear I had been feeling turned to barely-controlled panic.

He wasn't mad at me for bringing the gifts of hot chocolate. This was much, much worse.

He needed *more* of it.

Oh, crap. I couldn't just offer it to him as a gift. I would insult him, and more than likely we would die where we stood.

I needed to find a way, and find it quickly, to get the Silicon Suckers more hot chocolate and let the Great One feel as if he was paying a fair price.

I nodded and somehow, keeping my voice from cracking in the dry air, I said, "A great leader worrying about the well-being of his people. It is an honor to be in your presence."

I took the pack from my shoulder and took out the three thermoses, holding them in my hands and not allowing even the pack to touch the ground.

Beside me, Patty followed my lead and did the same.

"For the honor of meeting with the Great One," I said, "the leader of all Silicon Suckers, we have brought this special gift. I hope it will help while we work out a more lasting solution and a fair and equitable trade."

"I can only thank you for your generosity," he said.

Without any indication of a movement from the Great One, six other Silicon Suckers came out and each took one thermos and carried them away like carrying gold from the room.

After they had left I spoke again.

"May I be so bold as to ask how much of the precious substance is needed to supply the great beings of the race of Silicon Suckers with their needs?"

He stared at me for a moment and I began to wonder if I had gone too far with my question.

Then he said, "We would need four times the amount of your generous gift every moon cycle, plus the payment for the land we are already receiving."

I tried to look serious. Thirty-four thermoses full of hot chocolate. "That is a large amount," I said. "But it is possible. But I must ask for something in return."

"Of course," he said.

I had an idea on what we might trade for, but I had to be very careful in presenting it.

"My people are also in great need in this area for..." I stopped and looked pained. "...I am sorry, I cannot use such language in front of the Great One."

He motioned for me to continue.

"We are in need of plain water. We are a very different people, with different needs. We must have plain water to survive. Is there an area in your lands which is not usable to your people because of too much plain water that we might trade?"

"Something important to my people in exchange for something important to your people," he said.

I only nodded. Thankfully he saw my purpose and I had not insulted him by asking for what was, in essence, poison to his people.

"Poker Boy, there is a reason my people sing your praises."

"Thank you, Great One," I said.

A map of the area around Las Vegas appeared in the air between us. Some areas were colored in gold for Silicon Sucker lands. Black for human lands. Gray for land that neither party controlled.

I knew the Silicon Suckers protected their own lands fiercely when needed, and no building was allowed within one hundred yards of any border to their property.

Of course, no humans in Las Vegas government knew that. The map had been formed by treaty decades before by the Gods of Land Use and the Silicon Suckers. The gods in that area made sure nothing was allowed to be built on the Silicon Sucker lands.

The Great One pointed to a small area colored red off to one side of the old Boulder Dam highway. It did not seem to be attached to any other area of Silicon Sucker lands.

"We were forced to abandon a growing castle in this area due to large pools of the evil liquid under the area. I would like five times your most recent gift every moon cycle in trade for the entire area."

He had upped the amount expecting me to bargain. Again, I needed to not insult him by giving in too quickly.

"Forty containers of the precious liquid every moon cycle?" I asked.

He said simply, "Yes."

I pointed at the large area of red off the old highway. "My people will find much of what we need here?"

"You will find much of the poison there," he said.

I didn't want to tell him that the precious liquid he was asking for was based on the poison we called water.

"Twenty-eight additional every moon cycle," I said. "And if we find what we must look for on the land, we will increase the amount to forty total in twelve moon cycles."

He nodded. "Your terms are acceptable."

The red coloring of the land on the map turned to blue and then the map vanished.

"The first payment will be delivered tomorrow morning," I said, "to the area near the entrance to this castle at sunrise, and then at sunrise every moon cycle after."

The Great One bowed and Patty and I bowed also.

"This exchange has given my people a new beginning," he said. "It will allow my people to reproduce and spread and build many large new castles. You will both always be honored guests as long as I rule."

With that he turned and walked away.

For a moment I felt the elation that we had survived the meeting. Then his last words came back strong, like someone was shouting them in my head.

Hot chocolate helped these creatures have baby Silicon Suckers?

Wow, I had not known that. No wonder I had never seen any children. I had never thought of it before.

What had I just done?

Patty and I followed a guide out of the building and back up the wall toward the entrance above. All the paths and tunnels teamed with Silicon Suckers, far, far more than I had ever seen before.

Was all this population growth from just a few thermoses per month of hot chocolate?

Oh, man, what would forty every month do?

What had I done?

Was I setting up a future war between mankind and Silicon Suckers? I sure hoped not.

Outside, after Patty kissed me for a job well done and we put on our shoes in the already hot sun, I told her my worry.

She just laughed in that way she does that makes me relax. It's one of her very special superpowers I'm sure.

Then she said, "I could really use a couple glasses of water and a large breakfast."

"You don't think this is serious, do you?"

"They don't dare expand into our areas and fight with us."

"And why not?" I asked as I jumped us from the hot desert to our favorite booth in the air-conditioning of The Diner. I didn't want to call for Stan and Laverne until I understood what Patty was saying.

"There weren't that many of them moving around last time I was down there," I said as we slid into the booth, the cool vinyl seat feeling wonderful. "That's only after six months of regular hot chocolate use. Imagine after a year?"

Again Patty laughed. "Trust me, they have to treat us well."

"And why?" I asked as Madge headed our way with large glasses of water she must have had ready.

"Because if they don't," Patty said, patting my hand on the table top like I was two years old, "we just cut off their supply of hot chocolate."

"Oh," was all I could think to say.

THE LAST MAN

A VERY EARLY
BUCKEY THE SPACE PIRATE STORY

DEAN WESLEY SMITH

The last man on Earth sat alone in a room. There was a knock on the door...
—Fredric Brown "Knock"

ONE

There was a knock at the hotel room door.

A faint, feminine knock.

"Don't panic now, Buckey, you old space pirate," I said to myself out loud. "It might be the wrong room."

I said that.

Out loud.

I really did.

Another faint knock.

I couldn't believe I was doing this. Me, Buckey, the last man on Earth.

Alone in a room.

With someone knocking at the door.

Exactly like the old Fredric Brown science fiction story.

Damn Molly, anyway.

This was all her doing.

A simple costume party. That's how it all started. Just a simple party at a co-worker's house in one of those subdivisions that smelled of mowed lawns and sounded like young children on tricycles.

In this particular subdivision, the owners had had enough money to build houses that didn't look exactly alike, but not enough to really hide the similarity with massive amounts of walls, shrubs and trees.

Middle income, I think it's called.

Chances were it was going to be a boring party, so I had decided that I would try to liven things up with Buckey.

Not that Buckey hadn't been out of the closet before. He had, but only at last year's SuperBigCon science fiction convention. I figured people who didn't know anything about science fiction would think him wild.

In reality, Buckey's white boots, white tights, giant-plumed white hat, and jewel-studded saber were pretty tame at sf conventions. There the costumes tended to run from merchants from Zantar's three red suns to the belly dancers of Cain, who wore only small flashing lights in strategic places.

Those lights could really hypnotize a guy, let me tell you.

I ended up right about the suburban costumes. There were a lot of men dressed as gorillas, women dressed in Victorian dresses with small black masks, and one couple dressed as Groucho and Harpo Marx.

Buckey really stood out.

Except for Molly.

TWO

Another knock at the door.

This time harder, more insistent.

I licked my lips and tried not to think about the dry taste in my mouth. Every time I got nervous, my mouth dried up like a desert. Only this time, I didn't know whether to be excited or afraid. I was Molly's last man on Earth, alone in a room. Should I let whoever was knocking in?

Or just sit here?

What did Fredric Brown do in his story? I think he just had his character say "Come in."

I didn't want to do that yet.

I just hoped it was Molly knocking.

It was supposed to be. It was her room.

It was her idea.

I first saw Molly while talking to a woman dressed like Queen Anne. The Queen had great breasts and the dress pushed them together and up and made the soft skin seem like it was about to explode.

The dress seemed to be straining to hold them back and I was making a play at being on stage when the dress let go.

Then Molly walked in.

Actually, she did more than walk in. She made an entrance.

She couldn't have done better with trumpets blaring. Every male head, including all the gorillas', turned to watch her.

She wore what I suppose could be called an alien costume. But not just any *Star Wars* or *Star Trek* alien costume. No way. It was a costume like none I'd ever seen.

And after years of going to science fiction conventions, I'd seen a lot of them.

Two well-muscled men, dressed as slaves and wearing only loin cloths, backed into the room in front of her, sprinkling small flower petals on the shag carpet and showing lots of cheek.

Molly wore a crown of pearls embedded in gold. Golden stands of hair flowed from under the crown and formed a triangle directly in the middle of her forehead pointing down her nose. She had large blue eyes, no eyebrows, and pearls hanging from her ears.

I figured right then that whatever she used to cover the rest of her body had to have been painted on. A complete flesh-toned suit.

But no matter how hard I stared, and trust me, I stared, I couldn't see any sign of nipples, belly button, or pubic hair.

Damn thick paint.

Most amazing costume I had ever seen.

Buckey Junior liked it a lot. He perked right to life.

"I am Maiden Molly," she said, and her voice, soft and husky, made Buckey Junior twitch even more. "I'm the Sex Queen of the planet Frost. I'm here looking for the last man on Earth."

"Right here, my lady," I heard myself shout before I even had time to think.

I strode across the room with the biggest strides I could take, left hand resting on my saber.

I reached her, pulled my plumed white hat off with a flourish, and did a deep waist bow in front of her. "Buckey the Space Pirate, at your service, your Majesty."

I had more courage than I thought I had. Who knew?

She looked me up and down, taking in my saber, my boots and where Buckey Junior saluted her costume.

Then she nodded slowly.

"Yes," she said. "Yes indeed. You might very well be the one."

Lucky me. But now what the hell was I going to do?

"Thank you, my lady," I said as best I could with my suddenly dry mouth.

For good measure, I did another deep waist bow, brushing my plumes across the floor.

I let my eyes move slowly up her costume as I stood. Not one sign of a seam in the cloth or for that matter, even the cloth itself. It was skin tight from her toes to her hair and hid everything without exception.

And I knew exactly what I was looking for.

"You will be tested," she said. "To see if you really are the last man on Earth. Meet me. One hour."

"But, where?"

She nodded her head slightly at one of her muscle men and he handed me a hotel room key. The key was for room twenty-three in the Flamingo Hotel. That was about five miles from here. A nice place. Not the best in town, but not cheap.

"Do not be late," she said and turned and left as the other men and gorillas cheered.

I stood open-mouthed, watching, as her royal ass swayed out the front door, followed closely by her two henchmen.

I looked back down at the key. I just hoped the two servants weren't invited to the test.

I made it to room twenty-three in less than half an hour.

THREE

Another knock.

Now, I didn't really know if I wanted to go through with it. Old Buckey Junior still liked the idea of peeling off that skin tight costume and getting to those hidden secrets, but part of my mind kept trying to tell me something wasn't right.

Another insistent knock.

Buckey Junior won.

I licked my lips. "Come in," I said, just like in the story.

A henchman opened the door and stepped back.

Maiden Molly walked slowly into the room, this time without flowers at her feet. She was still just as impressive.

The henchman pulled the door closed and stayed out in the hall.

Right then I noticed that she was damn tall. I stood six feet. She had to top six-six. She wore a peach smelling perfume and her breasts were even bigger than I remembered from the party. Still no sign of nipples, though.

She looked me right in the eye and I looked right back. Her eyes were green, with slightly cat-like irises. Neat effect. I figured she did it with contacts.

After a long few seconds, I decided I had better just keep playing along with her game. After all, she had paid for the room.

I took off my hat and did another deep waist bow. "Your Majesty," I said. "It is an honor."

Buckey Junior was hoping it was going to be a lot more.

"Yes, I imagine it is," she said, not even cracking a smile. "Are you ready for your test?"

"And just what might that be?" I asked. Her attitude was turning Buckey Junior right off.

"To see if you are the last man on Earth. Now, get undressed and we will begin."

She reached up and took off her crown of gold and pearls and set it carefully on the nightstand beside the bed. Her hair was soft, peach-fuzz looking, and it became obvious that the triangle of hair on her forehead was going to stay right in place.

Weird woman.

I laid my hat on the chair beside the television.

She turned and faced me. Slowly, her body started to glow a faint orange. Her skin seemed to be melting right before my eyes.

I blinked as hard as I could, but it didn't stop what I was seeing.

Slowly, large pink nipples formed on her breasts, her bellybutton sunk into place, and blonde soft hair appeared between her legs.

"Wow!" I said. "How'd you do that?"

"You are not undressed," she said. "How can we start?"

She moved to the head of the bed and stripped the bedspread and sheets from the bed.

I stared at her beautiful ass, huge chest, and soft skin. No matter how that costume worked, there was no way I was going to pass this up. Besides, Buckey Junior was screaming to be let out.

It took a long ten seconds to get out of the rest of my costume.

"Join me," she said and patted the bed.

I tried to remain as dignified as I could as I sat down, but what I really wanted to do was take a running jump at her. Buckey Junior just remained standing at attention.

She reached over and took hold of Buckey Junior. Her hands felt warm. I let out a deep sigh and started to reach for her.

She stopped me. "The test will be to see if you have any control. Or, in other words, to see how long you can last. Understand?"

I nodded.

So did Buckey Junior.

"Then let's begin. Lay out flat."

I did as I was told without her ever letting go of Buckey Junior.

She knelt beside me and put her soft lips around Buckey Junior, sucking him quietly into her soft throat.

Right at that moment, I thought Buckey Junior was going to let me down. Not that I'd blame him. Not at all. It felt so damn good. But my mind screamed hold on.

Hold On!

And Buckey Junior held on.

Not that it wasn't touch and go there for a moment with her mouth moving slowly up and down and up and down. But Buckey Junior resisted doing his fire hose impression and let my mind take back over at least for the moment.

I reached out and pulled her hips toward my face. She hesitated for only a moment, then swung her leg up and over and sat down right on my nose.

Bullseye!

At that moment Buckey Junior almost went off unannounced. But somehow, he held on again and I started to explore the new world that covered my face. Maiden Molly stirred slightly as I made first contact and then began a slow, grinding motion with her hips.

I figured if I had died right at that moment, I wouldn't have to go anywhere to find heaven.

She kept up her vacuum pump imitation on Buckey Junior. I really don't know how Buckey Junior held on.

Absolutely amazing.

Finally, after what seemed like the shortest eternity that ever existed, Molly suddenly sat up, turned around and sat right down on Buckey Junior.

Again, another bullseye.

Buckey Junior shouted "Thank you!" right up my spine and through every nerve in my body.

Molly took my hands and placed them over her nipples, then started a slow belly dance number on Buckey Junior.

I let my hands do what came naturally and slowly Molly picked up speed.

After a short few minutes, Molly leaned forward, put her breasts against my face and started a fast up and down motion on Buckey Junior.

That was the end of the road for Buckey Junior.

Molly pumped faster and faster.

And finally Buckey Junior let go.

I saw stars swirling before my eyes and for a moment I really thought I was going to die.

But I didn't.

After a few more quick up and downs to make sure Buckey Junior was drained, Molly stopped, sat up and then stood beside the bed, leaving me and Buckey Junior feeling disappointed.

"You did not pass the test," she said.

"Huh?" I asked.

At that moment I was lucky to get that word out of my mouth.

I raised my head off the sheet and looked at her, which took all the energy I had left. I could still see stars spinning around the insides of my eyelids.

"You are not the last man on Earth," she said. "I am sorry."

Her skin glowed again and started to melt. Her nipples disappeared. She picked up her crown and carefully fitted it back on her head.

"How'd you do that? And what exactly did I do wrong?"

Not that I really cared. I'd had a great time. But her attitude was annoying.

And her costume had me worried.

"You did not last long enough. Just last week a baker in Nevada lasted forty minutes longer than you did. Unless I find someone better, he will be the last man on Earth. Not you. I am sorry."

"You mean the last man is the one who lasts the longest?"

"That is correct."

"Can I have another chance?" I patted the bed beside me. Buckey Junior gave a little jerk to show he was interested too.

"No. Only once per man."

She turned and headed for the door.

I watched her for a moment. I had to admit, this woman was kinky. Stranger than anyone I had met at a science fiction convention.

I sat quickly up in bed. "Wait!"

She stopped and turned.

"Just for my information," I said, "Could you tell me how close I came and why you are looking for this last man?"

"To be my mate, the King of the planet Frost. We have very long winters there. As for you..." She smiled for the very first time. "You did very well. Only seventeen men have lasted longer than you. Now, goodbye."

"Bye," I said weakly as she closed the door behind her with a sharp click.

Buckey, the Space Pirate, the seventeenth-from-the-last man on Earth sat alone in a room.

And after all that, I couldn't have done anything even if someone had knocked.

DINNER ON A FLYING SAUCER

DEAN WESLEY SMITH

DINNER ON A FLYING SAUCER

Ethel was lookin' at me like a skunk done crawled up my ass and was making a nest. I suppose I couldn't really be blamin' her. I figure that havin' dinner on a flyin' saucer would be a hard lump to swallow whole, especially when I smelled of whiskey and had lipstick-lookin' red marks all over my coveralls.

And, to boot, it was three in the mornin'.

Ethel stood there in the front door of the double-wide that I had bought and paid for with the sweat and hard work from my own bare hands like she owned the thing, leavin' me stuck on the second step halfway up to the porch like a dog after he rolled in the mud. She was makin' sure I didn't have a thought of goin' inside past her, even though it was cold and kinda real damp out.

Behind her, the light from the kitchen was showin' through her bathrobe and nightgown, outlinin' things that Ethel should *never* let be seen.

Now no disrespect to my wife, but Ethel is a big woman, taller by a pretty fine lick than my five-foot height. She never was much of a sight to look at at three in the morning, and this morning was no great exception to the rule. She had them there big curlers in her hair that jabbed me every darned time I rolled over in bed. She had on her flannel robe over her nightgown, and her favorite slippers with the pink furballs on the toes. Right at that moment her face was all screwed up like she was about to spit, and she had my shotgun cradled under her tits just like she carried it when she hunted.

At the moment I figured out real quick, I was the game, and if I didn't do a little scamperin', tellin' her what happened, I was going to end up with an ass-full of buckshot. Or worse yet, dead on my own front steps.

I held up my hands like I'd seen them criminals do on *Cops*. "Give me a chance to tell ya the story at least."

"Tell," she said, gesturing with the barrel of my gun.

"Can't we go inside so I can sit?" I didn't want to say nothin' about how the whiskey was makin' me feel right about then.

"Tell."

That time the gun gesture she made got her point out *real* clear like. She didn't care about no fog or cold or dark night. She just wanted to know where the hell I'd been and what the hell I'd been doin'.

I took a deep breath of the thick air and figured the best place to start my tellin' was at Benny's, a bar down on Owl Creek Road, right near the Miller place. Benny owned Benny's, ran it like every drop of booze was the most important drop of booze on the planet, never givin' no man a free drink for no reason. Cheap bastard, but a hard-worker and I liked him for that.

Benny had one of my elk heads, a seven-pointer, on the wall over the pool table. I was damn proud of that head, and spent many an evenin' in there drinkin' and starin' at it and makin' sure no one hit it with a pool cue.

"I was at Benny's," I told her.

Ethel snorted, clearly not surprised.

"Two Buds and then I left, I swear. I was aheadin' home for dinner by half-past six."

"Dinner got ate at seven," she said, the anger in her voice so strong that behind me I imagined I could feel the trees startin' to shake with fear. I know I was, but I couldn't be showin' her any weakness and I couldn't be upchuckin' no cookies from being sick on the whiskey. I had to keep on talkin' and talkin' fast.

"Tossed your dinner out at nine," Ethel said. "I let the dog eat it."

I wanted to ask her if the dog liked it, or if the dog was even still alive, but figured real quick-like to just not be saying anythin' real stupid with her still holdin' my shotgun. So I just nodded like I understood and kept on tellin'.

"I was walkin' down Owl Creek, headin' home after only two Buds, when this bright light comes at me from over the trees like a big bird diving for a rabbit. That there light just sort of hovered right smack over the road above me. I tell ya Ethel, that there light was so bright I had to go and cover my eyes."

She grunted.

I was sure she wasn't believin' me, but the story had to be as I started it, since changin' the tellin' now would cause me even more problems, and more problems at three in the morning, facin' an angry woman with a shotgun, is not somethin' any man wants.

So I just went right on, makin' the details real thick-like, cause I heard once that details make a story sound more right.

"And there was this wind," I told her, swingin' my arms up and around as if I was a warmin' up to throw something, "like that storm we had last winter that knocked down the chicken coop. I tell you, that there wind was real strong like, blowing dust into my face."

"No wind here," she said.

"The wind was a comin' right out of the light."

"Oh," she said.

"Then suddenly the light just sort of grabbed me and picked me up and sucked me through this big hole and into this really big room that was real dark considering it was inside the bright light."

She grunted and I didn't much blame her, since this was soundin' a might stupid to me. What on God's green earth had made me think tellin' her the truth about gettin' taken by aliens would stop her from shootin' me? But I was committed to the tellin' and I figured right then and there that the only way to get this out was to just tell her fast, before she decided I was too stupid to live and just shot me. Dyin' from a blast with my own shotgun just wasn't my idea of how to leave this life.

Takin' another deep breath to push back the whiskey-dizzies, I went on.

"I was frozen like a deer in a truck's headlights, standin' there starin' at three little gray guys, little fella's no taller than my belt, skinny, big long fingers, just like they had on the tee-vee in that movie we saw last year. You know the one with all them aliens?"

She stared at me and just said nothin' and when Ethel says nothin' I knew buckshot and a quick burial was a comin' next. You didn't go messin' with Ethel, and I doubted if Sheriff Bob would even bother to arrest her for killin' me once he heard why she had done it.

It was three in the mornin' and I was whiskey stupid and didn't have a lick of sense to begin with anyway, so I kept on tellin' her about the aliens.

"One of these little guys with only three long fingers took my hand and walked me across the room to a table and then pointed to a chair. I remember readin' in the *Enquirer* that they usually did things no man wants done, but they didn't seem to have read the same issue I read, which pleased me a might I can tell you. I sat right down let me tell you, since I was scared plain out of my wits and about ready to dump a big one in my pants."

Ethel just grunted and shook her head.

"The three little guys went around the table, each a sittin' on one of the other sides. They must have had booster chairs under them because they could see over the edge of the table and look me right in the face with their big, slanted eyes. The one closest to me pointed at the plate in front of him and then at me."

Ethel hadn't moved, even to shift her bulk from one swollen foot to the other, which for Ethel was some special thing. I knew that if I managed to get out of this alive I'd be rubbin' her feet for a week.

She made that gesture that said I should go on, so I did. "Right then

I noticed that the table was set like for a special Sunday dinner, with white plates, silverware, and food, lots of food, and it smelled real nice as well, like that wonderful turkey you made us last Thanksgivin'."

Figured a compliment or two couldn't hurt any, but it didn't even get her to blink, so I kept on with my tellin' real fast-like.

"It seemed they wanted me to try some of that there food in front of me, since the little fella next to me kept pointin' at the plate and then at me. The plates in front of them didn't have no food on them, but it seemed they wanted me to eat anyway. Now let me tell you, Ethel, I wasn't real pleased with the idea of eatin' no dinner fixed by little gray guys with three fingers who traveled in some beam of light. And I didn't hanker much to eatin' alone while they watched, but I figured I had no choice right about that point."

"You tellin' me you had dinner on an alien space ship?" Ethel asked, my gun moving in her arms more than I wanted it to move.

I ignored her question because that was just what I was about to tell her that I'd gone and done.

"When I picked up the fork on the outside like I had seen on that movie, they all clicked like a bunch of crickets, only louder, so I put the fork back down and they stopped clickin' and just stared instead."

Ethel just shook her head.

"It's gettin' cold out here," I said, easing my way up completely on the second step. "How's about I finish this at the table?"

"Keep on goin'," she said. "I don't want no blood in my house if I have ta go on and shoot ya."

I wanted to say it wasn't her damned double-wide, it was mine, since I had bought and paid two-thousand good, hard-earned money for it long before we had gone and gotten married, but contradictin' a woman with a shotgun had never been good thinkin'.

"Well, Ethel, let me tell you this," I said, going back to what had happened up there in that there spaceship, "I picked that fork back up and they went to clickin' again, stopped when I put it down, started when I picked it up, like there was somethin' really important about that there fork."

I took a deep breath and kept right on, not even lookin' at Ethel.

"Finally I got tired of playin' with 'em, so I just dug the fork into what looked like mashed potatoes with brown gravy and shoved a bite into my mouth like I hadn't eaten in days. Clickin'? You ain't never heard so much alien clickin', but I didn't much care because them there mashed potatoes were the best damned potatoes I had ever tasted, even better than the ones your Aunt Sarah used to make with that real butter that she took down to the church socials."

"You tellin' me you ate some alien's *food?*" Ethel asked.

"Every bite on the plate. Turkey drumstick, dressin', potatoes and gravy, roll, wanted to lick the plate it was all so good."

"You're eatin' while the perfectly good food I had worked hard to fix up for you sat gettin' cold on the table?"

"I couldn't help it," I said. "It weren't my idea to get sucked up into that light and set down at that table and clicked at. I just did as them there little fellas wanted me to do."

"And them there lipstick marks on your overalls?" she asked, swingin' my shotgun around to point at my chest that was covered in red marks that looked like a woman's lipstick. "Them from the little fellas as well?"

"They are at that," I said. "After I finished eaten that there food they had given me, all three of them got up and came over and started puttin' their three fingers on me all over and clickin' like mad. It was their fingers that left these here marks."

I pulled my coveralls away from my body and sort of held the chest part out for her to look at. "See, these here ain't no woman's lips. You can see for yourself they're alien fingerprints. Just look nice and close."

Again Ethel snorted and didn't move.

It was them there alien fingerprints that I was a hopin' would prove to her that my story was true and all. Alien fingerprints are damned hard to ignore I figure.

"So why did they want some fella like you?" Ethel asked.

"Directions," I said. "Them little guys were flat lost."

"The only place you know directions to is Benny's."

"Not true," I said. "Remember when we was lost two years ago, up in the hills and I got us out."

"Luck," she said, disgusted and waving the shotgun for me to go on tellin'.

"Well, it seemed that all their touching was a way of talkin'." I held out a section of my overalls to make sure she could still see the little red marks. "Ya see, them there little guys was warriors, soldiers, fighting in this big ol' war goin' on between them and these real ugly stick-like slug-creatures. I could see it all because it was like they was a runnin' a movie in my head."

I shuddered rememberin' it all, but kept on. "I could see the fightin' and killin' so clear, and let me tell you, them stick-slugs were ugly and really tall. Hell, I wanted to jump in right there and offer to help them there little gray fellas fight them ugly slugs. So I did."

"You did *what?*"

I took a deep breath and just kept on tellin' her the truth. "I up and said I'd help 'em in their war."

Ethel just shook her head and the shotgun swung around at me again. I wasn't going to get a chance to die for them gray guys. Ethel was going to kill me first. And I bet they didn't give out no ribbons for gettin' killed tellin' your wife the truth.

"Let me just finish, will ya?"

She shrugged, so I went on.

"Like I said, them little fellas was really lost, so that's all they wanted, but let me tell you, they was touched I offered to fight with them."

"You're the one who's touched," Ethel said.

"You just go and wait until them there big tall slug fellas start marchin' up the driveway. They fire light beams that can cook ya faster than Uncle Ben's barbecue pit."

She snorted. Not a good sign when Ethel starts snortin'.

"Look, I am knowin' you don't believe any of this, but what I saw when them there little gray guys touched me really opened my eyes, let me tell ya. This here is the battlefield. This country, this planet. All around us, right here, only not really here where we can see it, but yet right here. You know, like when a dog can hear a whistle and we can't?"

Ethel didn't say anythin', which was a degree worse than snortin'.

I pointed at a tree. "One of them there tall skinny slugs could just come right out of that trunk right there and we'd both be dead. Them little gray guys called it somethin' like multi-dimension or somethin' *Twilight Zone-ish.*"

Ethel glanced at the tree.

"But the little gray guys seem ta know when the tall stick-slugs are a comin' and where and they keep 'em from doin' that, which is why I up and offered ta help."

"How can an idiot like you help them?" Ethel asked, disgusted.

"Guide," I said. "They showed me a map of the area and somehow, with all the clickin' and touchin', got me to understand they was a lookin' for a dock at Steven's Lake. I pointed right on one of their maps where it was at and we got there in a flash of white light, and let me tell you, just in time to stop them there stick-slugs from comin' out. Stick-slugs blow up like popcorn under the little gray guys' weapons, which would be just horrible for huntin' but great for killing enemy stick-slugs. After they was all done fightin', I was a hero and they offered me more food, but I told 'em I had to be gettin' on home."

"So, how come you're not still fighten' with them if you're such a hero?"

"I said I'd try to get more help and then be here when they needed me."

"Help?" Ethel asked. "You're gonna' tell other folks this story?"

"Sure," I said. "Told them there little gray guys I would, get more guides, get a few folks like me workin' for 'em. So they let me go, right back through the white light and onto the road where they'd taken me. I sort of staggered back to Benny's and since it was right before two in the mornin', I caught Benny before he closed up and had a couple of whiskies to calm my nerves. And then I came straight on home, I swear."

I put up my right hand like I was on one of them tee-vee court shows where people argue and yell and have all sorts of fun.

Ethel just shook her head and stepped toward me, grabbing my overalls and lookin' at the red marks. Then finally she said, "You're sleepin' with the dog."

"Now hold on there," I said, but she swung the shotgun around to point directly at me.

"It's three in da morning," she said, "and you been drinkin' and playin' pool and missed my dinner because you're a damn fool drunk. And if that there raspberry rubbin' don't come out of your overalls, I'm goin' ta make ya wear them anyway."

She turned and before I could get another word out of my mouth, she went inside and slammed the door on me. Can't say as I blamed her for not believin' my story.

I turned and whiskey-stumbled down off the two steps and headed for the dog house which I had built when we got the mutt a few years back. It weren't really no dog house, just a lean-to against the chicken coop, but the dog liked it and who was I to argue with a dog. I was a goin' to be covered in fleas by mornin', but I suppose that's not as bad as an ass full of buckshot.

I had made it halfway to the doghouse when a bright light hit me from overhead, a wind whipped up dust and dirt, and then the next damn thing I knew I was back in the alien ship with the three little fellas clickin' at me. I was swayin' dizzy-like from the whiskey and the ride on the light.

I can't say I was happy to be seein' them again so fast, but after facin' Ethel and that shotgun, they looked pretty darned harmless.

This time they wanted me to try some really nice-tastin' ice cream. Strawberry, with swirls right in there of some sort a chocolate. Ethel would end up even bigger if she ever laid her hands on the fixin' for that there stuff. They studied every move my spoon made like I was an artist at the ice-cream-eatin' event in the alien Olympics.

And I can tell ya, my spoon did some real fancy dancin'. After three full dishes of the stuff, I waved off a fourth, then with them gettin' more red marks on my coveralls, I told them where Deacon Creek Falls were. They let me lay down and catch a few winks while they went and killed more stick-slugs, since ice cream and whiskey don't match if you do much movin' around after, and I couldn't see how I'd be much use in a fight throwin' up and all.

They finally woke me up with a bunch of loud clickin' and shot me through the light back by the dog house.

It was a comin' up on dawn and Ethel was already up and cookin' breakfast, so I just went on inside. She pointed at the table just like them aliens had, only without clickin', and served me my favorite breakfast, buttermilk pancakes smothered in maple. She never mixed up a batch of buttermilks unless something was wrong, or she really needed somethin' from me. And after the tellin' of my story, I had no idea what that might be.

I ate as much of them as I could, and let me tell ya that wasn't no easy chore after a night of doin' nothin' but eatin'.

I kept waitin' for her to say whatever she wanted, because with Ethel I could always tell when something was runnin' around on her mind, but she just watched me eat in silence, no talkin', no clickin' and didn't say nothin' about my story, and I didn't go tellin' her about my ice cream visit to the little fellas and hours of sleep on the alien ship. I figured she wouldn't have believed me no-how.

Besides, there was just no point in gettin' in even more trouble for not sleepin' in the doghouse.

Finally, after I just couldn't eat another bite she spoke her mind. "You go back, get me them recipes."

I stared at her like she had gone and lost her grip on reality.

"Recipes?" I asked. "There's a war on, woman."

"I don't care about no war," she said. "You can help them or not, make me no mind. But I want them alien mashed potatoes recipe, and the dressing one if you can get it, too. Monthly social is a comin' up and..."

She stopped like she knew I knew what she was a sayin'. I couldn't believe my luck. She had just up and gave me a free ticket to husband heaven. She needed me to get her somethin', and from the looks of the buttermilk pancakes, she was a willin' to pay. I was goin' ta be eatin' good for a week. And havin' my beer toted to me in my chair in front of the tee-vee. And no more doghouse for stoppin' at Benny's every night. Any darned time I wanted somethin' all I had to say was I was a tryin' to get her them there alien recipes.

"Next time them little fellas come and get me for some eatin', and guidin'" I said, nodding to her real serious and all, "I'll ask them. How does that sound ta ya?"

She gave me her sad smile and shook her head, which puzzled me for a moment. Then she stood, moved over to the stove and pulled out my shotgun from a spot she'd hidden it.

"You were supposed to be a sleepin' in the doghouse," she said, pointing the gun right into my face, "so where was ya? And don't go tellin' me ya went back to them aliens for dessert. There ain't no aliens, no recipes, just you, an old drunk lyin' to his wife. So no lyin'. Where was ya? Widow Matti?"

I should have known Ethel wouldn't have gone and believed me, since she never read *The National Inquirer*. She didn't know them there gray guys got folks from all over the country ta help them in their big fight with the tall stick-slugs.

The visions of my husband heaven left me like a cat being chased by a dog. Now she thought I was a cheatin' on her with the widow Matti.

But I had to tell her the truth. I just couldn't think of anythin' else while lookin' down the barrel of my shotgun.

"I'm not a cheatin' on ya. Them there little fellas took me in the light again, gave me ice cream, asked directions to Deacon Creek Falls, and let me sleep on the floor. I swear!"

The red in her face sort of crawled up from her thick neck like a burner on the stove gettin' hot.

I held up my hands as the business end of that shotgun sort of got bigger. "Okay, wait, wait, I stumbled into the woods to toss my cookies and passed out near the woodpile."

"Checked there," she said, her face gettin' redder and startin' ta look like a ripe tomato.

I was about as desperate as a man could get, and my brain was a workin' on too little sleep and too much food and didn't seem ta be helpin' like it was supposed ta be in a husband crisis. So, without really doing much thinkin' I shouted out what she wanted ta hear.

"Okay, okay I was at widow Matti's cabin, and she rode me like a cowboy rides a bull, and I can even show you her spur marks in my side if ya want."

Ethel's face was about as red as I had ever seen it.

I glanced around at the door, figurin' that if I made the outside and ducked right, she might miss me enough with the shot for me to live. But if Ethel was anythin', she was a fine shot, and I just wasn't that fast.

I was just about to make my break when suddenly the build-up exploded, but not like I had 'spected. She burst out laughin' and lowered the shotgun.

I stared at her, more stunned than I had remembered feelin' starin' at them there three little gray men inside the light. She was laughin' and shakin' her head and the flesh on her arms was a movin' in all sorts of directions like waves on a beach. It was like Jay Leno had just told a joke right there in the kitchen.

"What's so danged funny?" I asked after she managed to catch a breath.

"Your story," she said, startin' to laugh all over again. After a moment she just shook her head. "You and the widow Matti. Now *that's* funny."

"Why is *that* so danged funny?" I asked.

The widow Matti had given me a few looks, but I sure hadn't told Ethel that, and I wasn't a bad-lookin' man, even if I didn't shave much and wore the same shirt for a few days in a row.

"Stick with them aliens servin' ya food story," Ethel said, shaking her head and startin' to clean up the kitchen. "And when I tell ya ta sleep in the doghouse, you better get your ass in there real pronto-like."

I opened my mouth to say somethin' real smart back in return, then decided that anythin' I might say wasn't real smart at that point, which is a good rule to follow just about any time with Ethel, but especially now after I had lied to her about bein' ridden by another woman, so instead I just sat right there at the kitchen table and nodded like a toy dog in the back window of a pick-up truck.

Still, it hurt that she didn't believe her own husband would be somethin' the widow Matti might ride some night. The widow had taken on old Chester from the service station, or at least Chester claimed she had every time he had a few too many drinks.

I believed Chester, yet my own damned wife didn't believe me about the widow Matti or about them there aliens either. Or the war with the tall stick-slugs. Maybe next time them little guys took me up into the light for dinner and directions, I *would* ask them for the recipe for them there mashed potatoes.

Then I'd give that there recipe to the widow Matti.

I bet the widow Matti would be real grateful like, and maybe give me a ride like she'd done to Chester. Especially when she found out I was a real war hero and all, keepin' the world safe from them stick-slug invasions.

The widow Matti would go and believe me. And then that would show Ethel.

TEN STORIES

BY

KRISTINE KATHRYN RUSCH

SKIN DEEP

KRISTINE KATHRYN RUSCH

SKIN DEEP

"More pancakes, Colin?"

Cullaene looked down at his empty plate so that he wouldn't have to meet Mrs. Fielding's eyes. The use of his alias bothered him more than usual that morning.

"Thank you, no, ma'am. I already ate so much I could burst. If I take another bite, Jared would have to carry me out to the fields."

Mrs. Fielding shot a glance at her husband. Jared was using the last of his pancake to sop up the syrup on his plate.

"On a morning as cold as this, you should eat more," she said as she scooped up Cullaene's plate and set it in the sterilizer. "You could use a little fat to keep you warm."

Cullaene ran his hand over the stubble covering his scalp. Not taking thirds was a mistake, but to take some now would compound it. He would have to watch himself for the rest of the day.

Jared slipped the dripping bit of pancake into his mouth. He grinned and shrugged as he inclined his head toward his wife's back. Cullaene understood the gesture. Jared had used it several times during the week Cullaene worked for them. The farmer knew that his wife seemed pushy, but he was convinced that she meant well.

"More coffee, then?" Mrs. Fielding asked. She stared at him as if she were waiting for another mistake.

"Please." Cullaene handed her his cup. He hated the foreign liquid that colonists drank in gallons. It burned the back of his throat and churned restlessly in his stomach. But he didn't dare say no.

Mrs. Fielding poured his coffee, and Cullaene took a tentative sip as Lucy entered the kitchen. The girl kept tugging her loose sweater over her skirt. She slipped into her place at the table and rubbed her eyes with the heel of her hand.

"You're running late, little miss," her father said gently.

Lucy nodded. She pushed her plate out of her way and rested both elbows on the table. "I don't think I'm going today, Dad."

"Going?" Mrs. Fielding exclaimed. "Of course, you'll go. You've had a perfect attendance record for three years, Luce. It's no time to break it now—"

"Let her be, Elsie," Jared said. "Can't you see she doesn't feel well?"

The girl's skin was white, and her hands were trembling. Cullaene frowned. She made him nervous this morning. If he hadn't known her parentage, he would have thought she was going to have her first Change. But the colonists had hundreds of diseases with symptoms like hers. And she was old enough to begin puberty. Perhaps she was about to begin her first menstrual period.

Apparently, Mrs. Fielding was having the same thoughts, for she placed her hand on her daughter's forehead. "Well, you don't have a fever," she said. Then her eyes met Cullaene's. "Why don't you men get busy? You have a lot to do today."

Cullaene slid his chair back, happy to leave his full cup of coffee sitting on the table. He pulled on the thick jacket that he had slung over the back of his chair and let himself out the back door.

Jared joined him on the porch. "Think we can finish plowing under?"

Cullaene nodded. The great, hulking machine sat in the half-turned field like a sleeping monster. In a few minutes, Cullaene would climb into the cab and feel the strange gears shiver under his fingers.

Jared had said that the machine was old and delicate, but it had to last at least three more years—colonist's years—or they would have to do the seeding by hand. There was no industry on the planet yet. The only way to replace broken equipment was to send to Earth for it, and that took time.

Just as Cullaene turned toward the field, a truck floated onto the landing. He began to walk, as if the arrival of others didn't concern him, but he knew they were coming to see him. The Fieldings seldom had visitors.

"Colin!" Jared was calling him. Cullaene stopped, trying not to panic. He had been incautious this time. Things had happened too fast. He wondered what the colonists would do. Would they imprison him, or would they hurt him? Would they give him a chance to explain the situation and then let him go?

Three colonists, two males and a female, were standing outside the truck. Jared was trying to get them to go toward the house.

"I'll meet you inside," Cullaene shouted back. For a moment he toyed with running. He stared out over the broad expanse of newly cultivated land, toward the forest and rising hills beyond it. Somewhere in there he might find an enclave of his own people, a group of Abandoned Ones who hadn't assimilated, but the chances of that were small. His people had always survived by adaptation. The groups of Abandoned Ones had grown smaller every year.

He rubbed his hands together. His skin was too dry. If only he could pull off this self-imposed restraint for an hour, he would lie down in the field and encase himself in mud. Then his skin would emerge as soft and pure as the fur on Jared's cats. But he needed his restraint now more than ever. He pulled his jacket tighter and let himself into the kitchen once more.

He could hear the voices of Lucy and her mother rise in a heated discussion from upstairs. Jared had pressed the recycle switch on the old coffee maker, and it was screeching in protest. The three visitors were seated around the table, the woman in Cullaene's seat, and all of them turned as he entered the room.

He nodded and sat by the sterilizer. The heat made his back tingle, and the unusual angle made him feel like a stranger in the kitchen where he had supped for over a week. The visitors stared at him with the same cold look he had seen on the faces of the townspeople.

"This is Colin," Jared said. "He works for me."

Cullaene nodded again. Jared didn't introduce the visitors, and Cullaene wondered if it was an intentional oversight.

"We would like to ask you a few questions about yourself," the woman said. She leaned forward as she spoke, and Cullaene noted that her eyes were a vivid blue.

"May I ask why?"

Jared's hand shook as he poured the coffee. "Colin, it's customary around here—"

"No," the woman interrupted. "It is not customary. We're talking with all the strangers. Surely your hired man has heard of the murder."

Cullaene started. He took the coffee cup Jared offered him, relieved that his own hand did not shake. "No, I hadn't heard."

"We don't talk about such things in this house, Marlene," Jared said to the woman.

Coffee cups rattled in the silence as Jared finished serving everyone. The older man, leaning against the wall behind the table, waited until Jared was through before he spoke.

"It's our first killing in *this* colony, and it's a ghastly one. Out near the ridge, we found the skin of a man floating in the river. At first, we thought it was a body because the water filled the skin like it would fill a sack. Most of the hair was in place, hair so black that when it dried its highlights were blue. We couldn't find any clothes—"

"—or bones for that matter," the other man added.

"That's right," the spokesman continued. "He had been gutted. We scoured the area for the rest of him, and up on the ridge we found blood."

"A great deal of it," Marlene said. "As if they had skinned him while he was still alive."

Cullaene had to wrap his fingers around the hot cup to keep them warm. He hadn't been careful enough. Things had happened so swiftly that he hadn't had a chance to go deeper into the woods. He felt the fear that had been quivering in the bottom of his stomach settle around his heart.

"And so you're questioning all of the strangers here to see if they could have done it." He spoke as if he were more curious than frightened.

Marlene nodded. She ran a long hand across her hairline to catch any loose strands.

"I didn't kill anyone," Cullaene said. "I'll answer anything you ask."

They asked him careful, probing questions about his life before he had entered their colony, and he answered with equal care, being as truthful as he possibly could. He told them that the first colony he had been with landed on ground unsuitable for farming. The colonists tried hunting and even applied for a mining permit, but nothing worked. Eventually, most returned to Earth. He remained, traveling from family to family, working odd jobs while he tried to find a place to settle. As he spoke, he mentioned occasional details about himself, hoping that the sparse personal comments would prevent deeper probing. He told them about the Johansens whose daughter he had nearly married, the Cassels who taught him how to cultivate land, and the Slingers who nursed him back to health after a particularly debilitating illness. Cullaene told them every place he had ever been except the one place they were truly interested in—the woods that bordered the Fieldings' farm.

He spoke in a gentle tone that Earthlings respected. And he watched Jared's face because he knew that Jared, of any of them, would be the one to realize that Cullaene was not and never had been a colonist. Jared had lived on the planet for fifteen years. Once he had told Cullaene proudly that Lucy, though an orphan, was the first member of this colony born on the planet.

The trust in Jared's eyes never wavered. Cullaene relaxed slightly. If Jared didn't recognize him, no one would.

"They say that this is the way the natives commit murder," Marlene

149

said when Cullaene finished. "We've heard tales from other colonies of bodies—both human and Riiame—being found like this."

Cullaene realized that she was still questioning him. "I never heard of this kind of murder before."

She nodded. As if by an unseen cue, all three of them stood. Jared stood with them. "Do you think Riiame could be in the area?" he asked.

"It's very likely," Marlene said. "Since you live so close to the woods, you should probably take extra precautions."

"Yes." Jared glanced over at his well-stocked gun cabinet. "I plan to."

The men nodded their approval and started out the door. Marlene turned to Cullaene. "Thank you for your cooperation," she said. "We'll let you know if we have any further questions."

Cullaene stood to accompany them out, but Jared held him back. "Finish your coffee. We have plenty of time to get to the fields later."

After they went out the door, Cullaene took his coffee and moved to his own seat. Lucy and her mother were still arguing upstairs. He took the opportunity to indulge himself in a quick scratch of his hands and arms. The heat had made the dryness worse.

He wondered if he had been convincing. The three looked as if they had already decided what happened. A murder. He shook his head.

A door slammed upstairs, and the argument grew progressively louder. Cullaene glanced out the window over the sterilizer. Jared was still talking with the three visitors. Cullaene hoped they'd leave soon. Then maybe he'd talk to Jared, explain as best he could why he could no longer stay.

"Where are you going?" Mrs. Fielding shouted. Panic touched the edge of her voice.

"Away from you!" Lucy sounded on the verge of tears. Cullaene could hear her stamp her way down the stairs. Suddenly, the footsteps stopped. "No! You stay away from me! I need time to think!"

"You can't have time to think! We've got to find out what's wrong."

"Nothing's wrong!"

"Lucy—"

"You take another step and I swear I'll leave!" Lucy backed her way into the kitchen, slammed the door, and leaned on it. Then she noticed Cullaene, and all the fight left her face.

"How long have you been here?" she whispered.

He poured his now-cold coffee into the recycler that they had set aside for him. "I won't say anything to your father, if that's what you're worried about. I don't even know why you were fighting."

There was no room left in the sterilizer, so he set the cup next to the tiny boiler that purified the ground water. Lucy slid a chair back, and it creaked as she sat in it. Cullaene took another glance out the window. Jared and his visitors seemed to be arguing.

What would he do if they decided he was guilty? He couldn't disappear. They had a description of him that they would send to other colonies. He could search for the Abandoned Ones, but even if he found them, they might not take him in. He had lived with the colonists all his life. He looked human, and sometimes, he even felt human.

Something crashed behind him. Cullaene turned in time to see Lucy stumble over her chair as she backed away from the overturned coffee maker. Coffee ran down the wall, and the sterilizer hissed. He hurried to her side, moved the chair, and got her to a safer corner of the kitchen.

"Are you all right?" he asked.

She nodded. A tear slipped out of the corner of her eye. "I didn't grab it tight, I guess."

"Why don't you sit down. I'll clean it up—" Cullaene stopped as Lucy's tear landed on the back of his hand. The drop was heavy and lined with red. He watched it leave a pink trail as it rolled off his skin onto the floor. Slowly, he looked up into her frightened eyes. More blood-filled tears threatened. He wiped one from her eyelashes and rolled it around between his fingertips.

Suddenly, she tried to pull away from him, and he tightened his grip on her arm. He slid back the sleeve of her sweater. The flesh hung in folds around her elbow and wrist. He touched her wrist lightly and noted that the sweat from her pores was also rimmed in blood.

"How long?" he whispered. "How long has this been happening to you?"

The tears began to flow easily now. It looked as if she were bleeding from her eyes. "Yesterday morning."

He shook his head. "It had to start sooner than that. You would have itched badly. Like a rash."

"A week ago."

He let her go. Poor girl. A week alone without anyone telling her anything. She would hurt by now. The pain and the weakness would be nearly intolerable.

"What is it?" Her voice was filled with fear.

Cullaene stared at her, then, as the full horror finally reached him. He had been prepared from birth for the Change, but Lucy thought she was human. And suddenly he looked out the window again at Jared. Jared, who had found the orphaned girl without even trying to discover anything about the type of life form he raised. Jared, who must have assumed that because the child looked human, she was human.

She was rubbing her wrist. The skin was already so loose that the pressure of his hand hadn't left a mark on it.

"It's normal," he said. "It's the Change. The first time—the first time can be painful, but I can help you through it."

The instant he said the words, he regretted them. If he helped her, he'd have to stay. He was about to contradict himself when the kitchen door clicked shut.

Mrs. Fielding looked at the spilled coffee, then at the humped skin on Lucy's arm. The older woman seemed frightened and vulnerable. She held out her hand to her daughter, but Lucy didn't move. "She's sick," Mrs. Fielding said.

"Sick?" Cullaene permitted himself a small ironic smile. These people didn't realize what they had done to Lucy. "How do you know? You've never experienced anything like this before, have you?"

Mrs. Fielding was flushed. "Have you?"

"Of course, I have. It's perfectly normal development in an adult Riiame."

"And you'd be able to help her?"

The hope in her voice mitigated some of his anger. He could probably trust Mrs. Fielding to keep his secret. She had no one else to turn to right now. "I was able to help myself."

"You're Riiame?" she whispered. Suddenly, the color drained from her face. "Oh, my God."

Cullaene could feel a chill run through him. He'd made the wrong choice. Before he was able to stop her, she had pulled the porch door open. "Jared!" she called. "Get in here right away! Colin—Colin says he's a Riiame!"

Cullaene froze. She couldn't be saying that. Not now. Not when her daughter was about to go through one of life's most painful experiences unprepared. Lucy needed him right now. Her mother couldn't help her, and neither could the other colonists. If they tried to stop the bleeding, it would kill her.

He had made his decision. He grabbed Lucy and swung her horizontally across his back, locking her body in position with his arms. She was kicking and pounding on his side. Mrs. Fielding started to scream. Cullaene let go of Lucy's legs for a moment, grabbed the doorknob, and let himself out into the hallway. Lucy had her feet braced against the floor, forcing him to drag her. He continued to move swiftly toward the front door. When he reached it, he yanked it open and ran into the cold morning air.

Lucy had almost worked herself free. He shifted her slightly against his back and managed to capture her knees again. The skin had broken where he touched her. She would leave a trail of blood.

The girl was so frightened that she wasn't even screaming. She hit him in the soft flesh of his side, then leaned over and bit him. The pain almost made him drop her. Suddenly, he spun around and tightened his grip on her.

"I'm trying to help you," he said. "Now stop it!"

She stopped struggling and rested limply in his arms. Cullaene found himself hating the Fieldings. Didn't they know there would be questions? Perhaps they could explain the Change as a disease, but what would happen when her friends began to shrivel with age and she remained as young and lovely as she was now? Who would explain that to her?

He ran on a weaving path through the trees. If Jared was thinking, he would know where Cullaene was taking Lucy. But all Cullaene needed was time. Lucy was so near the Change now that it wouldn't take too long to help her through it. But if the others tried to stop it, no matter how good their intentions, they could kill or disfigure the girl.

Cullaene was sobbing air into his lungs. His chest burned. He hadn't run like this in a long time, and Lucy's extra weight was making the movements more difficult. As if the girl could read his thoughts, she began struggling again. She bent her knees and jammed them as hard as she could into his kidneys. He almost tripped, but managed to right himself just in time. The trees were beginning to thin up ahead, and he smelled the thick spice of the river. It would take the others a while to reach him. They couldn't get the truck in here. They would have to come by foot. Maybe he'd have enough time to help Lucy and to get away.

Cullaene broke into the clearing. Lucy gasped as she saw the ridge. He had to bring her here. She needed the spicy water—and the height. He thought he could hear someone following him now, and he prayed he would have enough time. He had so much to tell her. She had to know about the pigmentation changes, and the possibilities of retaining some skin. But most of all, she had to do what he told her, or she'd be deformed until the next Change, another ten years away.

He bent in half and lugged her up the ridge. The slope of the land was slight enough so that he kept his balance, but great enough to slow him down. He could feel Lucy's heart pounding against his back. The child thought he was going to kill her, and he didn't know how he would overcome that.

When he reached the top of the ridge, he stood, panting, looking over the caramel-colored water. He didn't dare release Lucy right away.

They didn't have much time, and he had to explain what was happening to her.

She had stopped struggling. She gripped him as if she were determined to drag him with her when he flung her into the river. In the distance, he could hear faint shouts.

"Lucy, I brought you up here for a reason," he said. Her fingers dug deeper into his flesh. "You're going through what my people call the Change. It's normal. It—"

"I'm not one of your people," she said. "Put me down!"

He stared across the sluggish river into the trees beyond. Even though he had just begun, he felt defeated. The girl had been human for thirteen years. He couldn't alter that in fifteen minutes.

"No, you're not." He set her down, but kept a firm grasp of her wrists. Her sweater and skirt were covered with blood. "But you were born here. Have you ever seen this happen to anyone else?"

He grabbed a loose fold of skin and lifted it. There was a sucking release as the skin separated from the wall of blood. Lucy tried to pull away from him. He drew her closer. "Unfortunately, you believe you are human and so the first one to undergo this. I'm the only one who can help you. I'm a Riiame. This has happened to me."

"You don't look like a Riiame."

He held back a sharp retort. There was so much that she didn't know. Riiame were a shape-shifting people. Parents chose the form of their children at birth. His parents had had enough foresight to give him a human shape. Apparently, so had hers. But she had only seen the Abandoned Ones who retained the shape of the hunters that used to populate the planet's forests.

A cry echoed through the woods. Lucy looked toward it, but Cullaene shook her to get her attention again. "I am Riiame," he said. "Your father's friends claimed to have found a body here. But that body they found wasn't a body at all. It was my skin. I just went through the Change. I shed my skin just as you're going to. And then I came out to find work in your father's farm."

"I don't believe you," she said.

"Lucy, you're bleeding through every pore in your body. Your skin is loose. You feel as if you're floating inside yourself. You panicked when you saw your form outlined in blood on the sheets this morning, didn't you? And your mother, she noticed it, too, didn't she?"

Lucy nodded.

"You have got to trust me because in a few hours the blood will go away, the skin you're wearing now will stick to the new skin beneath it, and you will be ugly and deformed. And in time, the old skin will start to rot. Do you want that to happen to you?"

A bloody tear made its way down Lucy's cheek. "No," she whispered.

"All right then." Cullaene wouldn't let himself feel relief. He could hear unnatural rustlings coming from the woods. "You're going to have to leave your clothes here. Then go to the edge of the ridge, reach your arms over your head to stretch the skin as much as you can, and jump into the river. It's safe, the river is very deep here. As soon as you can feel the cold water on every inch of your body, surface, go to shore, and wrap yourself in mud. That will prevent the itching from starting again."

The fear on her face alarmed him. "You mean I have to strip?"

He bit back his frustration. They didn't have time to work through human taboos. "Yes. Or the old skin won't come off."

Suddenly, he saw something flash in the woods below. It looked like the muzzle of a heat gun. Panic shot through him. Why was he risking his life to help this child? As soon as he emerged at the edge of the ridge, her father would kill him. Cullaene let go of Lucy's wrists. Let her run if she wanted to. He was not going to let himself get killed. Not yet.

But to his surprise, Lucy didn't run. She turned her back and slowly pulled her sweater over her head. Then she slid off the rest of her clothes and walked to the edge of the ridge. Cullaene knew she couldn't feel the cold right now. Her skin was too far away from the nerve endings.

She reached the edge of the ridge, her toes gripping the rock as tightly as her fingers had gripped his arm, and then she turned to look back at him. "I can't," she whispered.

She was so close. Cullaene saw the blood working under the old skin, trying to separate all of it. "You have to," he replied, keeping himself in shadow. "Jump."

Lucy looked down at the river below her, and a shiver ran through her body. She shook her head.

"Do—?" Cullaene stopped himself. If he went into the open, they'd kill him. Then he stared at Lucy for a moment, and felt his resolve waver. "Do you want me to help you?"

He could see the fear and helplessness mix on her face. She wasn't sure what he was going to do, but she wanted to believe him. Suddenly, she set her jaw with determination. "Yes," she said softly.

Cullaene's hands went cold. "All right. I'm going to do this quickly. I'll come up behind you and push you into the river. Point your toes and fall straight. The river is deep and it moves slow. You'll be all right."

Lucy nodded and looked straight ahead. The woods around them were unnaturally quiet. He hurried out of his cover and grabbed her waist, feeling the blood slide away from the pressure of his hands. He paused for a moment, knowing that Jared and his companions would not shoot while he held the girl.

"Point," he said, then pushed.

He could feel the air rush through his fingers as Lucy fell. Suddenly, a white heat blast stabbed his side, and he tumbled after her, whirling and flipping in the icy air. He landed on his stomach in the thick, cold water, knocking the wind out of his body. Cullaene knew that he should stay under and swim away from the banks, but he needed to breathe. He clawed his way to the surface, convinced he would die before he reached it. The fight seemed to take forever, and suddenly he was there, bobbing on top of the river, gasping air into his empty lungs.

Lucy's skin floated next to him, and he felt a moment of triumph before he saw Jared's heat gun leveled at him from the bank.

"Get out," the farmer said tightly. "Get out and tell me what you did with the rest of her before I lose my head altogether."

Cullaene could still go under and swim for it, but what would be the use? He wouldn't be able to change his pigmentation for another ten years or so, and if he managed to swim out of range of their heat guns, he would always be running.

With two long strokes, Cullaene swam to the bank and climbed out of the water. He shivered. It was cold, much too cold to be standing wet near the river. The spice aggravated his new skin's dryness.

Marlene, gun in hand, stood next to Jared, and the two other men were coming out of the woods.

"Where's the rest of her?" Jared asked. His arm was shaking. "On the ridge?"

Cullaene shook his head. He could have hit the gun from Jared's hand and run, but he couldn't stand to see the sadness, the defeat in the man who had befriended him.

"She'll be coming out of the water in a minute."

"You lie!" Jared screamed, and Cullaene saw with shock that the man had nearly snapped.

"No, she will." Cullaene hesitated for a moment. He didn't want to die to keep his people's secret. The Riiame always adapted. They'd adapt this time, too. "She's Riiame. You know that. This is normal for us."

"She's my daughter!"

"No, she's not. She can't be. This doesn't happen to humans."

A splash from the riverbank drew his attention. Lucy pulled herself up alongside the water several feet from them. Her skin was fresh, pink and clean, and her bald head reflected patches of sunlight. She gathered herself into a fetal position and began to rock.

Cullaene started to go to her, but Jared grabbed him. Cullaene tried to shake his arm free, but Jared was too strong for him.

"She's not done yet," Cullaene said.

Marlene had come up beside them. "Let him go, Jared."

"He killed my daughter." Jared's grip tightened on Cullaene's arm.

"No, he didn't. She's right over there."

Jared didn't even look. "That's not my Lucy."

Cullaene swallowed hard. His heart was beating in his throat. He should have run when he had the chance. Now Jared was going to kill him.

"That is Lucy," Marlene said firmly. "Let him go, Jared. He has to help her."

Jared looked over at the girl rocking at the edge of the riverbank. His hold loosened, and finally he let his hands drop. Cullaene took two steps backward and rubbed his arms. Relief was making him dizzy.

Marlene had put her arm around Jared as if she, too, didn't trust him. She was watching Cullaene to see what he'd do next. If he ran, she'd get the other two to stop him. Slowly, he turned away from them and went to Lucy's side.

"You need mud, Lucy," he said as he dragged her higher onto the bank. She let him roll her into a cocoon. When he was nearly through, he looked at the man behind him.

Jared had dropped his weapon and was staring at Lucy's skin as it made its way down the river. Marlene still clutched her gun, but her eyes were on Jared, not Cullaene.

"Is she Riiame?" Marlene asked Jared.

The farmer shook his head. "I thought she was human!" he said. Then he raised his voice as if he wanted Cullaene to hear. "I thought she was human!"

Cullaene took a handful of mud and started painting the skin on Lucy's face. She had closed her eyes and was lying very still. She would need time to recover from the shock.

"I thought they were going to kill her," Jared said brokenly. "There were two of them and she was so little and I thought they were going to kill her." His voice dropped. "So I killed them first."

Cullaene's fingers froze on Lucy's cheek. Jared had killed Lucy's parents because they didn't look human. Cullaene dipped his hands in more mud and continued working. He hoped they would let him leave when he finished.

He placed the last of the mud on the girl's face. Jared came up beside him. "You're Riiame too, aren't you? And you look human."

Cullaene washed the mud from his shaking hands. He was very frightened. What would he do now? Leave with Lucy, and try to teach the child that she wasn't human at all? He turned to face Jared. "What are you going to do with Lucy?"

"Will she be okay?" the farmer asked.

Cullaene stared at Jared for a moment. All the color had drained from the farmer's face, and he looked close to tears. Jared had finally realized what he had done.

"She should be," Cullaene said. "But someone has to explain this to her. It'll happen again. And there are other things."

He stopped, remembering his aborted love affair with a human woman. Ultimately, their forms had proven incompatible. He wasn't really human, although it was so easy to forget that. He only appeared human.

"Other things?"

"Difficult things." Cullaene shivered again. He would get ill from these wet clothes. "If you want, I'll take her with me. You won't have to deal with her then."

"No." Jared reached out to touch the mud-encased girl, but his hand hovered over her shell, never quite resting on it. "She's my daughter. I raised her. I can't just let her run off and disappear."

Cullaene swallowed heavily. He didn't understand these creatures. They killed Abandoned Ones on a whim, professed fear and hatred of the Riiame, and then would offer to keep one in their home.

"That was your skin that they found, wasn't it?" Jared asked. "This just happened to you."

Cullaene nodded. His muscles were tense. He wasn't sure what Jared was going to do.

"Why didn't you tell us?"

Cullaene looked at Jared for a moment. Because, he wanted to say, the woman I loved screamed and spat at me when she found out. Because one farmer nearly killed me with an axe. Because your people don't know how to cope with anything different, even when *they* are the aliens on a new planet.

"I didn't think you'd understand," he said. Suddenly, he grabbed Jared's hand and set it on the hardening mud covering Lucy's shoulder. Then he stood up. There had to be Abandoned Ones in these woods. He would find them if Jared didn't kill him first. He started to walk.

"Colin," Jared began, but Cullaene didn't stop. Marlene reached his side and grabbed him. Cullaene glared at her, but she didn't let go. He was too frightened to hit her, too frightened to try to break free. If she held him, maybe they weren't going to kill him after all.

She ripped open the side of Cullaene's shirt and examined the damage left by the heat blast. The skin was puckered and withered, and Cullaene suddenly realized how much it ached.

"Can we treat this?" she asked.

"Are you asking for permission?" Cullaene could barely keep the sarcasm from his voice.

"No." The woman looked down and blushed deeply as some humans did when their shame was fullest. "I was asking if we had the skill."

Cullaene relaxed enough to smile. "You have the skill."

"Then," she said. "May we treat you?"

Cullaene nodded. He allowed himself to be led back to Jared's side. Jared was staring at his daughter, letting tears fall onto the cocoon of mud.

"You can take her out of there soon," Cullaene said. "Her clothes are up on the ridge. I'll get them."

And before anyone could stop him, Cullaene went into the woods and started up the ridge. He could escape now. He could simply turn around and run away. But he wasn't sure he wanted to do that.

When he reached the top of the ridge, he peered down at Jared, his frightened daughter, and the woman who protected them. They had a lot of explaining to do to Lucy. But if she was strong enough to survive the Change, she was strong enough to survive anything.

Cullaene draped her bloody clothes over his arm and started back down the ridge. When he reached the others, he handed the clothes to Marlene. Then Cullaene crouched beside Jared. Carefully, Cullaene made a hole in the mud and began to peel it off Lucy. Jared watched him for a moment. Then he slipped his fingers into a crack, and together the alien and the native freed the girl from her handmade shell.

ALIEN INFLUENCES

KRISTINE KATHRYN RUSCH

ONE

The corridor smelled stale. John huddled against the display panel, replacing microchips with the latest models—more memory, more function. The near-robotic feel of the work was all that mattered: pull, grab, replace; pull, grab, replace. They should have had a droid doing this, but they gave the work to John, a sure sign that his contract was nearly up.

He didn't mind. He had been on the trader ship for nearly a month, and it was making him nervous. Too many people, too close. They watched him as if they expected him to go suddenly berserk and murder them all in their sleep. He wouldn't have minded if their wariness was based on his work as a bounty hunter. But it wasn't. It was based on the events on Bountiful, things he had done—and paid for—when he was little more than a child.

Footsteps along the plastic floor. He didn't move, figuring whoever it was would have nothing to say to him. A faint whiff of cologne and expensive illegal tobacco. The captain.

"John, someone to see you."

John looked up. The captain stood on the other side of the corridor, the lights from the display giving his skin a greenish cast. Once John had fancied this man his friend, but John hadn't had any real friends. Not since he was fifteen years old. The day Harper betrayed him. The day they took Beth away.

"I will not see anyone," John said. Sometimes he played the role, the Dancer child everyone thought he was. The one who never spoke in past tense, only present and future, using the subjunctive whenever possible. The one who couched his thoughts in emotion because he had nothing else, no memory, no ethics, no soul.

The captain didn't even blink. "She flew in special from Rotan Base."

John stood and closed the display. A client, then. The time on the trader ship would end sooner than he expected.

He followed the captain through the winding corridors. The ventilation system was out. The entire ship smelled of wet socks and too many people. Down one of the corridors, the techs were discussing whether they wanted to fix the system or whether they wanted to wait until next planetfall. John would have argued for fixing it.

The captain stopped at his personal suite and keyed in the access code. John had never seen this room; it was off limits to all but the captain himself. John stepped in, but the captain remained outside. The door snicked shut.

Computer-generated music—technically proficient and lifeless—played in the background. The room itself was decorated in whites, but the lighting gave everything a reddish cast. The couch was thick and plush. Through open doors, he could see the bed, suspended in the air, cushions piled on top of it. A room built for comfort, and for seduction.

A woman stood at the back of the room, gazing out the portals in the stars. Her long black hair trailed down her back, her body wrapped in expensive silks. She looked the part of the seductee, although she was the one who wanted to hire him.

John never hired out for anything but bounty work. He would tell her that if he had to.

"I would like you to work for me, John." She didn't even turn around to acknowledge him. He felt his hackles rise. She was establishing herself as the adult, him the child in this relationship. He hated being treated like a child. The claustrophobia inched back on him, tighter than it had been in months.

He leaned against the door, feigning a casualness he didn't feel. He wanted her to turn around, to look at him. "Why should I work for you?"

"Forgive me." This time she moved, smoothing her hair as she did. Her face was stunning: full lips, long nose, wide eyes. And familiar. "I'm Anita Miles. I run an art gallery on Rotan Base. We specialize in unusual objects d'art..."

He stopped listening, not needing the explanation. He recognized her face from a hundred vids. She was perhaps one of the most powerful people in this sector—controlling trade and commodities. Her gallery sold anything that could be considered art. Once she sold a baby Minaran, claiming that since the species was nearly extinct, the Minarans could only be appreciated in an aesthetic way. He couldn't remember if she had won or lost the ensuing lawsuit.

Baby trader. The entire galaxy as an art object. If she had been in business when he was a boy, what would she have done with the Dancers?

"Why would I work for you?" he repeated.

She closed her mouth and gave him a once-over. He recognized the look. *How much does he understand? I thought I was explaining in clear terms. This was going to be more difficult than I thought.* "You're the best," she said, apparently deciding on simplicity. "And I need the best."

He often wondered how these people thought he could bounty hunt with no memory. He shook off the thought. He needed the money. "What will you pay me?"

"Expenses, of course, a ship at your command because you may have to travel a bit, and three times your daily rate which is, I believe, the equivalent of four hundred Rotan zepeatas."

"Eight hundred."

Her expression froze for just a moment, and then she had the grace to flush. John crossed his arms. Too many clients tried to cheat him. He took them on anyway. If he tried to avoid those who treated him like a Dancer, he would have no business.

"I'm not a Dancer." He kept his tone soft, but made sure the sarcasm was there. "I wasn't even raised by them. Just influenced. The trial is over, and I've served my time. When they released me, they declared me sane, and sane for a human being means an understanding of time and an ability to remember. After that little stunt, I won't work with you for anything less than five times my rate, one month payable in advance."

The flush grew, making those spectacular eyes shine brighter. Not embarrassment after all. Anger. "You tricked me."

"Not at all," John didn't move. He felt more comfortable now with this little hint of emotion. He could ride on emotion, play it. That he had learned from the Dancers. "You had expectations. You shouldn't believe everything you hear."

For a moment, she drew herself up, as if she were going to renounce him and leave. But she didn't. She reached into her pocket and removed a credit flask. She must have needed him badly.

She handed him two chips, which he immediately put into his account. One hundred and twenty thousand zepeatas. Perfect. He smiled for the first time. "What do you want from me?" he asked.

She glanced at the portals, as if the stars would give her strength. The story was an embarrassment, then. An illegality perhaps, or some mistake she had made. "Several weeks ago," she said, "I acquired a Bodean wind sculpture."

Awe rippled through him. He had seen Bodean wind sculptures once, on their home planet. The deserts were full of them, swirling beautifully across the sands. No one knew how to tame them; they remained an isolated artform, on a lone planet. Someone must have figured out a way to capture them, wind currents and all.

"That's not the best part," she said. Her tone had changed. She still wasn't treating him like an equal, but she was closer. "The best part is the mystery inside the sculpture. My equipment indicates a life form trapped in there."

—*If we grow up, we'll be able to leave. We won't be trapped here. With them. On Bountiful. If we grow up...*

He shook the memory voices away, made himself concentrate on her words. Something inside the sculpture. A bodeangenie? But they were the stuff of legends. Traders to Bodean claimed that the sculptures originated to capture little magical beings to prevent them from causing harm to the desert. When the Interspecies Alliance went to study the sculptures, however, they found no evidence of life in or around them.

His hands were shaking. She trapped things and called them art. "You don't need me," he said. "You need a specialist."

"I need you." She turned, her hair spiraling out around her. Beautiful, dramatic. "The wind sculpture's been stolen."

TWO

Sleep. Narrow trader bunk, not built for his long frame. Dream voices, half remembered:

... *we'll be able to leave...*

... *the Dancers do it...*

... *It'll hurt, but that won't matter. You'll grow up ...*

... *Stop, please ...*

... *Just another minute ...*

... *Stop!!! ...*

... *the other hand...*

... *ssstttooooppp ...*

He forced himself awake, heart pounding, mouth dry. The trapped feeling still filled him. He rolled off the bunk, stood, listened to the even breathing of the other sleepers. He hadn't had the dream since when? The penal colony? The last trading ship? He couldn't remember. He had tried to put it out of his mind. Obviously that hadn't worked.

Trapped. He had started the spiral when she said the word trapped. He leaned against the door, felt the cool plastic against his forehead. The memory voices still rang in his head. If someone had listened, then maybe...

But no. The past was past. He would work for her, but he would follow his own reasons.

THREE

Her gallery was less than he expected. Shoved into a small corner of the merchant's wing on Rotan Base, the gallery had a storefront of only a few meters. Inside hung the standard work by standard artists: an Ashley rendition of the galaxy, done in blacks and pinks; a D.B. portrait of the shynix, a red-haired, catlike creature from Yster; a Degas statue of a young girl dancing. Nothing new, nothing unique, not even in the manner of display. All the pieces were self-illuminated against dark walls and stands, a small red light beside each indicating the place for credit purchases.

The gallery was even more of a surprise after she had told him her tale of woe: she claimed to have the best guards on Rotan, an elaborate security system, and special checking. He saw no evidence of them. Her storefront was the same as the others, complete with mesh framing that cascaded at closing each evening.

The gallery smelled dry, dustless. He wanted to sneeze, just to see particles in the air. The air's cleanliness, at least, was unusual. He would have to check the filtration system. The sculpture probably didn't disappear at all. Some overeager viewer probably opened the container, the wind escaped, and the sculpture returned to the grains of sand it was. No great mystery, certainly not worth 120,000 zepeatas. But he wouldn't tell her that.

Anita threaded her way through the displays to the back. He felt himself relax. There he would find the artwork he sought—the priceless, the illegal, the works which had made her famous. But when the door slid open, his mood vanished.

Crates, cartons, holoshippers, transmission machines, more credit slots. The faint odor of food. A desk covered with hardcopy invoices and credit records. A small cache of wine behind the overstuffed chair, and a microprocessor for late night meals. A workspace, nothing more.

She let the door close behind them, her gaze measuring him. He was missing something. He would lose the entire commission if he didn't find it.

He closed his eyes and saw in his imagination what his actual vision had missed. The dimensions of the rooms were off. The front was twice the size of the back. Base regulations required square sales—each purchased compartment had to form a box equal on all sides. She had divided her box into three sections—showroom, back workroom, and special gallery. But where?

Where something didn't fit. The wine. She sold wine as art—nectar of the gods, never drinking it, always collecting it. Wine didn't belong with the boxes and invoices.

He opened his eyes, crouched down, scanned the wine rack. Most bottles came from Earth. They were made with the heavy, too-thick glass that suggested work centuries old. Only one didn't belong: a thin bottle of the base-made synth stuff. He pulled it, felt something small fall into his hand. He clenched his hand to hold it as the wall slid back.

Inside was the gallery he had been expecting.

Holos of previous artifacts danced across the back wall. In those holos, the baby Minaran swam. He wondered where it was now; if it could feel happiness, exploitation. He made himself look away.

A tiny helldog from Frizos clawed at a glass cage. A mobile ice sculpture from Ngela rotated under cool lights. Four canisters in a bowl indicated a Colleician scent painting. He had only seen one before; all he had to do was touch it, and he would be bathed in alien memories.

More valuables drifted off in the distance. Some hung on walls, some rested on pedestals, and some floated around him. None had the standard red credit slot beside them. They were all set up for negotiation, bargaining, and extortion.

"Impressed?" She sounded sarcastic, as if a man with his background could not help but be impressed.

He was, but not for the reasons she thought. He knew how much skill it took to capture each item, to bring it onto a base with strict limitations for importing. "You have your own hunters. Why hire me?"

She tapped on the helldog's cage. John winced. The dog didn't move. "I would have to hire a hunter no matter what," she said. "If I removed one of my own people from normal routine, I would have to hire a replacement. I choose not to do that. My people have their own lives, their own beats, and their own predilections. This incident calls for someone a bit more adaptable, a freelancer. A person like you."

He nodded, deciding that was the best answer he would get from her. Perhaps she had chosen him, and not one of his colleagues, on a whim. Or perhaps she thought she could control him, with his Dancer mind. It didn't matter. She was paying him. And he had a being to free.

FOUR

Working late into the night so that the dreams would stay away, he did the standard checks: exploring the gallery for bits of the sculpture; contacting the base engineers to see if sand had lodged in the filters; examining particulate material for foreign readings. Nothing. The sculpture appeared to have vanished.

Except for the small item he had found near the wine cache. He set it in the light, examined it, and froze. A sticker. Lina Base used them as temporary IDs. Stickers weren't the proper term. Actually, they were little light tabs that allowed the bearer to enter secured areas for brief periods of time, and were called stickers because most spacers stuck them to the tops of their boots.

He hadn't touched one since he left Lina Base nearly two decades before. The memories tickled around his head: Beth, her eyes wide, hands grasping, as Harper's people carried her away; sitting on his own bed, arms wrapped around his head, eyes burning but tearless, staring at his own sticker-covered boots—signifying temporary, even though he had been there for nearly two years.

Dancer mind. He snorted. If only he could forget. He was cursed with too much remembrance.

He set the sticker down, made himself move. He had to check arrival records, see who had come from Lina Base, who frequented it. Then he would know who took the sculpture.

FIVE

The next morning, he walked into the gallery. The showroom was filled with Elegian tourists, fondling the merchandise. The security system had to be elaborate to allow such touching without any obvious watchful presence. The room smelled of animal sweat and damp fur. No wonder her filtration system was good. He pushed his way through, and let himself into the back.

Anita was cataloging chip-sized gems that had arrived the day before. She wore a jeweler's eye, and didn't look up when he entered.

"I need that ship," he said.

"You found something?"

He nodded. "A lead. Some traders."

This time she did look up. The jeweler's eye gave her face a foreign feel. "Who?"

A small ship out of Lina Base named *Runner*. Owned by a man named Minx. He worked with four others on odd jobs no one else wanted—domestic cats from Earth to a colony of miners on Calmium; a cargo of worthless moon rocks to scientists on Mina Base. No records older than twenty years. No recording of illegal trading of any kind.

But he didn't tell her that. He still wasn't sure if he was going to tell her anything.

"No one you'd know," he said. "If it turns out to be them, I'll introduce you."

She removed the jeweler's eye. Her own eye looked less threatening. "You're working for me which gives me the right to know what you've found."

"You *contracted* with me," he corrected. "And I have the right to walk away any time I choose—keeping the retainer. Now. Do I get that ship?"

She stared at him for a minute, then put the eye back in. "I'll call down," she said.

SIX

The ship was nearly a decade old, and designed to carry fewer than five people in comfort. He had computer access, games and holos, as much food and drink as he wanted. The only rule was not to disturb the pilot —for any reason. He guessed she had found out about his past, and wanted nothing to do with him.

He slept most of the time. His way of escape on ships. When he was awake, they reminded him of the penal ship, of the hands grabbing, voices prodding, violence, stink, and finally isolation ostensibly for his own good. When he was asleep, they were the only places that allowed him rest without dreams.

His alarm went off an hour before landing, and he paced. He hadn't been to Lina Base for twenty years. He had left as a boy, alone, without Beth, without even Harper, the man who had once been his savior and became his betrayer. Harper, who had healed his mind and broken his heart.

When the ship landed, John didn't move. He was crazy to go back, crazy to look at the part he had been avoiding. No job was worth that, especially a job he only half-believed in.

You have to face your past, face yourself. And once you see clearly what happened and why, you must forgive yourself. Only then will you be whole.

Harper's voice. John shook himself, as if he could force the voice from his head. He had promised himself, when he left Lina Base on the penal ship, that he would never listen to Harper again.

He had a job. His stay on Lina Base would be short.

He drew himself to his full height, and let himself out of his room. The pilot was at the door. She stopped moving when she saw him, her gaze wary. He nodded. She nodded back. Then he went out of the ship before her.

The docking bay had shiny new walls, and state-of-the-art flooring. But it smelled the same: dusty, tangy, harsh with chemical cleaners. He gripped the railing, cool against his hand.

... cringing in the back of the ship, safe behind the upholstered chairs. Voices urging him to get off, and he knowing they were going to kill him. They believed he had done something wrong, and he was going to get a punishment worse than any his parents could dish out ...

"You okay?" the pilot asked.

He snapped back to the present. He was not twelve, not landing on Lina Base for the first time. He was an adult, a man who could handle himself.

Down the stairs into the base. No crowds this time, no holoteams, no reporters. No Harper, no savior, no friends beside him. Only ships and shuttles of various sizes. Lina Base had grown since the last time he had been here. Now it had three docking facilities instead of one. It was one of the main trading bases in the galaxy, and had grown instead of declined when the officials closed Bountiful to any and all aliens. He stopped, remembered. If he went to one of the portals, he would be able to see Bountiful, its deserts and mountains etched across the surface like a painting, the Singing Sea adding a touch of blue to the art.

Odd that he missed the place when as a boy all he wanted to do was leave it.

"You seriously okay?"

"Yes." He whirled, expecting his anger to deflate her concern. Then understood that she was speaking from obligation. He was her charge until he left the docking bay, and she didn't want the responsibility of handling him.

"Then get to Deck Three for inspection and hosing. They need to clean this bay for other arrivals."

He nodded, felt a bit numb at her lack of concern. Procedures. After an outbreak of Malanian flu almost three decades before, Lina Base had become fanatic for keeping unwanted elements off the station. During his first visit here, he had been quarantined for three Earth months.

He turned his back on the pilot, sought the elevator, and took it to a tiny corridor on Deck Three. There, a blinking light indicated the room he was to use. He went inside.

The room was better than the one they had given him as a child. This one had a couch, and a servo tray filled with beverages. He stripped, let the robot arms whisk away his clothes, and then stepped under the pale blue light in the corner of the room.

Streams of light invaded his orifices, tickling with the warmth of their touch. He closed his eyes, holding himself still, knowing that on some bases they still used hand searches, and wondering how he could ever stand that when he found this procedure so invasive. When the light had finished, he stepped into the autodoc and let it search him for viruses, traces of alien matter, alien materials, and—probably—alien thought.

Alien influences...

A shiver ran through him. He had been twelve years old. Twelve years old and not realizing what they had done was abnormal. Not human. Yet he was still human enough to feel terror at separation from all that he knew. Knowing, deep down, that the horror was only beginning.

The autodoc was beeping, and for a long moment, he was afraid it had found something. Then he realized that it wanted him to leave its little chamber. He stepped back into the main room and retrieved his clothes—now cleaned and purified—dressed, and pressed the map to find out where he was and where he wanted to be.

SEVEN

John huddled in the shuttle records bay. Dark, cramped, smelling of sweat and skin oils, it was as familiar as any other place on the base. Only this was a different kind of familiarity. Every base had a records bay. And every base had an operator like Donnie.

He was small, wiry, scrawny enough to be comfortable in such a small space. His own stink didn't bother him—he was used to being alone. He monitored the traffic to and from the base, maintained licenses, and refused admittance if necessary.

"Left just as you were docking," he said. His lips barely parted, but his teeth were visible—half fake-white, half rotted. "In a hurry, too. Gave 'em the day's last slot."

The day's last slot. No other craft could be cleared for leaving then, until the next day. John clenched his fists. So close.

"Where did they go?"

Donnie checked the hard copy, then punched a button. The display on the screen was almost unreadable. He punched another button, lower lip out, grimy fingers shaking.

"Got a valid pass," he mumbled.

The shiver again, something a bit off. "Where?" John asked.

"Bountiful."

The word shimmered through him. Heat, thin and dry; deep flowery perfume; the rubbery feel of Dancer fingers...

"You done?" Donnie asked.

John took a deep breath, calmed himself. "You need to get me to Bountiful."

"Nope." Donnie leaned back in the chair. "I know who you are. Even if Bountiful were open, I couldn't let you go there."

Trapped. This time outside of Bountiful. John's fingernails dug into his palms. The pain kept him awake, sane. He made his voice sound calmer than he felt. "Where do I get the dispensation?"

Donnie gazed at him, scared of nothing, so secure in his small world of records, passes. "Level Five. But they won't help—"

"They will," John said.

EIGHT

He put in a call to Anita, told her to hurry or she would never get her sculpture back. She would pull the strings and dole out the cash. He would spend his time digging out information about the traders.

Lina Base's paranoia about its traders led to a wealth of information. He spent half an Earth day alone with a small computer linked up to the base's mainframe.

And found the information he had already known, plus some. Lina Base was their main base of operation. They were well known here, not popular. Two men worked with Minx: Dunnigan—trained as a linguist, and Carter—no formal training at all. The women, Parena and Nox, provided muscle and contacts. They had gotten the jobs on Calmium and Mina Base. And they had all hooked up twenty years ago.

After Bountiful was closed to aliens.

When Minx had to expand his operation.

When Salt Juice had become illegal.

Salt Juice. That little piece of information sent ripples of fear through John. Food. He had to get food. Take care of himself. He stood, unable to stop his mind.

Salt Juice had started it all.

The very smell of it gave him tremors, made him revert, close all the doors on himself, close out the memories and the emotions and the pain. He would focus on the future for protection, Dancerlike, and no one—except Harper, base kiddie therapist—had been able to get in. The only way to keep himself intact, human, was to take care of his body so that the damaged part of his mind could recover.

He went to the cafeteria.

Wide, spacious, with long windows open to space, and hanging plants from all sides, the cafeteria gave him a feeling of safety. He ordered off the servo, picked his table, and ran the credit voucher through. His food appeared on the table almost before the voucher stopped running. He walked over, sat down, and sniffed.

Roast chicken, steamed broccoli, mashed potatoes. Not a normal spacer's meal. Heaven. He made himself eat, feeling the food warm the cold places inside him. As he nourished himself, he allowed his mind to roam.

Salt Juice had been one of the most potent intoxicants in the galaxy. It was manufactured on Bountiful, using herbs grown by the Dancers. Those herbs were the main reason for the dispute with the Dancers—and when the colony finally learned how to grow them without Dancer assistance, they tried to wipe out the Dancers.

With the help of children. Poor, misguided children. Lonely little children who only wanted to leave the hell they were trapped in.

Once Lina Base discovered the scheme, Bountiful was closed. The best herbalists and chemists tried to manufacture Salt Juice away from the colony, but it proved impossible. A good thing. Later they learned that the drug everyone thought addiction-free had some nasty side effects.

Minx traded in Salt Juice.

Then moon rocks, cats. Worthless cargo. But Calmium's northern water supply had a drug as pure as crystal meth. And the Minaran skin was poison which, taken in small amounts, induced a dangerous kind of high.

The five were drug runners. Good, competent, skilled drug runners.

So the bodeangenie had more than artistic value to them. They also had some kind of stimulant value. He leaned back. What kind, he was sure he would find out.

NINE

But things happened too quickly. The call came from Anita. She had bought him a window—three Earth days—and she let him know that it cost her a fortune. He smiled. He was glad to put her money to good use.

He located the pilot, and together they flew to the place from which he had been banned for life.

TEN

Once again, he sat in his room on the ship, far from the uncommunicative pilot. He was glad for the solitude, even on such a short trip. He hadn't been to Bountiful since he was twelve. Then he had hated the planet, wanted nothing more than to be free of it. But the freedom he obtained wasn't the freedom he expected.

... *The plastic frame dug into his forehead. Through the portal, he could see Bountiful, swirling away from him. They had isolated him, considering him the ringleader—and perhaps he was. He hadn't understood the depths of their anger. He was experimenting, as they had, only he was trying to save the others ...*

He sighed, and walked to the portal. Bountiful loomed, dark and empty. Only five humans on the planet. Five humans and hundreds of Dancers, thousands of other species. After the announcement of the murders, the authorities had declared the planet unsafe, and closed it to all colonization. Even researchers needed special dispensation to go. The Dancers were too powerful, their thoughts too destructive. He shook his head. But the Dancers hadn't been the real problem. Salt Juice had.

Without Salt Juice, the Dancers would never have become an

endangered species. Without Salt Juice, the colony wouldn't have made money, and wouldn't have tried to protect that base by allowing ill-conceived killings to go on. The colonists had tried to blame the Dancers for the murders to exterminate the entire species; the intergalactic shock had been great when investigators discovered that the murderers were children.

Salt Juice. He still remembered the fumes, the glazed looks in his parents' eyes. Colonists weren't supposed to indulge—and none did—but they all suffered from Salt Juice intoxication because of their exposure during manufacturing. Perhaps if he had had a better lawyer, if the effects of Salt Juice were better understood at the time, he would have gotten off, been put in rehabilitation instead of incarcerated.

A slight ponging warned him that the shuttle would land soon. He dug in his duffel and removed the sand scarf, and some ointment. The woven material felt familiar, warm, a touch of the past. As children they had stopped wearing sand scarves, and he had gotten so crisped by Bountiful's sun that he still had tan lines. He was older now, and wiser. He would wear the offered protection.

His throat had gone dry. Three days alone on Bountiful. The pilot wouldn't stay—probably due to fear of him. He strapped himself in, knowing it was too late to turn back.

The shuttle bumped and scuttled its way to a stop. Already the temperature inside changed from cool to the kind of almost cool developed when the outside air was extremely hot. John unstrapped himself, put on the sand scarf, and rubbed oil over his exposed skin. Then he slung the duffel over his back, got up, and went into the flight deck.

The pilot made an exasperated, fearful noise. John ignored her. Through the windows, he could see the Salt Cliffs and the Singing Sea. The shuttle landed where they had always landed, on the edge of the desert, half a day's walk from the colony itself. He realized, with a shudder, that no one lived on the planet but the natives. The five traders and the sand sculpture were the aliens here.

He had no plan. He had been too lost in his memories.

"Familiar?" the pilot asked. Her expression was wary. She knew his history. Perhaps she thought that once he set foot on the planet, he would pull out a Dancer ritual knife and slice off her hands and feet.

He didn't answer her. "You're coming back in three days?"

She nodded. Her hands were shaking on the controls. What kind of lies had the authorities made up about Bountiful to keep the curious away? That one touch of the desert sand would lead to madness? That one view of the Dancers would lead to murder?

"Wait for me. Even if I'm not here right away, I'll be coming." The words sounded hollow to his own ears. She nodded again, but he knew at that moment that she wouldn't wait. He would have to be here precisely on time or be stranded on Bountiful forever. Trapped.

The child inside him shivered.

He tugged on the duffel strap, adjusting it, and let himself out. A hot, dry breeze caressed his face. The air smelled like flowers, decaying flowers too long in the sun. Twelve years of memories, familiarity and fear rose within him—and suddenly he didn't want to be here anymore. He turned to the shuttle, but the bay door had already closed. He reached up to flag her down—and turned the gesture into a wave. He was not twelve any more. The adults were gone. The colony was gone. He was the adult now, and he wouldn't let himself down.

ELEVEN

The traders made a brilliant decision to come to Bountiful with the wind sculpture. Here they had a ready-made empty colony, a desert filled with sand, and winds aplenty. They could experiment until they were able to duplicate whatever effect they needed, or they could use the planet as a base from which to travel back to Bodean. No one would have caught on if Anita hadn't started the search for her sculpture.

The colony's dome shone like a glass in the sunlight. The walk wasn't as long as John remembered. Still, he would have loved an air car. Air cars had always been forbidden here; they destroyed the desert's delicate ecological balance.

He stopped in front of the dome, stunned to see it covered with little sand particles. In another generation, the dome would be a mound of sand, with no indication that anything had ever existed beneath it. The desert reclaimed its own.

He brushed the sand aside, feeling the grains cling to the oil on his skin. The dome was hot, hotter than he cared to touch, but still he felt for the fingerholds that he knew would be there.

And found them. Smaller than he remembered, and filled with sand, but there. He tugged, and with a groan, the section moved. He slipped inside, bumping his head on the surface. He was a man now, not a boy, and crawling through small spaces wasn't as easy as it used to be.

Once inside, he closed the hatch, and took a deep breath. The air wasn't as stale as he had expected it to be. It tasted metallic, dusty, like air from a machine that had been turned off for a long time. Decades, probably.

The traders had been in here. Of course they would know that the dome could be breached from the outside. Bountiful's colonists had had a terror of being trapped in the desert.

All he had to do was go to the municipal plant and track them from there. So easy. He would have to wait three lousy Earth days together for the shuttle pilot to return.

He turned onto a street and started walking. He had made it halfway down the block before the things he saw registered, and his emotions stopped him.

The houses hadn't collapsed. They were old-time regulation colony homes, built for short-term, but used on Bountiful for nearly a century. The lawns were dead. Brown hulks of plants remained, crumbling now that the air had come back on.

The lawns, the gardens, had been the colonists' joy. They were so pleased that they had been able to tame this little space of land, turn it into their ideal of Earth. Plastic homes with no windows, and Earth flowers everywhere. The dome used to change color with the quality of the light: sometimes gray, sometimes blue, sometimes an odd sepia to protect the colonists from the UV rays.

All of that gone now. No voices, no hum of the Salt Juice factory, no movement. Just John on a long empty street, facing long empty ghosts.

There, on the house to the left, he and the other children had placed Michael Dengler's body. He had been the last one, the true failure. It had seemed so logical that if they removed his head along with his hands, his heart and his lungs, that he would grow taller and stronger than the adults. But like the others, he hadn't grown at all.

John sank to the ground, wrapped his arms around his head as if he could shield himself from his own memories. He and the others weren't covered under the Alien Influences Act. They weren't crazy. They were, according to the prosecuting attorney, evil children with an evil plan.

All they had wanted to do was escape. And they thought the Dancers held the secret to that escape.

He remembered huddling behind the canopied trees, watching the Dancer puberty ritual, thinking it made so much sense: remove the hands, the heart and the lungs, so that the new ones would grow in. He was on a different planet now, the third generation born in a new place. Of course he wasn't growing up. He wasn't following the traditions of the new world.

The attorneys asked him, over and over, if he believed that, why hadn't he gone first? He wanted to go last, thinking that the ultimate sacrifice. Dancer children didn't move for days. He didn't understand the adult reaction—the children weren't dead, they were growing new limbs. Or at least, that was what he thought. Until Michael Dengler. Then John had understood what he had done.

He stayed on his knees for a long time. Then he made himself rise slowly. He did bounty now. He traveled all over the galaxy. He had served his sentence. This was done, gone. He had a wind sculpture to recover, and the people were within his grasp.

He made himself walk, and concentrate on the future. He found where they got in. Another section had been dislodged, letting too bright sunlight into the dome. Footprints marred the dirt, and several brown plant stalks were newly broken. Being this close usually excited him—one of the few excitements that he had—but this time he felt empty inside.

His breathing rasped in his throat. He had a dual feeling: that of being watched and that of being totally alone. The hairs prickled on the back of his neck. Something was wrong here.

He followed the footprints to the municipal building. The door was open—an invitation almost. He couldn't go around to the windows, since there were none, and most buildings didn't have another doorway. He braced himself, and slipped in.

The silence was heavier in here. The buildings always had a bit of white noise—the rustle of a fan, the whisper of air filtering through the ceiling. Here, nothing. Perhaps they had only found the controls for the dome itself. Perhaps they wanted it quiet so that they could hear him.

The walls and floors were spotless, so clean that they looked as if they had been washed days before. Only the dirt-covered tracks of the traders marred the whiteness, a trail leading him forward, like an Earth dog on the trail of a scent.

He followed it, willing to play out his little role in this drama. Some action would take his mind off the remains of the colony, of the hollow vestiges of his past.

He rounded the corner—and found the first body.

It leaned against the wall, skin toughened, mummified into a near skeleton. For a minute, he thought it had been there since the colony closed and the air shut down. Then he noticed the weapon in its left hand. A small hand-held laser, keyed to a person's print. Last year's model.

He made himself swallow and lean in. One of the traders. For a minute, he couldn't determine which one. He ripped at the clothes, discovered gender—male—then studied the wrinkled, freeze-dried face.

Not the old trader, Minx, who had run Salt Juice. One of the younger males. Tension crept up his back. He held himself still. He had seen this kind of death before, but where?

The answer required that he let down some internal shields, reach into his own memory. He did so slowly, feeling the hot spots, the oppression the colony imposed on him. Then it came:

A cadmium miner on one of the many cargo ships he had worked for. The miner had slipped into the hold, trying to get safe passage somewhere, not realized that to get out of those mines, he needed a series of shots, shots that protected him from the ways that the mining had destroyed his body, processes that wouldn't start until the mining ended.

The captain of the cargo ship had leaned over to John, expressed the view for the entire ship. "God," he said, "I hope I don't die like that!"

John touched the corpse again, figuring if he was contaminated, there wasn't much he could do about it. Amazing that he didn't die when he left Cadmium. They had been away from that planet for years. Amazing that the death would come now, here, in this faraway place, with a weapon in his hand.

He took the laser from the body, ran the diagnostic. It worked. He pocketed it. Better to use that weapon than his own. Cover his tracks, if he had to.

The footprint path continued down the hall. He brushed off his hands, and followed it. All the doors were closed, locks blinking, as if they hadn't been touched since the colony was evacuated.

He followed the trail around another corner, and found another body: this one a woman. She was sprawled across the floor, clothing shredded, blood everywhere, eyes wide with terror. No desiccation, no mummification. This time, the reek of death, and the lingering scent of fear.

She appeared to have been brutalized and beaten to death, but as he got closer, he realized that she didn't have a scratch on her. John's throat had gone dry, and his hands were shaking. He had never before encountered anything as odd as this. How did people die on a dead planet? Nothing here would do this, not in this fashion, and not so quickly. He knew about death on Bountiful, and it didn't work like this.

He pulled the laser out of his pocket and kept going. The dirt path didn't look like footprints any more, just a swirl of dirt along a once-clean floor. He half-expected a crazed trader to leap out from behind one of the doors, but he knew that wouldn't happen. The deaths were too bizarre, too different to be the work of a maniac. They had been planned. And a little scared voice inside told him they had been planned for him.

TWELVE

John reached the main control room, surprised to find it empty and silent. Lights blinked and flashed on a grid panel nearly two centuries old. He checked the patterns, figuring how it should run on guesswork, experience with old grids, and a half-worn-down diagram near the top of the room. His instincts warned him to absorb the knowledge in this room—and he was, as quickly as he could.

A door slammed somewhere in the building.

His skin prickled. He whirled. No one visible. No sounds. Nothing except the slight breeze caused by his own actions. He moved slowly, with a deliberation he didn't feel. He checked the corridor, both directions, noting that it was empty. Then he left the main control room. There was nothing more he could do inside. He walked toward the direction of the slammed door. Someone else was alive in here, and he would find that person. He didn't know what he would do then.

His heart was pounding against his chest. Death had never frightened him before. He had never felt it as a threat, only as a partner, an accident. He never saw the murders as deaths, just failed experiments. No one he loved had ever died. They had just disappeared.

Another body littered the corridor. He didn't examine it. A quick glance told him the cause of death. Parts were scattered all over, hanging in the ritual position of Fetin killings, something he had seen too much of in his own exile.

The fourth body was crucified against a wall, upside down, blood still dripping onto the pristine floor. Perhaps he was wrong. One madman with a lot of determination, and perhaps some kind of toxic brain poisoning from a drug he wasn't used to. One man, Minx, the old trader, under the influence of the Bodean wind sculpture.

He hated to think Minx had done this in a rational frame of mind.

John had circled nearly the entire building. From his position, he could see the door, still standing open. Minx had to be outside, waiting for him. He tensed, holding the laser, setting his own systems on alert.

The dirt spread all over the floor, and a bit on the walls. Odd, without anyone tracking it. Was Minx's entire body grimy? John crept along as quietly as he could, trying to disturb nothing. Seemed eerie, as if Minx had been planning for this. It felt as if he had been watching, waiting, as if John were part of a plan. Even more eerie that Minx had managed to kill so many people in such diverse ways—and in such a short period of time.

It made no sense.

John reached the front door, and went rigid, except for a trembling at the very base of his spine. Minx was there, all right, waiting, all right, but not in the way John expected.

Minx was dead.

The blood still trickled from the stumps where his hands used to be. His chest was flayed open, heart and lungs missing. Head tilted back, neck half cut, as if whoever did this couldn't decide whether or not to slice it through.

He hadn't been there when John went into the building. Minx couldn't have died here—it took too long to chop up a human being like that. John knew. He had done it half a dozen times—with willing victims. Minx didn't look willing.

The blood was everywhere, spraying everything. Minx had to have died while John was inside.

To kill an adult the size of Minx would have taken a lot of strength, or a lot of time.

The shivering ran up John's spine, into his hands. *I didn't mean to kill him!* the little boy inside him cried. *We just wanted to grow up, like Dancers. Please! I didn't mean...*

He quashed the voice. He had to think. All five were dead. Something—

"John?"

He looked up. Beth stood before him, clutching a Dancer ritual blade. It was blood-covered, and so was she. Streaks had splattered across her face, her hands. He hadn't seen her since she was fifteen, since the afternoon the authorities caught them comforting each other, him inside her, her legs wrapped around him like a hug.

The first and last time John had been intimate with anyone.

She had hated the killings, never wanted to do them. Always sat quietly when Harper made the group talk about them. Three years of sessions, one afternoon of love. Then prison ship and separation, and him bounty hunting, alone, forever.

"Beth?" He knew it wasn't her, couldn't be her. She never would do anything like this, not alone, and not now so many years in the future. He walked toward her anyway, wanting to wipe the blood off her precious face. He reached for her, hand shaking, to touch that still rosy cheek, to see if it was as soft as he remembered, when his hand went through her.

She was as solid as wind.

Wind.

She laughed and grew bigger, Minx now, even though he remained dead at John's feet. "Took you long enough," the bodeangenie said. "And you call yourself the best."

John glanced at the body, the ritual knife, found the laser in his own hand. A laser could not cut through wind.

"No," the bodeangenie said. "It can't."

John stopped breathing. He took a step back as the realization hit. The bodeangenie was telepathic. It had been inside John's head, inside his mind. He shuddered, wiped himself off, as if in brushing away the sand he brushed away the touch, the intimacy that he had never wanted. Had the others died of things they feared? That would explain the lack of external marks, the suddenness. That would explain all except Minx. Minx, who died of something John feared.

Then the images assaulted him: The trader ship, full of sweat, laughter and drink, hurtling toward the planet; the traders themselves dipping into the bodeangenie like forbidden fruit, using him to enhance their own powers, tap each other's minds, playing; the Dancers stalking out of the woods, into the desert; John, sitting in the cafeteria, his memories displayed before him; Anita, counting credits, peering into the bottle; the trap closing tight, holding him fast, a bit of wind, a bit of sand, a bit of plastic . . .

John was the bodeangenie's freedom if Bountiful didn't work. He could pilot the traders' ship back to Bodean, back to the 'genie's home. Fear pounded inside his skull. He didn't want to die like that. He had never wanted to die like that...

He slid to his knees, hands around his head as if to protect it. Harper's voice: *If you want protection, build a wall. Not a firm wall, a permeable one, to help you survive the alone times. The wall must come down when you need it to, so that things don't remain hidden. But sometimes, to protect yourself, build a wall.*

The sheets came up, slowly, but easier than he had hoped because they were already half there. The bodeangenie chuckled, Beth again, laughter infectious. She went to the dome, touched it, and John saw Dancers, hundreds of them, their fingers rubbing against the plastic, their movement graceful and soft, the thing that had given them their name.

"Three choices," the bodeangenie said. "Me, or death, or them."

A little light went on behind his wall. The bodeangenie thought the Dancers frightened him. The 'genie could only tap what was on the surface, not what was buried deep, no matter what its threats.

Wind, and sand, and plastic.

John hurled himself at the dome, pushing out, and sliding through.

The Dancers vanished as if they never were. He rolled in the sand, using all his strength to close the dome doors. The bodeangenie pushed against him with the power of wind. His muscles shook, his arms ached. The bodeangenie changed form, started to slip out, when John slammed the portal shut.

Trapping the 'genie inside.

The bodeangenie howled and raged against the plastic wall. The side of the dome shook, but the 'genie was trapped. A little boy appeared in his mind, alone in a foreign place, hands pounding on a door. *Let me out*, the little boy said with John's voice. *Please I didn't mean to—*

His words, his past. Trapped. The 'genie was trapped. It had to be or it would kill him. Trapped.

John started to run, as if that would drown out the voice. Across the sands toward the forest, toward something familiar. The sun beat down on him, and he realized he had forgotten his scarf, his ointment, his protection. The little boy kept pounding, sobbing. Torture. He wouldn't be able to survive it. Two more days until the shuttle arrived.

He could take the traders' ship, if he could find it.

The forest still looked charred, decades after the fire that happened just before John left the planet. But the canopied trees had grown back, and John could smell the familiar scent of tangy cinnamon. Dancers.

No!!! the little boy screamed in his head.

They came toward him, two-legged, two-armed, gliding like ballerinas on one of the bases. They chirruped in greeting, and he chirruped back, the language as fresh as if he had used it the day before.

His mind drifted into the future, into emotion, into their world.

I would like to stay, John said, placing his memories behind him. *I would like to be home.*

THIRTEEN

Sometimes he would wake in the middle of the night, stare through the canopies at the stars, and think: *Someday I will touch them.* Then he would return to sleep, incident forgotten.

Sometimes he would be touching a Dancer's hand, performing a ritual ceremony, and a child's scream would filter through his mind. He would drop the knife, plead apology, and wonder at it, since none of the others seemed to mind.

He loved the trees and the grass, but the hot, dry wind against his face would make him shiver. Sometimes he would think he was crazy, but usually he thought nothing at all.

FOURTEEN

Perhaps days, perhaps months later, John found himself in the desert, searching for small plants. Food, he was thinking, he would like food—when fists, a little boy's voice, pounded their way into his mind. *Let me out, please let me out.* Puzzlement, a touch of fear, and something against a block—

The memories came flooding back, the shuttle, the bodeangenie. He sat down, examined his fried skin. Human. No matter how much he wanted to be Dancer, he would always be human, with memories, guilt, and regrets.

The bodeangenie was still trapped. The shuttle was long gone, and John was trapped here, presumed dead, doomed to die if he didn't get out of the harsh sun and eat human foods instead of Dancer foods.

He looked back into the forest. He had no memories of the last few days (months?). Dancer thought. Dancers had no memories. He had achieved it, ever so briefly. And it would kill him, just as it nearly killed him when he was a boy. They were his drug, as potent as Salt Juice, and as deadly.

Please...

He stood, wiped himself off. The trader shuttle was hidden near the Singing Sea. The bodeangenie was trapped, the planet closed. He was thought dead, and Anita had lost her money.

Beth rose in his mind, pleading against the dome.

Beth. Her screams, his cries. Nights clutching a pillow pretending it was her, wanting the warmth she provided, the understanding of shared experience, shared terror.

Trapped.

The adults had punished him because he felt trapped, abandoned, because he had killed to set himself free.

Like the bodeangenie.

John was the adult now.

He sank to the sand, examined his sun-baked skin. Much longer, and he would have died of exposure. He was already weak. His need to run, his longing for the Dancers, had trapped him as neatly as he had trapped the bodeangenie. He had been imprisoned so long that even when he had freedom, he imprisoned himself.

Beth and a handful of children huddled near the edges of the dome, waiting for him. Children he had killed, others he had destroyed. The 'genie was using their memories to reach him, to remind him how it felt to be trapped.

He needed no reminding. He had never been free.

He got up, wiped the sand off his skin. His clothing was tattered, his feet callused. He had been hiding for a long time. The 'genie wasn't able to touch the Dancer part of his mind.

John started to walk, feet leading him away from the Dancers. He glanced back once, to the canopied forest, the life without thought, without memory. Alien influence. The reaction was not human.

And he was all too human.

Please! I didn't mean...

Yes, he did. Just as the 'genie did. It was the only way they knew how to survive.

The sand burned under his bare feet. He wasn't too far from the dome. Perhaps that was how the 'genie's thoughts had penetrated. Saving him. Saving them both.

John nodded, a plan forming. He would take the 'genie back home on the trader ship, using Anita's credits for fuel. She would know that he was alive then, and she would be angry.

Then he would deal with her, and all the creatures she had trapped. He would find the Minaran, free it; free the little helldog. He would destroy her before she destroyed too much else.

Sand blew across the dome's surface. Almost buried, almost gone. He got closer, felt the presence inside.

Please...

In his mind's eye, a half-dozen children pushed their faces against the plastic, waiting for him. Beth, a woman now, held them in place. No 'genie. Just his past. Face it, Harper had said.

He had been running from it too long.

He reached the dome, brushed the sand away, searching for a portal.

The 'genie needed him. It wouldn't kill him. Wind couldn't pilot a spaceship alone.

"I'm coming," John said.

And inside the dome, the children rejoiced.

GLASS WALLS

KRISTINE KATHRYN RUSCH

ONE

Beth touched the warm glass window. Inside, the baby Minaran swam, its small head rounded and sleek, its eyes open and friendly. When she had first passed the cubicle, the baby rested on its back on a rock, basking in fake sunlight. Its fur was white, its fins slender but strong.

Odd that it would have a cubicle all to itself just inside the human wing. Odder still that the cubicle had been a banquet room a few days before.

She leaned her face against the glass, wishing she could go inside. The poor little thing had to be lonely. If she could hold it and feel its warm, wet fur against her skin, she might be able to ease the loneliness —both of their loneliness—for just a short time.

"Beth!"

Roddy's voice. She jumped away from the window and stood, hands clasped behind her back. She kept her gaze trained downward, away from the Minaran in the cubicle. Roddy hated it when she ogled the guests.

"What are you doing in the main lobby?" He stood beside her. She could smell peppermint on his breath. He had just had a cup of his favorite—expensive—tea. "Did someone call for you?"

She shook her head. How many demerits this time? Or maybe he would take a week's worth of tips. The diamond square pattern on the carpet ran together. She blinked, making sure her eyes were tearless.

"You know I don't like having the personal staff in the lobby. It creates a sleazy atmosphere. Some of our patrons would prefer to ignore people like you."

As you would, she thought. She finally raised her head, saw Candice at the lobby entrance, watching the entire exchange. Roddy wore a black suit, very twentieth-century retro, fitting in perfectly with the decor in this half of the human wing. Except for the Minaran.

"I was walking through," Beth said, "and I saw the Minaran. What's it doing here?"

"That's none of your business," Roddy said. "When you were hired on, you were told not to ask questions—"

"Beth was not hired," Candice said. She started down the incline into the lobby. Roddy didn't move. He froze, just like Beth had, when faced with his boss. "Let's not have this discussion in the lobby, hmm? My office, please."

Except for the Minaran the lobby was empty. The next ship was twenty minutes behind schedule. The staff was having its break, preparing for the mid-afternoon rush.

Beth and Roddy followed Candice around the registration desk. Her office was a spacious room with a view of the docking ships and the stars beyond. She had to have been at Hotel Andromeda for most of her life—and had to have been a valued employee—to attain a view like that.

"Sit down," Candice said as she slipped into the wide leather chair behind her desk. Her office, too, was done retro. Beth didn't want to sit in the leather chair on the other side of the desk—she hated the feel of the material against her skin; it brought back too many unpleasant memories—but she did anyway. Roddy sat beside her, perched at the edge of the chair as if he were going to spring up any minute.

"The lobby is not a place for dressing down an employee," Candice said, folding her jeweled hands together and leaning forward on the desk. "We are striving to make our guests as comfortable as possible, and they don't need to see dissention among the staff. Is that clear?"

Roddy nodded.

"Good. You may go."

Roddy leaped out of the chair as if it had an ejector seat. He was gone from Candice's office in the time it took her to turn to Beth. "You know better than to stand in the lobby when you're not working."

"Yes." Beth looked at her hands. They weren't as well groomed as Candice's. The years of hard labor would always remain in the form of yellowed calluses, bent nails, and scarred skin.

"The Minaran fascinates you."

Beth didn't answer. When she stared at the creature, memories crossed within her. Memories of the investigator—what was his name? Shafer?—who had killed so many Minarans and destroyed her world, too. Memories of being trapped, naked, in a cubicle the same size for her first real journey into space, the other prisoners passing her, jeering, and tapping on the clear plastic. She had hated it, hated it, and not even the memory of John got her through.

All that combined in loneliness so deep that sometimes she thought nothing would fill it.

"Beth?"

Beth looked up. Candice's voice was harsh, but her eyes weren't. Candice was the only nice person Beth had met on the staff. The rest treated her like dirt, like she was worse than dirt, like she had no value at all.

"You have more demerits than any other staff member. Your ten-year service contract has grown to sixteen. If you don't watch yourself, you could be indentured to the hotel for life."

Beth shrugged. She had nowhere else to go. Meager as it was, the hotel was more home to her than any other place she had lived. Any other place except Bountiful, among the Dancers.

Candice stood up, and shoved her hands in the pocket of her suit

She was a big woman, and powerful. "I would like to make you a project, Beth. I think you're smarter than any other person on the staff. I can send you to an alien no one knows anything about, and you can discover its sexuality and please it within a matter of hours. If this system ran on merits instead of demerits, I suspect you would have been out of here in five years, instead of accumulating enough trouble to keep you here indefinitely. But I need to know if you're willing."

"What do you want from me?" Beth's voice felt rusty, as if she hadn't used it for days.

"I want to train you to become my assistant. You would act as liaison between all branches of the hotel, and you would mostly work in New Species Contact. You would discover what a species needs to feel most at home, and work with the design and personal staff to accomplish that."

Beth clasped her hands together. She had never done anything like that. She could barely speak to other people. Imagine if she had to speak to other species. Normally she went into their rooms and became like a Dancer, absorbing the emotions of the other being and flowing with them until she found what they wanted. Then she would leave, and Dancer-like, forget everything that had happened. "I don't know design or diplomacy."

"I would train you."

Beth shook her head once and stood. "If you knew about me, you wouldn't offer this."

"I know you came to us from a penal ship. I know you were in for murder."

"No." Beth reached out and touched the edge of Candice's desk. The wood was smooth and warm, like the glass around the Minaran's cubicle. "I was convicted under the Alien Influences Act. Some friends of mine and I saw Dancer puberty rites and tried them on each other, not realizing that when you cut off a human's hands, heart and lungs, they die. Because of us, the Intergalactic Alliance closed its second planet—Bountiful—and ordered that humans never have contact with Dancers again. And we were scattered into isolation, away from aliens.

That's why the hotel had to get special dispensation to buy my indentured servitude contract."

"But no aliens have influenced you since," Candice said.

"That's because," Beth kept her voice soft, "that's because I haven't let them."

TWO

Beth went back up to her room by the back way, so that she wouldn't see the Minaran, and be tempted to stop again in the lobby.

The hallway outside her room was quiet. She pressed her finger against her door and it slid open, revealing her haven. Her room was not done retro. A sleep couch floated in the middle, mimicking the weightlessness of space. Nothing decorated the walls, not even a holo-jector, vid screen, or sound unit. It had taken her nearly two years to accept the room as a haven instead of a punishment—by that time, she was used to its spareness. It gave her eyes a rest from the business in the remainder of the hotel.

She took off her shoes and waved at the bed. The motion made it float down to her, and she climbed on it, letting the softness take her. When she had no assignments, she usually slept. Sleep protected her from her memories, protected her from her life. She closed her eyes and felt the bed rise to its place in the center of the room.

The Minaran swam behind her closed eyelids, its little white body begging for her attention. Minarans were not space-faring creatures, so they had no place in the hotel. So of course the hotel would have to build something special.

But someone would have had to bring the creature here. Someone would have had to travel with it, provide it with accommodations, alter a vessel in order to carry it in space. Someone had a lot of money invested in that one little creature.

Odd. Too odd.

Beth opened her eyes and stared at the blank ceiling. Still the sense of the Minaran did not leave her. Minar, the creature's home planet, had been closed, like Bountiful. The Minarans were an endangered species, like the Dancers.

She sat up so fast the bed rocked and nearly tossed her out. Like the Dancers, Minarans were protected species—no one was allowed to remove them from the planet. And this one was a baby, since it was the size of a small cat. Adult Minarans grew to the size of adult male lions, like the kind kept in the Earth zoo on the fifteenth level.

Her knowledge of the Minarans came from the holos that the hotel had shown her when she arrived. The Minaran sequence was the most graphic, hordes of colonists sweeping down on the defenseless animals because the colonists believed that the Minarans had killed a few humans. The colonists had poisoned the Minarans' environment, and the creatures had died in agony as the chemical balance of their watery home shifted. Eighty percent of the creatures died before someone figured out that the colonists were killed by environmental factors that had nothing to do with the Minarans at all.

The holo was a cautionary piece about the power of erroneous beliefs. If hotel staff suffered from the same kind of prejudices the colonists had, guests would die on all levels, from ignorance to lack of care, to well-intentioned "security" measures.

That's what had been striking her as odd, more than the cubicle in the lobby. The entire staff knew about the Minarans, knew about the illegality of transporting them, and still gave this one a place of honor in the lobby.

She had seen a lot of strange things in the hotel, and she had ignored most of them. She couldn't ignore this one.

The Minaran's wide, round eyes haunted her in a way that no one had since she left Bountiful, almost two decades before.

THREE

She didn't want to see Candice, because Candice would ask her to change her decision. Beth wasn't qualified to work in such a sophisticated position. She didn't want anyone harping on her, forcing her into a place she didn't want to be.

A place she wasn't able to be. Working with the aliens required thought. And Beth worked hard at losing thought and memory while she did her job.

Before she could do anything about the Minaran, though, a summons came from Roddy. The summons was merely a beep inside her neural net. She had screamed so when they attached the simple system that the doctors were afraid to try anything more complex. Roddy hated the fact that he had to direct her in person, but she refused to let anyone ever again mess inside her mind.

His office was two levels down from her room. She hated it. She hadn't recognized the design when she first saw it, almost a decade before, but then she had done some research.

Roddy had chosen nineteenth-century retro, Victorian period, England. His office smelled of tobacco and liquor, both substances now banned in large intergalactic areas like the hotel (unless some guest requested them for his pleasure). Rich reds and dark woods covered the walls and carpet. The furniture was heavy, so heavy that Beth wondered how it met regulation. Roddy's stiff suits and muttonchop whiskers looked natural here, as did his distaste for her and the others like her.

"We had a request from Amphib," he said, his back to her. Steam rose from a cup on his desk, and she recognized black tea, as difficult to get as the peppermint stuff he usually drank. "I've forgotten. Do you swim?"

He hadn't forgotten at all. He just liked to toy with her. She wouldn't give him the satisfaction of emotion in her answer.

"Yes, sir."

"Good." He turned. Between his fingers, he held a pipe, unlit, of course. His gaze was cold. "We wouldn't want you to drown, like Tina did last year. We can't afford more scandals like that."

"Good swimmers can drown in only a few inches of water if they get knocked unconscious," Beth said. Keeping her tone flat had become more difficult. Tina had taught her how to swim when she first came to the hotel almost a decade before. Careless sex, violence, or some kind of accident had caused Tina to die.

"I suppose." Roddy leaned against a shelf filled with antique books. "We had a request from a Ratoid. It seems it heard about our interspecies service from a satisfied friend. I have a vid in the next room if you want to see how it's done among consenting Ratoids—"

She shook her head. She had discovered that information vids often interfered with her flow, her opportunity to do her work. "What room?"

He handed her a card with a floor plan and a duplicate of the print which would open the Ratoid's lock. "In all fairness," he said, "I should let you know that Ratoids achieve orgasm underwater. I trust you can hold your breath for long periods of time?"

Beth bit back a response—she usually held her breath the entire time she was in his office—and snatched the card from his hand.

She worked her way through the maze of levels. At least the Amphibs were close to the human quarters. The atmosphere, oxygen levels, and room design weren't all that different. The various amphibs from a number of worlds required a pool instead of a bathroom. They had adjusted to beds and sofas and other human comforts.

Finally, she climbed up a flight of rough-hewn stairs and pushed open a door. The air that greeted her was thick with humidity and smelled faintly of stagnant water. The Amphib section had several kinds of water pools—stagnant, spring-fed, saltwater, acidic, and freshwater. Some Amphibs did well with chemical water treatments. Others died.

She pushed back her hair with one hand and paused in front of the door. Stagnant water. Yuck. Then she took a deep breath and reached to the part of her mind where the Dancers lived.

Dancers—long flowing bodies that looked as if they danced instead of walked. Wide eyes, a faint tang, and a chirp. No memories, none at all, just instinct and free-flowing emotion. Affection, warmth, curiosity, and touch. She still remembered their touch, rubbery and soft at the same time. She had wanted to be a Dancer when she was young. Now she became one each time she walked through a guest's door.

Inside, large creature, beautiful creature with jeweled skin. Not jeweled. Water dappled. Air smells fetid. Stagnant water. Her skin tingles, wondering how it will feel pressed up against the creature's. It speaks—a rumble she does not understand. She steps forward, rubs her hand on its jeweled skin, feeling water, feeling coolness, feeling slime. Her entire body heats. The creature pulls away her clothes, and together they dive into the green algae, floating on the surface of the pool...

FOUR

And when she came to herself, she was standing on the rough-hewn steps, her clothing carelessly wrapped around her. She smelled rank—decayed water and something else, something even more foul. Her body felt heavy, tired, used, like it always did when these things ended. She lifted a hand, and found it coated with black slime. A shudder ran through her, and she ran the remaining distance to her apartment.

A beep echoed inside her net. Roddy. He wanted to see her humiliation. Odd he could think after all these years she could still be humiliated. Odd that she could. So many of the others shut off their skins as if their brains had been developed with an on-off switch. Hers must have malfunctioned. She always came to herself frightened and disgusted.

Her apartment door opened and she let herself inside, discarding her clothing, climbing into the tiny bathing cubicle, and setting the water temperature near scalding. Washing didn't make the feeling go away, but it did give her some of her dignity back. She never could remember what happened, but that never changed her feeling that what did happen was wrong.

The beep echoed again. She put on a different outfit and checked herself in the tiny mirror. No trace of the Ratoid remained.

On the surface.

She was about to let herself out when the door swung open. Roddy stood there, hands on his hips. "I've been summoning you," he said.

"I just finished. I was coming."

"You finished almost an hour ago."

He was watching, then. She wondered how many times he watched, and how it made him feel. It made her feel even more used.

"I don't know what couldn't wait until I got cleaned up."

"The Ratoid wants you back, later. It is bringing in a number of guests, and wants you for entertainment."

She couldn't suppress the shudder. The last time she had participated in an interspecies orgy, she had nearly died. Roddy knew that. He knew how she feared another encounter. Maybe he was still punishing her for glancing at the Minaran. Or maybe he wanted her to know how much he resented the interaction with Candice, earlier.

"It's against regulations to perform with an alien twice in one day." She put one hand on the undecorated wall to anchor herself.

"You are in too much trouble to quote regulations to me." His jaw was set, his mouth in a sideways line. She didn't like the way his eyes glittered.

"The regulations protect the hotel." She kept her voice soft, but the muscles in her arm tensed. "Too many humans died from repeat contact. Sometimes the alien touch is like a slow-acting poison. I remember when Steve died—"

"I had the autodoc check out the Ratoids," Roddy said. "You'll be fine."

"No." Beth felt dizzy. She had never stood up to Roddy before—to anyone before. She wondered if the Minaran swimming in its little tank felt the same trapped anger that she felt so dangerously close to the surface. "No," she said again.

"This kind of action will allow me to hold your contract forever."

"That gives me a lot of incentive to work harder," she said, and pushed her way into the hall. The air felt cooler there. She strode toward the lobby, not looking back. She had no plan, no idea in mind. She just had to walk.

It wasn't until she stopped in front of the Minaran that she realized she had had a plan after all. It swam up to her, examined her for a moment, then swam away and climbed up on the rocks, its back to her. She wanted to tell it she knew how it felt, trapped in there, on display, with no one to love it, no one to hold it, no one to understand its dreams —and its nightmares.

"Pretty, isn't it?"

The voice was soft, deep and human. Beth turned and looked up into the face of an older woman. Her hair had been painted in small geometric squares of black and silver, and her skin in complementary shades of brown and cream. She wore a rich purple dress that accented the bizarre geometry that some thought fashion.

"You brought it here." Beth made herself look away. The Minaran had hunched into itself, as if it were frightened of the woman.

Assumptions. Human assumptions. Something the hotel warned them never to make.

"I figured this would be a good place to find it a home." Her voice had the warmth of an Amphib sauna, but her silvery eyes glistened with chill. Beth saw, over the woman's shoulder, Roddy gesturing at her frantically. She ignored him.

"Wasn't it at home on Minar?"

The woman laughed. "So sweet and amusing." She tucked a strand of hair behind Beth's ear. Beth shuddered. "I thought you were the one that liked touch."

Beth stiffened. This was a guest. She couldn't contradict a guest. "I'm off duty," she said.

The woman's eyes twinkled for the first time. "I thought staff never went off duty." Her smile grew wider. "Would you like to please my little Minaran there? It looks quite lonely."

Inside the cage? Trapped behind invisible walls? Beth pushed away, trying not to be rude, but her entire body had started to shake.

She bobbed her head once, and walked away, turning her back on Roddy, whose face had turned purple with anger.

FIVE

In her dream, she dove into the Minaran's tank. The water was cool against her skin. The creature rubbed its furry face against her breasts, seeking comfort, seeking milk. She pushed it away. She wanted friendship, but not touch.

She hated touch.

She swam underwater to the rock in the center of the pool. Then her fingers gripped the hard surface and she pulled herself up. Artificial sunlight caressed her body, warmed her, comforted her as she hadn't been comforted since she left Bountiful.

Except for John. Hands tentative, gaze soft. They hadn't known what they were doing. But the Lunar Base psychological staff had. They burst into the room, pulled two lonely teenagers apart and kept them separate forever. Since then, she had never touched another human being in love.

The Minaran pushed its face against her arm. Its muzzle was wet, brown eyes liquid. It chirped at her, then dove back under the water. When it rose again, it was on the other side of the rock. Its loneliness radiated from it. The round eyes looked sad.

She rolled over on her stomach, covering herself as best she could.

The Minaran used its fins to pull itself on the rock and cuddle next to her. She tried to push it away—it was too human, too cute. She didn't want touch, didn't want touch, didn't want—

Beth woke up, heart pounding, skin crawling. She put her head between her knees, made herself take deep breaths. Ever since she saw the Minaran, the nightmares were coming thick and fast. Opening a little door that would best remain closed.

Trapped. The little creature was trapped. No being deserved to be imprisoned, bartered, and sold. No being. No one.

Not even her.

She eased the bed toward the ground so that she could climb off. Then she stood barefoot on the cold floor, hugging herself as she stared at the four bare walls surrounding her.

SIX

The next morning, she made her way into the docks. Willis was there, working in a small cubicle, head bent over a small screen. When he saw her, he grinned and waved. She made herself wave back.

"Going to take me up on it?" he asked, voice jaunty, eyes filled with too much hope.

Beth made the smile stay on her face. "Someday," she said. Usually she felt nothing when she spoke to him. This morning she felt a bit sad.

The large docking bay was over cool. Goose bumps rose on her arms. Marks from hundreds of shuttles covered the floor, and the bay doors had dents in them from accidents missing the path. Through the double protection windows, she could see a dozen ships orbiting around the hotel.

"Knew it wasn't my charm," he said, careful not to touch her. Willis had tried to touch her once years ago, and she had screamed so loudly that Security arrived. They both got demerits for that incident. "What can I do for you?"

"Your office," she said, and made herself put her hand on the small of his back. His face flushed, but he still didn't touch her back. He had offered to buy her contract from the hotel, indenture her to him, and then throw the contract away once they were in space—no strings. Only they both knew that he wanted her love forever, and she had no love to give.

A soft female voice echoed in the bay. *Next arrival in thirty-six minutes. Next arrival...*

Willis closed the door on the sound. Beth reached up and shut off the interhotel com. Willis's flush left his skin and he tamped back something, probably willing his net to stop monitoring the conversation.

She hoped it worked. His net was twenty times more sophisticated than hers.

"Can you get a message off the hotel for me?" she asked.

He started, then sat down. "I didn't know you knew anyone away from here."

She shrugged, unwilling to implicate him more than she had to. She handed him a small chip encased in plastic. It had taken her more than two hours to put the package together and to hide her steps. "Instructions are on here," she said. "Could you do it once you're out of hotel range?"

"Not leaving with me?" he asked, a little too seriously.

"After this," she said, "I'm probably not leaving at all."

SEVEN

Every morning after that, she stood at the edge of the lobby, watching the Minaran swim. Its fur had grown coarser, and its eyes less bright. Its energy was flagging, and she began to wonder if she had taken action in time.

Sometimes, as she stood there, Candice came up beside her and stood, too. They never spoke, but Beth felt as if Candice wanted her to say something, to reconsider her decision. Roddy would catch Beth standing there and a few minutes later her net would beep, summoning her to darker and smellier parts of the hotel. She went, but came to herself with unusual bruises and once, a limp on her left side.

And she didn't see the woman again, not until the day the Intergalactic Police showed up at the hotel. They had used the securities entrance, and tripped no alarms, used no buzzers. One minute the lobby was empty, the next it swarmed with uniformed creatures—most investigating the cubicle holding the Minaran.

Beth inched her way into the lobby and stood off to one side, knowing that she looked shoddy and hurt. Roddy was nowhere around, but Candice buzzed into the room, all efficiency and smiles. Only her shaking hands betrayed her fears.

"Officers?" Candice said, her voice carrying, warning the staff to keep the guests away.

A burly man grabbed a computer clip from a four-armed humanoid and approached Candice.

"Ma'am. I need to see the Manager on Duty or the highest person in charge of the hotel."

"Right now, that's me," she said. "The others are sleeping or attending a conference off surface. Would you like me to contact—?"

"No." His voice boomed in the small area. The Minaran had stopped swimming, and had retreated to its rock. Beth wished she could do the same. "I came to inform you that you and your hotel are in violation of Galactic Code 1.675: kidnapping, imprisonment, and trafficking of an endangered species."

"The Minaran?" Candice asked. She turned toward the cubicle. Beth could see her struggle for control.

"We're also looking for a human, Candice Arrowsmith."

Candice straightened. "I'm Candice Arrowsmith."

"Then you shouldn't look so shocked, Ms. Arrowsmith. You will receive a commendation from Galactic Services for risking your job and contacting us. The Minaran will be returned to its rightful home, and the guilty parties will stand trial for this."

Candice's gaze caught Beth's. She opened her mouth as if to speak to Beth. but then another officer called her away.

Beth watched for another moment, saluting the little Minaran mentally. "At least," she whispered, "one of us is free."

EIGHT

The intergalactic police took only three hours to remove the Minaran and clear the lobby. Hotel workers dismantled the cubicle, and, by afternoon, the space housed a banquet room again. Beth watched through a double-paned window as a shuttle took the woman who had kidnapped the Minaran away.

Maybe the little creature would go back to its family. Maybe it would find someone to love it, to hold it, to give it the comfort it needed—

A hand touched her shoulder. Beth jumped. She turned and saw Candice standing behind her, face ashen and worn with the stress of the day.

"My office," Candice said quietly.

Beth followed her in there. The normally neat office had papers strewn about Screens on all four walls blinked with waiting messages. In addition to the strain of talking with the officers, Candice's neural net was probably going crazy—she had all her superiors to answer to.

She closed the office door and slumped in her chair. Beth remained standing. She didn't know what Candice could do, but she would do something. Still, out there, the little Minaran was going home.

"I saw your face when they came in," Candice said. "What were you thinking?"

Beth knew better than to play dumb. She knew about the other things they had installed in her net, in the pain centers, things they promised to remove when her contract was up. "I knew they wouldn't believe me, even with all the evidence in front of them. That woman was rich, wasn't she? Rich enough to have the entire hotel at her feet."

"So you used my name."

Beth shrugged. "I figured you'd get in trouble otherwise, if someone else reported the violation. This is the first time I've ever seen the hotel party to such a big crime."

"And you have the right to place a moral judgment on the rest of us? Did this come from your experience on the penal ship?" Candice didn't move, but her words had the force of blows. Beth resisted the urge to duck.

"I know what it's like to be trapped, with no escape," Beth said. "Like that Minaran. There's no worse thing in the world."

Candice remained quiet for a long time, refusing to meet Beth's gaze. Beth continued to stand, unmoving, until Candice signaled that it was all right.

"You know I can never offer you a position of authority here again," Candice said.

Beth nodded. "I could never exercise authority," she said. She wouldn't punish or she would be too harsh. She would run in fear of some creatures and worship others. And she would never, ever, allow a creature to imprison another, no matter how much money was involved.

Candice sighed. "Leave me now," she said. "I have a mess to clean up."

NINE

Beth spent the next three days in her room, leaving only to eat. She received no summons from Roddy, no word from Candice. The other staff would not speak to her, and even the robotic units kept their distance. If Candice had wanted a way to punish Beth, this was it.

Finally, someone knocked on her door. Beth grabbed a robe, and sent her bed up to the center of the room. Then she let the door slide open. Willis was there, bouncing from foot to foot, slapping papers against his hand.

"Orders from above," he said. "You're supposed to come with me."

Beth stared at him for a moment, heart hammering. The last time, they had dragged her away from John, still naked, kicking and screaming. The time before that, they had taken her off the planet with the other children, promising them that they would be taken care of. They were taken care of, all right. Analyzed, tried, viewed galaxy-wide, then sent on separate penal ships to parts unknown.

She hadn't done anything illegal. The hotel had no right to send her away.

"Get dressed," he said, "and pack up. It's okay. I'll turn my back."

His smile faded as she still refused to move. "It's okay," he repeated. "They're setting you free."

He handed her the papers, and she saw her name all over them, with "completed" stamped across the pages. She separated them out, ran her fingers across them, wondering, wishing, it was all true.

"You need a proper net," he said. "If you had a proper net, you wouldn't have to look through the documentation. We'll see what we can do once we're away from the hotel. We got to remove those pain receptors, anyway. Now get dressed."

He stepped outside and let the door close, true to his word. She packed numbly, touching the papers from time to time, feeling her hands shake.

When they had let her out of solitary—late one night when the other prisoners were asleep—she had refused to crawl out of her corner. She believed that once she put a foot on the real floor, the guards would beat her for trying to escape. She believed she wasn't worthy of emerging. She believed she could live nowhere else than that clear plastic hole.

She glanced at the bed, at the empty walls, at the room that had been her prison since she arrived at the hotel. "I didn't do it for me," she whispered, knowing Candice couldn't hear her.

But Candice didn't have to hear. She knew. She spent her life in the job she had offered to Beth, reading aliens, understanding their needs, pleasing guests and making sure that even unspoken wishes were granted. The one time she had made a mistake—allowing that woman in with her Minaran prisoner to broker a sale—she had received an out. Beth had saved her. Beth had freed the Minaran.

She took one small case, and kept her papers clutched in her hand. Then she slid the door open.

Willis was still there, back to the door, shifting from foot to foot.

"Where're we going?" Beth asked, the words almost sticking in her throat. She remembered the feeling of near-surface panic, and had to prevent herself from searching for guards.

He smiled and took the bag from her. "Wherever the lady wants."

Where ever she wanted. The concept was beyond her. Once she had had dreams of seeing other places, other lives. But she had left those dreams on Bountiful, with the Dancers. Since then she had wanted nothing but to be left alone.

"Don't worry," Willis said quietly. "You'll think of someplace you want to be."

And for the first time since she arrived at the hotel, she favored someone with a real, heartfelt smile. Willis flushed, and started down the hall, keeping his physical distance, saying nothing, but walking beside her in companionable silence.

Any place she wanted. Thank you, Candice, she thought, and wished that she had a functioning net so that she could send a true message. But Candice wouldn't want to hear. She wanted Beth to disappear in the chaos following the arrival of the Intergalactic Police. She wanted Beth gone so the incident would blow over and go away.

Beth gave a little skip. Any place she wanted. She gazed out of one of the hall portals at the darkness of space, a view she used to ignore. Any place she wanted. Or no place at all.

"I'm joining you, little guy," she whispered to the Minaran. "We're free."

THE INJUSTICE COLLECTOR

KRISTINE KATHRYN RUSCH

THE INJUSTICE COLLECTOR

Record of Proceeding
Incident at Gray's Brook
Injustice Collector 0080 Presiding

Testimony of Requesting Party

They trusted us with their children.

Later, they claimed they trusted us because we resembled animals from their world. Canines. I have seen representations of such things, and the resemblance is superficial.

We are thinner, taller, and we do not stand on all fours. (Many of my people were insulted by this implication—that we could not walk upright—but I was more insulted by the look of the beasts: shaggy, unkempt, and that appendage at the base of the spine—the tail—looked vaguely ominous to me, as if the creatures were slapped together by a careless scientist.)

It is true that we do not have bald skin as the humans do; ours is dusted attractively with fine hairs, making each of us distinctive. Our noses are larger and our mouths open beneath them—perhaps the most canine of our features—but we, as a people, have come to resent the word "snout."

As for the rest, we do not see ourselves as too different from the humans. We use our arms in much the same way, we have hands, we wear clothing. It is true that we do not wear shoes, but the bottoms of our feet are tough and hair-covered. We do not injure as easily as the humans do.

Which, I suppose, is the heart of the problem.

————

They came half a season ago. Their ships were shiny and silver, made of materials we had not seen before. Their leaders offered to teach us how to create such materials, but the lessons never happened—one of many such incidences. Among my tribe, the humans have become known as the People of Broken Promises.

The humans created a settlement on the ice plain, not realizing, of course, that we were in summer, and the plain was at its best. Trees flowered, insects buzzed, and a thousand varieties of summer vegetation grew across the expanse. The air, thick with humidity, was nearly unbearable to us; to them, it spoke of comfort—the "tropics," "paradise," and other words that we did not then know.

We did know that soon the fall would come with its rains, destroying all but the hardiest of plants. Those would die in the cold, buried beneath the sheet of ice that gave the plain its name.

We doubted the humans would survive the fall, let alone the cold. We did not tell them of the cycle, believing that such warning would reward ignorance.

That is why we did not contact the Injustice Collector at the theft of land.

We believed justice had taken care of itself.

————

Interruption in the Proceeding

Two Cycles into the Requesting Party's Testimony, A Breach of Protocol:

Breach of Protocol by the creatures known as human require in-depth reporting methods not employed in two centuries of Injustice Collecting. The humans, it seems, are unfamiliar with the concept of Justice/Injustice. They believe such decisions might be rendered on the small scale, and as a result, have appealed to me in unorthodox ways, which under rules 7765 and 11,235, I am obligated to report.

As a result, my presence will intrude on the record of these proceedings. I beg the Review Board's indulgence.

—INJUSTICE COLLECTOR 0080

Explanatory Note:

This meeting is taking place, as is customary in cases of cultural disputes, in the Great Hall of the Collecting Ship. Four members of the Requesting Party, both male and female, stand to the left. Twenty members of the Non-Requesting Party stand to the right.

Both sides have been instructed in the rules of the proceedings, although for the two days of rules' instructions, only two of the humans attended.

Since the number of humans has grown significantly, I can only assume the added 18 were not briefed by their colleagues.

[*An Aside*: Working conditions are barely tolerable. The Great Hall barely accommodates all of these bodies. As is mentioned in the opening testimony, these human creatures are as large as the MugwL. The crowd presses against my Decision Desk. The temperature in the Great Hall has risen significantly. The Collecting Ship's systems are not designed to accommodate so many heat-giving sources in such a small area.

[To complicate matters, both the MugwL and the humans have distinctive—and competing—odors. The MugwL's fur stinks of rone spice—a sharp peppery scent that invades the nostrils—and the humans, beneath the coating odor of soap, give off a musk that burns the eyes. When I inquired, I was told that such an odor is called a "nervous sweat" and it cannot be controlled. Human suggestions to control the temperature were ignored as untenable. My suggestion that some of the human party leave was met with severe protests. However, if the stench worsens, I will be forced to cut the human presence in half.]

The Non-Requesting Party is inattentive and disrespectful. They speak without tone—in something called a "whisper"—and believe they cannot be heard.

They have obviously not met an Injustice Collector before. They seem to believe that because I am small and do not have features they can readily identify, I am somehow less than they are.

Already, I can see why the MugwL find them so intolerable.

The Breach of Protocol began when the MugwL Representative stated, "That is why we did not contact the Injustice Collector at the theft of land."

The "whispering" rose to an intolerable level, and one human, not one of the original two (I believe, since it is hard to tell—the bald skin is, as the MugwL implied, offensive), cried out,

"We didn't steal! We asked permission to settle there!"

The MugwL Representative continued over the disturbance, adding his phrase, "We believed justice had taken care of itself."

At which another of the humans, one of the tallest, turned toward the MugwL so quickly that I feared violence.

"You fucking bastard," the human said—and judging by its tone, the words "fucking bastard" are an insult. "First you kill our children, now you tell us it's our fault! Judge, this is all wrong. You gotta hear our case—"

I clapped two of my hands for silence, and to my surprise, the human complied. Perhaps it was the spray of red light that flew from my fingertips. That seems to impress the lesser species.

As I clapped with two hands, I used the other three to set the collection bag beneath the Decision Desk. It became clear to me in that moment that the humans do not understand the proceedings.

I do not sit in Judgment, therefore I am not a Judge. I merely listen to the reports and determine to whom the Injustice has occurred. Then I collect it.

Or rather, the bag does. Most of my efforts go toward corralling the bag.

I try to explain this to the humans again (more confirmation that the initial human representatives did not report back to their colleagues), but the humans did not seem to understand.

More "whispering" occurred, and a common sentence wound its way through the Non-Requesting Party: *It's obvious that we have suffered the injustice. Our children are dead.*

If matters of Justice/Injustice were so easily determined, there would be no need for the Decision Desk. Again, I explain, but the humans seem confused.

They seem to believe that the decision is a judgment which I would therefore make. They do not seem to understand the distinctions required by the customs of the Alliance.

I call for a recess, insist that both Parties leave the Ship, and order scrubbers into the Great Hall to attempt to alleviate the stench.

Then I transmit my request for assistance to the Board of Governors.

I tell them I am concerned that I might commit an Injustice myself.

———

Excerpts from the 500-page Gubernatorial Response to Inquiry Presented by Injustice Collector 0080 in regard to Non-Requesting Party Involved in the Incident at Gray's Brook
[Requesting Party Reference: MugwL Case 3345678221]:

. . .

The self-named Humans are an unknown, unstudied species. A careful search of the records reveals that they have never been a Requesting, Non-Requesting, Peripherally Involved, or Bystanding Party in any Justice/Injustice proceeding...

Cases involving unknown, unstudied species must proceed as if the species is sentient, according to Justice/Injustice standards...

...and so, to satisfy your request, we had to return to the earliest records of Justice/Injustice proceedings, in which species now known to us [but which were, at the time of the proceedings, unknown] established Justice/Injustice Precedent...

...what the early Injustice Collectors learned was that the bags did not accept as an Injustice cases presided over by an Injustice Collector in which a Party of Unknown Sentience did not understand the intricacies of the proceeding...

Therefore, certification continues in the Incident at Gray's Brook, also known as Requesting Party Reference: MugwL Case 3345678221.

———

Record of Proceeding
Incident at Gray's Brook
Injustice Collector 0080 Presiding

Testimony of Requesting Party
[*continued*]

Human children are curious creatures. They share some traits with the adults of the species, but no one would intuitively understand that such a small creature, less than a meter in length at first appearance, would eventually become the towering figures now standing to my left.

In fact, we had no idea at the time of the incident that the creatures called "children" were also a type of "human." We believed them to be a related Earth species, rather like the Canine we had referred to in our previous remarks.

It is counter-intuitive to believe these creatures would grow at such an astounding rate. It is also counter-intuitive to believe that a group traveling the great distances that the humans traveled would bring the young of the species, carrying with it the very future of the species itself.

We therefore request that the surviving children join this proceeding as the Bystanding Party—

————

Interruption in the Proceeding

Eight Cycles into the Requesting Party's Testimony, A Breach of Protocol:

This protocol breach [and, I am certain, all others] are caused by the factors listed in the Second Cycle breach described above. I see no reason to repeat that finding here. In future breaches, I shall simply describe the breach, and continue with the Report of the Proceeding.

If any member of the Review Board has an objection, I refer

him to the Board of Governors' Response to the Official Inquiry on the Humans [attached above].

—*INJUSTICE COLLECTOR 0080*

"Your Honor," said the human who, before this morning's proceedings, introduced himself [they assure me that this creature is a male] as the one in charge. At my request, he wears a large red badge which lists his designation: John Graf. I do not know what these words stand for; I know only that I am to use them whenever I refer to the human with the red badge. "You can't let them do this."

The "them" in that sentence refers to the Requesting Party. The "this" refers to the introduction of the "children" as the Bystanding Party.

I cite regulations, as I have done for days now. The "humans" apparently have a short attention span. We discussed the rights of the Requesting Party in regards to the Bystanding Party on the first day of the explanatory proceedings.

"No, sir," the John Graf human said, "I'm afraid *you* don't understand. By our laws and customs, the only people who speak for our children are their parents."

I do not know this word "parents" and I tell the John Graf so.

His bald skin turns an alarming shade of red, nearly the color of his badge, and I am concerned that my words have harmed him physically. The "whispering" begins again, and I beg for silence.

Then I tell the John Graf that he may recess for medical treatment if he so desires.

His tiny features press together, as if he is trying to make them into a MugwL face. "I'm in perfect health, Your Honor."

He sounds—and I am merely guessing—offended. I look down at the bag which I have stored under the Decision Desk to see if it detects an Injustice that I may have inadvertently caused, but it hasn't even twitched.

"I just find it appalling that you don't know what parents are," the John Graf says. His voice has risen to an intolerable level. "I'm opposed to a legal proceeding when our cultures are so different that we have to explain something as basic as parenthood."

I hold up my middle hand. "We are discussing 'parents,' not 'parenthood.' Please do not confuse the issue."

He makes a blatting sound, like the wind through a malfunctioning weezer engine.

"I am not confusing any issue," he says. "You people are. We can't continue with this charade any longer."

Another concept I do not know. But I do not ask him to explain it, since I am beginning to agree with the MugwL's characterization of the humans as People of Broken Promises. I ask the John Graf to explain "parents" and instead, he confuses the issue by adding two more unknown words into the proceedings.

No explanation of "parents" appears to be forthcoming.

"We're leaving," the John Graf says.

The nineteen other humans nod in agreement. They all turn toward the Great Hall doors, but I do not open them.

"You cannot leave when the Proceedings are underway," I tell them. "The doors will only open in case of Recess or Final Determination."

[*An Aside*: I wish for nothing more than the opening of doors and the disappearance of the humans. The stench seems worse this day. My eyes have been burning since the presentation began.]

"We refuse to participate any longer," the John Graf says. "This is a joke!"

Joke. Another new word. I choose not to focus on it, but on the preceding sentence.

"You cannot refuse to participate," I remind him. "The time for that is past. You had from the moment the Request for a Justice/Injustice review was made to the Board of Governors to the moment the Collecting Ship arrived to demand a cancellation. You did not make such a demand. So the proceeding must continue."

"Another stupid law no one bothered to tell us about," the John Graf says, waving his arm downward, as if he is compacting a pile of snow.

"We should've just killed the fuckers," one of the other humans says, rather loudly. This is not a "whisper." I believe it was meant to be heard. "Blasted them all to hell and back for what they did to the kids."

Murmurs of agreement thread through the human crowd. The MugwLs look at me as if they expect me to stop it.

They should know better. If the humans take action, I can only observe. If the MugwLs or their survivors then believe that the human action was wrong, they can make yet another request for an Injustice Collector. I will become a Peripherally Involved Party, and will not sit on the Decision Desk.

[*An Aside*: I confess that such a change would please me. I find this case taxing, and would like as much as the humans for it to end.]

"It could've been an accident," says the John Graf. "It's pretty clear we don't understand these aliens any more than they understand us. I'm not going to be in charge of a genocide, even when—"

"Even when they kill our kids?" the other human asks.

The John Graf expels air, and shakes his head from side to side. He is clearly in charge, but the others do not agree with him. I fear trouble of a type I am not equipped to deal with.

I glance down. The bag has turned a light lavender. It is getting greedy. I slam its top closed with two of my hands, using the other two to twist the top into a knot. The bag fades, but I worry that this is just an act.

The John Graf is leaning close to his compatriots. "We've been here for fifty years," he says, as if this is important.

It sounds strange to me. The MugwL claimed in his opening testimony that the humans had only been here half a season, and I see no evidence to the contrary.

But the other humans do not disagree with that characterization. In fact, many of them nod which, as their representatives informed me on the first day, is a sign of assent.

"This is our home. Our children were born here," the John Graf is saying.

I am leaning toward the conversation, even though I hear it more clearly than the "whispering." The MugwL watch me as if they expect me to do something about this exchange.

At least the MugwL are smart enough to know that I will not interfere.

"Leaving is not an option," the John Graf says. "We must peace-fully co-exist."

"Even if they kill our kids," the vocal human states. Although the words sound like a question, they are not.

"That's what we're here to determine," the John Graf says. "Whether it was intentional or not. Right?"

At this last, he turns to me. He seems to be expecting a Judgment again, but I do not give it to him.

Instead, I do as I have done before. I recite the law and the history. "The MugwL have requested our presence because they believe an injustice may have occurred."

"Hell, yes, an injustice occurred," says the vocal human. "They murdered our children. That's an injustice."

"But you did not request the proceeding," I say. "They did."

The vocal human starts to answer, but the John Graf steps in front of it. [Him? The genders are difficult to determine. I shall cease trying until I am told with certainty which of the six known genders I am dealing with.]

"Because of us," the John Graf says. He looks over his shoulder at the MugwL.

The two of them stand, hands together, heads bowed, as is proper procedure. Emotion does not cross their faces. Only the slight change in their peppery odor tells me that they are reacting to this at all.

"We went to them," the John Graf is saying to me, "right after the deaths. My people wanted an arrest, some kind of charges, sanctions—a few, like Victor here, wanted to take matters into their own hands. But we want to peacefully co-exist. So I want to handle this by the book. I go to MegrP, their leader, and I say just that, we need to handle this properly so that we stay allies. He listens, then asks if I think an injustice has occurred. And I say hell, yes. Our kids are dead. He nods, and says he will contact you."

I let him speak, even though the history of the request is not relevant. That too was explained in the first two days, and apparently not conveyed to all of the humans.

"Nonetheless," I say when it becomes clear that the John Graf is done speaking. "They are the Requesting Party, and it is by their aegis that I am here."

"So?" the John Graf asks.

"So you must let the proceeding continue."

"What, so they can tell you their side of the story without us saying ours? How fair is that?" His voice has risen to nearly intolerable levels. "It's our kids that're dead, us that've suffered here, and it sounds like we'll suffer some more when Fall—however you people define your seasons—eventually shows up and washes our homes away. *That's* Injustice, Mr. Collector. We haven't done anything wrong."

"This is not a Judgment," I say yet again. "This is a Justice/Injustice proceeding."

"Yeah," the John Graf says, "and I thought that meant a finding of fact. You know, the truth will out and all that. Some impartial person would investigate, maybe even go to the crime scene, interview some MugwLs and the surviving kids and find out what happened. But if I understand your rules right, you're just going to let this guy talk—and he wasn't even there. Then you'll make some kind of judgment, and we're done. That's not Justice, Mr. Collector. That's just plain wrong."

The bag is a darker shade of purple. I use my middle arm to check the knot. The knot is tight. The bag will not get loose.

"This Proceeding was Requested," I say. "It must continue. When it is finished, you may seek this 'investigation' and 'judgment,' perhaps from your own people. This Proceeding is what it is, and I cannot make it anything else."

[*An Aside*: although, in some ways, the Proceeding has become something else. It resembles the Proceedings of the early Alliance rather than modern Proceedings, partly because of these protocol breaches.]

"We have spent more than Eight Cycles here," I say. "If we continue at the pace, we will be here until Fall. The Requesting Party must complete his testimony. If there are no further objections, I shall send my staff for the Bystanding Party, and we shall—"

"But there are objections," the John Graf says. "The very objection that started me. Children can't be here without their parents' permission. And no parent is going to allow a child to take place in this farce."

Again with the unexplained words. I chose to ignore them.

"What your people want now does not matter," I say. "All that matters now is the Proceeding itself. These 'children' are, at the request of the Requesting Party, the Bystanding Party, and by our regulations, required to be here. You cannot change centuries of law simply because you do not agree to it."

"What'll happen to the children?" the John Graf asks.

I am at the end of my patience. "We discussed Bystanding Parties on the first day. Consult with your representatives. We shall indulge you no longer."

The John Graf clenches his hands into fists and does not step away from the Decision Desk. The vocal human moves its head from side to side.

"Told you we should've blasted them," it "whispers." Its gaze is on mine as it speaks, and I know the comment is somehow directed toward me.

"Proceed," I say to the MugwL representative, and he does, with obvious relief.

———

Record of Proceeding
Incident at Gray's Brook
Injustice Collector 0080 Presiding

Testimony of Requesting Party
[continued]

As I said more than Eight Cycles ago now, the humans trusted us with their children. This was not a trust we asked for or even understood. We had no desire to interact with the humans, but their intrusiveness forced us into relations.

They asked questions; they tried our food (and complained when it made them ill); they even came into the village during Privacy Cycles, demanding attention. All of that, we accommodated. We listened, we spoke, we spent time with them at their request.

We did not ask them questions, knowing that our lack of interest would show them they were not wanted. Yet they seemed to ignore that message.

Part of the problem, we assumed, was that they always sent new representation. The early Elders vanished, replaced by other Elders, and now we are being introduced to yet a new set of Elders. Even though the shiny silver ships the humans arrived in seemed small, they carried a multitude of beings, so many that we often found ourselves confused.

We did not even note the presence of "children" until late in the days of the first set of Elders. Then the Elders brought small creatures to us, and showed us the "children" proudly. We believed they had been sent in another mission, that the humans, in their folly, thought they could add their native creatures to our environment.

We did not know that these creatures were the young or that they were somehow created without waterbaths and the freezings of six winters. We did not know that the young could be created off the world the humans call Earth.

―――――

Interruption in the Proceeding

Nine Cycles into the Requesting Party's Testimony, The Arrival of the Bystanding Party.

This interruption is one I had requested when I insisted the Requesting Party continue with its Testimony without all Requested members present. The "children"—some thirty of them of various sizes and shapes—have been brought in by two Collectors-in-Training and five robotic helpers.

Like the other humans, the "children" do not seem to understand the proceedings. Since explanation did not work with the older humans, I do not believe it will work with the younger, and chose not to take the two days to reiterate the rules and regulations.

If any member of the Review Board has an objection, I refer him to the Board of Governors' Response to the Official Inquiry on the Humans [attached above].

—INJUSTICE COLLECTOR 0080

In the midst of the arrival of the Bystanding Party, the humans committed yet another protocol breach. I note this here, but do not place it into the record as a secondary interruption since this is an interruption of an interruption.

Nonetheless, I report it here:

"I object," says the John Graf. "These children have no legal rights here. Their parents must be present."

[*An Aside*: there are now fifty humans, two MugwL, two Collectors-in-Training, five robotic helpers, and the bag in the Great Hall. Even if I complied with the John Graf's demands, the additional humans [if, indeed that's what these "parents" are] would not fit into the room. I do not mention this. I have ceased arguing with the humans.]

"The 'children' are the Bystanding Party," I say. "If the Bystanding Party does not understand its function here, I suggest it choose one representative member, and set the rest free. The representative member will listen to the testimony, will spend time with the Collectors-in-Training to gain an understanding of the rules session which was missed, and will, if need be, relay the Justice/Injustice to the remaining members of the Party."

"Your Honor," one of the "children" says. It has a high voice with many overtones, "our parents don't want us here."

Again, I ignore this. "We shall recess for One Cycle while the Bystanding Party picks its representative."

And so we do.

———

[*An Aside*: After the Great Hall empties, and the Scrubbers enter, attempting to clean the vile stench from the air, I look down at the bag. It is a faint lavender.

[It senses my attention, and sends me this message: *There have been too many protocol breaches all ready. This proceeding will fail its Review. Let me take the Perceived Injustices now in the interest of time, and it will save us all more Cycles of this.*

[I note the communication here in an aside, since it is within the bag's rights to make such a communication. Each case I have administered has included such a communication.

[Only this time, I actually contemplate the bag's request. This procedure *is* unusual and will receive great attention from the Review Board. I am tempted to save all of us the trouble and allow the bag this one indulgence.

[Apparently it senses my hesitation and turns a violent purple. The color change and the shimmering hatred that rises from the bag's porous exterior remind me that, no matter how logical a bag's argument, the bag is always concerned with its own power. Too many Injustices, even Perceived Ones, might overload the safety protocols, and the bag would be freed.

[There are fifty bags within traveling distance of this sector. One free bag could free the others—that's how the Attwne System dissolved.

[I reject the bag's request, but note my hesitation here, in case the Review Board would like to bring me up on charges for even considering it.

[By the time the Representatives return—two MugwL, two human [as I note with relief], and two "children" of the larger variety—the bag is again pale lavender, and I have made certain the knot and the imprisoning devices are fixed securely.]

———

Record of Proceeding
Incident at Gray's Brook
Injustice Collector 0080 Presiding

Testimony of Requesting Party
[continued]

By the time of the Incident at Gray's Brook, we had already been to the human settlement six times with the express purpose of seeing the "children." The "children" gather every other Cycle in a building called the "school." There they sit while a full-sized human passes knowledge to them via three different means—vocal communication, printed communication, and written communication.

The system seems inefficient to us, and is part of what led us to believe the "children" were another species. We now believe that the human young are not born with the knowledge of the community implanted in the brain. The knowledge must be transferred by these inefficient means.

Since we use these means only with inferior creatures, ones that we hope to domesticate, we place this assumption of ours before the Decision Desk as a simple Misunderstanding, not an Injustice.

———

Interruption in the Proceeding

Eleven Cycles into the Requesting Party's Testimony, A Breach of Protocol: Cause of breach is, as noted above, human ignorance.

—*INJUSTICE COLLECTOR 0080*

"I don't suppose anyone wants to explain that distinction," says the John Graf. I believe he is referring to the distinction between the "Misunderstanding" and the "Injustice."

We have explained this, taking days—not cycles—to do so. But I weary of reminding him of that, so say nothing.

After a moment of silence, the John Graf says, "I thought not. Why do I even try?"

———

Record of Proceeding
Incident at Gray's Brook
Injustice Collector 0080 Presiding

Testimony of Requesting Party
[continued]

Just before the Incident at Gray's Brook, one of the human Elders came to our Village Council and requested a "field trip" in which their "children" would see how we tend our own young. This "field trip" as best we could understand it was an educational venture designed to exemplify the distinctions between our two species.

It took the humans several visits to explain the need for such an event to us. Even so, we are uncertain as to whether we sufficiently understand it, and believe on this point that the Non-Requesting Party might like a voice.

———

[*An Aside*: I offer the opportunity to the John Graf. He raises and lowers his shoulders.

["This isn't a proceeding, it's a joke, and we're here under protest," he says by way of explanation.

[The MugwL seem to find this response as unsatisfactory as I do. But that does not stop their testimony. Their representative continues.]

———

To understand what transpired next, we must explain a distinction that we have learned over this half-season of dealing with the humans. In their language, "day" means "cycle." Their concept of time is different from ours in significant ways, ways we do not yet completely understand.

We have come to realize that even though we speak the same accepted Alliance tongue, our understandings break down at even this most basic level. Some of our scientists postulate that the humans have a summer's lifespan, although others believe this to be impossible based on the humans' ability to learn Alliance languages and travel in space.

This digression stems from our attempt to understand the humans' extreme reaction to the Incident at Gray's Brook and our culpability, if any, in it.

———

Interruption in the Proceeding

Eleven Cycles into the Requesting Party's Testimony, A Breach of Protocol: Cause of breach is, as noted above, human ignorance.

—INJUSTICE COLLECTOR 0080

"Culpability, hell," says the other human representative quite loudly. "We'll show them culpability."

———

Record of Proceeding
Incident at Gray's Brook
Injustice Collector 0080 Presiding

Testimony of Requesting Party
[continued]

At the time of the incident, our young were in the waterbath. The waters are at their lowest this time in the season, and the fetal pods are clearly visible.

The waters are also quite warm and, in the words of one of the "children," "inviting" although, it must be noted for the record, the MugwL heard no such invitation.

The "children" asked if it was permissible to touch the pods. We apparently did not understand the nature of their question. We told them that, indeed, it is always permissible to touch the pods.

We did not, however, expand the answer, expecting more questions. Apparently, however, the "children" are unlike the humans in more ways than knowledge and size.

The "children" did ask one other question. They asked if the water was harmful.

The question was, on its surface, unnecessary. If the water was harmful, would we have put our fetal pods into it? Of course not. We answered the question we believed was asked. We answered according to our biology and our customs. We did not realize that the "children" could not frame their questions correctly.

Again, we plead Misunderstanding, not Injustice.

————

Interruption in the Proceeding

Eleven Cycles into the Requesting Party's Testimony, A Breach of Protocol: Cause of breach is, as noted above, human ignorance.

—INJUSTICE COLLECTOR 0080

"Lying manipulative bastards," says the other human representative.

The John Graf puts his hand on the other representative's arm. The other representative moves away.

————

Record of Proceeding
Incident at Gray's Brook
Injustice Collector 0080 Presiding

Testimony of Requesting Party
[continued]

The devastation was stunning and terrifying. The people who witnessed the deaths are not the same. They cannot go near the human settlement; they are appalled at the very mention of humans. This emotion grew worse when it became clear to all concerned that the "children" are also human young.

———

[*An Aside*: for the first time, the MugwL representative is having trouble controlling his voice. It breaks. This is the first obvious sign of emotion from the MugwL and it is quite moving.

[I do not look at the bag, waiting at my feet, below.]

———

The "children" shed their clothing with a rapidity that startled us. Then they plunged headfirst into the water. A few jumped feet first.

We had never seen anyone but registered tenders step into water, and even then, they followed distinct and important protocols.

These "children" followed no protocols at all. They drenched themselves and arose, laughing—a sound that is the same among both of our species (something we did not know and did not want to learn in this context).

Then the laughter turned to shrill, high pitched sounds that the humans later identified as sounds of extreme fright. The "children" had rested their feet on the pods—a few "children" had gone underwater and touched the pods with their hands—and the pods—the pods—

The pods absorb food through the exterior shell. It supplies the fetal material and maintains the growth necessary for development. Anything that touches the pod becomes food, unless certain protocols are followed.

Even the tenders do not touch the pods without wearing special equipment, equipment that we did not bring on our "field trip" with the "children."

We managed to save five of the children, but ten of them—ten of them—

We learned, to our dismay, that human blood is red. When combined with water and flailing limbs, bubbles are created, making a pinkish foam.

Many of us still see this foam in our dreams.

————

Record of Proceeding
Incident at Gray's Brook
Injustice Collector 0080 Presiding

Citing of the Injustice[s]

According to custom, I place the bag on the Decision Desk. The bag maintains its composure above the desk; the bag's porous outer layer is now a creamy white.

Then I state the interrogatory: What do you believe are the Injustices in this Incident?

The Non-Requesting Party attempts to respond, but is silenced. The Bystanding Party simply shifts from foot-to-foot as if the proceedings do not concern either representative. The Requesting Party look at the bag with great fear before replying:

"The Injustices are, as we see them, as follows: One Injustice occurring against the Requesting Party, and one Injustice occurring against the Bystanding Party."

————

Interruption in the Proceeding

---

*Eleven Cycles into the Requesting Party's Testimony, A Breach
of Protocol: Cause of breach is, as noted above, human ignorance.*

—INJUSTICE COLLECTOR 0080

The John Graf steps forward. "What the—?"
  He does not finish his own sentence.

————

Record of Proceeding
Incident at Gray's Brook
Injustice Collector 0080 Presiding

Citing of the Injustice[s]
[continued]

"The Injustice against the Requesting Party is this: The humans should
have explained to us the nature and vulnerability of their young. In
this, they should have explained the purpose of "children" and the
caring of them. We should not have been responsible for beings we
know nothing about.

————

Interruption in the Proceeding

Eleven Cycles into the Requesting Party's Testimony, A Breach of Protocol: Cause of breach is, as noted above, human ignorance.

—INJUSTICE COLLECTOR 0080

"Right," the other human representative says, surprising me with his agreement. "Go ahead. Blame the victim."

———

Record of Proceeding
Incident at Gray's Brook
Injustice Collector 0080 Presiding

Citing of the Injustice[s]
[continued]

"The Injustice against the Bystanding Party is more severe. It is this: Although these human young, these "children," are adaptable enough to survive their youth away from their home world, they are not strong enough to face challenges inherent in space exploration. It took less than a season to wipe out ten of these youth. One can only surmise how many more will die before the Fall comes and the floods—"

———

Interruption in the Proceeding

Eleven Cycles into the Requesting Party's Testimony, A Breach of Protocol: Cause of breach is, as noted above, human ignorance

—INJUSTICE COLLECTOR 0080

."For Crissake," the John Graf says, using yet another unknown phrase. "We did not bring the children here. We gave birth to them here. We're colonists for God's sake. We're building a life here. Can't you people understand that? My father explained it all when the ships landed. He told you what we were doing, and you agreed to let us have the land. You agreed to let us live here. And all our studies said it was safe. There's no injustice in that. Don't you get it? We're just living—"

―――――

Record of Proceeding
Incident at Gray's Brook
Injustice Collector 0080 Presiding

Citing of the Injustice[s]
[continued]

According to custom, I place another hand on the bag, and ask: Does the Bystanding Party accept the Injustice claimed in its behalf?

The representative of the Bystanding Party has to be prodded by the John Graf. The representative of the Bystanding Party appears startled, then says, "I dunno."

Again, faced with the ignorance of the humans, I cite the Gubernatorial Decision, accepting that response as an affirmative, and continue with the procedure.

"In this case," I intone, "as in all cases of this nature, the final decision on the Injustices will be made by the Wiwendian." I add for the humans, "the Wiwendian is what you have casually heard us refer to as 'the bag.' It is, instead, the true Injustice Collector, in that it feeds on such violations, needing them to survive. We feed the Collector, so that it and its people will not create new Injustices, simply for the sake of devouring them. In stating this old truth, I remind us all of the oaths we have taken to maintain Justice in our universe."

I place my remaining hands on the bag, and undo the knot I tied in its opening. "Do you accept these Injustices?"

There is a whooshing, and the bag turns a light lavender. The Injustices white and blue, swirl away from the Requesting Party and the Bystanding Party. For a moment, I believe I see something red near the Non-Requesting Party, but the redness vanishes.

The bag accepts the Injustices and then fades to its normal color. I place the bag beneath the Decision Desk once more, and declare the proceedings complete.

———

But the proceedings do not exactly end. I add these events as an addendum to my report:

"That's it?" the John Graf asks. "You ask a silly question of a *bag* and then it changes color and we get to go? That's all that happens? We spent months of our lives here for that?"

The time reference confirms yet again the MugwL's impression of time differences between the humans and our various species. More study will be needed to ascertain if this is, indeed a fact.

"Yes," I tell the human. "The Proceeding has ended."

"But nothing has changed," the John Graf says.

"On the contrary. The Wiwendian—we—have taken the known Injustices from this world. The slate is clean. You may begin again."

"Begin what?" the other human asks. "Our children are gone. We've gotten no satisfaction here. You let those people—those murderers get away with feeding our kids to their pod thingies."

I signal my Collectors-in-Training. "I have done my work according to the laws and customs of our Alliance. I have responded to the Requesting Party, brought the Wiwendian, and collected injustices. If you perceive any violations, you may bring them up with the Review Board."

I have, of course, added this for the humans' benefit. It is more explanation than I usually offer after a decision has been rendered.

I feel the humans' displeasure and empathize with it, but even they must realize that nothing brings back lost lives.

That, perhaps, is the ultimate Injustice, but one so common that the bag usually rejects it.

"My assistants will explain how to file your petitions with the Review Board," I say as I open the doors to the Great Hall. The rush of cool air is marvelous. "But not in here."

The Collectors-in-Training usher the humans out, but they are not the ones that stop at the doors. The MugwL do, and as they do, they let out their own sounds of fear and displeasure.

I rise, peering over their heads.

In the distance, smoke rises from the MugwL village. Too much smoke, accompanied by leaping flames.

The John Graf looks upset. He puts his arms around the "children" and leads them outside.

But the other human, the vocal one, stops, turns and looks at me, not the MugwL. I do not know human expressions, but this one seems, in some way frightening—the raised eyebrows, the half-contained amusement.

"On my world," he says, "when systems break down, only one kind of justice remains. We call it street justice."

And then he leaves.

The MugwL cry and wail, claiming their village is gone. My Collectors-in-Training still usher them out, and finally close the door.

I am alone, except for the bag. The bag that wants to collect these Injustices, in a Preliminary fashion, to save us a trip.

If my bag is any indication, the Wiwendians are becoming dissatisfied with our agreement to feed and house them in exchange for controlling their somewhat destructive talents. But that is an aside.

I would have refused its request on principle—one finished Proceeding is enough for any Collector—but principle is not my real reason for saying no.

I say no because I do not want to preside over another Proceeding involving humans. Too messy, too many chances for mistakes.

The red floating above them as the bag collected the Injustices disturbs me. Red is usually the color of violation. The Injustices from the MugwL and the "children" were not red.

The humans have a rawer, more passionate sense of Injustice than we do.

There is already so much Injustice in the Alliance that we barely maintain our hold on the Wiwendians. My Wiwendian already finds the human sense of Injustice attractive. Other Wiwendians will as well.

The humans will give the Wiwendians too much power.

Together, they will destroy everything.

And I fear that, after this Proceeding, they have already started.

BROKEN WINDCHIMES

KRISTINE KATHRYN RUSCH

BROKEN WINDCHIMES

I first heard non-Pané music in an alley behind an auditorium in Lhelomika. Lhelomika, the arts capitol of Djapé, made me nervous. The last two times I had performed there, I shivered as I hit each note—not with cold, but with fear.

That afternoon, I walked outside the auditorium, trying to calm myself. From a nearby building, I heard a raspy male voice—a deep unaltered adult male voice—attempting to sing a melody. Some instruments I could not identify provided a music bed behind the voice.

The instruments were more harmonious than the voice, even though they did not hit pure tones. But the voice held me. It sang of a wonderful world, one that had beauty in its simple existence.

Strangely, the harshness of the voice, its lack of tone and musicality, provided a contrast to the lyrics so profound that it accented them.

I stood outside the building, listening as the song played, knowing that this was human music and it was forbidden to me. If Gibson, my manager, caught me, he would chastise me. Male sopranos who performed as long as I had—some twenty years now—were rare, a commodity worth millions.

Each day that I survived in my rarified position as performer—a living windchime, as the Pané called us—was a victory. I knew my time was limited.

Maybe that was why, when I made it through that evening's performance with no mistakes, I hid in my study and searched for that song on the forbidden human databases.

I didn't find it for months.

When I did, I listened, rapt, as stunned as I had been the first time at the simple beauty of contrast, the way that the flaws added to the whole.

The Pané would never accept flaws.

I knew it, and ignored it.

And some would argue, that was the beginning of the end.

———

I sang my last concert before a packed hall in Tygher City. The auditorium there, made of bone and thin membranes almost like skin, had acoustics so perfect that a sigh made on stage could be heard in each seat, in every row. Only the best performers got a berth in Tygher City, and I'd played there for fifteen of my twenty-five summers.

On this evening, I sang three solos accompanied by the Boys' Choir, all in the second half of the concert, and all written by Tampini.

Tampini composed for male windchimes, accenting their technique and vocal range. His work, very Pané, was rarely performed outside of the Tygher City auditorium, since it was one of the few places on Djapé that had the acoustic sensitivity for his works.

The auditorium in Tygher City made me nervous. A note, missed by as little as one-one-thousandth, would receive silence, the Pané version of a boo. Even timing that did not follow the score to the letter—say, a half note extended to a dotted half simply for interpretation—had gotten more than one performer thrown off the stage.

So I had dreaded the performance for weeks, and shaved my involvement from six solos to three. Even then, I couldn't lose the feeling of impending doom.

I had mentioned that to Gibson, and he had laughed at me, telling me I worried too much. Still, he had the on-site doctor take my temperature and give me a thorough going over to make certain there were no alien viruses coursing through my system. They couldn't give me any medication to keep my blood pressure steady because medication might make an alteration, even a slight one, in my vocal chords. Nor could they feed me to keep my blood sugar up, because food coated the throat, disturbed the stomach, and occasionally caused gas.

More than one performer had lost his berth in Tygher City because of a nearly silent swallowed belch.

All that preparation, all the careful rehearsal—my time monitored so that I didn't overdo—, and still I approached the edge of the shell-like stage with trepidation.

It didn't show, of course. I walked on stage with a fake confidence born of years of performing. I wore a blue robe that contrasted with the chorus's white, and reflected the natural interior light of the bone auditorium as if we were outdoors.

The Pané crowded in their seats, squat and attentive, their heads down so that they could hear better. They were oddly malleable creatures, mostly cartilage, their skin a translucent gray that showed the shadows of their internal organs.

Their faces, it was said, took a lot of getting used to; eyes askew, mouth hidden, and the ridges that looked like sheet wrinkles, covering the bulk of their skull. The Pané looked normal to me, but I really couldn't remember the times before I arrived on Djapé. Like so many of my companions, my voice came early. Someone discovered my hollow, fluted soprano before I had turned three.

The first part of the set went well. The boys' choir had a sweetness that the adult male sopranos lost. Or perhaps it was the innocence in their faces, the love of singing that also got lost after years of performing.

The children took on Tampini like he was meant to be sung, with precision and grace and harmonies that sent shivers up my spine. The Pané remained motionless, so attentive that they barely seemed to breathe. I sang the first solo, the hardest of the three, with a clarity of tone that I hadn't realized I could achieve.

The problems started in the second solo which was, really, more of a descant. I felt a thickness at the back of my throat, as if phlegm were creeping in. I had the desperate urge to cough, but consummate performer that I was, I did not. Coughing ruined the vocal chords and had to be avoided at all costs. Clearing the throat and shouting had the same effect, and I hadn't done any of those things in my memory.

But I wanted to, right there on stage, in front of five thousand rapt Pané.

When the second Tampini ended, and I was allowed to walk backstage before taking my second bow, I swigged the warm water Gibson kept for me. It cleared the throat slightly, refreshed me enough, and got rid of the urge to cough.

In fact, I had forgotten all about it as I started into the third solo.

This last, a Pané favorite, always seemed the least musical to me. The boys provided a choral backdrop, usually made up of thirds and fifths, while I let my four-octave voice explore its range. At the time, I was the only man on Djapé who could hit the E above High C, and Gibson exploited that as often as he could, having me sing show-off pieces like Tampini's Aria in E Major.

The aria had an optional arpeggio section, and Gibson always made me include it at Tygher City. To the human ear, the arpeggios sounded like little more than exercises, going from E major to Bb minor, and on through every possible variation, until the mind wearied and human listener grew bored.

But the Pané heard overtones and undertones we could not. A series of arpeggios like that apparently created harmonies that lingered, pleasing the Pané like no other musical trick could. Any performer who could do the Aria in E Major and do it well was a guaranteed celebrity on Djapé.

The aria had become my signature piece, much as I despised it.

I was right in the middle of the C Major arpeggio when my voice cracked.

It didn't break the way voices do when they change—I'd heard that a few times, and it was a horrible thing, especially the look on the boy's face when he realized his treatment was faulty, and the thing that he had lived his entire life for, the thing that defined him, was vanishing.

No. Instead, my voice cracked with exhaustion, leaving a hole between the G's. Even though I found High C, felt it position properly in my vocal chords, the note did not emerge. Instead, there was a wisp of air, a near-silence, almost a hiss that was audible throughout that galaxy's most sensitive auditorium.

The audience gasped. It was a hideous, non-human sound. The Pané attempted to imitate us, out of a sense of courtesy, but it backfired. Their gasp was closer to a roar, emerging from the throat and not the diaphragm.

It was a sharp, shocked sound, one in such a low register that the Pané couldn't hear it.

But I could, and it terrified me. They had made the sound in my presence maybe a hundred times before, but never once directed at me.

Still, my training paid off. I did not lose my place or my concentration, and when High C was part of an arpeggio again, I hit the note with the same clarity and purity that I had always had.

I finished the piece and walked off the stage to lukewarm applause, knowing that my career was finished.

Gibson, to his credit, tried to smooth the moment over as if it hadn't mattered at all. His puffy face looked pasty in the backstage lights, and his hair seemed even thinner than before.

He put his fleshy hands on my back, easing me toward the dressing room.

"No need to worry," he said. "We'll get it checked out. You just should have told me."

Told him what? My voice had never broken, never failed me, not even when I'd gone on stage with fevers, and mysterious Pané-originated illnesses.

I had never failed before—not in twenty-two years.

I had no idea how to react.

Neither did anyone else.

————

I received three days of testing, all in the port city of Énané, as far from the Pané music scene as we could get. Énané was the site of the largest human enclave on Djapé, and as such, a place that most Pané escaped as soon as they could.

The Pané found most humans large, smelly, and loud; we had been of no use to them at all until they discovered our musical abilities, centuries ago. At first the Pané thought the abilities mindless, simple pleasant sounds that we made almost unconsciously. Over time, however, the Pané realized that we purposely made music, that we had control over the notes, the order in which they were sung or played, and the interpretation of those notes.

Still, it took time for the Pané to understand what we were doing—and time for us to understand the Pané. Their highly evolved hearing found pleasure only in the diatonic scale, and then mostly in notes above Middle C.

Certain instruments—the organ, for example, and the harpsichord —caused the Pané pain when played in that register. Flutes, clarinets, oboes could be tolerated, but brass instruments could not. Stringed instruments, particularly the violin, were banned on Djapé. While humans heard the violin as an expressive instrument, imitative of the human voice, the Pané heard it only as a scraping of bow on string, a grating sound that was so repulsive to them that, legend has it, the first Pané who ever heard one murdered the violinist.

Human music had strict limits, and had to remain in the human enclave. Until the Pané discovered the soprano—the male soprano.

And Pané were particular about their male sopranos. Falsettos, tried once and quickly abandoned, were almost as offensive as a violin. Irish tenors fell into the same category. The male soprano had to have had a clear voice from boyhood, and that voice couldn't be tainted by anything that would offend the sensitive Pané ear.

No human ever learned if the Pané were truly as sensitive as they claimed or if they were, like all true collectors, so fussy that they couldn't stand the idea of tampering with a pure voice. For the Pané were collectors of the worst sort.

They could not create music of their own. Their vocal chords did not produce song and they could not envision music. Djapé itself had many musical aspects—from the ice caves of Windsor to the Trilling Beetles of Lahonia—but nothing formal, nothing creatively musical.

The Pané didn't know that music could be created purposely until the first humans arrived on Djapé, centuries ago. I never learned how the alliance between the Pané and the humans was formed, nor did I know, then, how it was maintained.

No one answered those questions, often pretending they didn't hear them. Instead, I got to study music management and practice my scales.

The older I got, the less any of that appealed to me, and I could tell no one. By that point, I was Djapé's biggest human star: a favorite windchime who could perform in the most difficult venues at the best hours.

All of that ended for me with a single missed note, a crack, a lost C, scarcely noticeable to human ears, and serious flaw to the Pané.

I had enjoyed my success, and while I had always known that I would one day cease being the biggest star, I had hoped to remain respected—the kind of performer called out for a nostalgic review or, if my voice had suffered the effects of age, a commentary on past performances, often done before an audience.

I had even imagined my retirement—on the rugged coastline between Énané and the Causée Mountain—where I would teach advanced students (only those who had the capability of becoming stars) and where I would occasionally deign to review an up-and-coming performer, give someone a small lift, like I had gotten early on, enabling him to become a performer the Pané might worship.

None of that was possible now. I knew it, and my assistants knew it. One afternoon, I caught Gibson leaving the compound in the company of a boy. The boy, at that indeterminate age between twelve and twenty, had a softness that belonged only to the human musicians on Djapé. When he saw me, he flushed.

If I had needed confirmation of the severity of my situation, I had it then. Gibson—who only handled the best—was looking for a new client. As soon as he found the boy he could develop into a star, Gibson would be gone.

I fled to the garden, pushing my way past the leafy foliage until I found my favorite stone bench. It was tucked into a side corner, not tended often, because the small lemon and orange trees didn't need as much day-to-day care. I huddled on the bench, put my hands behind me, and turned my face to Djapé's hot sun. I wasn't supposed to do that either—something about the light and my skin—but I didn't have to listen to Gibson any more.

He was leaving.

And I was shaking.

I had never before been on my own.

———

He caught me, hours later, in the study, listening to the song I had heard in the alley so long ago. I had found it, startled at its age. The singer was a 20th century American composer, and trumpeter named Louis Armstrong. Until that evening, I'd always listened to Armstrong on headphones, secretly, hiding him. He was a revelation in surround sound—a gravelly voice that would make the Pané recoil in fear.

Gibson acted as if he were still my manager, as if he were not going to leave me at all. "What's this?"

I hadn't heard him come in. I had been lost in the archaic slang of the Armstrong.

My back had been to Gibson, but I did not whirl to face him as I would have done just the day before. Instead, I waited until the end of the phrase, then touched the sound file built into my desk. The music paused mid-note.

"Is that what destroyed your voice? That garbage?" Gibson had apparently continued speaking over the music, and I hadn't noticed. Now that the music was off, his voice was much too loud.

I turned, as I would toward a fan, folding my hands together over my robe.

"Have you noticed," I asked, keeping my voice at its usual whisper, "that we listen to very little music in this house?"

"Pané-inspired music is not restful to human ears," Gibson snapped. "When you are not performing or practicing, you need to relax."

He had said that a thousand times, maybe more. I nodded. "How is the new client?"

Gibson's eyes narrowed. I had never spoken to him like that before. "It was a lunch."

"It was an audition," I said. "We've been together for twenty-two years. You owe me the courtesy of honesty."

He glanced at the sound file and I knew what he was going to say. He was going to make this about me, about my words, about my problems. *Did you imitate this so-called singer? What were you thinking?*

In the past, I would have answered him humbly. I would have let him take my music away.

He turned away from me, but not before I saw guilt cross his face. He sank into the couch and put his feet on the ottoman. He seemed relaxed, but he was not. The fingers of his left hand drummed against the multi-lined Pané-made upholstery.

"I only move up," he said. "The moment I start the spiral downward, even with a client I care about, I lose my clout."

I crossed my arms, hiding my clenched fists beneath my biceps. Spiral downward. Loss of clout.

Loss of everything.

Not only would I lose my career and my dreamed-of future, I also would lose the only family I had ever known.

Perhaps, deep down, I had felt that I could hold him here, with guilt, with logic, with sheer affection.

Even with a client I care about. Client. Care. Not friend. Not love.

He had held himself distant from me, even when I was a three-year-old prodigy with a spectacular voice. Even then he had evaluated my every note, my every performance, and if he hadn't felt I was on an upward path, he would have left.

I was shaking, but I tried to control it. I did not want him to see the effect his words were having on me.

"You have enough money, you know that. You don't have to work again, if you don't want to. That's why I taught you how to handle and understand finances. That's more than most managers would have done for you."

He sounded defensive. He *was* defensive. But he was also right. He had forced me to study things I had not wanted to learn. Money, business, even booking schedules.

Teaching me how to survive the inevitable decline. Always with an eye toward the next client, the next project. Remaining on the upward spiral.

"You can retire now," he said. "If you don't go back on the stage, no one will remember that moment of silence. No one will think you left because of the mistake."

"You don't need to lie to me," I said, not bothering to soften my voice. He wasn't going to manage me any longer and I wasn't going to listen to his directives. Childish, perhaps, but at that moment, small rebellions were all that I had left.

He plucked at the couch, his head down. His hair was thinning on the sides. He would need some reconstruction, and he didn't even realize it.

"All right then." He took a deep breath as if he were steeling himself against what he had to say. "The best thing you can do is retire. The Pané will remember, and so will the musical community. But they'll also remember that you had achieved top celebrity status once. For a little while, you were perfect."

The shaking was growing worse. I leaned against the desk just so that I could brace myself. I had to concentrate on my breathing, just like I used to do before a concert.

"You won't be able to get the best students," he said, "but you'll get the cream of the beginners. It'll be a good life. Not as glamorous as it had been before, but good."

Glamorous? He thought that performing in front of the Pané was glamorous? I remembered no glamour. Just concert halls and round eyes, watching, the hush as I walked onto the stages specially built for the new kind of music, the way my back ached after hours of holding myself rigid, and the headaches I had when I finished a successful concert.

Perhaps he enjoyed the meals, the hotels, the traveling, but I saw little of it. I couldn't mingle—the dry air in Pané restaurants made my throat tickle—and I rarely saw the outside of my suite, since the Pané didn't want to spend time with performers away from the concert halls.

"You still have a future," he was saying, understanding me well up until the last, "just not the one you were expecting."

He stood and met my gaze for the first time since he had come into the room. I finally saw him clearly, realizing that what I had always taken for intensity had been a reserve, an unwillingness to let his emotions get wrapped up in his business.

"I've done the best for you I could," he said, "although I don't expect you to understand that."

Then he nodded once and headed out of the study. I gripped the sides of the desk, my legs weak.

When he reached the door, he stopped. "And you might want to destroy all of that non-Pané music. It will only dilute your purity and should anyone find out you've been listening, corrupt your reputation. On other worlds, perhaps people still enjoy that stuff. But music on Pané has its own traditions, ones you were created especially for. Remember that."

Then he left, closing the door behind him.

I sank onto the overstuffed chair beside the desk. Created. He had said created. I thought I had been found.

I wondered what else I did not know about my own life.

I suspected it was a lot.

———

After Gibson left with his new prodigy, I hid in the gardens and listened to every piece of music I could find—that is, every piece composed with humans, not Pané in mind.

I was stunned by the depth and breadth of it. The mixture of voices fascinated me—female sopranos and altos, and unaltered male tenors and basses.

I wasn't sure I liked the deep sound, but it entranced me nonetheless. Such freedom existed out there, away from Djapé, where this music was created.

Such freedom and so many opportunities.

It took me months, but I finally decided to make those opportunities my own.

———

I planned my escape from Djapé meticulously. I studied everything I could about travel routes off planet. Human settlements were more numerous than I realized, and I had hundreds of choices.

The problem wasn't where to go, but how to get there. Very few human transport ships ran between Djapé and other worlds. The performers couldn't travel to non-Pané approved worlds for fear of tainting their performances—or, more accurately, for fear of the perception of taint that would forever follow them from the trip.

Managers, handlers and merchants came and went with ease. But the successful managers and handlers hired their own transport. The merchants traveled on the cargo ships that supplied the small human colonies scattered across Djapé.

The supplies, I learned, were more numerous than I expected. Very little human food grew in Djapé's soil, and the Pané would not let humans disfigure the areas around their enclaves with greenhouses or hydroponic gardens. I learned that most of the food I had eaten throughout my life on Djapé had been imported, just as most of the material I wore and most of the furniture I sat on.

The Pané did not want humans to contaminate their world, even if they did want humans to perform for them. This so-called contamination included any kind of infrastructure. They allowed us our towns, but not industry or agriculture or even a real form of government.

Yet they expected us to police ourselves.

So much of what we needed on Djapé came from a space station called the Last Outpost. The Last Outpost was not the last human outpost in this sector, or in truth was in an outpost any longer. It was the only station between the nearest human-controlled world and Djapé, and it had become a community in and of itself.

Humans lived and worked on the Outpost. Entire generations had never left, tending to the ships, as well as to the diplomatic needs of the human community on Djapé.

Wherever humans lived and worked, they also needed entertainment.

All of my research confirmed that the best musicians in the sector rotated in and out of the Last Outpost. The Outpost had more bars, concert halls, and theaters than any other space station in this region— more, some said, than any other human-sponsored station.

The musically inclined (at least among the humans) actually vacationed at the Last Outpost to take in all the forms provided there. The Outpost itself was considered a music capitol by all three neighboring human worlds.

It even had its own conservatory, as well as a university with the best music department in the sector, and more informal instruction than any other city outside of the great and mythical Earth.

Gibson would not have approved, but Gibson no longer controlled me.

No one did.

And it was with that heady sense of freedom that I finally left

Djapé, the place I had lived since I was three years old.

———

The trip was not what I expected. The single transport that occasionally stopped on Djapé would not arrive for another two years. So I hired a cargo ship.

It was small and cramped, but the human crew left me to my own devices. We made the trip in thirty-six uneventful hours—a short time, it seemed to me, to make the transition from one life to another.

During the last few hours of the trip, I watched the Outpost appear in a portal. My research had told me the Outpost was unusual, but nothing had prepared me for the size of it. Interwoven rings, dozens, maybe a hundred, grew out of a small square station built centuries ago in this part of space. Each ring had a specialty and each ring had its own warren of buildings, living quarters and businesses.

For that reason, I hired a porter to meet me at the docks. He was a slight man with dark hair and a thin, petulant mouth. He brought a large cart with him, one that seemed to operate under its own power. When he saw that I had only two bags, he appeared surprised.

"Well, now," he said as I came down the cargo ship's passenger ramp, "this's the first time I've been called out for something I can carry in my own two hands."

My cheeks heated. I wanted to ask him if I had made some kind of social gaffe, but I did not. Gibson used to tell me that the only way others knew a man was uncomfortable was for him to admit it. *Performers,* Gibson said, *were never uncomfortable; nor did they make mistakes. They simply did things their very own way.*

I was already doing things my own way. My clothing marked me as different as well. On the cargo ship, no one wore robes, but I had nothing else. Here, too, in the docking area, I was the only person whose clothing flowed around his sandaled feet.

The porter took my bags and set them on his cart. They seemed somewhat forlorn there, as if they were waiting for a dozen other bags to join them. The porter helped me onto a seat at the front of the cart. He sat in the middle, pressing screen commands that were nearly invisible from my vantage.

We lurched forward, and I headed into my very first strictly human enclave. I sat stiffly, hands folded, as we left the nearly empty docking area, and emerged in the Last Outpost itself.

A cacophony greeted me. We went from clanging echoey near-silence to an amalgam of unrelated sounds. Voices carrying on dozens of conversations, children laughing, music blaring overhead. Our cart glided above the polished floor, but other carts had actual wheels that clack-clacked as they moved around us. People stood in front of open doors, hawking wares inside.

Shoppers merged with foot traffic and all the carts, talking, pointing, joking. Blue dresses jarred against orange pants which jarred against green hats. Brown coats, lavender shirts, white bandannas—no one wore the same uniform. No one wore the same colors.

The cart veered sharply to the left. Building facades lined the curved walls, each building a clear construct with a strict design code. Some were white with columns around the doors, others multi-colored, some with tiny round doors, others with irises that webbed open as something went by.

Those passing now were predominantly human, but some were not. One group of bipeds were covered in fuchsia-colored feathers. I couldn't tell if the feathers were a kind of clothing or part of their bodies. Others who passed had flippers instead of limbs, and still others waved their eyes on stalks, peering at me as if I were the exotic one.

"Short timers stay here," my porter said. "Those who come to the Outpost regularly have apartments in the permanent ring."

The permanent ring had an exotic sound to it. I tried to imagine living forever in this noisy, busy place, and found I could not. I had seen no windows since we docked.

Even if there were windows, they would only show darkness. I had always craved warmth and sunlight. I could not imagine being without them forever.

The cart glided into an archway. Dozens of other carts floated in the small space, all at varying height. The carts hummed, all at different frequencies, clashing and grating against my ears. The air here smelled slightly metallic, which meant that the gliders themselves gave off some kind of discharge.

The porter lowered his glider to a space in front of white double doors. The doors were carved with the name of the hotel in black flowing script.

I stepped gingerly off the glider onto a platform in front of the doors. Inside, lights as bright as the afternoon sun in my garden back home greeted me, soothing my jangled nerves.

I turned, about to grab the bags, when the porter grinned at me. "Door to door service," he said and lugged them inside.

I followed.

The lobby of this hotel—if one could call it a lobby—was cavernous. It felt like an outdoor spa. The bright lights hid the ceiling—above me it looked like a gigantic sun had obliterated the sky. Plants that I did not recognize, most of them green, grew out of the floor, grouping around the furniture, and adding a minty scent to the already perfumed air.

The tension left my shoulders and I felt, for the first time since I left Djapé, that I could relax.

The porter led me to a black marble podium, one I would not have seen without him. It was hidden by the leafy plants, which parted as we approached.

The porter set down my bags and extended a small silver disc. "Just a thumbprint," he said, "to verify it's you and your account will be charged."

I placed my thumb against the disc, which lit up. Then he nodded to me, pocketed the disc, and disappeared through the leaves.

I felt a slight pang at seeing him go. To assuage it, I turned to the podium. A lighted menu appeared above it. I checked myself in, then followed the written instructions. My bags were already moving on some kind of walkway toward my cabana.

I followed them.

My cabana resembled a small house. In fact, if I had not known I was on a station in space, I would have thought I was in some open but exotic domed colony somewhere.

The cabana had six rooms and two levels. Floor-to-ceiling windows covered the walls on the exterior side. The view constantly changed as the station slowly rotated.

I explored cautiously. The room that intrigued me the most was the dining area off the courtesy kitchen. A table sat on a clear floor, in a platform that extended out from the ring. When I sat on one of the chairs, I felt as if I were floating just outside of the station.

I finally understood how someone lived on the Outpost without feeling trapped or claustrophobic. I had known that the place was huge —one of the largest of its type anywhere in the sector—but I had thought that the darkness and the cramped quarters would make it feel like an underground cavern.

Instead, I felt like I was in a magical place, one that held the promise of a great future.

For the first time in months, I was at peace.

———

I mapped my assault on the Outpost's musical venues as if I were planning a military campaign. In part, I knew that I would be an outsider, and I didn't want to call too much attention to myself. So my earliest visits would be at venues not too far from the guest ring.

But also, I didn't want to hear exceptionally exotic music. I was much more interested in music history, old Earth forms, truly human music with no alien influence whatsoever.

The first venue I chose was small and intimate, something called a blues club. The club itself was in a part of the Outpost called Saloon Central, a ring devoted mostly to clubs, bars, and restaurants that also dabbled in intoxicating substances.

I chose a table in the back away from the lights. A menu offered items I'd never heard of, from green chili to tamales to barbeque brisket

—all, the menu claimed, authentic foods, but authentic to what I did not know. The air smelled tangy and sour, a scent that wasn't quite bad and wasn't quite good.

I ordered a beverage from a list I'd never heard of, something non-intoxicating called a C'cola, also considered "authentic" and a bowl of that day's special steak-and-potato soup.

Then I settled back and waited for the entertainment to begin.

The musicians did not file on stage as I had expected. Nor were they wearing matching clothing. In fact, they looked as though they were wearing their normal everyday dress. They carried instruments I had not seen before.

Slowly lights came up on the stage, revealing what I believed to be a percussion set—drums, was it called?—and some sort of keyboard instrument. I recognized two guitars and some kind of woodwind—a saxophone?—as well as a bass. Brass players—trumpeters?—sat near the percussionist in the back.

A rotund man sat on a stool in the center, one leg extended, the other supporting one of the guitars in the curve of its belly. The bass player sat on the right.

The remaining players sat near the side, holding their instruments down, all except the lone woman, who stood beside the rotund man in the center.

They crowded around their instruments, chatting so softly I couldn't hear them. Then the rotund man in the middle picked seven notes on his guitar.

They were almost a command to play music.

The others seemed to heed that command. The bass player plucked a long note. The keyboardist added a rolling chord, and the percussionist tapped one of the flatter instruments in the same rhythm the rotund man had played.

With the other hand, the percussionist played one-and-a-two-and-a-three, which then got picked up by the brass, almost as if they were answering the initial line.

It seemed disorganized. The music was loud. I could feel each instrument in my sternum, the bass line in particular so forceful that it seemed to propel my heart to a new rhythm.

Each time the rotund man played his signature line, he changed it. The changes made me uneasy, and once I caught myself looking to see how the Pané were reacting.

Only there weren't any Pané in the room.

Just humans of all sizes, most of them nodding their heads to the one-and-a-two beat carved (and kept) by the percussionist. Then the rotund man changed octaves, playing the same seven notes, only varying the motif, as if he were composing the song on the spot. When he reached the end of that variation, all the pieces came together: the original motif, the answer, and the percussion into one dramatic note, followed by a prolonged rest.

At that moment, the woman whirled toward the audience as if she suddenly realized we were there. She sang to us as if she were talking to us. Only she made the words fit that original motif. Her singing was low, in the same register as the rotund man's strings, and repeated in the same rhythm.

At the moment she hit the end of the sentence, the instruments joined her, just the same way they had joined the rotund man when he started the song.

She was swaying to the music. The entire ensemble swayed, as if they couldn't help themselves. I glanced at the audience. They were swaying too.

I was the only one who wasn't moving, and it took me a moment to realize the strain that was causing me. I literally had to hold myself in place, each muscle tense, so that I wouldn't move.

Movement caused the vocal chords to slip, the breath to fail, the wrong muscle to tighten at the wrong moment. If a performer moved, he ran the risk of making a fatal error.

Of course, in Tygher City, I had made a fatal error without moving anything except my lungs, my diaphragm, my throat, and my mouth. So even that theory, the theory of passivity, had been wrong.

Now the musical conversation had three parts: The woman, who sang her part as if she were making it up on the spot, the rotund man who continued his variations, and the rest of the musicians who either built a bed beneath her phrases or an answer to his.

I looked around again, afraid that someone would stop the music because of its myriad flaws, but no one did. Everyone was staring at the stage, bobbing their heads or tapping their fingers. Behind me, someone yelled, "Sing it, Sister!" and the woman didn't stop, she didn't chastise him, she didn't even seem to notice.

I turned and looked. The man at the door, the one who had taken my credits, didn't do anything, and neither did the servers.

Apparently, it was all right to yell in this place. Just like it was all right to move even when you were on stage.

They got to the end of her lyrics, following a similar, but not the same motif that the rotund man had set up with his strings. She created her own variations, and explored them with her voice, which grew louder and more raspy as the words became more fraught.

Finally, she told us she was done, and the music did as it had before: all the instruments came together in a single note, punctuated by a prolonged rest.

Then the other man—the one who had been talking with the woman—stepped forward and actually spoke to us, as if the rest of the musicians weren't there at all. What he was saying responded directly to her lyrics. He was answering her, like the musical phrases answered each other.

The complexity made my head hurt. The music had only gone on for a few minutes, but it felt as if time slowed down. Each phrase took on import, each beat seemed to reveal something new to me.

This wasn't music, not as I had heard music. This was something other, something visceral, something real.

The music came to that climactic pause again, and as it did, he and the woman turned to each other, mixing their lyrics together in a conversation—his words mimicking the background instruments' one-and-a-two rhythm, hers on that seven-note motif, so the entire opening of the piece, which had seemed so impromptu and random to me suddenly had purpose.

They had planned this, maybe even practiced each section, yet somehow retained a spontaneity that put me on edge, frightening me with its sheer audacity.

Only no one else seemed to think it audacious. They all seemed to expect this—the melody, the response, the not-quite-musical singing, the raspiness, and the increasing violence of the music, as the man and woman played at anger with each other.

I knew they were playing, yet as the music grew louder and louder, that anger seemed real. It was there in the strings, in the power of the keyboard, in the bass line, in the harder and harder rhythm of the percussion player.

I shifted my chair backwards, leaning against the wall, unable to go any farther. Never had music itself made me so uncomfortable—not the way it was performed, not the errors (of which there were dozens)—but the actual power of the notes, the force of the rhythm, the way that each sound built on every other sound creating so much emotional power that I became overwhelmed.

Finally, the song ended. The sound reverberated throughout the room, and slowly faded. I let out the breath I hadn't realized I was holding, my heart racing.

They started another song—this one with three hard beats from the percussionist, and then the entire group of musicians weighed in.

I couldn't handle more music. My heart already felt like it was going to explode. I'd felt more violent emotions in that six-minute song than I had felt in months—maybe since I saw Gibson with his new protégé. Or maybe even before that.

I pressed my thumb against the payment screen, then staggered out, stepping into the wide corridor. It seemed too bright after being in that club. People strolled past, some arm in arm, others having discussions. Tables filled with diners sat outside a few of the restaurants.

No one looked at me oddly. Apparently a man staggering out of the blues club wasn't unusual. I leaned against a nearby pillar and tried to catch my breath.

My heart wouldn't slow. My entire stomach churned.

I had had no idea that music had such intrinsic power. I had known that it was different, just from the recordings. But I had heard that difference in an intellectual way—with a fascination that different musical traditions could have such unbelievably different rules.

But I had never thought of music as an emotional pursuit—something that could control not only how I felt, but how I breathed.

Faintly, from inside the club, I could hear the wail of the rotund man's guitar, the rasp of the woman's voice. I stayed against the column, a safe distance away.

How had I missed this? I had devoted my life to music. And now it seemed as if I had only known a small part of it.

When I finally caught my breath, I wandered back to my cabana, and climbed inside that floating dining room.

I sat there without the lights on, staring at the blackness beyond—a blackness that wasn't entirely dark, because of the light from stars I couldn't identify. I sat in silence.

Only there was no silence.

Because inside my mind, I kept hearing that seven note motif.

Finally I tried it myself. It wasn't as easy as it sounded. My notes were pure and somehow wrong. I sang the line again, and heard how inappropriate my voice was. The woman's voice had been lower than mine. My voice was high, as high as the guitar on its fourth octave.

So I warbled the motif, like the guitar had done, and heard something in my own voice that hadn't been there before:

A wail. Almost a moan.

It caught me, and pleased me, and frightened me, all at the same time.

Ah, yes, the Pané had been right: other music corrupted. Other music changed.

I smiled softly to myself and sang the seven notes over and over again, each time making them different.

Each time, making them mine.

———

Of course I went back: I couldn't help myself. Night after night, I listened to the same group of people playing different songs in different combinations of instruments.

At first, I couldn't stay very long. I sat rigidly and fled when the panic got too great. But slowly, I found myself relaxing. The toes of my right foot started tapping, only to stop when I noticed, or my head bobbed ever so slightly, just like everyone else's in the audience.

Gradually, over the space of a week, I managed to stay for seven songs. When they ended, the group left the stage, although their instruments remained. The audience remained as well, which I thought odd. The other patrons ordered more drinks, talked among themselves, even talked with the musicians—which shocked me. On Djapé, we musicians could not speak to the Pané. It was expressly forbidden unless the Pané spoke to us first.

I ordered another C'cola (those things were addicting) and watched the interactions. After about twenty minutes, the musicians meandered toward the stage, always led by the rotund man. When he sat on his stool, one knee supported his instrument—which I now knew as an electric guitar. The music dictionary I consulted called it "an outmoded instrument that uses an amplifier [which, in original instruments, used dangerous electric current] to make the vibrations of the strings louder or to alter them altogether).

I had looked up the blues as well. The definition told me why I had felt some unease. Central to the music was something called "blue notes," notes that fell somewhere between natural and flat on the third, fifth, and seventh degrees of a C Major scale. Those blue notes had the effect of holding the listener between the major and minor modes, without quite achieving either of them, providing either a sense of unease or, in most cases, a feeling of loss, of incompleteness.

The blues, then, was composed of half-flatted notes—abominations to the Pané.

Which made sitting in this venue, dim and claustrophobic, feel like rebellion to me.

It was as I had that thought that the musicians started up again, this time with an up-tempo piece. The singer—if he could be called that— was the rotund man. He had the most nasal voice I had ever heard. He seemed to sing from his throat instead of his diaphragm. And yet his vocals had power.

He sang three verses, then repeated the melody on his guitar, creating his own arpeggio in the middle of it all. The usual male singer had joined the trumpet player in the back, playing a smaller version of the same instrument, with a higher pitch and a brighter tone.

The various sounds these people could make with their instruments, the way that they answered each other and yet made everything seem casual amazed me. This time, this song, caught me, and I couldn't stop my toes from tapping or myself from swaying. I kept breathing too, which I hadn't in some of the earlier songs.

I relaxed into it, feeling, for the first time, like part of the audience. Before that, I had felt like an observer, an alien myself, someone who couldn't quite understand the experience everyone else was having.

I wasn't sure I still understood it, but I appreciated it—and with this song, I realized it had become part of me, so deep a part that I couldn't control my own physical response to it.

But I could finally move. I didn't have to be rigid any longer.

And that, more than anything, seemed like a victory to me.

―――

After that night, I managed to stay for the entire show. I got used to the cuisine, falling in love with the brisket and the steak-and-potato soup. I nodded to the doorman as I came in, and after a week, the waitress no longer had to give me a menu. Instead, she asked me which of my favorites I preferred, and brought me C'colas whenever my glass was empty.

The music had become an obsession for me. I'd been coming long enough to hear the musicians play some of the same songs over and over again. But startlingly, terrifyingly, they never played the songs in quite the same way.

The first time they changed a motif or played the electric guitar in place of the saxophone, I felt frightened. Had I, for the first time in my life, misremembered a piece of music? But later that same evening, as they played yet another song differently, I realized they had no set track. Unlike the music we performed for the Pané, there was more than one way to play these songs.

And that seemed like such a revelation to me that I finally felt I needed to consult with someone. Someone who knew what they were doing.

I wanted to talk to the rotund man.

———

I approached him after what he called a "set." He was always the first to climb onto the stage and the last to leave. After the first set of that evening's entertainment, he sat alone on his stool. He had unhooked his guitar from its strange amplifier, and he was plucking at the strings.

As I got closer, I could hear them, faint and precise.

He was tuning the guitar.

"Excuse me," I said. "May I ask you a question?"

He looked at me. Sweat beaded his forehead and lined the circles underneath his eyes. Up close, I saw that his shirt was drenched as well.

It was hot on the stage. The heat from the small bar seemed to gather here. The amplifier, which I stood beside, seemed to give off some heat of its own.

"Sure," he said, his fingers flat against the strings on the guitar's neck. He no longer picked at it. "What do you need to know?"

I wasn't sure how to ask the question. I felt awkward and young, something I hadn't felt around music in a very, very long time.

"You never play songs in the same way," I said.

293

He waited.

"Isn't that—is that—isn't that...?" I didn't know how to finish the question. It kept getting jumbled in my mind between two separate thoughts: *Isn't that wrong? Is that disrespectful?*

Finally, instead of choosing between those thoughts, I blurted, "Doesn't music have rules here?"

"Rules," he repeated. He studied me for a moment. "Of course music has rules. It's all about rules."

"But you don't follow any of them," I said.

His eyes narrowed. He leaned back, his head tilting. It was as if he saw me for the very first time.

"Should you even be here?" he asked.

I flushed and lowered my head. I didn't want him to think I had deliberately stepped out of my place—whatever that place was.

"I don't know," I said. "If there are rules about who can be in this club, no one told me. If I'm supposed to leave—"

"No," he said. "That's not what I mean. You're one of those unfortunates, right? From Djapé?"

I raised my head. He was staring at me as if I were as alien to him as his music was to me.

"Unfortunates?" I repeated.

"One of those—what're you called?—castrati? Castrato? You...dress like one." He wasn't originally going to say dress. He was going to say "sound" or "speak." Others had said the same thing to me on the Outpost.

I had learned not to correct their ignorance, and to suffer their questions with as much grace as I could muster.

"I was raised on Djapé," I said cautiously.

"Which means you're one of their musicians, right? And from what I understand, they don't want you off the planet, let alone in a place like this, listening to us."

His words weren't harsh. They had a compassion and an interest that no one had shown me before.

"They no longer care what I do," I said.

"You got yourself fired?" His eyebrows went up. "I didn't know that was possible."

"No, I wasn't fired." My flush deepened. "I swallowed a note."

"You what?" He was leaning forward now. "What does that mean?"

"It means that I am no longer a trustworthy soloist, so my singing career is over." I spoke with a dispassion that surprised me. "I could have taught, but I chose instead to travel. I've never seen any place other than Djapé."

He frowned. "And you think this is where you should be?"

My heart was pounding as if his percussionist had gone back to work. "I've never heard music like this before. I had planned to go to other clubs, different venues. But I came here first. I've never heard anything like this. Not even on the old recordings. Your music is...evocative."

Words were so inadequate.

"And different," I said. "And technically, it shouldn't be. Technically, it's wrong."

"Wrong," he repeated.

My breath caught. Had I insulted him? I hadn't meant to.

"Each time you play," I said, "the songs are different. Are you making a statement by refusing to play the correct version of the song? Is it a rebellion?"

"The correct version of the song." He kept repeating my phrases as if we weren't speaking the same language, as if he had to hear the words in his own voice before he understood them. "What do you mean, the correct version of the song?"

"The composer's version," I said. "Surely, someone wrote it down or recorded it, showing how it should be played."

He blinked at me. "Don't you improvise on Djapé?"

"Improvise?" It was my turn to parrot him. I shook my head. "Humans lived under constraints on Djapé. Our lives were prescribed. We were not to deviate from any standard procedure. So, I suppose the answer is no, we did not improvise."

His eyes twinkled, as if my response amused him. "I meant musically," he said. "I was wondering if anyone taught you improvisation. But after what you just said, I doubt it now."

"Improvisation is a musical term?" I asked.

He nodded.

"You're making fun of me now," I said. "Music can't be improvised. It is all about precision and accuracy."

He rested an arm over the front of his guitar. "What would you have to be accurate about?"

"Following the composer's wishes," I said. "Making certain each note is hit precisely and held for the exact moment specified in the score."

"Seriously?" he asked.

"Yes," I said. "That's why I am asking you about your styles. Do the composers of your songs have more than one preferred text? Or are you making some kind of protest with your music? Is this an aspect of the blues that is accepted like half-flatted notes?"

"This—you mean improvisation?" he asked.

I shook my head. "Playing each song in a different manner than you played it the time before."

"We improvise," he said. "We let the music move us and we do what we feel when we feel it."

I couldn't wrap my brain around the concept. I was shaking my head as we spoke.

"Look," he said, "music follows rules. You were talking about them a minute ago. Haven't you taken theory?"

"I have sung," I said. "I haven't studied. There are theories to music?"

"Hundreds of them, just among humans alone, depending on the culture. We work out of a European Western tradition, based in ancient Earth texts. Blues evolved about a thousand years after the first known instances of repeated Western music. I would think you would be familiar with it. You're part of that tradition."

"I am?" I asked.

"Castrati," he said, "were extremely popular in opera—you know opera, right?"

I shook my head.

He raised his eyebrows. "I thought they were having you sing opera on Pané."

"No," I said. "We sing music specially written for and approved by the Pané."

"Man," he said, then grinned. "See? Even I have something to learn about music."

"You were saying something about opera and the musical tradition," I said.

"I was talking about castrati," he said. "They were really popular in the two hundred years before anyone ever thought of the blues. The castrati sang women's parts in Italian opera, but that probably doesn't mean anything to you since you don't know what opera is."

He shook his head in clear astonishment.

"Damn, I always thought you were following the operatic tradition. I thought you guys were singing the women's parts."

"Women do not sing for the Pané," I said. "It is forbidden. They are allowed to sing for humans in saloons, but only in the all-human areas."

"Weird," he said. "Fascinating, but weird."

Some of the other musicians had come back onto the stage.

"Look," he said. "I can't teach you anything about music or music theory or music history in a twenty-minute break. But we can continue the discussion at the conservatory tomorrow. I teach a three p.m. class in American folk songs, spirituals, and the blues. You could sit in if you want."

"I would like that," I said.

He extended his hand. I had seen this before on the Outpost. It was a sign of greeting and trust. I took his hand in mine. His skin was rough, as if it were made of a different substance than mine. His fingertips actually scraped my skin.

"I'm Jackson Scopes," he said. "Come find me tomorrow."

"I will," I said after I introduced myself. "And thank you."

I went back to my seat, thinking I wouldn't be able to concentrate on the music. But the rotund man—Jackson—started to play an eight-note combination on his electric guitar. Trumpets soared over it, added sixteenth notes and a glissando that sent shivers down my back. Then the percussionist joined in, and the woman started to sing.

I was lost, unease forgotten. The music swept me away, and I spent the rest of the evening in my chair, tapping my toes and reminding myself to breathe.

————

The conservatory had its own ring. It was a smaller ring that encircled a section of the large higher education ring. Apparently, the conservatory had once been part of the higher education ring, like the two colleges and the university, but the conservatory became so famous and attracted so many students, that it needed additional space.

I hired a driver to take me to the conservatory, and I was glad that I did. As his two-person taxi glided through the corridors of the Outpost, he showed me the higher education ring, the conservatory, and the connectors on a glowing map that mostly covered one window. He was trying to give me instruction so that in the future, I could find the area myself, but all he managed to do was confuse me.

Still, I thanked him as he left me off in front of the American Wing of the Old Earth Campus on the Conservatory. Jackson's classroom wasn't far from the main doors. It was bigger than I expected, like a concert hall only with the stage at the bottom of the room, so that everyone looked down on the professor.

The students sat close to the front, so I remained in the back. Jackson stood in the very center of that lowered stage. Diagrams floated around him. All of them were music notations on a familiar five-line staff.

As Jackson touched each staff, music surrounded us. The notes on the staff moved as the music moved, showing us the notation that signified what the music was doing.

298

We were listening to a five-note melody, played in different lengths and different rhythms. Jackson got rid of the lyrics so that we could concentrate on the sound. The sound made me as uncomfortable as the blues had when I first heard it.

Even though the music seemed simple, with its variations on the same five notes, the sound produced was not. The song was something he called a spiritual, a father of the blues.

While I followed the moving notes, stunned at the variations rhythm could bring to the same piece of music, I didn't understand half of what he told us.

I didn't mind. I felt exhilarated as the class ended—not because of all I failed to understand, but because of what little I did.

Music had more depth and history than I had ever expected. What I had learned on Djapé was a small, narrow subset, one that had more to do with Pané tastes than human tastes.

As the class ended, I silently promised myself I would ask Jackson how I enrolled in the conservatory. I wanted to begin all over again, learn music anew.

The music ended, the notations disappeared, and slowly the students filed out. I remained in my seat. Jackson finished compiling his materials up front, placing the small discs in his pocket, and then climbed the stairs to me.

"What did you think?" he asked.

"I am stunned at all that I do not know," I said.

"And you want to learn, right?"

"Yes," I said.

He nodded. "Getting into the conservatory is hard—and expensive."

"Money is not a problem for me," I said.

"Finding space in a class, especially since you've already had a career, might be difficult. But I know who you can talk to."

He signaled me to get up.

"Come with me," he said. "I want to introduce you to the chief administrator of the Old Earth Wing."

"I assume from his title there are other wings?"

Jackson nodded as he led me out of the classroom. "The conservatory specializes in music from a variety of places. Mostly we focus on human forms, but there is a Pané wing, another wing for the Escarbemantes, and a few others. I don't listen to much alien music. I barely listen to human music of the post-colonial era. Mostly I listen to Old Earth forms."

As we passed door after door, I heard snatches of music. Some of it grand, with dozens of instruments, and some of it simple. A baritone sang arpeggios in one of the rooms.

We climbed four stairs to a floor that reminded me of my cabana. Floor-to-ceiling windows showed a truncated view. I could see the vistas of nearby space, but they were eclipsed by a walkway and a bit of the Higher Education Ring.

Couches covered the floor, with tables alongside. Scores floated by, tempting me to touch them so that I could hear the music they so clearly depicted.

"You can listen to anything you want," Jackson said, "so long as you use one of the private earcubes. We don't want you to disturb other passers-by."

The cubes sat on a nearby table. They were tiny, about an eighth the size of my smallest fingernail.

I looked longingly at them.

"Later," he said, "I'll get you permission to use one of the conservatory's music libraries."

"Thank you," I said. "You're being quite kind."

"Not really," he said. "You just intrigued me with your questions. I'm fascinated by the way you think."

He leaned into a door on the wall opposite the windows and called to someone named Felix.

A man came out of the door. He was tall, with a narrow nose and wide eyes. His lips narrowed when he saw me.

"This is the singer I told you about from Djapé," Jackson said. "He was quite well known—"

"You're early," Felix said to me as if I had done something wrong.

My face warmed. "I'm sorry. I didn't realize we had an appointment."

Jackson looked at Felix in confusion. Felix was frowning at me.

"I told your people we'd contact you when we were ready," Felix said. "We're not ready. We only have two. Normally we don't contact you until there are five or more."

"I'm sorry," I said again. "You must have me confused with someone else."

"You're from Djapé," Felix said. "You're here for the sopranos?"

My breath caught. "Boys?"

"What else?" he asked. "We should get another shipload in a month or so, and I'm told there are more on that."

"More sopranos?" I asked, my mouth dry.

Jackson was looking back and forth at us as if he didn't know what was going on. I didn't exactly either, but I had an inkling.

"We don't know if there are sopranos," Felix said. "But the incoming ship has an orphan wing. There are possibles. I thought you were going to wait until we could screen them."

Jackson took a step back from me. "I thought you didn't know anyone here."

"I don't," I said.

"Then what's this?" Jackson asked.

"I'm not sure." I folded my hands in front of my robe and leaned toward Felix. "You think I'm here to take boys back to Djapé?"

"Why else would you come?" Felix said.

I swallowed. "I came to the Outpost because of your music."

"I caught him listening to blues, Felix," Jackson said. "No true castrato from Pané would contaminate himself with human music."

"Then why is he here?" Felix asked.

I bowed, as I had been taught to do when I was most offended. I rose slowly, and said, "I am a windchime. I performed in the highest halls of Djapé, but my voice has failed me. I am a true castrato, as you say, but I am not here to bring others to Djapé. I am here to learn."

Felix blinked at me as if he couldn't quite believe what he was hearing. "Learn what?"

I folded my hands in front of my robe. "The forbidden music."

I said that last in a whisper. It was the first time I had admitted it to myself.

"You were offering him *kids*?" Jackson asked. "What the hell is that?"

Felix gave him a sideways glance. It looked furtive to me. "We have an agreement with the human musical colony on Djapé. If we encountered pure boy sopranos, we notify them. The Pané's tastes are so particular that they go through singers as if they were made of crystal. One bad shake and they've shattered."

The description was so accurate that I shuddered. It was one of the reasons we were called windchimes. A single crack, tiny and nearly invisible, could ruin a windchime's tone forever.

"You think it right to send a child into that mess?" Jackson asked.

"Why not? It's better than hiring them out to freighters at thirteen. That's what happens to most of the kids who come through here." Felix looked at me. "You lived a luxurious life, right? You have money. You're well off."

"I have money," I said.

"So you came for what?" Felix asked. "Reconstruction and reeducation?"

"Reconstruction is possible?" I asked.

"Sure," Felix said. "That's what most of the has-beens do when they get here. They get repaired and they go on to live normal lives."

"Without their voice," I said.

"Usually, they end up with a very musical voice," Felix said. "It is just a male voice. An adult male voice."

"Without the purity," I said.

"Humans rarely care about purity of tone," Felix said. "We outgrew that before we left Earth's solar system."

"It's Pané affectation," Jackson said, as if he were trying to convince me.

My breath caught. I thought of myself, singing those blue notes all those weeks ago, how odd my voice sounded. Yet how rich.

Both men were watching me. "You didn't come here for that either, did you?" Felix said.

I shook my head. "I came to see if I could enroll in the conservatory."

"Why?" Felix asked. "You already know Pané music."

"Jackson tells me there is an entire musical history I do not know. I would like to learn it."

Felix studied me for a moment. "You're not here for the boys?"

"No," I said. "Although I would like to meet them."

"Why?" Felix sounded wary.

"I am curious," I said.

"I can't believe this," Jackson said. "You sell children to the Pané?"

Felix straightened his back. "You know how the Children's Ring works. Don't sound so shocked."

"We don't usually sell children to aliens who'll disfigure them," Jackson said.

It was as if I was not in the room.

"We do not sell," Felix said.

"Maybe not outright," Jackson said, "but don't tell me there's no quid pro quo."

Felix shifted from foot to foot. "The Pané have generously agreed to fund the education of the other children. It's a small price to pay for the artistic richness we have given them."

"Artistic richness?" Jackson asked. "Those kids don't get a choice."

"It is what it is," Felix said. "They don't get a choice about being orphaned either."

I felt dizzy. I had no memories of my life before Djapé, although Gibson told me that I had come from another community and my parents were dead.

I am your family now, he had said to me in my earliest memory.

Only he wasn't family. He hadn't ever been family, only a man hoping to get rich off my talent.

"Have you always done it this way?" I asked Felix.

"I inherited the program," Felix said, with a glare at Jackson. "I wasn't sure I liked it at first either, but I toured the facilities on Djapé. Those kids live in luxury."

Jackson shook his head. He looked like he was about to speak.

"How long has this system been in place?" I asked.

"A century or more," Felix said. "I can look it up for you."

"So I came through here?"

Both men looked at me as if they suddenly realized that their discussion existed in more than theory.

"All human musicians get approved at the Outpost," Felix said.

"Just like the other merchandise." Jackson's face was red, but not with embarrassment.

With anger.

"I've heard no complaints," Felix said.

"That doesn't make it right," Jackson said.

"Ask your friend," Felix said. "Are you dissatisfied with your life?"

I did not know how to answer that question. My life was what it was. I couldn't imagine it any other way.

But then, I had little experience of other lives. What I knew about the universe, I had learned in the small human enclaves on Djapé.

"He's here, isn't he?" Jackson said. "Isn't that proof enough of dissatisfaction?"

"He's here because he did something to upset the Pané," Felix said.

"That's true," I said.

Jackson frowned. "Swallowing a note was enough to torpedo an entire career?"

"The Pané expect perfection," Felix said as if I weren't there. "That humans can achieve it, even for a short period of time, is nothing short of miraculous."

The warmth in my face increased. I didn't want to think about the Pané. But I did want to understand where I came from.

"Let me see the boys," I said.

"So you *are* here to take them back," Felix said.

"No," I said. "I had never thought of my life before Djapé. I would simply like to see what it had been like."

"Then you should see all of them," Jackson said.

Felix frowned. I thought he was going to say no, but he surprised me.

"Jackson is right," Felix said. "You should see all of them. Even the ones who aren't going to leave the Outpost."

My heart did a small flip, like it did when Jackson's musicians played a particularly interesting line of music.

"I would like that," I said. "I would like it very much."

————

They called it the Children's Ring, but Felix told me that wasn't accurate. Not all children on the Outpost lived here, only the ones without family.

It was still a dangerous sector. People died all the time, leaving their children untended. Many children died, abandoned and alone.

Even more came to the Outpost, searching for some way to survive.

Eventually, the Outpost set up an area for them, complete with teachers and caretakers. If they were old enough, the children had to agree to live by the Outpost's rules—education and care in return for years of service wherever the Outpost deemed appropriate.

If the children weren't old enough to make a decision for themselves, they were offered for limited adoption. The limited adoption period lasted no more than two months. If no one took the children, they were then placed in the Children's Ring and expected to follow the same rules as all the others.

"Limited adoption?" I asked as we settled into one of the Conservatory's glide vehicles. Felix handled the controls. His position gave him all kinds of privileges within the Conservatory and parts of the Outpost. "What exactly does that mean?"

"The child doesn't have to become part of any family," Felix said. "But the person who sponsors the adoption guarantees the child's education and livelihood. Most of the children who go to Djapé do so under terms of a limited adoption."

"So I had one," I said.

"Most likely," Felix said. "This plan has been in place for decades."

I swallowed hard. My throat constricted. Still, I managed to ask, "Could I trace mine?"

"If you're still using the name you had when you arrived on the Outpost," Felix said. "And the only way to know that is to look."

Jackson sat in the back of the glide car. He wasn't watching either of us. Instead, he watched the door fronts pass us by. We had gone by several musical departments, all part of the Conservatory, and all of them leading into areas as large as the Old Earth Music Department.

The glide cart left the Conservatory through one of the bridges that led to the Higher Education Ring. We went through two other bridges between rings, each more crowded and cramped than the last, until we ended up in the Children's Ring.

It had straight walls and no apparent windows into the space beyond. The walls were decorated with multicolored rectangles. It took me a while to realize that those rectangles were doors.

Felix glided the cart past schools, religious buildings, and storefronts, finally stopping at a wide building with double doors marked *Auditorium*.

"This is the induction center," he said. "Children spend their first week or so here, as they learn the rules, figure out where they fit, and get tested."

My shoulders were rigid. My hands, clasped over my stomach, were pressed so tightly together that my fingers ached.

"Tested for what?" I asked.

"Their various aptitudes," Felix said.

"To find out if they're musical," I said.

"Musical, mathematical, or have a facility for languages." Felix glided the cart into a pole that had locks along the edges. "As well as hundreds of other skills and talents."

"So they all have a place," I said, feeling more relieved than I expected.

"Of course not," Jackson said. "Some kids are too young to have skills. Others are too traumatized to even try."

He sounded bitter. He was clearly familiar with this place. I shifted on my seat so that I could see him.

"What happens to those children?" I asked.

"They're the ones who usually get shipped off by freighter at thirteen," Jackson said. "If they survive that long."

"Survive?" I asked. "Children die here?"

"It's not health," Jackson said. "It's cooperation. You have to work within the machine. If you don't, then you get moved."

"Moved where?" I asked.

"There is an area for troubled children," Felix said. He let himself out of the cart onto one of the glide platforms. He hit the button, sending himself down.

I felt disoriented. Felix hadn't wanted to discuss the troubled children. Jackson wasn't looking at me either.

"They die in the area for troubled children?" I asked.

Jackson shrugged one shoulder. "They don't thrive."

"How do you know this?" I asked.

He turned toward me. His expression was bleak. "You and I both came through this place. You received a limited adoption and lost body parts. I was trouble. I worked a freighter."

"But you have a teaching position now," I said. "You play music every night."

"Where do you think I learned about the blues?"

"They play blues on freighters?" I asked.

Jackson smiled faintly, almost contemptuously, and shook his head. "Did you like living on Djapé?"

My garden rose in my mind. And the music, playing softly in my study. The forbidden music. The way my back tensed before I went on stage. The feeling of relief and terror that happened as my voice cracked.

"I don't know," I said.

"I hated the freighter," he said. "I hated what Felix calls the Trouble Area. You didn't hate Djapé."

"Hate is a strong word," I said.

"And I've noticed that you don't use strong words." Jackson shrugged. "Go visit. See what you think."

My heart was pounding.

"How do I get down?" I asked.

"Touch the pole," Jackson said. "Your glide platform will appear next to the door."

I had to lean forward to touch the pole. It vibrated slightly under my fingertips. Within seconds, the platform appeared beside the car, a square bit of flooring that looked unstable to me. Still, I let myself out, balancing myself with my hands on the pole and the glide car.

"Are you coming?" I asked Jackson.

His face was gray. He looked vaguely ill. "No."

I studied him for a moment, but he didn't meet my gaze any longer. Instead, he looked at the neighborhood as if he had never seen it before.

I left him. The platform took me down slowly. It felt rickety, as if I moved wrong, I would fall.

I held myself rigid. The platform landed, and I staggered slightly to the left.

Felix was waiting beside the double doors.

"Did Jackson try to talk you out of coming?" he asked.

"No," I said. "But he's not going to join us."

Felix gave me a sideways, somewhat distracted grin. "You know he grew up here."

"He told me," I said. "I didn't expect it."

"You should have. I think a good fifty percent of the permanent workforce came through the Children's Ring."

He pulled the doors open, stepping inside. The interior was dark compared with the main thoroughfare we'd traveled along.

"Did you?" I asked as I followed him into the dimness.

308

"No," he said. "I'm one of the lucky ones. I was hired for my expertise."

"With children?" I asked.

This time he did look at me in surprise. "In Ancient Music, particularly Earth forms."

"I'm surprised the Outpost found that a valuable skill."

"It wasn't the Outpost," he said. "It was the Conservatory. They needed someone with a broad range of knowledge to handle the Old Earth Department. All human music was born on Earth. Those forms are the most important."

"All human music," I said slowly. "Even what we sang on Djapé?"

"Especially what you sang there," he said. "The diatonic scale—the eight whole notes—comes from Ancient Greece. The hexachords that you also sang were developed in Europe in what was called the Middle Ages, and arpeggios, especially those sung in descending order, which were first developed in a period called the Renaissance."

"But I was told that the Pané had unique musical tastes," I said.

"Most humans do not listen to pure notes or broken chords and consider them entertainment. To humans, they are part of a great whole, a symphony or a song. To the Pané, they are the entire performance."

We had gone deep into the building. It had no windows. Only doorways marked with numbers running alongside the hallway. Eventually the hallway opened up, revealing another set of double doors.

"I contacted the headmistress here," he said. "The boys are waiting for you."

He made it sound like I was still going to choose them. My stomach clenched.

"They don't think I'm going to adopt them or anything, do they?" I asked.

He shook his head. "They only know that you want an audition. That is what you want, isn't it?"

I wasn't sure what I wanted. "Is that what you do when someone comes from Djapé?"

"Scales and arpeggios only," he said. "Would you like to hear that?"

It was what I understood. But I didn't want to set up the wrong expectations.

"Whatever they have prepared is fine," I said.

He made a small grunt, as if I had disappointed him, and then we stepped through the doors.

I had expected an auditorium—something with a stage and chairs. While this room was large, it was nothing more than an empty space. The floor did slope downwards slightly, but that seemed to be more of a design flaw than anything else.

A woman stood to one side and when she saw us, she waved a hand. A group of boys filed in. They ranged in age from about ten to four or five. At the end of the group, four women brought in very little children. The women held their hands as the boys half-walked, half-tumbled forward. Some were so young that they hadn't mastered walking very well yet. Others had obviously been raised in zero-g and weren't used to walking in gravity.

"Only boys?" I asked.

Felix gave me a withering look. "No other aliens care about our music. And the Pané only want male sopranos."

I almost protested again that I was not here for the Pané, but I did not. He had thought I was interested only in the children that might go to Djapé—and maybe I was.

"We'll start with the little ones," Felix said. "Let's just go one by one."

Each little boy paraded forward. At the urging of the woman who had led him in, he would sing a diatonic scale. All of the little ones had beautiful voices, but only one sang with such purity that my hair stood on end.

He was tiny, with big brown eyes and hair cut so short that it stood straight up on top. He didn't seem to understand why anyone wanted him to sing, but all the woman had to do was name the note and he sang it with clarity and such accuracy that if I tested the note mechanically, I would have found him to hit the center of the pitch—no variation, not even a fraction of a fraction off.

"He's one of the two, isn't he?" I softly asked Felix. Felix nodded.

I walked up to the boy and crouched.

"Sing after me," I said, and proceeded to sing the C Major arpeggio that I had destroyed in Tygher City.

The boy sang with me—C-E-G-C-G-E-C—his notes so pure and fresh that shivers ran down my spine.

He didn't know what he was singing. He was just making sounds. Lovely sounds, but nothing more.

The older boys watched, rapt. The youngest boys squirmed, held fast by the women who had brought them in. Everyone was staring at me.

"Thank you," I said to the little one who sang for me.

He gave me a wide grin, and then ran back to his handler. He hugged her thigh.

I frowned as I saw that. He had made a connection here, whether he had known it or not. He would not be able to hug a woman like that on Djapé. Not without special permission.

Then I stood, and backed up.

"Let's hear the rest of you," I said.

The woman who had called them all in clapped her hands together. They looked toward her. Then she waved her hands in a fashion that seemed to give them direction.

One quarter of them started. They sang in perfect unison, singing the entire verse. Then they started over, and when they got to the end of the first line, another quarter of the group started at the beginning. When the second group got to the end of the first line, the third quarter chimed in. And when they reached their line, the final quarter joined.

I had never heard the song sung this way—and it became instantly clear that the song had been designed to be sung like this. The harmonies were lovely, the boys' voices strong.

And like a perfect chorus, no voice stuck out.

One of the oldest boys on the side closest to me sang with such complete joy that my eye went to him immediately. He smiled as the harmonies grew more intense and his body swayed as if he were listening to one of Jackson's performances in the blues' club.

The boys finished and the chords echoed through the auditorium. Now I knew how the place had gotten its name. Its acoustics were perfect.

"Let's hear it again," I said, "but this time, with only one person from each group."

I didn't care who the first three were, but I wanted to hear that joyful boy. So I picked three others from the sections and him. He had been in the final group, so he would have a solo at the end, but he wouldn't start.

The boy who started wobbled his way through the opening line. He was clearly terrified, his throat closing and constricting the notes. He didn't lose pitch, but his tone was muddy.

The second child joined, then the third. The fourth—the boy I was interested in—tilted his head back and opened his mouth, blending perfectly. Again he sang with joy.

As each part dropped out, his became stronger. At the end, he sounded like the entire chorus all by himself.

And like that little boy who sang for me, this boy had a purity of tone that sent shivers down my spine.

"You're amazing," Felix said to me. "You found the other one."

It wasn't hard. I had grown up listening to voices like that. But I nodded.

"Thank you," I said to the boys. "Thank you all."

I thanked the women as well, and they nodded at me. Then the one who had directed the chorus asked Felix if they could leave. He looked at me.

I nodded, and the boys filed out.

"Satisfied?" he asked.

But I wasn't. I felt even more uncomfortable than I expected—not because this performance raised memories. It didn't. But because of the children themselves.

I must have been as young as that first boy when I left the Outpost. I had no memory of a time before Djapé, and I had vague memories of imitation singing, much like I had the boy do for me. It was the way the youngest children learned to sing in the Pané style.

But the older boy bothered me. He had already learned music—this culture's music—and he loved it.

"You can't send that older child to Djapé," I said to Felix. "The Pané will destroy him."

Felix frowned at me. "You can't know that."

"I know it better than you," I said. "They'll teach perfection, not enjoyment. Each note is an exam, not a linked unit with any other note. He may spend years there, but he'll never be a top-level performer, and he will learn to hate his gift."

Felix glanced toward the door the boys had left from.

"So that's why you wanted to come," he said. "To prevent children from going to Djapé. I told you how entrenched this system is, how the Pané money helps the other children—"

"Yes," I said. "You told me, and I believe you. The youngest one is exactly what they want. He is a mimic. He makes sounds, pure sounds, not music. He is a human windchime, and they will love him."

Felix was still watching me warily. "I still hear hesitation in your voice."

I sighed. I was guessing at this last part. "He has affection for the woman who brought him here. You shouldn't break that up."

"Women can't contaminate the performers," Felix said.

"You could argue that she's already had an influence, and it can't be heard in his voice. Make her a deal-breaker."

He stared at me. "You guarantee that the Pané will like him?"

"Yes," I said. "I spent my entire life in that system. I know what they're looking for."

"You realize his happiness isn't an issue," Felix said.

"It seems that happiness isn't an issue for anyone here," I said, not telling him that I never thought of happiness either. "But if he has someone to care for him, he'll perform better, and maybe he'll survive longer than some of the others who come to Djapé."

Maybe he wouldn't have a horrible realization, like I had, that the person he thought cared about him only cared about his perfect voice.

"Why would he survive longer?" Felix asked.

"Fear," I said. "Voices shatter from the sheer terror of making a mistake. I was raised to be perfect or I would be rejected. Maybe if he has someone who cares for him as him, he will not be afraid of such rejection. His voice won't constrict. He'll perform from strength, not from terror."

Felix continued to stare at me, and then he shook his head. He grinned, just a little. "You want my job?"

"I know nothing about Old Earth," I said.

"Picking voices for the Pané," he said.

"No," I said before I could edit my response. "I want to study every form of music possible. I want to break the habits I learned on Djapé, not embrace them."

"So you're a lot more like that older kid. You love music," Felix said.

I thought of those stolen moments in my study, the revelations in the blues club, the odd sound to my own voice as I tried that seven-note opening.

"I was nothing like that boy," I said. "I was a windchime, just like the little one. But I stumbled on some recordings, and they changed me."

The recordings had frightened me too, but I wasn't going to tell Felix that. They had frightened me because they had contaminated me, and I had let it happen.

I might even have let that vocal break happen, just to escape the repetition of performance, the nightly striving for perfection.

"If you sent the older boy to Djapé, you would change him in the wrong way. The younger one, he would have the good life you told Jackson about. And if the younger boy chooses something different when he gets older, then so be it. But you would be forcing the older child into a mold that doesn't suit him."

"One child, not two," Felix said, almost to himself. "They're not going to like this."

"One child who sings longer. One child who loves what he does. Usually you send two because one will break, right?"

He looked at me. His gaze was measuring. It was as if I had uncovered a secret even he didn't want to acknowledge.

"It's always been that way," he said. "You send two, one breaks. And no one has been able to predict the break."

"Because you have to know what life on Djapé is like, and you don't know that," I said.

"But you do."

Too well.

"Don't send the one who'll break," I said. "Send the woman instead."

"They hated women's voices," he said as if I didn't know.

"She's not going there to sing," I said. "She's going to make sure he does."

"By taking care of him," Felix said. He turned away from me, but not before I saw the relief on his face.

"Yes," I said.

"Are you telling me no one takes care of these children?"

"No, I'm not saying that." I looked at the door where the children had filed out. I had no idea what level of care they received here. I supposed I could ask Jackson.

"Then why send the woman?" Felix asked.

"The children get good care," I said, "but they—we—are commodities. And if we break, no one puts us back together."

"Is that what happened to you?" Felix asked.

"As an adult," I said. "But I know it happens to the young ones. I've seen it."

"What happens to them then?" Felix asked.

I frowned. I didn't exactly know. The ones I had seen got led off-stage, never to perform again.

"They grow up to become support staff, I think," I said. "I don't exactly know."

Sadly, ironically, I had never thought about it before.

Felix walked to the front of the room. He was clearly thinking about what I said. He clasped his hands behind his back, paced as if he were retracing the boys' steps, and then walked back to me.

He nodded. "I can make this work. I know I can."

His mood seemed suddenly lighter. I let out a small breath of air I hadn't realized I had been holding.

Maybe this all disturbed me more than I wanted to admit. Such a big system, and these boys were only a small part of it. The entire Outpost had developed around the orphans. And if they had been farmed out throughout the decades, then they had an impact throughout the entire sector.

But Felix clearly wasn't thinking of that. He was thinking of our discussion. He clapped a hand on my back and led me out of the auditorium. As we walked down the hall, he said,

"If I do this, you'll have to agree to listen to the future candidates."

It wasn't a question. It was a command. I bristled at commands.

"I already said I don't want your job," I said.

"I'm asking you to consult," he said. "In exchange for the right to study at the Conservatory."

I wanted to say no, but that might have been a reaction to his preemptory statement. I also wanted to study at the Conservatory. I wanted to study human musical traditions. I wanted to learn everything I could about the art I had just so recently discovered.

I could do some of that simply by attending the bars, clubs, and concert halls on the Outpost. But the last week of listening to Jackson's performances had raised questions too complicated to answer in a single night's performance.

Still, I wanted to make my own decision—and not one based on Djapé or the Pané or sending boys to a life just like mine had been.

"I want to think about it," I said.

My silence must have told Felix about my ambivalence. He

nodded.

"Fair enough," he said.

———

I spent the next three days thinking about Felix's offer. Only I wasn't thinking so much about the trade as I was about myself. I had never done a lot of self analysis. I was just stumbling onto it here, and it felt as uncomfortable as the music I first heard in the blues club.

Windchimes did not feel emotion. Windchimes simply let air pass through their instrument, achieving a purity of sound that was in their very nature. Not because they had brought the emotion to the surface. Not because they had felt anything, except maybe a cold breeze.

The fear came because the instrument could become flawed. The chimes could crack, the wind could shatter a delicate part of the glass itself. And then nothing, not even the most careful repair, could remake the sound.

Sound was notoriously fickle. Its perfection was short-lived.

Perhaps that was why blues had intrigued me so much. The blues did not seem to recognize perfection.

The blues seemed to spurn it.

The older boy had felt emotion when he sang. The younger boy had not. He hadn't even thought of music as anything other than sounds that traveled through his instrument, through his voice.

Perfection could be trained. It could be achieved by a blessed few. I had done so. That child might be able to as well.

Oddly, at least to me, I felt less conflicted about choosing the children than I did about my own motivation for doing so. When I left Djapé, I hoped to leave permanently. I had kept my home there, yes, because I was afraid (that word again!) that I would not survive the universe outside of the one I had known.

But I could survive here, even if I did not join the Conservatory. I could spend the rest of my life here, listening to music, discovering new theories, and learning to use my voice in a new way.

I did not go to the blues club during those three days, but I did go back to the Children's Ring. I asked for—and received—my records.

Apparently Gibson, who had taken me from the Outpost, had kept my name.

I had been three, just like he said. One of ten survivors of a mid-space collision between a passenger ship and some kind of space debris. The pilots survived. A few of the crew had taken the children first to a secure area. By the time they were ready to take the parents, they realized that the back section of the ship had opened to the coldness of space.

All of the children had been brought to the Outpost, where the authorities had followed standard protocol: they had searched for the remaining family. Some of the children had grandparents and aunts and uncles. I had had no one, except the two people traveling with me. People who were listed only by their names, and the fact that they were traveling to the Outpost to look for work.

"Charity cases," the woman who helped me with the records said. "Sometimes the Outpost does that. It funds a ship of job seekers. It's hard to get good workers out here, and even harder to keep them."

"So I would have ended up on the Outpost no matter what," I said.

She nodded. "And probably not have been tested for music. You would have lived with your parents and most likely had minimal education. You would have ended up as they had."

"Dead?" I asked.

She laughed. "No," she said. "Whatever jobs they found themselves in were the jobs you would have been considered for."

"Work is hereditary here?" I asked.

She shook her head. "But families tend to follow the same paths. The new jobs are filled by the children from the Ring—the talented children of the Ring, of course."

Her comments sounded self-serving to me, so I investigated them, and found, indeed, that employment studies of the Outpost had shown the most driven employees were not members of the families who lived here, but the children who had been orphaned. They had learned competition, the value of hard work, and how to maximize their own skill set.

Which was what I was now trying to do. I had a beautiful voice—albeit unconventional for the Outpost—and a growing love of all types of music. A curiosity that had gotten me in trouble on Djapé and might serve me well here.

A curiosity that seemed to grow the more I learned.

After the three days, I returned to Felix and accepted his offer. I would help him choose the right children for Djapé and he would guarantee me a permanent place of study in the Conservatory.

But I did have one condition. If I felt a perfectly pure boy soprano would be destroyed on Djapé—and there were no others to take his place—the Pané and their human minions would be told that there were no boys in that group. Fewer children would go to Djapé, but those who would might actually have a chance at long-term musical (and personal) survival.

Felix agreed. He offered to take me to dinner to celebrate, but I refused.

Instead, I went to the blues club.

Jackson's band was at the end of a song. Instead of fading out as he usually did, Jackson started a completely different song. The band members looked at him, and then the percussionist grinned. He caught the syncopated beat. So did the bass player. The saxophonist did his own riff. The female singer grabbed a tambourine off the percussionist's table and tapped it against her hip on the off-beats.

I made my way to my usual table. The waitress was already setting down my C'cola when Jackson started singing, *Playin' With My Friends*. I had heard it before, but never so energetically.

He was looking at me as he played, inviting me through the lyrics of the song, to join them on stage. He even beckoned as he sang that I could pick any song I wanted to, so long as it was the blues.

I shook my head and sat down. He grinned at me, and stopped singing, playing a variation on the melody that I had never heard before. The entire band played without a singer for another fifteen minutes, various versions of the same song, with each instrument taking the melody—except the percussionist, who kept the same syncopated beat to the entire piece.

It was one of the most interesting—and welcoming—songs I had ever heard them do. By the end of it, I was clapping with the tambourine's beat like everyone else.

Finally Jackson eased out of the piece, followed by the bass. The percussion, tambourine and trumpets finished it off with a flourish. Then everyone bowed, and threaded off the stage.

Jackson leaned his electric guitar against his stool. He climbed down into the audience as well, and startled me by coming to my table just as the steak-and-potato soup did. He ordered his own C'cola and a side of brisket.

"Why didn't you come up?" he asked. "I know you can sing."

"Not like that," I said. "Try as I might, I can't achieve a half-flatted note."

"Achieve it?" He raised his eyebrows. "You don't achieve notes. You sing them."

I shrugged. "I can't sing them either."

"Lemme hear you," he said. "Come on up to the stage."

I shook my head. "You have an audience."

"So?" He finished his C'cola as he stood, then set the glass on the table. "Come on."

"The last time I sang for anyone," I said, "I swallowed a note."

He laughed. "Hell, we're lucky if we even hit them."

That was true. I exhaled, and I stood reluctantly. My stomach had clenched, but to my surprise, my throat hadn't.

I climbed onto the stage and stood with my back to the small crowd. "What do you want me to try?"

"Something Pané," he said. "Something you're used to."

"No one here will like it," I said.

He nodded. "I want to hear it."

So I sang part of Tampini's Aria in E Major. I hit each note perfectly. They sounded too large in the club, ironic, I thought, considering the power of the blues band before me.

Jackson was grinning. "That's Pané music, huh?"

I nodded. "It's certainly not blues," I said.

"So sing for me," he said. "This line."

He sang the opening lines of the song that the band had just done. I sang as softly as I could, knowing how embarrassingly strange my pure high voice sounded.

"Keep going," he said, as I faded out. "You know the words."

And I did. Music stayed in my head. So I sang the opening lines of *Playin' With My Friends*, and he built a bridge underneath me with the electric guitar. Shivers were running down my spine.

I had always thought I was a windchime, but Jackson's song was making me into something else. As I sang, the other band members filed back on stage. They picked up in the middle as if they had never quit, only I was singing the melody. Jackson kept the bridge beneath me, and I kept my back to the audience. We played through all three verses and two renditions of the chorus, and then Jackson nodded at me to stop.

The band played twelve more bars and stopped as well. There was a moment of silence—the Pané version of a boo—and then someone clapped. Others followed. The applause was so steady and fierce that it threatened to overwhelm me.

I hadn't moved. Jackson had to set down his guitar and grab me by the shoulders, turning me around. The audience was on its feet, clapping and stomping and asking for more.

"But it's not the blues," I said to Jackson.

"Not the old-fashioned kind, that's true," he said. "This is something new. That's what they're applauding. Something different."

"Is that good?" I asked.

He extended a hand to the still applauding crowd. "What do you think?"

I thought I had never experienced a reaction that so moved me. The Pané's pleasure allowed me to keep my job. Here I had no job. I had experimented—and it had succeeded.

"Join us for another song?" he asked.

I started to shake my head, then changed my mind.

"Just one," I said, "and no more."

Five songs later, winded and covered in sweat, I staggered off the stage. The waitress brought me a fresh bowl of soup, some water, and another C'cola. The audience congratulated me and asked me when I was going to sing again.

Jackson grinned. "He'll be back," he kept promising.

"I can't," I said to him as he sat back down at my table. "I don't sing like you do. There's no music like this."

"Precisely," he said. "That's what's so wonderful about it."

"It doesn't follow any rules," I said.

"So there can't be perfection," he said.

I stared at him for a moment, stunned at what he just said. No perfection? Not even a little?

"We'll start slowly," he said. "One night a week. We'll put a sign out front, and call it the Pané Blues."

"Isn't that a contradiction?" I asked.

"Music loves dissonance," he said. "You just haven't learned that yet."

He was right. I hadn't learned dissonance. But I had a hunch I would.

And if my previous experiences on the Outpost were any example, I might actually come to love it.

"One night," I said, "and no more."

He grinned. He knew, as well as I did, that my vows that night weren't holding up.

I wasn't sure I wanted them to.

I was acting without thinking, just like I had done in that concert in Tygher City, when my voice broke. My perfection broke. My life broke.

And became something new.

Something flawed.

Something better.

BONDING

KRISTINE KATHRYN RUSCH

BONDING

This part of K'dar'ak smelled like wet wool. I pulled my parka hood around my face, thankful for the chill. Heat always accentuated odors. I glanced over my shoulder. My companion, George, was studying a snow mural as if he had never seen anything like it before. I couldn't see the backup team, but I knew they were there. This was a part of my job that I both welcomed and feared. Done right, we'd break another ring. Done wrong—well. Done wrong, no one really cared.

No one but us.

George stuck his mittened hands in his pockets and the thermal lining sealed around them. He nodded toward me, his breath visible in the thin air. K'dar'Ak's atmosphere was barely tolerable for humans, but that didn't stop us from settling the place. Anytime there was money to be made, humans would gather. These beautiful towns, carved out of snow and k'dar, a hard grainy wood-like substance, would disappear if the funds ran out.

I took a deep breath, feeling the chill in my lungs. It felt as if I could never get enough air, even though all the studies said I could. I just hadn't acclimatized. I had arrived on K'dar'Ak only last night; George had figured my breathless state and my chill-crystalled skin would mark me as a newcomer, and make me less suspicious.

I hoped so. I hated working at a disadvantage.

George had also figured that my small frame, my high-pitched voice, and my wide eyes would have a similar effect. Most people saw me as younger than I am. That, combined with my girlish presence, made them dismiss me, just as they would dismiss a young boy who came into their midst.

I rounded the corner, out of sight of George and the backup squad. This was so that my contact wouldn't get nervous. I had three different security implants, tiny chips—each more undetectable than the last—and I activated all of them before continuing.

The wet wool smell increased. Someone had once told me it was caused by a combination of the building materials and the snow. K'dar'Ak looked like no place I'd ever seen before. The homes were small and round—igloo-shaped, some Earth historian once told me—but the k'dar formed the frame. A thin porous material also native to K'dar'Ak stretched over that frame, and then the locals let snow gather all winter, spending much of their leisure time creating murals on the exterior walls. I'd watched one local work that morning, using tools I'd never seen, creating lines in the snow, using one tool to melt the edges around the line, and then another to freeze the line solid. A few humans used snow paints to decorate their murals, but those weren't as pure as the native murals. Each native mural looked different, even though the colors used were white, light gray, and white again.

George told me that a lot of humans hired locals to create their murals. I didn't doubt it. The process looked laborious and it seemed strange to me, to work on a piece of art all winter only to have it melt in one day in the Sudden Spring Thaw.

Yet all of the houses I passed had murals on their western walls. It wasn't custom to have them on the east. A lot of the homes glowed from within, meaning someone was home. Flagsticks with metal tags stuck out of the snow near the front doors, giving the house numbers.

I went to Number 84A, just as I was instructed.

The door was three steep steps down and in an enclave built from k'dar and shell. I stood on the threshold and knocked, even though I knew it wasn't local custom. I was supposed to be from the Moon, Armstrong to be exact, and customs there came from the Western Alliance on Earth. It was best to keep up the pretense in all ways.

The door opened. A small man with a wispy brown beard stared at me. His eyes were extended slightly, as happened to humans born on K'dar'Ak, and his skin showed evidence of a dozen broken capillaries. His features marked his age at less than twenty; K'dar'Ak's human habitation began only twenty-one years ago.

"*G'dit?*" he asked in Kiddy, which was what outsiders called the local variation of one of the native tongues. He had asked me what I wanted. I pretended not to understand.

"Do you speak English?" I asked, making my voice even breathier than usual. "Or maybe Cantonese?"

"English," he said. The word was heavily accented: It sounded more as if he had said *Ang Leash.*

"Excellent," I said. "I'm Marisa Creelman. We've been exchanging e-mail."

When he didn't respond, I made my lower lip tremble.

"From Armstrong? On the Moon? Isn't this the—"

"Yes," he said and ushered me inside.

There the air was so hot as to be almost oppressive. It smelled of wood smoke and garlic. The locals here used a fire pit to cook a lot of their meals. It had the extra advantage of warming the homes. K'dar was easy to grow, and added a flavor to the food that had become a delicacy on Mars, the Moon, and Earth. The locals had standard cooking devices, of course, but anyone who'd spent a lot of time on K'dar'Ak prided himself on his ability to cook in a fire pit.

The light inside was diffuse and thick with particles. It took my eyes a moment to adjust. The living area was divided into an entertainment grouping, a dining room, and a kitchen. Through a curved doorway were more rooms. I assumed that was the sleep area.

In the center of the entertainment area, three infant Ce'narks rolled over each other. They were round and still had their white fur. They looked healthy enough, although I wouldn't be able to tell until I got them to our unit.

The man followed my gaze. "Lucky you came today," he said. "Two spoken for."

I felt a shiver run through me. I hoped the backup team had heard that. If we did this right, we would get not only the distributors, but some of the buyers as well.

"Have they chosen their creatures?" I asked, keeping my voice girlish and eager.

He shook his head. "Too risky. Must always be done in person. Sometimes people change their minds."

He was looking at me as he said that last, as if he sensed something, my sadness perhaps. I'd always had trouble hiding it on cases like this. "The Ce'nark is for my brother," I said, to cover the emotion. "I told you he was ill, didn't I?"

The man frowned. "Better he be here, then. Ce'narks only bond a few times."

"But these are babies," I said. "Surely they're unbonded."

He shrugged. "Found them. Do not know what happened to their unit. Perhaps bonded and died. Perhaps."

"These are litter mates?"

"No," he said, then his frown grew deeper. "Do not know. Found together."

"Oh, so they must be." Probably not. Probably they were captured, their parents killed. That was the normal way of these things. The sadness filled me again.

Where was the backup team?

"You should see closer."

I didn't want to, but I could tell he was getting suspicious. I had to stall somehow. I glanced at them. The Ce'narks were the size of basset hounds. They would grow double that size, get fangs, and lose some of the rolly polly cuteness that made them so popular among humans. But that would happen gradually. Ce'narks had a life span of fifty plus years, and didn't lose their baby cuteness until they were nearly ten. Then they were abandoned, and often died, because the bonding was broken.

"You said you found them. Does that mean they don't have paperwork?"

"Told you in e-mail these were not official."

"But how am I supposed to get them to Armstrong?"

He measured me for a moment. "You have coin?"

Coin. I hadn't heard that term in years. "Credit," I said. "Earth funds, mostly European Union currency, although I can get it transferred into Galaxy Exchange."

"Good enough." He was watching me. "If you have coin, you can get papers."

"But they won't be official."

"You want official, buy from authorized store."

And, we both knew that the authorized pet stores did not sell infant Ce'narks. "My brother really wants this."

"Then you use coin."

"Credit," I said.

"Credit," he said, nodding.

"You can set me up with the papers?"

"Yes," he said.

"And they'll be official enough to get the Ce'nark from here to the Moon?"

"Yes," he said. "Done it before."

That was enough. That was more than enough. Where was the backup?

"You want to see now?"

I couldn't think of an excuse to stay away. I didn't glance at the door—I was too much of a pro for that—but I was counting the seconds. A vibration tingled through my skin. The signal. They were delayed.

He crossed his arms. "You don't want Ce'nark, do you? Why you here?"

I swallowed. I was on my own for a few more minutes. "I—I don't want to bond to my brother's pet."

He tilted his head. "You have no choice. It bonds on the way to Moon."

"Then it's not worth the sale to me. It needs to bond to my brother."

"They bond more than once. Three, sometimes four."

"But you said you didn't know how often—"

"These are babies. They not bond much yet."

Still nothing. The vibration continued, soft and subtle. Something in that worried me.

"Come." He took my arm and led me to the Ce'narks. I couldn't even activate my own emergency warning. Damn. I would have to play along with this.

I walked toward the babies. They smelled faintly of cinnamon and fresh bread—another early selling point to humans. Later, when the Ce'nark went through puberty, the scents would solidify into something closer to spoiled milk, something only the toughest human nose could handle.

"Aren't they cute?" I said, mostly because it was expected of me, and dropped on my knees outside the cage.

The Ce'narks all looked at me, their round orange eyes liquid and somehow lonely. They had brown snouts and small thin lips over rounded teeth. Ce'narks were usually fed by their parents for the first five years. They didn't get their real teeth until they were seven.

"What do I feed it?" I asked.

"Which one?" he said.

"Hmm?"

"Which one you want? Then we talk food."

The vibration had stopped. The backup was coming. League rules didn't allow me to make an arrest until they arrived. In fact, I wouldn't be making the arrest at all. It kept my face off the vids, nets and links, kept my undercover intact.

"That one," I said, pointing to the thin one in the back. It did appeal to me. Its face was rounder, its eyes wider. It had been staring at me since I arrived.

"Good," he said, and reached into the cage. Before I realized what he was doing, he picked up the Ce'nark and placed it in my arms.

I swore under my breath. The Ce'nark was warm and its skin soft. Its fur was even soft, with that silky thin texture that long-haired human newborns had. It snuggled against me, rooting in the way of mammals, looking for a nipple, looking for food. Its bones stood out in sharp relief to its skin, and the nails on its toes were flaking. It was malnourished.

"What do I feed it?" I asked again.

At that moment, the door burst open. The backup team was in. Five men and two women. George was behind them, looking at me with great disapproval.

The leader of the backup team and another team member took my contact outside to make the live net record of his arrest. Three of the men and one of the women searched the rest of the dwelling for accomplices and information. The remaining woman placed the other two Ce'narks in specially constructed cages. I crouched, trying to hand her mine, when she shook her head.

"It's yours now," she said.

"Mine? But I can't—"

"You have to," she said, her tone flat. "It's already bonded."

———

Ce'narks ate pulped branches of local bushes called mikiles mixed with snow and some leaves for flavor. Unfortunately, the mother Ce'nark was the one who pulped the branch, and it wasn't until infant Ce'narks started to die in large numbers that our scientists realized the mother's saliva was an essential part of the infant's nutrition. A formula was developed that imitated the saliva's benefits, as best as humanly possible of course. There were several side effects, most considered fortunate by human authorities. The severest was that any Ce'nark infant raised on the formula would grow up sterile.

Luckily our team had been planning to pick up live Ce'nark infants, and had a small compound prepared. The two unbonded infants were placed in a wide cage filled with snow and several warm beds to mimic their homes in the wild. The bonded infant remained with me.

Lenie Davis, the woman in charge of the Reclamation Unit, had given me a Ce'nark tank, and instructed me to sit in it. The tank had a self-contained snow-filled area, and a warm sleepers' area. It covered half my tiny living quarters, barely leaving me enough room for the bed.

I sat inside the tank, cradling the Ce'nark, and tried to feed it the formulaic paste that Lenie had given me. The Ce'nark sniffed the paste, and then would reach toward my mouth as if to take it from my lips. The creature wouldn't eat from my hands.

"You'll have to feed it properly." Lenie's clipped British vowels gave her voice an air of command that no one else in the unit had.

"Properly?" I asked, knowing somehow what she meant.

"It wants to eat the way it was taught. It'll die if it doesn't." She came around the tank so that I could see her. She was wearing a gray single piece made of soft fur, the uniform of the Reclamation team. It mimicked, as best as humanly possible, the skin of an adult Ce'nark.

"Why don't you do it?" I asked.

"Because it's bonded to you."

I gazed at the little creature. It touched my mouth again, and mewled. I sighed.

I was thirty-five years old, unmarried, and childless. On purpose. I had joined the undercover squad when I was fifteen so that I wouldn't have any ties. I didn't need any ties. I had seen, in the Colony Riots on the Moon, what happened to people who were tied to others. My entire family died in those Riots. It was an experience I didn't need to have again.

"Can't it bond to someone else?"

"Maybe," Lenie leaned over the edge of the tank. "But do you really want to risk its life on that?"

I stared at her. We had had this discussion twice, and apparently she was ready to have it the third time. We had no idea how this Ce'nark was taken from its family. That bond remained. That bond would always remain. But if it had bonded to its kidnappers or to anyone else along the way, we couldn't tell. And Ce'narks only bonded a few times. Those bonds were life. A Ce'nark didn't eat without someone bonded near it, or drink, or sleep. Unbonded Ce'narks died within days.

Lenie hypothesized that the unbonded pair we had in the other tank had, in reality, bonded to each other. That would create a problem later, if their families were found. It might solve a problem if their families were not.

"Rather frightening to know you hold someone's life in your hands, isn't it?" she asked.

"It happens to me a lot," I said, and I wasn't bragging. That Ce'nark trafficker owed his life to me. I could have killed him after he confessed and not gotten in trouble. There was precedent for that.

"Yes," Lenie said. "I suppose it does. You choose to kill or not to kill. But I'll wager you've never been forced to nurture before. That's as important to life as your usual choice."

I knew that. I knew it and had always avoided it. I was not a nurturer. "Maybe I could watch while you—?"

The Ce'nark put its fur-covered fingers in my mouth, stood on its hind feet and peered inside. It mewled again.

"No," Lenie said. "You have to."

I grimaced, looking at the pink paste that coated my right hand. "This stuff won't hurt me, will it?"

Lenie laughed. "No."

I raised my hand, wincing as I did so, the smell of cinnamon, burnt plastic, and pond scum wafting toward me. The little creature drooled as it watched.

I scraped the paste off my hand with my teeth, then leaned

forward, careful to keep my tongue away from the stuff. Not that it mattered much. The paste tasted like it smelled, and it had the consistency of overcooked oatmeal.

The Ce'nark cooed and fished a handful out of my mouth with its little fingers. Its tiny nails dug into my gums.

"Ouch!" I said, pulling back.

The Ce'nark stopped and looked at me. I had to be going crazy. It looked concerned.

"I—um—it's all right," I said.

The creature chirruped, then mimicked my action, scraping the paste into its mouth with its teeth. It chewed happily for a moment, then rooted in my mouth for more.

This was the most disgusting procedure I had gone through in twenty years of undercover work on six planets. And that was saying something.

"You're getting the hang of it," Lenie said. "You'll be a bond-pair in no time."

"I think we already are," I said, then cursed as my tongue hit the remains of the paste. I was wrong. The stuff tasted worse than it smelled. Like someone had added one part vermouth and two parts fish oil to the cinnamon, burnt plastic, and pond scum.

The Ce'nark made a sound between a giggle and a chirrup—it seemed delighted by the look of disgust that I made—and then it scraped the last of the paste out of my mouth.

"How do I teach it to stay clear of the gums?" I asked.

"They don't have gums," she said. "Not like we do. It's not a natural motion. We don't want to teach it too much in the hopes it can return to the wild."

"In the meantime, I lose half the protective layer over my teeth."

"We have a salve for it."

The Ce'nark patted my face with its clean hand, then climbed off my lap and went to its warm sleeping nest.

"You'll have to follow it, and tuck it in," Lenie said.

"For heaven's sake—"

"It's a Ce'nark ritual. Why do you think early colonists took to the beasties?"

I glared at her then followed the Ce'nark. The marvels of modern technology. The sleeping nest somehow mimicked the hot air pockets found throughout the snow-covered wilds of K'dar'Ak. The Ce'nark only lived in the north, and in the summer had to sleep elsewhere. Nothing lived in the southern climes of this hemisphere. The entire ground there was steam muck and air so hot that it could burn the skin off an unprotected human in a matter of minutes.

I patted the Ce'nark three times, then smoothed its fur. It ran a pink-coated blue tongue over its lips, smacking them slightly, then cooing at me. After a moment, its eyes closed and it assumed the rigid, death-like posture the Ce'narks held in sleep.

"I'll never get used to that," I said.

"Vestigial hibernation," Lenie said. "One of those once-important traits that isn't necessary any more but remains encoded. Rather like our need to put on fat six months of every year."

I patted the Ce'nark once more for good measure, then stood. My knees cracked as I did so. "I do know something about Ce'narks," I said.

"Oh?" Lenie asked.

"I knew that last one."

She smiled, but it didn't quite reach her eyes. "You can get out of there now."

I did. Climbing out of the tank was harder than getting in. The plastic walls were higher on the inside than on the out. The flooring was recessed inside the tank.

I had to lever myself over the edge. Lenie didn't give me any assistance.

"I'd offer you something to drink, but my entire kitchen and living area has been subsumed by this damn tank."

She nodded, and sat at the edge of my bed. I couldn't leave the Ce'nark. To do that would kill it also, if it hadn't bonded with anyone else. In their first three years of life, infant Ce'narks were never alone.

I hadn't known that when I walked toward that cage this afternoon. If I had, I wouldn't have gone near the little creature.

"I've been speaking to your supervisor," she said. "The arrest was a good one. You got the leader of one of the animal theft rings on K'dar'Ak, as well as several of his accomplices and buyers. The folks upstairs think there'll be a lot more arrests before this is through. Good job."

I continued standing, leaning against the wall so that I could see her clearly, as well as the tank. I crossed my arms. "So why are you telling me this instead of George?"

She looked down at her hands, spread out before her as if she were examining her nails. "George sent me."

"Obviously. Why?"

"I reviewed the vid record of this arrest. You did everything by the book. You could have avoided touching the Ce'nark, but that would have meant that we would have lost the accomplices and probably the buyers. We would only have captured the supplier, and that's not enough, certainly, to justify the expense we went to."

"I know that," I said, keeping my voice deliberately dry.

She raised her head. "I'm trying to tell you not to blame yourself."

"For?"

"The choices you're now going to have to make."

I felt the muscles in my back tense. "Go on."

"These Ce'narks are young, and still quite close to their original bondings. If the suppliers didn't touch the families, the Ce'narks have a good chance of being returned to the wild."

"Excellent." I didn't want a Ce'nark around. It didn't suit my job.

"For now," she said, "you're being assigned to the Reclamation team."

"Nice try," I said, "but I stay with the undercover unit."

"It's not an offer," she said. "It's an order. You can log on later to verify."

A chill ran through me. Things didn't usually work this way. Usually a service requested me, and I could choose or deny the job.

"Why?" I asked.

She nodded toward the tank. "It may take us a week to find its family unit. We may not find any of its family at all. If that's the case, the Ce'nark will die without its bonded caretaker."

She left the third option unsaid, the most likely option. That the Ce'nark's tribal unit had been slaughtered during the theft of the infant.

I was being manipulated into a place I vowed I would never go. "It's young. Why don't we see if it can bond to someone else before we leave the base? Then you can take it into the wild and I can go to my next assignment."

She shook her head. "It's too risky. If it fails to bond, we've wasted precious time. Judging from the infants' behavior and from the way that this one bonded to you, they'd only been in custody a day, maybe less."

"Nonsense," I said. "The supplier contacted me a week ago, promising me an infant Ce'nark."

"That's right."

"And he said he had one."

"That's right too. He was probably monitoring a tribe, and he knew that he could get the infants fresh before you arrived. That way they wouldn't seem too sickly for the buyer, and if they later died unbonded they would die due to the buyer's 'lack of care' rather than the supplier's carelessness."

"Ruthless son of a bitch," I muttered.

"Exactly," she said. "But what that means is that the tribe is probably still in the area. We can find them. But we're almost out of time."

"And I have to come with you."

"With your infant." She stood. "It's either that, or you get to keep it. Do it my way and you may get your old life back. Do it your way and you're assigned to desk duty until you die or the Ce'nark bonds to someone else."

I glanced at the small sleeping creature. It was cute, right, but that was all. Cute and vulnerable and worrisome. It had no place in my life.

"I don't want to do this."

"Think of it as part of your undercover assignment," she said. "I'll download the information you need, as well as the equipment you'll be required to bring along. And I'll make sure we have the materials for care of the Ce'nark."

"You're not going to take no for an answer, are you?"

"Why should I?" she asked. "If you keep that Ce'nark, we've undermined the point of that entire raid."

"We still would have arrested the supplier and his team."

"And kept a Ce'nark for a pet, something we've railed against for nearly a decade now. How hypocritical is that?" She glanced at me. "Not becoming attached, are you, Marisa?"

I snorted. "No."

"Good," she said. "Because it wouldn't make any difference if you were. The Ce'nark is going home."

She headed toward the door. "See you in the staging area at 0500 sharp."

And then she let herself out. 0500. That gave the Ce'nark some sleep and me almost none. I sat on the edge of my bed near the warm spot that Lenie had left.

I didn't want to go with a Reclamation team. I had managed to avoid that part of my training by volunteering from my first undercover assignment. I was as unprepared as a rookie, and I hadn't had that kind of disadvantage in years. I wouldn't be in charge of the unit; I'd be the junior member.

With a Ce'nark that ate seven meals a day.

I winced at the thought of that paste. Then I got up, grabbed my palmtop, and scanned the information that Lenie had downloaded for me.

———

When I showed up at the staging area, my tongue was numb from the taste of that paste. The Ce'nark was cooing and pointing, although I didn't know if the gesture meant anything or not. If it were a human child or a monkey, I would have known its interest in its surroundings by those gestures. But it was neither, and the more time I spent with the creature the clearer that became.

We had both been up an hour. I spent some of that time feeding the Ce'nark and the rest trying to catch it to get it out of the tank. If I had known that the little thing wanted to run after it ate, I would have fed it last, then carried it out of the tank. As it was, I arrived at the staging area exhausted and more than a little annoyed.

The Ce'nark wrapped all four of its limbs around me and hid its eyes against my shoulder as we stepped into the light.

The staging area was an unheated bunker, empty except for the team—six of us, counting me—and the lightweight white glider trucks especially built for work on K'dar'Ak. We were given two trucks for this mission. One to remain at the point of entry as a backup and guard, and the other to go in as far as the environmental laws allowed.

We didn't want to scare the Ce'nark, but we did want to find them.

I wore a white parka and snow pants. The parka had attached mittens that doubled as hand warmers and a self-sealing hood with a five-hour oxygen supply. The pants had a boot feature that could, in a pinch, cover the feet with a thin layer of thermal material. It wasn't great protection, but it would do if something did happen to my regular boots.

We also had emergency rations stored flat in the pockets, enough to get us through two days of great conservation. The trucks carried most everything else, including our daily rations and heat tents, as well as small tank for the unbonded Ce'narks. Lenie informed me that my Ce'nark would sleep with me "just like in the wild."

I had no rational response to that, so I said nothing. I got into the truck as assigned. The seats were long and unpadded. There were no windows. There was a small cold tank for the Ce'nark to use as it needed. We were only supposed to be traveling a short time, but there was no guarantee. If we found a trace of the tribe, we might be following it for most of the week.

Four of us rode in the back of this truck. Lenie and one other rode with the other two Ce'narks in the second truck. I sat nearest the tank. The Ce'nark kept its face hidden in my parka, clinging to me as if it thought I would leave in an instant. The truck rose, then clanged as the wheels folded beneath it, setting off on a smooth glide. The movement made the Ce'nark cling even harder, and I wondered if I would be bruised in the morning.

The others were trained Reclamation workers. Two women, Hildy and Betty, sat side by side, and spoke quietly in a language I didn't know. The only man in this group, Nathan, slept. No one talked to me. They all avoided looking at the Ce'nark.

The Ce'nark's breathing eased, and I realized that it too slept. Despite my own lack of sleep, I sat stiffly, not quite comfortable on the rough seats, going over the mission.

They had denied me a weapon, worried, I suppose, that I would accidentally kill Ce'narks. I knew better than that, but expected the treatment. I was the rookie after all, and I was the one bonded to a Ce'nark, justifiably or not. It was, according to the manual I had downloaded sometime during the night, so taboo among Reclamation officers that any who made such a mistake were banned from the core for life.

Thank the higher powers that I was working enforcement undercover, not Reclamation. I would lose this badge as soon as I lost the creature.

My chances of that were pretty good. Reclamation had reintroduced 85% of recovered Ce'narks to the wild. Ce'nark family units had a definable DNA trace, as well as a distinct pheromone, easily measured. The Reclamation units used the pheromone to make sure the recovered Ce'narks were with the correct family; if the unit had any concerns at all, it would take a DNA sample, usually from hair in the nest, and confirm from there.

Recovered Ce'narks were usually tagged with green environmental bracelets for easy visual identification, and a subcutaneous chip so that the movements of the tribes could be monitored. The chip had the added benefit of letting the Reclamation folks know if any Ce'nark found dead was one accidentally placed with the wrong family group. So far that had never happened.

I had one of the bracelets for my Ce'nark. It had already received its subcutaneous chip, in its initial examination after it was brought to the Reclamation site.

The Ce'nark's warm body seemed to grow even hotter in sleep. Its even breathing inspired my own; its primary heart, pounding against mine, seemed to calm me as well. Before I knew it, I had fallen asleep. I didn't wake up until we reached the field site, nearly three standard hours later.

———

The field site was several kilometers past the village where I found the Ce'narks. We parked the trucks beneath some k'dar, their snow-covered branches providing great cover. We would have to go the rest of the way into the forest on foot.

The drivers remained with the trucks and were instructed to remain linked with us at all times. They were to monitor net-links, the open vid chips, and sound as well. At any sign of trouble they were either to send for help or to come in after us.

That part of the plan seemed fairly standard to me. Traveling in such a large group—seven humans, counting me, and three Ce'narks—seemed unusual. Lenie had brought a specially built glide sled for the unbonded Ce'narks, as well as glide shoes for us. We weren't to leave a trace of ourselves on the snow-covered landscape, except, of course, if we needed to camp. Even then, we had to follow special double-blind procedures.

As the group started its preparations, I fed my Ce'nark and winced as it nicked my gums again. At least I was getting used to the taste of that damn paste. When it was done, the Ce'nark patted my face with its clean hand, and tried to climb down so that it could run around.

I didn't let it go.

As I climbed out of the truck, extending one hand for balance and keeping the other beneath the Ce'nark so that I didn't drop it, I paused and watched the efficient movements of the team. It was clear I wasn't a part of the group; I was there only as the Ce'nark's bonded pair, an inconvenience, an embarrassment. I said nothing as I put on my glide shoes beneath my boots and tested the strength of the glide field before leaving the staging area.

The air here was even colder than it had been in the village, but the wet wool smell was gone. Only processed k'dar smelled that way. Here, in the wild, it had an almost minty tang, a freshness that I associated with my springs in Canada instead of the dead of winter on the coldest side of one of the coldest planets we had yet discovered.

As the fresh air hit us, the Ce'nark raised its head. It made a guttural sound, almost a question against the back of its throat. It looked around, and then wailed so loud I nearly dropped it.

"What the hell did you do?" Lenie asked.

"Nothing." I kept my hand on the Ce'nark's back, patting it as if it were a newborn human that needed to be burped. The wail continued for another minute longer, and then faded into a hiccup. The Ce'nark rested its head on my shoulder and brought one of its hands up to its face. It peered at the nearby forest through its splayed fingers, and its breathing grew rapid.

The other Ce'narks, already in their sled, raised their heads at the sound of the wail. They too splayed their fingers over their faces and looked to the woods.

"I've never seen anything like that," Nathan said softly. The only other man on the team, Luc, put his hand over his face, splayed the fingers and looked as well.

"It creates a slight distortion," he said. "You can separate out the lines of the k'dar from the snow itself this way."

"You think they're looking for more Ce'nark?" Betty asked.

"It seems likely."

"Never speculate," Hildy said. "You know that." And Lenie nodded, but they all looked in the direction of the woods, the direction we were going to go, the direction that had so disturbed my Ce'nark.

Its primary heart was beating so rapidly that I worried for its health. Behind the primary beat was a softer counter rhythm, the secondary heart, the feature that someone had once told me gave the Ce'nark their incredible resilience to any sort of external damage. It took a direct wound through one of the hearts to cripple a Ce'nark. It took wounds through both hearts to kill one instantly. Otherwise, Ce'narks did not die suddenly in the wild. They died in their nests of old age. Often they lingered after one heart failed, sometimes for years, and tended the young in the warmth of the sleeping nests while the parents and bonding pairs hunted and searched for food.

It was an efficient system. Or it had been, until we came along.

Lenie squared her shoulders. "Let's go," she said, and pushed off the nearest truck.

Moving in glide shoes was a lot like skating. It required balance and rhythm and a bit of grace. Betty and Nathan pulled the Ce'nark sled. Luc kept pace with Lenie, and Hildy brought up the rear. I remained in the middle, my balance slightly compromised by the Ce'nark who protested at the unusual movement. It pulled its hand off its face and clung to me as we went, squeaking softly under its breath as we went into the first row of k'dar.

K'dar did most of its growing in the winter, adding bark and long trailing branches covered in snow. Going into a k'dar forest was like going into a tunnel made almost entirely of ice, bark, and snow. There was no wind here, and sounds made a strange echo.

We left no imprint on the snow's crust, but the signs of the supplier's team were everywhere. They didn't use glide shoes because they didn't have to. They used regular boots and left footprints behind them. As we passed over their trail, Luc pointed down. I looked as I passed. There was the track of an illegal ground vehicle on the snow's surface. They had taken the Ce'nark out rapidly in some sort of mechanized conveyance. That set the timeline for the kidnapping of the Ce'nark as sometime between my on-planet call, and my arrival at the supplier's door two hours later.

Luc led us over the track. Betty peered at everything with the intensity of someone who was making a record. My Ce'nark whimpered, its face buried against my shoulder, its small hands clinging to me so tightly that I was afraid it would rip holes in my parka unit.

By the time we reached the end of the k'dar tunnel, the other two Ce'narks were holding each other, faces buried. The minty tang was gone from the air as if it had never been. It was not replaced by another smell—and that was odd. It almost felt as if there were a smell overlying the tang, but it wasn't something that I could identify.

The track beneath us veered to the right. Luc followed it, disappearing through a small opening in the k'dar canopy. Lenie followed. Nathan and Betty had trouble getting the sled through, but they managed. I started into the canopy when my Ce'nark screamed. It let go of me and grabbed the frozen branches rooting us in place. Hildy had to glide halfway up a nearby branch to avoid hitting us.

"What the—?" she asked.

I didn't know but I had a guess. I patted the Ce'nark's back, murmuring soothing noises, and slowly tried to disengage its fingers. Every time I loosened one, its grip tightened. Finally, in exasperation, Hildy broke the branches my Ce'nark held.

"We weren't supposed to leave signs of our presence," I said.

"As if that's going to matter," she said, looking at the track we were following.

She had a point. I moved before the Ce'nark had a chance to grab more branches. I glided a few meters, and stopped at the opening to a clearing.

Lenie and the others had stopped here too. The Ce'narks in the sled were completely woven together, their heads hidden inside the tangle of limbs. It was a protective posture; if they had been on the snow, they would have blended in.

Sort of.

For the snow was pocked and melted and covered with black, frozen Ce'nark blood. The remains of half a dozen Ce'narks—I could guess that many by the heads—littered the snow.

My Ce'nark was trembling in my grasp, its head pushing against my chest as if it wanted to hide inside.

I knew that feeling. It had haunted my dreams for decades. I had tried to hide my face in the stomach of a man who had pulled me out of the remains of my family's bungalow. I was emaciated and covered in week-old blood. I remembered nothing from the moment the raiders slaughtered my brother—the last of the family to die—and the man's arms around me one week later.

Nothing, except the need to bury myself, to hide, to never, ever come out.

"I had no idea they killed this way," I said, mostly to keep myself in the present. I knew that the raiders sometimes slaughtered adult Ce'narks, but I hadn't realized that they had used high-powered laser guns with a wide charge that effectively exploded the animal's entire abdomen, exploding both hearts at once. "Now how do we find—?"

I wasn't able to finish the question. An adult Ce'nark leapt from the frozen top of the k'dar, and landed on Luc's back, stabbing him through the neck with a sharpened k'dar stick. Dozens of other Ce'narks dropped around us. Hildy screamed behind me, the sound cut off abruptly. Nathan and Betty crouched protectively near the sled and Lenie started in their direction. Five Ce'narks—the size of small adult humans—barred her way, growling and waving sticks at her.

She stopped, looked at us, and held her hands out in a gesture of peace.

I turned, hoping to lead the way back. Hildy was on the snow behind me, a stick through her open mouth. She was batting at the edge of the wood feebly, but it was clear the effort wouldn't work. I crouched beside her, and she grabbed my hand.

My Ce'nark kept clinging to me, and the other Ce'narks stared at me, but did not approach.

Behind me, Lenie screamed. Her scream mingled with another, and then another, this one male. The Ce'narks were attacking Nathan and Betty too.

But not me.

They stared at me. Their orange eyes were flat and their fangs bared. It was hard to see them against the white ice covering the k'dar branches. Their sticks were the only things that marked them as Ce'narks. Their sticks, their orange eyes, and the green bracelets around their right wrists.

Hildy's grip loosened on mine. Her eyes were open and glazed. I'd seen that look a hundred times before, first on my family, and then on others.

I shook myself. If I didn't stay here, in the present, I would die with the group. The present. I turned toward the Ce'narks. Never in all our contact with them, had we encountered Ce'narks that attacked. I had learned that in my reading the night before.

So what made these—?

A Ce'nark raised its stick, its green bracelet flashing against the white snow.

The bracelet. I shivered. I was having trouble breathing, but I figured that was as much from the atmosphere as from my own adrenaline.

I slid my hand out of Hildy's, and headed for the sled. The Ce'narks followed. Nathan was defending himself with a bloodied stick. Lenie was rolled in a ball, a stick protruding from her hip.

Betty was missing.

I noted all of that in a matter of moments. I grabbed the sled and pulled it into the clearing—

—as a heat explosion destroyed branches above me. The drivers. They were coming to help us as instructed.

The last thing we needed was help. It would only make things worse.

"Stop!" I yelled. "Stop!"

I saw the first, his head coming through the canopy, the Ce'narks hurrying toward him.

"Go away!" I screamed. "Now!"

"But—"

"Go! They're defending themselves. They'll slaughter you!"

He didn't have to be told twice. His head disappeared so fast I realized he too was using illegal snow equipment. I continued pulling the sled into the bloody clearing.

Then I stopped, leaving it in the center. I disentangled the Ce'nark from me—it wailed as I did so—and placed it with the others. It sat at the edge of the sled and rocked, its mouth open in a circle of pain.

I left it there—I left all three of them there—and backed away. The adult Ce'narks were watching me, but they weren't going to the infants.

They weren't attacking any more either.

I sat down, even though my pumping adrenaline told me not to. I sat down, and I waited. They watched me. It was a stalemate, punctuated by the shivering sobs of the two clinging infant Ce'nark. I had to let the adults know that this was not a trap. They had their children back. They didn't have to fight us.

I studied them for a moment, my gaze on the sticks. Their orange eyes met my gaze, and it seemed as if they were waiting too. But for what?

My Ce'nark was watching me as well, rocking, its mouth still open. They all expected me to do something. But what? Did they think I had set up a trap? How did I convince them it wasn't?

And then I knew.

I reached inside the pocket of my parka and removed the bracelet for my Ce'nark. I held it up in front of attacking Ce'narks.

And then I tossed it toward the sled.

The bracelet spun in mid-air. It looked foreign and out of place, gray against all that white. It rose high, crested, and fell. It didn't land in the snow. It broke the crust and slipped in, disappearing beside the sled.

My Ce'nark looked at me and raised its hands toward me like a child wanting to be picked up. The adult Ce'narks looked at it, then looked at me, and scurried across the destroyed expanse of snow.

They surrounded the sled, grabbed the two unattached Ce'nark infants, and hurried away, leaving mine. It still reached for me.

"Go." The voice was soft, raspy, almost a whisper.

It was Lenie. She had crawled closer to me, one hand on her hip. She had left a bloody trail in the snow.

"Go to it," she said. "They wouldn't take it. That means it has no one."

But me. That was what she implied. No one but me.

I crossed the snow, my heart pounding. There was no sign of the other Ce'narks. It was as if they hadn't been here at all.

I bent toward it, and it grabbed me, nearly pulling me down. Then it climbed up my parka until it was inside my arms, holding my neck and forcing my face beside its. It ran its hands over my skin, touching me as if it had thought it would never see me again.

It was trembling.

So was I.

It didn't look at the bodies in the snow, the Ce'nark bodies, but I did. And I thought I recognized the faces. The mother. The father. The siblings. All destroyed.

Forever.

I wrapped my arms around the Ce'nark, and carried it back to the group. As I did, I used my security links to signal the drivers that it was safe now. A vibration ran through my arm, signaling their affirmative response. They would be coming soon, with something to get the wounded out of here.

While I waited, I performed some rudimentary first aid on Lenie, used snow to stop Nathan's bleeding, and found Betty uninjured but pinned by sticks through her clothing deep within the canopy. Luc and Hildy were dead.

Through it all, the Ce'nark shuddered against me, its tiny hands clinging so tightly that at one point, I thought it would shut off my air. The drivers showed up, and loaded the wounded into the trucks.

The Ce'nark and I sat up front. No one spoke to me. They look at the Ce'nark as my failure, the deaths as my fault. No one saw that without me, the entire team would have died.

But I didn't say anything. I couldn't say anything. When we

returned to the compound, I went to my room and fed the Ce'nark in its tank.

And waited.

———

The downloadable information on infant Ce'narks had to do with their physical care, but not their emotional states. My Ce'nark was unwilling to let me go. I had to sleep in its nest, take sponge baths because Ce'narks couldn't cope with warm water, and feed it by hand every two hours. Nothing seemed to ease its need to hold me, nothing at all.

Five days into my ordeal, Lenie showed up. She was limping, but otherwise seemed fine. She came into my room without waiting for an invitation, and sat on my bed as she had before.

"You saved our lives," she said. Somehow the acknowledgment, coming so late, meant little. I had had time to think, and I realized that my actions were only a small part of the drama that had taken place in the k'dar woods.

"The Ce'nark saved you," I said. "They looked at me as one of them, a part of a bonded pair."

She sighed and stood. "The Ce'narks learned that behavior from us. I reviewed the vids. They were wearing bracelets. They were some of the Ce'narks we returned to the wild."

"They were defending themselves."

She looked at me.

I shrugged. "It's not speculation. It's obvious." I shifted my Ce'nark to my other arm. I was finally beginning to get used to its weight. "Now you can seal off the k'dar forests, use the video proof that Ce'narks are violent and dangerous."

"And condemn hundreds of them to death when their bonded humans abandon them?" she asked.

"They won't be abandoned," I said. "Not if you word the release right."

She closed her eyes. "Human-raised infants are fine?"

"Yes."

"A ruling that will lead to more poaching."

"I doubt the poachers will live through it," I said.

Her eyes opened. The Ce'nark had changed. We had changed them. By stealing their young, slaughtering their adults. By bringing death into their midst.

She raised a hand, and ran it along my Ce'nark's head. "Have you named her yet?"

"Her?"

She tilted the Ce'nark's head slightly, revealing pink ridges in the throat. "Her. The sexual characteristics are forming now."

"She won't let me go. I think she's traumatized."

Lenie's gaze met mine. Then she looked away, and held out her hands as if they were more interesting than our conversation.

"The vid gives us more information than we've ever had on Ce'narks in the wild." She was telling me something, something else beneath her words. "They use tools. They can communicate well enough to plan an attack."

"They waited in ambush," I said.

"They understood what you were telling them when you threw that bracelet. They understood that we were returning the infants, not stealing them." She closed her hands into fists. "We thought because of the rigidity of their bonding, because infants in captivity retained their infant behavior as adults much like domesticated Earth animals, that they had limited intelligence. We were wrong."

I waited. I had never heard a Reclamation officer admit a mistake.

"Do you know what this means?" she asked.

I did. It meant a higher level of prosecution for anyone caught kidnapping infant Ce'narks. It meant murder charges for anyone who killed one.

It meant that, good intentioned or not, we had enslaved a sentient race.

I wrapped my arms around my Ce'nark. She sighed and leaned her head against me. "What do I do about her?"

"I don't know," Lenie said. "This is new to us. We have to throw out most of what we know."

I said, because I had to, because I couldn't keep quiet: "There were tests, you know. That slaughtered group of Ce'narks. It was her family."

"I doubt she'll ever bond again." She didn't look at me as she said that. She wiped her hands on her skirt, and then she stood. "I'm sorry, Marisa."

I stood too. I didn't know what else to do. She had just made it clear to me that everything was different now. To abandon my Ce'nark was to condemn her to death. And if I did that, I would be charged with the murder of a sentient being.

I placed my hand on the back of the Ce'nark's head. She snuggled closer. As if I could have abandoned her anyway. I had taken my job to prevent the harming of innocents, not to harm them myself. I just hadn't expected to have to care for one, especially not one as delicate as my Ce'nark.

"What happens to me now?" I asked. "I mean, I've got her."

"Yes," Lenie said. "You do."

"And I can't give her up, can I?"

Lenie shook her head.

"She changes everything."

Lenie's smile was gentle. "Infants usually do."

———

I work on Earth now. Iceland, Finland, Norway. Some parts of Siberia, Alaska and any other cold climate my bosses can think of. Most of the Ce'nark owners live in these climates. Those that don't are rich enough to create the proper natural environment for the Ce'nark in the hottest climates. Someone else worries about them.

My job is subtler now. I infiltrate Ce'nark shows and vet clinics; I start neighborhood clubs for Ce'nark owners. Some I educate in the art of caring for another sentient being. Others I turn in for all sorts of flagrant abuses.

Celine, my Ce'nark, has slowly come to like this life. She has spotted problems long before I ever would. I guess her early life attuned her to them.

Oh, she still has nightmares. Awful, horrible nightmares. Sometimes I hear that wail echoing from her tank. I wake her and hold her, and she shivers in my arms.

And sometimes, truth be told, she wakes me in just the same way, from a nearly identical dream.

There was a reason we bonded. A reason she chose me above all the other humans she saw. We're just beginning to understand that Ce'nark see even more than we do when they look at someone else. They see matching patterns. They see similar needs.

They communicate on several more levels.

She doesn't like Earth. There are too many humans here for her, and we're much too violent. We've always been more violent than Ce'narks have.

I've promised her an early retirement. Lenie's promised me work in Ce'nark research on K'dar'Ak. But I doubt I'll take her up on it. I don't like the quiet life. It gives me too much time to think. Too much time to feel. And neither Celine nor I like to feel much.

We're alike in that too.

I'm still not sure I understand nurturing. But I understand bonding. I just hadn't realized that humans did it too. We're not as obvious about it as Ce'narks, but we're just as rigid about it.

Only most of us haven't realized it yet.

Sometimes I miss the undercover work. But only sometimes.

Mostly I just wonder how I ever managed all those years—alone.

WHAT FLUFFY KNEW

KRISTINE KATHRYN RUSCH

WHAT FLUFFY KNEW

Fluffy knew she was a princess. Her person told her so. And Fluffy herself could see it, in her white, white fur, her long elegant whiskers, and her dainty paws. Fluffy had a soft bed that smelled of cedar. She had as much food as she wanted. People came to her house, and when she presented herself, they all spoke in awe of her beauty and petted her gingerly, as if they couldn't believe they were allowed to touch her sacred body. She bumped them gently to let them know that petting was preferred in her kingdom, and they usually responded with a laugh and a good ear rub.

Life was good. It didn't even matter that her people occasionally took in other cats. There had been other cats in her life as long as she was alive. She knew, however, that they weren't as great as she was. No other cat was as beautiful or as soft or as well loved. Other cats lived with her, and she tolerated them. She would have put up a large fuss, but her people had found a new palace, one with many rooms, and she rarely saw the other cats, except at feeding times.

Her routine was perfect in its simplicity. She spent her mornings in the kitchen waiting for someone to brush her, her afternoons sprawled on the couch in the warm sunshine, and her evenings on the nearest lap. Sometimes she watched the water droplets in the bathtub after her people took showers.

Nights were her special time. She prowled and explored, took food her people sometimes left near the sink, and occasionally slept on their soft bed. She was in her cedar bed at dawn just to make sure no one else used it, and then she was up, beginning her routine all over again.

Yes. It was a very good life.

Until *they* came.

———

"Please give the boys a thorough examination. I'll pay you extra. I know your time is limited when you do your house calls, and I appreciate the fact that so few vets do such a thing, but this has me bothered."

"Mrs. Winters, what's happened is tragic, but not uncommon. These adorable creatures are miniature lions. We think they're civilized, but they're not. And occasionally they remind us, often in particularly unpleasant ways."

———

They seemed to know who the weak ones were. Later, Fluffy found herself wondering: if she had known what *they* were going to do, would she have crushed *them* on that first day? Would she have stopped *them*? *They* were, after all, little bigger than a flea. But even fleas were hard to kill, weren't they? She had had fleas as a kitten, before she was elevated to her proper position, and she remembered the sudden sharp pain of the bite, the uncontrollable urge to scratch, the impossibility of catching a flea between your teeth. So perhaps she wouldn't have been able to do anything even if she had been paying attention. Even if she tried to stop the problem on the day it had started.

They went for her littermate, Streaker, and his little friend, Rook. Streaker's royal blood was diluted by his street tough father, a swaggering Tom that Fluffy barely remembered from her kittenhood. Her own father was a sweet white cat, a little on the fat side, just as her mother was. A "Pedigreed Pair," her former people used to say. The litter, they said to the people who would become her people, was ruined by the black-and-white kitten. A Tom had gotten to their precious girl at the right time. So they had to give the kittens away, unable to prove the purity of their bloodline.

Her people didn't care. They liked the black-and-white kitten with the impish streak, and they named him Streaker because he liked to run from one end of the house to the other for no apparent reason. He refused to show her the proper respect, slapping at her when she got in his way, or demanding that she give up her food. His little friend Rook, a long-haired tabby, showed many of the same behaviors. Rook was a stray her people had rescued, and to them he was kind. To her, he was as insensitive as her brother.

But she could avoid them — and often did. Streak and Rook spent most of their time together, sleeping, eating, playing. She spent most of her time with her human companions, as it should be.

So the afternoon *they* appeared, she thought nothing of it.

———

"Yes, but they've never done anything like this before. I'm beginning to wonder if something's wrong —"

"Trust me, Mrs. Winters. We get complaints like this all the time when housecats show their animal natures. There's nothing wrong."

———

It was summer. Her favorite window was open, the one overlooking the garden and the birds. She could smell flowers, which sometimes made her sneeze; other cats, which always made her curious; and birds, which usually made her want to be slightly energetic, in a wholly disgusting way. She, as her people always told her, was a princess, and didn't have to kill her own food. The boys, as her people called Streaker and Rook, didn't quite understand that, but the other two cats, Starlight and Cupcake, did. They preferred to sleep and eat, just as she did, and fortunately for her, weren't as good at attracting pets.

She had been asleep in the sun below her favorite window when *they* arrived. Rook and Streaker were sprawled in the door, playing their nasty little game: Trap Fluffy. If she hissed at them, they would jump on her and pull at her fur. If she pretended not to notice, they would leave her alone and eventually grow tired of the game. She had decided not to notice, and the hot sun had put her to sleep.

A slight whirring sound woke her up. She sat up, stretched and saw a tiny machine, rather like the ones her people watched on the box in the living room, a round machine that had doors and windows too tiny for any cat to use.

The fur rose on the back of her neck and she felt a hiss start in the back of her throat. But something warned her not to hiss. She didn't want to call attention to herself. Instead, she slipped beneath the couch, and watched.

The little door opened, and tiny human shaped creatures emerged. They were no bigger than ants. They spoke a strange language, stranger than the one her people used. It was much harder to understand. The creatures had other creatures held by silver threads — leashes as thin as spider webs and nearly as invisible. Fluffy watched as the bigger creatures unhooked the leashes, snapped their fingers, and pointed toward the door.

The smaller creatures flew across the room, like tiny flies on a mission. The larger creatures went back through the door. Fluffy heard a whirring sound, and the tiny machine was gone.

She adjusted her position under the couch, and saw the small creatures fly into Rook's left ear. Another group of them flew into Streaker's right ear.

And then the terror began.

———

"What about the alien virus?"

"Mrs. Winters —"

"Don't use that tone with me, Doctor. I've been doing some reading —"

"Tabloids."

"They mentioned it on CNN. They said that ever since those tiny spaceships landed —"

"There's no proof that those are spaceships, Mrs. Winters."

" — animals have been acting strangely. You told me yourself last month, when you gave Cupcake her shots that all sorts of strange things were happening to the animals in town."

"I was talking about illnesses."

"Well, so am I. Rook and Streaker haven't been acting normally, and I'm really worried about the other cats..."

———

Rook let out a yelp like a cat in severe pain, and Streaker shook his head as if something were biting him. Then they ran in opposite directions, and Fluffy didn't see them for the rest of the day.

Of course, she had to go back to sleep. The spot under the couch, despite the dirt, was much more comfortable than she had expected.

She didn't see the attack on the dog.

It was, or so her people said later in very excited tones, extremely strange. Their neighbor had brought his dog over when he came to get a package one of her admirers — the one who drove the loud brown truck — had left. Rook and Streaker bit the dog's legs and made him bleed before her people could pull them off. Her people apologized, but the neighbor got upset. Fluffy never did understand that part. It was just a dog, after all. She was more concerned about the smelly blood all over the kitchen floor.

Rook and Streaker licked it up, and smacked their lips as if they'd had a particularly tasty treat. Her male person had said it was fortunate the boys were up to date on their shots or the entire experience would have been a costly one.

The other cats chalked it up to Dog Phobia, but Fluffy didn't. She saw the look in their eyes. She had been their target many times, and she had never seen them look so sad after an attack. Usually they were gleeful. Instead, they smacked their lips and scratched their ears, and when they finally fell asleep, they whined.

A lot.

She made sure they were nowhere near her as she prowled and snacked later that night.

———

"One article, in the local paper, said a university researcher thought that the aliens were experimenting on mammals as test cases before they started experimenting on humans."

"Mrs. Winters, really."

"I know it sounds silly, but after what the boys did, I'm looking for any explanation. Please, Doctor. Take just a few moments. Examine them."

———

For the first three days, they tried to get outside, but her people were too fast for them. The boys were getting older and were well fed and didn't move as fast as they used to. Their people stopped them at the door, every time, usually with a foot blocking their way. And then they turned their attention on the other cats.

Cupcake, the obese Persian who wanted Fluffy's spot as princess of the house, found a hiding spot behind the dryer. Fluffy stayed close to her people because she knew the boys wouldn't attack her in public. But Starlight, the black and gold stray, wasn't so lucky.

The boys cornered Starlight behind the toilet, and had ripped out her throat before their people could stop it. Their male person took the boys and threw them in cat carriers. Their female person tried to save Starlight. She bundled her in a towel and took her to the Emergency Vet, a place Fluffy had — fortunately — never seen.

The boys spent the night in cages in the garage. Their people promised a Mobile Vet visit in the morning. Cupcake slept well for the first time in a week.

Fluffy woke once and shivered. The boys were wailing as if they had seen the end of the world.

———

"All right, Mrs. Winters. I'll examine them. But before I do, let me be blunt. Starlight was a very old, malnourished stray. She wasn't part of your cat family."

"Yes, she was."

"Not to the cats. And it might not have mattered even if they had known her well. Cats live in prides and have hierarchies. And one rule that exists from lions to barn cats is that the alpha male destroys the weak so that the rest have enough to eat."

"They have enough to eat."

"It doesn't matter. It's in the genetic code."

"We've taken in strays before and they've never — you know. Killed the cat."

"Maybe the other strays weren't as sick."

"You don't think you'll find anything, do you?"

"No."

———

Fluffy hated puzzles, and she really didn't like the boys. They harassed her and didn't give her the respect that royalty deserved. But she didn't like to hear anyone cry either. And her person was right: they hadn't killed Starlight. Those creatures inside them had.

She had to get those creatures out of the boys. And she had to do it without infecting herself or Cupcake.

The creatures had gone in the ear. The Mobile Vet had cold wet stuff that went in the ear. She had seen him use it on Starlight just last week. Maybe that would be enough to get the creatures out.

But how to tell her person and the Mobile Vet what she knew? They would think, if she wound around their legs, that she wanted pets. And even though they thought themselves superior, they never had mastered Fluffy's language, not like she had mastered theirs. The problem was she couldn't speak it; she hadn't seen the use for it until now.

Her person had brought Streaker in from the garage. He had dried blood on his muzzle and his eyes were wide and dark. He looked like a cat in pain to Fluffy.

Her person put Streaker's cat carrier on the kitchen counter, and started to open the gate. Fluffy had to act now. She took a flying leap — something she hadn't done since she was a kitten — and landed on the Vet's medical bag.

He made a small sound and her person spoke her name in that sharp reprimanding tone. Fluffy ignored her. Instead she scratched on the top of the bag until a corner of it pulled back. She put a paw under it, and clung as the vet tried to lift her off.

Instead, he helped her open the bag.

There were rows of needles inside, and lots of little vials. She tried not to watch when he worked on the other cats, and she could barely remember what he had done to Starlight's ear.

He hadn't used a needle. He had used a bottle. A small white bottle that liquid dripped out of.

She only had a moment. She batted a bottle aside, and it rolled along the floor. Then she wriggled out of the vet's grasp and jumped on the counter.

Her person reprimanded her again. Fluffy stopped in front of Streaker's cage and scratched her ear. He frowned at her. She scratched her other ear, and her person shoved her on the floor.

She landed with an unceremonious thump, and she had to pause to lick herself. No princess ever allowed herself to be shoved like that, not even in the name of justice.

From above, she heard the sound of a back foot thumping against a plastic cage.

Streaker had understood.

———

"They're too big to be earmites."

"Then what are they?"

"I don't know. But I'm going to take them to the lab with me and investigate. I'll leave this vial with you. If you see any more of them, scoop them up and bring them to me. Don't let them near the cats."

"Should we do the other cats?"

"Probably. Yes. Get them. We'd best make sure this is taken care of. Something this big in your ear would be painful. We don't want it to happen again."

———

For her troubles, she was grabbed, held by the scruff of the neck, and had cold liquid shoved down her ear, with instructions to have the same procedure repeated until the liquid was gone. Both the vet and her person were pleased to see that no creatures came out of her ears.

And then they went off to find Cupcake.

Streaker looked at her from his cage. She looked back. His eyes closed slowly. She had never seen a cat seem so exhausted — and so relieved.

———

"Doctor?"

"Mmm?"

"Are those bugs what made my boys kill Starlight?"

"I can't answer that for sure, Mrs. Winters. I don't know what these bugs are or what they do."

"But the boys, will they hurt my other cats?"

"Cats aren't like dogs, Mrs. Winters. Once dogs get a taste for blood, they usually must be kept outside or destroyed. Cats — the thing that your cats did — is natural. They hurt things one minute and cuddle with their owner the next. Will your cats be the same loving creatures you've always known? Of course. Will they hurt Cupcake and Fluffy? Not unless they get so sick that they're a threat to the pride. I would say that you separate your cats in the future when one of them gets ill. That'll ensure something like this will never happen again."

"So I can let them have the run of the house, and they won't hurt anyone again?"

"If you follow my instructions."

"I will. Oh, Doctor. How will I ever forgive them for Starlight?"

"Realize they're not human, and that human laws don't apply. What they did was right in the feline world."

"That doesn't work for me."

"Then blame it on the bugs."

———

Three days later, Fluffy was asleep in the sun beneath her favorite window. The boys were cuddled on the couch, still exhausted from their ordeal.

A whir woke Fluffy up. She rolled over and saw the tiny machine on the windowsill. The little door opened and the bigger creatures came out. They held tiny whistles in their hands.

The high-pitched sound woke up the boys. They glanced at Fluffy. She glanced at them. Then she reached up with one paw, and knocked the machines — and the bigger creatures — off the sill.

The boys jumped down beside her, and the hunt began.

It was Rook who discovered that if you bit one of the creatures halfway between its head and its feet and then threw it against the wall, it didn't move again. Streaker discovered that a paw through the door crushed the little machines.

But Fluffy was the one who figured out how to knock down machines mid-flight; Fluffy who figured out how to dodge the tiny rays of light that hurt more than a needle's prick; Fluffy who figured out how to flush the machines down the toilet so that they would be gone for good.

Because Fluffy knew if the creatures and their tiny machines succeeded in taking over Rook and Streaker, they might take over her. And if they took over her, and discovered how wonderful her life was, it wouldn't be long before they sent for more little machines and sent bugs into the ears of her people. And once they had control of her people, they had control of the entire world.

And Fluffy couldn't let that happen. In this world, she was a princess. And she would remain a princess — even if it meant dirtying her paws to do so.

The creatures hadn't known what they were up against.

But Fluffy knew.

And Fluffy won.

Just like she knew she would.

BLIND

KRISTINE KATHRYN RUSCH

BLIND

Felton Woods, outside the small coastal town of Seavy Village, Oregon, has a certain place in my memory. Whenever I think of it, I think of a particular moonlit evening when my brother Richard and I decided to dare the ghosts.

It was 1974. Richard was twelve. I was ten and small for my age. Usually, he thought of me as the annoying younger brother, but that night, he needed me. He had bragged to his buddies that he always went to Felton Woods on the nights of a full moon, and they hadn't believed him. So, as proof, he promised a Polaroid, taken near the fairy circle, with the moonlight shining all around and the pocket knife he always carried on a rock in the center of the circle.

Richard had lied, of course. In those days, Richard usually lied to puff himself up. Later, as an adult, I learned that such behavior was a sign of insecurity, but then I simply saw it as part of Richard. And I usually got dragged into the lies when he needed help proving he had actually been telling the truth.

I was a little enabler, and was just beginning to realize it.

The night of the full moon was a school night. The next day was the annual spelling bee—something I was good at that my brother was not—and I wanted to have a good night sleep. When Richard shook me awake, leaning across my bottom bunk to find me pressed up against the wall, I mumbled, "Don wanna," so many times that he climbed on the bunk and sat on me. We tussled silently in the dark so that we wouldn't wake our parents in the room next door, and finally Richard pinned my arms against my race car pillow cases.

"Give?" he whispered.

"No," I said, and tried to buck him off.

"I need your help, Scott," he said, and that got me to stop moving. He'd never asked for my help before.

"Yeah?" I said.

"Yeah." He got off the bed and threw clothes at me. I put them on. Then we snuck into the kitchen, got Dad's utility flashlight, and the new Polaroid, and tiptoed out the back door.

Our house was on a small hill that had an ocean view on one side and a view of Felton woods on the other. The moon was so bright that it seemed like Mom had left the porch light on. I could see Richard's shadow. I followed him across the yard, under the clothesline, and to the deer path that my father kept trying to block with fallen tree limbs and bags of clipped grass from our mower. Richard and I walked around the mass of limbs and grass, which, that late in the fall, had begun to smell ripe.

The path was narrow and steep and somewhere along it, I clutched small branches for support. A hawk swooped past us that night, and we heard an owl in the distance. I wasn't frightened, just surprised at the brightness of the moonlight and angry at Richard's assumption that I would do anything if he asked, no matter how stupid. The fact that the assumption was correct somehow made it worse.

I think Richard was scared, though. He went first and moved slowly, using that flashlight's beam as if it were a raygun that could zap anything in our path. His breathing was harsh and ragged, and more than once, he squealed softly as some creature darted through the grass. For the first time that I knew of, he had trapped himself well and good, and I probably would have remembered that night for the rest of my life

370

for simply that reason. But as it were, other things made the night just as memorable.

The fairy circle in Felton Woods was really just a clearing where no trees grew. What looked like the remains of an out-of-control camp-fire had left a dirt circle wide enough to fit four or five tents. In the center of that circle was a flat-topped boulder that looked as if it had grown, mushroom-like, from the blackness of the earth. In the middle of the day, sunlight streamed into the circle, illuminating the rock as if someone in heaven had placed a spotlight on its dark surface. The trees diffused the light everywhere else in the wood.

As we approached the fairy circle, we could hear the burble of Felton Creek. In the winter, the creek grew too wide and deep to cross, and sometimes it flooded the lower part of the wood. In the summer, the creek was little more than a trickle—and sometimes, in dry years, not even that. I didn't think I had ever been to the woods when the creek lived up to its name, and gurgled through its banks just like it was supposed to.

I was getting cold and tired and thirsty, and I knew, somehow, that Mrs. Yates had chosen Czechoslovakia as one of the place names we had to identify and spell. I always misplaced the "l" in that word, and as I walked, I tried to remember if it was C-z-e-c-h-l or C-z-e-c-h-o-l or—

Richard stuck out his bony arm to stop me, and I slammed right into it. "Hey!"

"Shh," he whispered, putting a finger to his lips in case I didn't get the message.

There was a sound over the burbling, a light wail, almost like the wind blowing through a poorly sealed window. I felt the hair rise on the back of my neck, and it took all of my strength not to grab Richard's arm.

Instead, I pushed it away and kept going down the path.

"Scott!" he whispered. "Scotty!"

My heart was beating too hard, and my throat had gone dry, but I continued walking. Part of my defiance came from my anger at Richard, and part of it came from my desire to get back home to bed.

But the largest part was that no sound, wailing or not, would get the better of me.

I could see clearly without the flashlight. The moon sent a silvery glow over the entire meadow. The rock in the center of the dirt circle shone as if someone had painted it with reflecting paint.

The wail had stopped.

"Give me your damn knife," I said, not bothering to whisper. Richard didn't seem to notice, nor did he seem to care that I had used a forbidden word. Instead he scrambled the rest of the way down the path, and handed me the knife.

I walked into the dirt circle and put the knife in the center of the boulder. The rock's flat surface wasn't flat up close. It had ripples, like chocolate frosting that had dried with the spatula marks still in it. I balanced the knife between the grooves, where its silver and pearl handle caught the moonlight, and then I walked out of the circle. I grabbed the Polaroid from Richard, brought the whole thing to my face, and found the knife through the viewfinder. The knife looked thin, insubstantial. I was too far away. Without moving the camera, I walked closer, until the knife was in the center of the frame.

Then I pressed the big red "shoot" button, and listened to the camera hum and whir as it processed the film. I hit the button twice more before taking the undeveloped pictures that had fallen to the ground and thrusting the camera back at Richard.

"There," I said. "We're done."

He wasn't looking at me. He was looking at his knife. It was lost in a shroud of ground fog which I could have sworn hadn't been there a moment before. The fog was shaped like a human being, bent over to examine the surface of the rock.

The sight took my breath away, but only for a moment. The air was getting chillier. Ground fog was always bad near water, and would get worse as a night progressed.

I didn't want to go up that path blind.

I walked back into the circle, and reached through the fog. The knife was higher than I had expected it to be. And colder. It dropped into my palm, and as it did, the ground fog rose, like a person standing up. I yelped, then backed up. My fingers closed around the knife, and I remembered to thrust it into my pocket, before I started to run.

Richard was already up the hill ahead of me. His feet had dug long holes in the path's dirt where he had slipped and slid as he hurried his way to the top. He was leaning against Mother's clothes pole, taking deep shuddery breaths. In his hand, he clutched the Polaroids, and the camera hung around his neck.

"Jerkwad," I said to him when I could breathe. "You left me down there."

"You shouldn't've gone back in that circle."

"Someone had to get your dumb knife." I pulled it out of my pocket and tossed it to the ground beside him. "Don't ask me to do anything again."

And then I stomped into the house, climbed back in bed, and shivered for the next hour. I fell asleep thinking how the fog had felt like fingertips brushing against my skin as the knife fell into my palm.

The next morning I misspelled Czechoslovakia, and was eliminated on the second round. I didn't know that Richard and the Polaroids were creating quite a stir among the sixth grade boys. I didn't know that a father of one of the boys specialized in paranormal research, and thought the photos were something special. I didn't know that he would write an article about our experiences in the woods— without talking to me—and would get us grounded for a month for a) going out at night alone and b) stealing the camera. I also didn't know that those photographs would haunt me for the rest of my life.

You see, on the photographs themselves, the ground fog appeared in its strangely human shape. It looked as if it were contemplating us, then as if it were interested in the knife. It appeared to reach out a clearly defined hand in the last photo, as if it were going to pick up the knife.

The *Skeptical Inquirer,* years later, agreed with me: what we had seen was ground fog. Other debunkers claimed everything from flawed film to poor photography (one even suggested that I had a thumb over part of the lens). None of which I tried to deny, although Richard did. I wanted no part of any of it.

But the believers had one frightened little boy—who grew up into a frightened man—on their side. They also had a bit of strange ground fog that didn't show up on the dirt around the boulder, only in that long thin strangely human column. They also had the stories about Felton Wood, which included strange disappearances, unexplained noises, and the inability for anything to grow in the circle where we had put the knife.

It all made for a great spook story, and if I had been inclined to believe in spooks, I might have let that memory of the chill, dank fog fingers against my palm convince me too. But since then I'd been in fog a hundred times, and sometimes it felt like little needles pricking my skin, and sometimes it felt like hands caressing my face, and sometimes it felt like cold damp air giving me chills.

I believe in nothing, but remain open to everything. Only I need more proof than a quick touch against the palm, a knife that felt as if it were dropped instead of picked up, and Polaroids of something that could be a ghost or could be ground fog or could be a flaw in film.

So, except for the occasional interviewer who would dig me up for a retelling of my experience, I didn't think about Felton Woods. At least, not until my brother died, and I found myself there one final time.

———

My brother Richard was the kind of man who succeeded young and allowed everything to go downhill from there. He was the star quarterback for the Seavy High Sailors, but his talents didn't extend beyond our small town. He married the homecoming queen, just like he was supposed to, but after high school, they both looked a little lost. He flunked out of Oregon Coast Community College, and she never went, pregnant at the time with the first of their three daughters. He got a job managing a store, and that became his career. When my parents died in a car crash on Highway 20, hit head-on by a tourist trying to pass in a no-passing zone, Richard asked me if he could move into their house instead of selling it. He didn't want to pay rent.

I had no objections. I had gone to MIT on a National Merit Scholarship, and had discovered the great world beyond the Oregon Coast. Until my parents' funeral, I hadn't been back. I saw no reason to spend my life in a town that couldn't pass a referendum to expand their two-room library.

My degree got me into computers back when you had to learn a second language to do so. I joined up with Microsoft when it was still a young company, and through its generous stock program, I became one of Seattle's many Microsoft millionaires. I never purchased additional stock past what the company allowed, and I used my dividends to buy into other companies. I retired at the age of thirty-two to manage my portfolio, and to see the world. By the time I returned home to attend my parents' funeral, I had already been to all seven continents, and I had just found my new avocation.

I became a historic crash site detective.

It started as a lark. I joined some friends of mine from MIT on a trip into the Mojave. They were looking for metal left by the crash of an experimental aircraft in 1958. They had used historic documents, some obtained through the Freedom of Information Act, to determine where the craft went down. They needed people to help them comb several square miles of desert, looking for bits of metal left to deteriorate in the sun.

I was the one who found the first piece. I saw it glinting beneath a bit of sagebrush. The metal was a shard of aluminum no bigger than a quarter, with the telltale green of aviation zinc chromate paint on one side.

From that moment, I was hooked. I went on subsequent trips, and soon became the coordinator for several more, since I was the man who had no nine-to-five job. We were all amateurs, and we all loved the work. Even after aviation historians began to take note of us, we still refused payment for the research. We were all very aware of the fact that our work came out of tragedy. We couldn't work modern crash sites—we were all too squeamish and would, I think, have been out of our depths—so we felt as if we were resurrecting the memories of men who had died long ago, in courageous ways.

Of course, along the way, we found things we couldn't identify. A scrap of metal near Barstow that could be crumpled and then would return to its own shape as if it had been ironed; a slip of paper that hadn't deteriorated over time, with the tensile strength equal to that of steel; and a bit of something that looked like a child's hair ribbon, that appeared pink to some of us, gold to others, and which shared some of the same color properties as an oil slick. Most of these we gave to colleagues in related industries, and we never saw them again. But sometimes, as with the items listed above, I kept the oddities, and put them in a safety deposit box, just so that I could remind myself there were things in the universe that human beings couldn't yet explain.

One of the things human beings couldn't explain was exactly how my brother Richard died. He was found near Felton Creek, a victim of exposure.

His wife had called me the day he was found. The conversation had been a strange one; she hadn't been crying, but I could hear tears in her voice. Behind her, other voices spoke softly, and I knew that her family had already rallied around her and the girls. They didn't need me, but she had almost begged me to come.

Perhaps she had been afraid that I wouldn't go to Seavy Village for my brother's funeral, even though I was only seven hours away by car. After all, I had told them repeatedly that I didn't plan to come back, and all our visits were on my dime in places around the world that I had chosen to broaden my nieces' horizons, to show them that there was more to life than a tourist town with only seven thousand permanent residents.

Or perhaps she had spoken to everyone that way, from me to the owner of the outlet franchise store that Richard managed. I had no way of telling, and I didn't really ponder the information. Not at first. When your older brother dies mysteriously and unexpectedly at the age of 37, you spend all of your time trying to accept the world without him. Even though I saw Richard as something of a failure, as a man who never reached his full potential, I also knew him as my older brother, as a constant so fine that life without him seemed like suddenly discovering that the sun was going to rise in the west for the rest of my life. It wasn't possible that I could continue without Richard, that one day I would be 37, and he would never get past that age. I thought we had time. To learn that we didn't, and that we never would have, consumed me so that I didn't even notice the drive.

Nor did I note that Seavy Village had gotten bigger, until I reached the outskirts of town and found houses there, dozens of them, new developments built up around what had once been a fairly ugly and poorly maintained 9-hole golf course. Now the course was part of a fitness center, and it boasted 18 beautiful holes. The houses, according to a sign, sold for $200,000 each, and all had views of either the mountains or the ocean.

The stores had changed, but they always did that, even when I was a boy. A modern library stood in what used to be the old city center, and across the street from it was the factory outlet mall where Richard had worked. Beside that was a six-plex movie theater, and several newly built hotels. Seavy Village no longer deserved its "village" moniker. It was a healthy and growing town.

The road to the house was the same. The state hadn't widened 101 yet—not that they could without damaging prime real estate (there is only so much land between the ocean and the mountains)—and so, even though the buildings were different, the twists and turns of the place where I had learned how to drive remained the same. I turned onto the side road that led away from the ocean to what had been my parents' house. When we were growing up, the small turquoise blue ranch-style building had been the only one on the ridgeline. Now there were houses on either side of the ridge, and down the road as far as I could see.

When I pulled up in front of the house, I had to park on the lawn. Half a dozen cars filled the wide driveway, and four more were also on the stretch of grass that had once held my mother's clotheslines. My youngest niece, Stacy, sat on a barstool inside the garage. She clutched a basketball in both hands. Her blond hair fell across her face, and for a moment, she looked like her mother had at the same age, pensive and pretty. Then she brought her head up, and I saw the blending of Richard in her face, the soft features that made her uniquely Stacy.

I got out of the car. She didn't smile at me. Instead, she dropped the basketball, ran across the driveway, and flung herself in my arms.

She was almost as tall as I was, and the impact of her thin body nearly knocked me over. She clung tightly and I held her back, realizing, for the first time, how much I needed this closeness as well. After Cindy's call, I had just gotten into the car and drove. I hadn't even told friends where I was going.

Finally, Stacy broke away. Her eyes were swollen from crying, and her cheeks looked chapped. With one hand, she tucked loose hair behind her ears.

"Don't believe them, Uncle Scott," she said. "They're all lying."

Whatever I had expected her to say, it wasn't that. "Who's lying?" I asked.

"Everyone." She bit her lower lip, scraping off the chapped skin with her teeth. Blood appeared on the side of her mouth, and I realized she'd been doing this since her father died. If she didn't quit soon, she'd rub her mouth raw. "They say Daddy left Mommy, but he didn't. I was with him that last night. He didn't plan to go anywhere."

I felt as if I were playing catch up. I touched the corner of her mouth. "You're hurting yourself, honey."

She jerked away as if I had burned her. "You don't believe me either."

"I didn't say that." I frowned. "It's just I don't know what happened to your dad, except that he was found dead."

"He was gone for a week, and then they found him in Felton Woods," she said.

"Was he murdered?"

She shook her head. "You know how he always had crazy schemes. They said this one just went wrong."

Crazy schemes, yes. But my brother never acted on the schemes, not as he grew older. Not after that little incident with the Polaroids and the knife in the fairy circle.

"What was the scheme?" I asked.

"I don't know!" her voice rose. "It wasn't like Dad. He never did anything dangerous. He wouldn't even let us go on those whale watching tours because he was afraid something would happen."

Just like our father. He had protected himself only to be killed on a routine drive, not an hour away from home.

I put my arm around her waist. "Let's go in, Stace, and see what's going on."

"You're not going to like it," she said. "I don't." But she came with me anyway.

The interior of the house smelled of dirty dishes, unwashed clothing, and casseroles thick with hamburger and American cheese. Voices came from the kitchen. I walked through the hallway decorated with school photographs, and into the living room. The large double-paned picture window with a view of the ocean remained the same as did the room's general contours. Otherwise it was unfamiliar. The furniture was old and faded, the couch shrouded in a green coverlet designed to hide furniture that needed upholstering. Richard and Cindy's wedding picture hung over the fireplace, and a large mirror hung over the couch, making the small room seem somehow smaller.

A dozen people stood in the center, talking, surrounding Cindy. She had put on weight since I last saw her, and her eyes were puffy as well. In her right hand she held a tattered box of Kleenex, and in her left, a stuffed dog that appeared new. The people around her had familiar faces, and some of them I recognized from Richard and Cindy's wedding almost twenty years before. My oldest niece, Heather, was leaning against the built-in bookshelf on the far wall, watching everyone. The middle niece, April, was nowhere to be seen.

Stacy came in the room behind me. Heather noticed me at that moment, but didn't leave her post.

"Mother," Stacy said. "Uncle Scott is here."

Cindy turned then, and came toward me, arms out. I let her hug me, but somehow I didn't need this hug like I had needed Stacy's. Stacy's had felt mutual. Cindy's felt as if she were trying to draw something from me, something I did not have to give.

As she pulled back, she held my upper arms in a vise-grip. "Oh, Scotty," she said. "At last."

I made myself smile, felt how insincere it was, how much even that small movement hurt. "I came as soon as you called."

She nodded as if she hadn't really heard me. "Now we can ask you," she said, and she turned to the others as if she were speaking for all of them. "What was Richard doing that last week? Why did he go see you?"

Her fingers bit into my biceps. I would have bruises in the morning. "He didn't come to see me, Cindy."

"Yes," she said. "Yes, he did."

I shook my head. Heather was staring at me, her pretty brown eyes dull. Stacy stood close to me as if she were protecting me.

"Come on, son," said Cindy's father. He had grown shorter in the intervening years. "No need to cover for Richard now."

"I'm not," I said. "The last time I saw him, Cindy, was in London. With you."

She was shaking her head, her eyes closed. This was clearly not what she wanted to hear. She let go of my arms.

"There's no need to lie, Scott," Cindy's mother said.

"I know," I said. "I'm not lying."

The room was silent. Everyone was watching me. Stacy slipped one slim hand in mine.

"Does someone want to tell me what happened here?" I asked. "Or should I leave?"

"No." Cindy took a deep shuddery breath and pulled herself together visibly. In that movement, I saw the remains of the slender girl who had managed, every halftime, to do a double twist ending in splits, even though the entire maneuver terrified her. "I'll tell you."

And so she did.

―――――

It all started when one of the producers for a cable television program called *American's Strangest Stories* contacted Richard about our night in Felton Woods. Felton Woods was making the national UFO websites because of all the strange disappearances that were taking place there. Dogs had vanished off leashes, children had gone missing, and adults also disappeared, all after saying they were going to Felton Woods. People claimed they saw the dogs disappear, but no one had actually seen the children or adults disappear.

Most of the people who had disappeared were tourists, and most of them had severe family problems. All of the children were involved in some sort of parental custody dispute. Local authorities seemed to think these things important; in all cases, the police found explanations other than mysterious events in the woods. No bodies were ever found.

When the producer came to visit, she was young, beautiful, and very businesslike. When she saw the battered Polaroids, and heard Richard's story, she had smiled at him condescendingly and asked if he had been to the woods lately. When he said he hadn't, she had thanked him for his time, offered him $250 for the use of the Polaroids on the show, and promised that she would call him for "deep background."

The show aired in April. She used the Polaroids, but never called him. His name wasn't even mentioned.

But the show had aired with the promise of a follow-up in the fall. Richard became obsessed with being part of that follow-up. It was all he could talk about. He felt that the phenomenon of Felton Woods had started with him—and here Cindy had bowed her head, then shrugged. "I'm sure he meant both of you," she had said—and he was determined to be sure he was still a part of it all.

And then Heather broke into the tale.

"He stopped coming home at night," she said. "Or if he came home, he would leave again."

"Usually with a flashlight," Stacy said from beside me.

Heather shot her a how-stupid-can-you-be? look. "He was seeing someone."

"He was going to the woods," Stacy said.

Heather shook her head.

"It doesn't matter," Cindy said. "What matters is that he disappeared a week before he died. He led me to believe he was going to see you, Scott, to see if you remembered anything else about that night."

I sighed. "He didn't even call."

"He had a girlfriend," Heather said.

"Did not," Stacy said.

"Girls." Cindy sounded tired. "I guess now we'll never know."

My brother could have had a girlfriend. He had been tempted once before, after our parents died, but he had been afraid of what an affair would do to his family. He and I spent many a late night on the phone, on my dime, while he discussed the lack of direction in his life.

He hadn't called this time.

"I don't understand," I said. "If you thought he was with me, how do you explain his death in Felton Woods?"

"Maybe you concocted a scheme, helped him like you used to, so the producer would come back. Maybe he did it wrong, or maybe he started without you, or..." Cindy's voice trailed off. Apparently I had been her last hope. Apparently she had convinced herself this silly story of hers was true, and she used it to prevent herself from seeing what seemed plain to her parents and the rest of her family.

But the whole thing seemed odd, and so did Cindy. At the time I attributed her behavior to grief. Later I would remember she had shown signs of it on our last visit, in London, six months before. A willingness to believe the strangest things. Accusations when no crime had been committed. The belief that Richard and I were somehow concocting schemes without her.

"Daddy couldn't have been having an affair," Stacy said. "I was with him that last night."

"You couldn't have been," Heather said. "You were too sick."

"I snuck out."

Heather shook her head. "You don't have to lie for him."

"I'm *not.*"

"Girls," Cindy said tiredly. She ran a hand through her limp hair. Everyone watched her. "Do you need a place to stay, Scott?"

The offer was half-hearted. She didn't want anyone else in her place, particularly the man who had blown her comfortable scenario all to hell.

"I reserved a room down at the Lodge," I said, even though I hadn't. Money talked. I would find some place to take me, no matter how full the town was.

She nodded. Her mother sat down beside her on the couch. "The funeral's tomorrow," her father said. "Viewing's tonight." And with those few words, I had been dismissed.

———

Stacy accompanied me outside. She was still holding my hand. "I want you to stay here, Uncle Scott."

"Your mom doesn't," I said. "Besides, you need your privacy."

She shook her head. "We need someone sane. April won't come out of her room. Heather stomps around like it's our fault Dad's dead, and Mom won't stop crying."

That made me want to stay even less. "Look, sweetie," I said, "as soon as I have a room number, I'll call you with it. If things get too bad, come on down, and I'll play you a mean game of gin rummy."

Her grin was quick, but shallow. I hadn't touched her heart. "Uncle Scott?"

"Hmm?"

"If I gave you my dad's notes, would you read them?"

"His notes?"

She nodded. "He was trying to do something, like you. He thought if he could prove—well, his notes say it better."

I didn't answer her one way or another. What I was listening to was behind the words. "That visit with the producer really shook him up, didn't it?"

She bit her bottom lip again, then stopped when she saw me watching. "He said he was turning forty and had nothing to show for it."

Ouch, I thought. What a thing to say to your daughter.

"He said you were the one who did everything. You were the one with the courage. Even that night in the woods, you were the one who put the knife on the boulder, you were the one who photographed everything, and you were the one who got the knife back when Dad ran away."

He had never told that full story before, not to anyone. I hadn't contributed to his lie, but I hadn't corrected it either.

"He had a great family," I said, not to enable him any longer, but because I didn't like the hurt in her eyes when she spoke of his failure. "I've never been able to find that."

"We're your family, Uncle Scott," she said. And at that moment, I realized she was right. They were my family. The only family I had. And they were a mess.

What had you been doing these last few weeks, Richard? What was worth your sacrifice?

"Have you read his papers?" I asked.

She shook her head. "He made me promise not to. And I couldn't show them to Mom or April or Heather. But he didn't make me promise not to show them to you."

So she had doubts as well. She was protecting her father, and doubting him at the same time. When I left, he had a few years on his own, and then Stacy had arrived, another little enabler.

Maybe that had been the reason she and I were always so close. Neither of us could stand up to Richard when he needed someone to help him get his way.

"What happened that last night?" I asked. "You said you saw him in the woods."

She ran a hand through her hair, a gesture so like her mother's that it stopped my breath. "I had a migraine," she said, and then she flushed so red that it looked as if her skin were going to explode. "I've been getting them lately."

Puberty, I wanted to say. It didn't scare me like it did her, but it explained her new height and her gawky poise. I wanted to tell her that migraines were normal, that at least three of my girlfriends had suffered the same thing, but I remained silent.

"I went to bed without supper. I get nauseous sometimes too."

I nodded.

"I fell asleep, and when I woke up, there was moonlight coming in my window." Stacy's room was on the far end of the house. After Richard and Cindy had moved in, they had added two rooms on the narrow space left on the lot. They had planned to build a second story, but never had the funds. I didn't respond to their hints for a loan.

"Something about the moonlight made me think of Dad, and that producer, and the whole mess. I missed him." She looked behind me, at the trail to the woods. "So I went down the fairy circle. He called my name. He was hiding in the bushes near the creek. I'd never heard him sound so scared."

"Was he all right?"

She nodded. "He had a tent and everything. He said he was waiting."

"For?"

"I don't know. But he said he'd be home as soon as he had proof. Then he told me to leave, said it wasn't safe to come into the woods alone. I knew that, but I wasn't thinking clear—the migraine, I guess— and besides, I wanted to see him. He walked me up the path, and hugged me." She swallowed hard. "And that was the last time I saw him."

I leaned against my car. "Why doesn't anyone believe you?"

A slight frown crossed her forehead. "There wasn't any tent when they found him, and the coroner says he might have been dead for a day or two. They say I dreamed the whole thing because I wanted my dad to come home. Mom said it wasn't possible for me to go down the hill, not after I'd taken one of her sleeping pills. But I slept, Uncle Scott, and then I woke up. I was woozy, but I was awake. I remember feeling cold and going down that path. I remember hugging him."

She sounded like she wanted to convince herself more than me, but I was willing to believe her, at least at this point. "Give me his papers," I said. "I'll see what I can find."

———

The papers fit into my briefcase. Apparently Richard hadn't bought a computer yet, or if he had, he hadn't used it for this. Everything was on yellow legal pads, covered in his tight narrow handwriting. Looking at it as I stuffed it in the briefcase made my heartache. My brother had been in trouble, and for the first time in his life, he hadn't come to me.

I managed to get a room in the Lodge after all. It was the off season, and because I was feeling so low, I decided to go for luxurious. They had a two-room suite, complete with living room, a gas fireplace and Jacuzzi, all with an ocean view. I took it, and lit the fire as soon as I entered the room. Then I set the briefcase aside, ordered dinner from room service, and pulled back the curtains.

It had started to rain. Another storm was building over the ocean, its clouds diffuse and elongated, indicating even heavier ran to come. Fall on the coast was always dicey—my least favorite season. Winter was cold and sunny, but fall was filled with storm after storm, making it feel as if the entire world were going to drown, one raindrop at a time.

While I waited for the food, I settled in the armchair near the fireplace and removed the legal pads. Richard had enough sense to date them, and so I put them in order, oldest on top. He had written a sort of diary beginning years before, with the first of the strange disappearances. Sometimes the gaps between notations were as long as six months, sometimes the notations appeared hourly.

I started to read, pausing only to open the door when my dinner arrived. Hours later, I turned the last page in the final notebook, leaned my head against the chair and closed my eyes. I knew I'd have to follow

386

my brother into the woods one final time, and this time, I liked the idea even less than I had when I was ten.

———

The funeral was a long, surprising affair. Richard had known the entire town, and some people had driven in from as far away as Portland to offer their respects. The minister gave a small eulogy, then opened the floor to anyone who felt like speaking. Most people did.

Cindy sat in the front row through it all, silent sometimes, sobbing at others. April sat beside her, a wisp of her former self. I wondered if she was eating—or if anyone had bothered to find out—and vowed to spend some time with her while I was in town. Heather kept a protective arm around her mother throughout the service, and Stacy leaned away from all of them, twisting a handkerchief in her right hand.

I sat one row back and startled several old ladies who had forgotten that Richard had a brother. I was slimmer than he had been, but we were balding in the same way, and most of them confused me for him, at least momentarily. I could see it in their eyes, the sudden surprise, covered quickly as they realized I was a relative.

After the funeral, everyone went to Richard's house. Someone had cleaned up the surface mess, although the bathrooms were still filthy and dust covered the bookshelves. No one seemed to notice but me and perhaps I did because my mother had been a stickler for cleanliness, and she was probably turning in her grave at the way Cindy kept house. When Cindy asked me, in hushed tones, if I minded that she and the girls remained in the family homestead, I offered to deed the place to her. The last thing I wanted was to make my brother's family homeless.

And then it was all over, leaving only the flotsam and jetsam of a life cut short. Cindy and I spent a day hunting for investments, not that there were many, and then we spent another figuring out how she would make ends meet. We came to no conclusions—she hadn't been able to hold a job for longer than six months since Stacy was born—and I felt as if I were more concerned about this than she was. Cindy spent part of our time together just staring at things as if she didn't see them. I was wondering if, in her mind's eye, she saw Richard instead.

I also took everyone out for meals, insisting that April come as well. She didn't say anything to me for the first two days after the funeral—I was beginning to think she couldn't talk at all—and then she screamed at me when I had, in her presence, suggested grief counseling to her mother. After that, April seemed a bit more like herself, but I was still worried.

Richard's entire family seemed lost without him.

I had always thought Richard a failure. I hadn't realized how successful he had been, and how that success had differed from mine. He bound people together. I achieved goals. Two different ways of living. He had hundreds of people at his funeral. I realized if I died suddenly, I would have only had a handful, and of that handful, most would have been Richard's family.

I wished I could tell him that. I wished I could apologize. But I had missed my chance, and for the first time, I felt as if I had let an opportunity slip by.

So I took care of his family as best I could, helped them pick up the pieces without treading on their grief. And then, when I felt I could do no more, I called my team.

———

They didn't want to come. They thought I was on a wild goose chase, and perhaps I was. So, for the first time in our joint history, I offered to pay them. And instead of refusing, they took me up on it.

At that time, the team still had its original members: Marietta Walker, an archivist for NASA; Tony Dryser, an historian who taught at Annapolis; Peter Bartell, an aviation historian who taught at Northwestern; and Joseph Harwell, a professional photographer. What they all had in common, besides an interest in U.S. test flight history, was that they attended MIT at the same time I did. I had been a peripheral part of their group, but in those days I was more interested in the inner workings of computers than in the adventures men had when they tried new aircraft.

The team came to Seavy Village in one large sports utility vehicle, rented at the Portland International airport, and driven, so the other three said, by Dryser as if he were expecting to get take-off orders at any moment. I got them all suites in the Lodge, and they piled in, energetic and resourceful, excited about a paid vacation at the coast.

I had forgotten, in the week I had been here, how exuberance felt. The entire town seemed depressed by Richard's death. My friends' energy almost seemed wrong.

Marietta hugged me when she saw me. She was a tiny woman built like a basketball player—all legs and torso—who somehow didn't make it to full height. She was wearing a white cotton t-shirt that accented her tanned skin, and army fatigue pants. The others hung back. They weren't as certain how to handle grief. None of them had experienced a serious loss, and since they'd known me, I'd lost my entire nuclear family.

When Marietta let me go, I let them all into my suite, and had room service bring us coffee and a snack. Dryser sprawled lengthwise on the couch, his thin frame—so appropriate to the desert—seemed out of place here. His wrinkled skin looked as if it might hydrate in the rain and suddenly make him full-faced and jolly.

Bartell was still dressed like the professor he was, tweed suit and scuffed shoes, his thinning blond hair combed to one side. He would dress like that until we went into the field, where he would don t-shirts and khakis and transform himself into a man of adventure. Harwell always looked like a man of adventure. His dark hair hadn't had a good cut in years, and that morning he had forgotten to shave. Only he was dressed appropriately for the coast, wearing a red and gray checked flannel shirt, faded blue jeans, and waterproof boots.

Harwell stood in the window, watching the ocean. Marietta perched on the arm of the couch, watching me. Bartell perused the books on the built-in shelves. Judging them was his manner of listening.

"You know," Dryser said, "you don't have to pay us the fee. Just room and board."

"Speak for yourself, Tony," Harwell said. "I'm losing a week of work here that I can ill afford."

"Scott doesn't look good, Joseph," Dryser said.

"But I'm well enough not to be talked about in the third person," I said. "I told you I'd pay for this, and I will. It's something I want to do, not something we normally do."

"We're just not used to proceeding backwards," Marietta said.

"That's not it." Bartell turned away from the books. "This feels too much like UFO-ology, and we've always stayed away from that."

I nodded. "You don't have to—"

"We're here," Marietta said.

Dryser put his hands behind his head. "Look at it this way, Peter. We're not investigating UFOs. We're investigating a death. Scott's brother died here."

"Of exposure," Bartell said, but gently so as not to offend me.

"Yeah," Harwell said. "What do the cops say about that?"

"They say he was having an affair. They say he was supposed to meet the lady in Felton Woods and either she didn't show or she did, and he fell asleep, dying in the cold. They also say he'd been there for a few days, but my niece claims she saw him—with a tent and gear—the night before his body was found."

"Whom do you believe?" Marietta asked.

I shrugged. "Today I believe Stacy. Ask me tomorrow and I might believe the police."

"So we're doing this for you," Harwell said.

"I guess. I have the feeling he wouldn't have been out there if not for me."

"How's that?" Bartell asked.

"You've got to read the notebooks," I said, and handed them to him.

———

The next morning, we went to Felton Woods. They looked smaller than I remembered. The trees were second growth, sometimes third, spindly things that bent in the wind. Leaves covered the ground, and several of the Doug firs looked sick. Felton Creek was high, past the burbling stage, and nearly to the flood stage. After two weeks of near solid rain, it couldn't be anything else.

The fairy circle was smaller too. I had thought it the size of a parking lot when actually only one car would have fit on it. The boulder was little more than a large rock. Only it looked odd. There were no other rocks near it, and no place it could have fallen from above. Someone or something had once moved it there.

The team stared at the dirt circle as if it were something dangerous. We were all in our rain gear, and we looked like something out of a 1950s horror movie—yellow slickers against wet, dark trees, and a rain-swept sky.

For a moment, no one seemed to know what to do. Then Marietta dug into her pack for the Geiger counter. Bartell walked down to the creek, careful to hold tree branches in case he lost his footing. Harwell began taking pictures. Dryser was watching me.

I was having second thoughts. Marietta was right. We were proceeding backwards. Normally, we picked a test flight that ended in tragedy—the pilot dead, the experimental plane destroyed—and we searched until we found pieces of it. Sometimes we found enough to reassemble the plane. Sometimes all we did was locate the crash site for the pilot's families. Those were the tough cases, watching full adults sob as they remembered the night their father never came home, as they realized, perhaps for the first time, that he never would.

Here we had a mysterious site and strange evidence that my brother believed pointed to a UFO. The circle was not maintained by the park. In fact, I could remember a campaign in the mid-seventies to attempt to grow grass in that space. It hadn't worked. My brother added that, the mysterious disappearances, and strange lights that sometimes flashed over the ocean and came up with UFOs. Dryser, when he finished reading the tablets, came up with a sigh. "Sounds like people should stay out of Felton Woods."

Marietta had closed her eyes after her reading. Bartell had agreed with the cops. "You'll probably find all kinds of drug paraphernalia there. Evidence of some kind of illegal nightlife in that place."

Only Harwell had said nothing. He asked me a bunch of questions about the Polaroids, and then he had asked to see the pictures. I had given them to him and he had stared at them for a very long time.

Marietta's Geiger counter clicked as she held the wand over the dirt circle. "Radiation," she said softly. "Very low levels."

"Christ," I said. "Is it dangerous?"

"It's always dangerous, old bean," Dryser said. "But if you're expecting sudden outbreaks of strange cancers, you've got the wrong idea."

"It's localized," she said. "It doesn't leave the circle. It doesn't even go down to the stream."

"Creek," I said automatically.

"Creek," she repeated. Bartell had come up from the creek side. He had heard the entire exchange.

"How long has this circle been here?" he asked.

"According to my brother, since the fifties."

"Not good enough," Bartell said. "We need to pinpoint when."

"And how do you propose we do that?" I asked. "This town has only had a library for the past ten years. Not even the high school had one when I was a kid."

"Jesus," Harwell said. "How did you study?"

"There was a bookstore down the hill that had a reference area. The owner let kids use it."

"You've got to be kidding," Marietta said.

I shook my head.

"Wow," Dryser said. "Who'd've thought anything'd be that backward twenty years ago?"

"You had a newspaper then, didn't you?" Bartell asked. "Someone had to notice this."

"We did," I said.

"And there'd be police records or something strange. Big dirt circles don't appear overnight."

"In England they do," Harwell said.

"Those're crop circles," Dryser said. "That's a different phenomenon."

"We don't know that," Marietta said. In her tone, she cited the first rule of investigation. Never assume.

"Listen, Peter," I said. "You're better at research than I am. You go, see what you can find."

"I'll help him," Dryser said. "I'm not going to get much here."

"See if there are aerial photographs of this place," Harwell said.

"Good thought," Dryser said, and then he and Bartell left.

Marietta traced the radiation around the point of the circle. Her readings didn't change. I scanned the area, as I usually did a crash site. Here I found used condoms, a hypodermic, bubblegum wrappers, and a Frisbee. Harwell continued to snap pictures.

I didn't know what I wanted from this work. Richard had known. He had come here, assuming that the circle had been burned into the ground by a flying saucer that came at regular intervals, and took people. He had hoped it might take him, but if his hypothesis were true (and I doubted it was), he would never have been taken. All the disappeared were in states of flux. They had no one place where they belonged. I would have had a better chance of disappearing than Richard ever would.

"We need a shovel," Marietta said to no one in particular.

"We need drier clothes," Harwell muttered.

"We need lunch," I said, and led them back to the SUV.

———

For the next three days, we researched and hypothesized and worked. We dug into the circle and found that the dirt and the radiation went down at least six feet, but we also discovered nothing else—no debris, no metal, no garbage. It was as if the dirt circle were completely pristine.

Aerial photographs taken during World War II showed a Seavy Village I didn't recognize, a small place that hadn't even grown near Felton Woods. The clearing wasn't visible at all in those photographs. When we used a magnifying glass, we realized the entire area was covered in trees.

The trees disappeared in 1955, and a perfect circle took their place. The topography maps showed an incline where the area was now flat. We had no aerial photographs for the years in between, so Bartell and Dryser had to search records until they found mention of the dirt circle.

The first mention appeared in the *Oregonian* in December, 1952. Apparently a loud explosion was heard in Felton Woods late the night of December 30, and fire crews were called to put out a raging fire near the creek. Local papers did not report this, nor did the *Oregonian* do any follow-ups. Later newspaper histories of Felton Woods mentioned the explosion, but never tied it to any of the strange events. Apparently no one knew what caused the explosion, nor did anyone try to figure it out.

The team got interested here. To them, this was less about UFOs than experimental aircraft. But Bartell researched missing experimental craft, and didn't find anything that had disappeared over Oregon at that time. He didn't even find anything that had disappeared in the Pacific Northwest.

Marietta believed that something with a nuclear payload crashed in Felton Woods and the Air Force kept it quiet. I didn't, though. A nuclear payload like the ones the U.S. used in the early fifties would have created a serious radiation problem, and more than a small circle of dirt and some trees would have been destroyed.

Late one night after the others had gone to sleep, Harwell knocked on my door. I was still awake, staring into the fire, and wondering if the fall storms would ever ease. I had just gotten off the phone with Stacy— she wanted to help us search the wood, but I had said no. The radiation worried me more than I wanted to admit—and I was thinking of turning on the television to see if I could take my mind off things for a while.

When I got up and opened the door, Harwell pushed inside. He had tied his hair back with a thin strip of leather. He wasn't wearing a shirt, and his feet were bare. He was frowning.

"Tell me," he said. "When you took those Polaroids, did you see the mist in your frame?"

"How the hell should I know?" I asked. "It was twenty-five years ago."

"Think," he said.

"Why? Do you have anything?"

"Not concrete. But tomorrow is a full moon, did you know that?"

Somehow those two thoughts had to be linked, but I didn't know how. "What are you thinking?"

He sank into the easy chair and stuck his feet toward the fire. "I took fifteen photographs of that rock. I had some geology in school. The thing doesn't look like it came from a stream bed or had water flow over it. In fact, it doesn't look any different from the rock you took a picture of."

"Should it?"

He swept a hand to the window. Rain poured down outside, dotting the pain. "Weather like this, and twenty-five years, not to mention an occasional flood from that creek, yeah. It should look different."

My mouth went dry.

"Now maybe I'm as nuts as—." He stopped himself and his eyes flashed an apology.

"As Richard," I finished for him.

"But that rock has bothered me from the beginning. So I started looking at your pictures. It's the knife that's different, right? Has anyone else ever placed a knife on that spot?"

"How the hell should I know?"

"No, I mean, those UFO freaks and those TV people and the Uri Geller fan club. The ones that contacted you."

"Not to my knowledge," I said, not quite sure what he was getting at. "And I think Richard would have made a note of it in his diaries."

"That's what I thought." He leaned forward. "So here's the thing. We replicate the experiment."

"What?"

"I'm no scientist," he said, "but it seems to me the best way to reproduce the results you got is to replicate the experiment. And we have the opportunity to do that tomorrow night."

"It's supposed to rain tomorrow night. It was clear and dry when Richard and I went down to the creek."

"All the better."

"But there can't be ground fog in these conditions."

"Sure there can."

"It's too cold, and too late in the year."

Harwell shrugged. "Then nothing happens. You can't say we didn't try."

True enough. And at least we would be doing something. Right now it felt as if we were spinning our wheels. It was strange to work backwards, strange to have a hypothesis about what might turn out to be nothing.

But I was afraid to return to the fairy circle in the moonlight. I told myself I didn't want to mess with an old memory, but that wasn't it. The fear I hadn't felt as a young boy I'd been feeling ever since. And it was a fear I didn't really want to confront.

Still the others, when consulted, thought it a good idea. I didn't mention my reservations. It wasn't fair, after all. I had asked them to come against their wills, and they had, for me. I couldn't back out on an experiment just because it made me feel uneasy.

That night, as I finally drifted off to sleep, I found myself wondering what I was afraid of, and being unable to answer the question.

———

The next day, a Saturday, dawned clear and cold. The ocean was an electric blue with yellowish gray white caps on its waves. Debris floated near the shore, the remains of several days of storms. The storm promised for this day was still out in the Pacific, moving slowly and possibly dissipating, according to the news.

I went to Cindy's for lunch. I told my team I wanted to check up on the girls, but I also needed to talk to Stacy.

The house was a mess. Even though it was after noon, Cindy still wore her bathrobe. She hadn't washed her hair in days. No one had done the dishes, either, and April was locked in her room once again.

Instead of talking to Stacy, I made her and Heather start the dishes. Then I made Cindy take a shower, and I knocked on April's door. She didn't answer, so I opened it. She was unconscious on the bed, and nothing I could do could wake her.

I thought about calling an ambulance, but I didn't. It was quicker in Seavy Village—or it had been when I was a boy—to drive her directly. I picked her up and carried her from the room. She was skeletal, and weighed next to nothing. The arm that dangled was no wider than a ruler, and I could see the outlines of all her bones.

"Tell your mom I'm taking April to the emergency room," I said as I slammed through the kitchen. Stacy ran beside me, asking what was wrong, but I was too angry to reply. They were all so wrapped up in their problems that they hadn't seen the girl starving in their midst.

I had seen, but I had thought it all past when April got angry at me. Instead, I spent my time in Felton Woods, just like her father.

I laid April on the back seat, and was about to get up front when Stacy let herself in. "Stay here," I said.

She shook her head. "She's my sister."

I didn't respond. Instead, I backed the car out, and headed down the road at a fast clip.

I still knew the back streets, and I got to the hospital in record time. They took April away from me, and Stacy and I sat for nearly an hour before Cindy and Heather came in, looking frightened.

"Is she going to be all right?" Cindy asked.

This was Richard's legacy, Richard's family, the very thing I had envied of him. "She's malnourished," I said. "She hasn't had anything to drink, they believe, in two days. She had slipped into a coma. She would have died if I hadn't knocked on that door."

Cindy put a hand to her mouth. "You must think I'm a bad mother," she said.

What was the Biblical phrase? It was as if scales fell from my eyes. "No, Cindy," I snapped. "I know you are."

She gasped, and so did Heather. Stacy grabbed my arm. "Uncle Scott—"

I shook away. If I stayed any longer, I would say more things I would later regret. "They stabilized her. I'll be back to visit her later."

And then I left.

———

I went back to the house, and finished cleaning, furious more at myself than at them. They lived their lives. I was the outsider who could see them clearly, and I had done nothing. Or what I had done, I had done wrong. I picked up the towels Cindy left in the bathroom, stripped the sheets of April's bed, and started a load of laundry. I finished the dishes, scrubbed the floors, put everything away, and still I found things to clean. The house hadn't had a complete going over in months, maybe years. My mother would have been appalled. I know I was.

They still hadn't returned when I finished. I almost went back to the Lodge, but something stopped me. I had come to the house to talk to Stacy, to ask for her help. But she was preoccupied now.

I was on my own.

I swallowed, wondering if I should call off the team, or if it was my own fear that was speaking yet again. I leaned my head against the wall, knew that everything was mixed up in my mind—the fairy circle, Richard's death, his family's disintegration. And mixed with it were my feelings for Richard and his for me, all of them focused on that one night, the night when everything changed.

Without even thinking about it, I turned and walked down the hall to what had become Cindy's bedroom. They had a two-sided bureau, and the left side had been Richard's. It had been as long as the two of them had been together. Cindy hadn't been able to do anything since he died. I knew she hadn't clean out his stuff.

It didn't take me long to find the pocket knife. It was hidden in the bottom drawer, inside an old pair of socks. Richard hadn't changed in all the years of his life. Whenever he wanted to hide something, he put it inside a sock in the bottom drawer. I wondered what else I would find, buried there, if I bothered to look.

I slipped the knife into my pocket, then, almost as an afterthought, I took the old Polaroid camera down from its place of honor on the nearby bookshelf. I glanced at the back, and saw that the camera still had some old film in it. I didn't know if the battery was fresh. I didn't care. Something about what Harwell had said about reproducing the experiment and replicating the results reverberated in my mind.

I called the team from the house, told them everything was still on for the night, and then I returned to the hospital. April hadn't yet awakened, but her prognosis was good. Cindy was talking to a child welfare officer, and Stacy looked terrified. Heather was asleep on the waiting room couch.

I stayed with them until Cindy returned. The welfare officer wanted to talk to me as well. We went to an empty room down the hall. She asked me what I thought would be best for the family.

"If I knew that," I said, "I would have already done it."

And then I left.

———

The team was waiting for me at the Lodge. Marietta took one look at my face and said, "We don't have to do this if you don't want to."

I shook my head. "We've come this far." Then I reached into my pocket, removed the knife and tossed it at Harwell. "May as well reproduce as much as we can."

He caught the knife, then turned it in his hand. With his thumb and forefinger, he pulled open the blade. "Shiny."

"Yeah," I said. "I don't think it was ever used."

But of course I had no way to know that. I had no way to know anything any more.

Marietta made me go to the cafe and have dinner. Then we waited until 11 p.m., which I figured would be about the time that Richard and I walked down the path.

We all piled into the SUV. and drove to the house. The lights were out, but Cindy's car was in the driveway. I made Dryser park on the road below the house, and I insisted on complete quiet as we snuck through the yard. I didn't want to scare Cindy, and I didn't want to wake Stacy. I didn't want her to join us. The last thing I needed, after that day's tragedy, was to have something happen to my youngest niece.

The path was narrow as always, and this time, no one had tried to block it with branches and cut grass. The ground was muddy and slick, and I indicated to the group to make sure their hands were on something firm before they took a step. The moonlight was as clear as it had been on that singular night in my memory, but the air was colder. I had forgotten gloves, and by the time I was halfway down the path, my fingers were raw.

The distance to the fairy circle from the house was much shorter than I remembered. We reached the dirt in only a few minutes. Bartell shut off our flashlight, and Harwell took out his camera. The whir/click of his work echoed in the small forest. I had the Polaroid around my neck, but I wasn't ready to use it.

My mouth was dry and my hands were shaking. I took the knife, and slowly walked into the middle of the fairy circle.

I expected to slip on muddy ground as I had been doing since I started down the hill, but within the circle, the dirt was crumbly, as if the weeks of rain hadn't happened. The air felt no different here; it was as cold and damp as it had been on the hillside. I bent over the rock.

It was as I remembered, shiny and solid, its seemingly flat surface not flat up close. Now the swirls on the surface didn't look so much like frosting as they did a deliberate pattern, not discernible to the casual eye.

I set the knife across two grooves as I had done all those years before, and then I walked away, picking up the Polaroid as I went. Harwell continued snapping pictures, and I did as well, focusing on the knife.

Beside me, Marietta gasped. So did Dryser. Harwell continued shooting and so did I. Square packets of film spit out of the ancient camera and Bartell caught them before they fell.

Finally I had used up all my film. Harwell had prepared; he had brought several cameras, all with new rolls. When one finished, he picked up another. I let the Polaroid fall to my chest.

The rock was completely covered in white mist. The mist seemed to be growing, expanding, until it filled the fairy circle. In the center was the boulder, the only solid item that I could see. Within the mist, someone—something—had picked up the knife. It floated, free, like the needle on a compass.

Dryser put his hand on my arm and pulled me away from the circle. Then he did the same for Marietta and Bartell. Harwell wouldn't move. He kept photographing everything.

A wave of cold came off that mist so intense that it felt like we had stepped into a deep freeze. Dryser kept backing us up until we could no longer feel the cold. Harwell was shaking. I went to him, grabbed him, and pulled him back as well.

At that moment, a face formed in the mist. It was obsidian, like the rock, and its eyes were yellow. It watched the both of us, and then it dissolved into particles.

"Son of a bitch," Dryser whispered.

"What?" Harwell asked. He looked out of his view frame and swore softly. "When did that mist show up?"

"The whole time," I said. "It's been there since I put the knife down."

"No," he said.

But it had. I picked up my Polaroid and looked through the

viewfinder. Nothing. The night was clear, and the moonlight was falling across the rock. Only the knife remained, floating above it, turning, pointing at us as it did so. When I removed the camera, the mist was back.

"That makes no sense," I said. "The viewfinder should see what my eye does."

"It puts one more barrier between the naked eye and the mist," Dryser said.

"Or maybe it's something else," Marietta said. "None of us are scientists."

"I wish we were," Bartell said.

Harwell cursed again, and then replaced a roll of film in one of his cameras. He kept shooting until all his film was gone.

"What do we do now?" he asked.

"We wait," I said.

"For what?"

I shrugged. I had no idea what was going to happen next.

———

We grew colder. The light dimmed as the moon set in the west. The mist was fading as well. At just about the moment I was going to give up, the knife tilted, point down, and fell into the rock.

It landed with a thud, and then the rock split open. Light poured out. Real light, not the silvery moon stuff. The obsidian face we had seen earlier appeared again, this time attached to a head, a neck and a torso with two arms. It pulled itself out of the split rock and stared at us, golden eyes blinking.

"What do we do now?" Marietta whispered. "Say we came in peace?"

The creature crawled off the side of the rock and along a diagonal through the air, as if it were walking along the side of a building. When it reached the end of the fairy circle, it jumped to the ground. It sat there, as if it were waiting for something.

"Like a person does when faced with a pack of wild animals," Dryser muttered. He had obviously been thinking the same thing I was.

"A person facing a pack of wild animals hauls out a gun," Bartell whispered.

"Not if he wants to tame them," I said. I crouched and reached out a hand. Marietta slapped it away.

"No," she whispered. "What would your family do if you died here too?"

I wanted to argue, but couldn't. Instead she reached out to the creature. Their fingers met, and then went right through each other as if they were two holograms attempting to touch.

"My god," she said, and brought her hand back.

The creature tilted its head. It seemed sad somehow, as if it wanted more. Then it stood and climbed up the air as if it were climbing on something solid. When it reached the edge of the rock, it dipped its head inside.

"What's it doing?" Dryser asked.

"Preparing to take us away," Marietta said.

"It's never hurt a group before," Bartell said.

"That we know of," I said.

Harwell was digging through his bag for more film. His movements were quick, frantic, as if he were looking for a gun.

The creature reached into the rock and grabbed something. Then it braced itself with its remaining hand, and sat up. Balanced on the other hand was a tray. Carefully, like an obsidian waiter in a futuristic cafe, it slid down the nothingness again, until it reached the edge of the fairy circle. Then it dropped the tray onto the ground.

We dove behind trees like extras in a bad war movie. I hit Marietta along the way, knocked her over, and had to drag her with me. We cowered, but nothing happened.

And when I peered around the tree, the entire fairy circle was dark.

"Found some film!" Harwell said.

"Too late," Bartell said. "It's gone."

Dryser grabbed a flashlight and shone it on the circle. Nothing was there, no mist, no obsidian creature. Even the rock looked normal.

Only the knife was missing.

"What did it throw at us?" Marietta asked.

"Let's go see," I said.

"Wait!" Harwell said. He came out from behind his tree, shooting pictures of the entire area. He crouched over the tray, and let out a soft whistle. "Any of this stuff look familiar?"

We came out of our hiding places. The tray was silver in appearance, highly polished, and on it were dozens of small items, from wedding rings to wallets, from dog collars to i.d. bracelets.

"My god," Bartell said.

"Ten to one the names in those wallets'll correspond with the names of the folks who've disappeared," said Dryser.

"What was that creature doing, bragging?" Harwell asked.

"Shut up and take pictures," Dryser said.

"Right." Harwell bent over the tray as if he were doing a spread for *House and Garden.*

"I don't think it was bragging," Marietta said. "I think it was apologizing."

"Apologizing?" I asked.

"Look," she said, pointing at the nearest wallet. "It's got some sort of water damage."

"That's not water," Dryser said. "That's frost."

"Or ice," Bartell said. "Water usually doesn't leave that white film on leather."

"Ice is water," Marietta said.

"We're speculating again," I said.

"What do you expect us to do?" Dryser said. "Knock on the rock and get facts?"

The cold was gone. The air felt normal. I glanced at him, then, without warning the others, stepped into the fairy circle.

"Scott!" Marietta said.

"Stop!" Bartell said.

I didn't listen to them. I crossed to the rock and knocked on it, just like Dryser suggested. The rock was cool to my touch. After a moment, I knocked again.

I thought I heard a corresponding sound coming from inside, but nothing happened. I knocked until the side of my hand was raw, and the rock never opened, never split again.

"Anyone got a knife?" I asked.

Harwell tossed me his. It was a Swiss Army knife, heavier than Richard's and not as pretty. I laid it across the rock as I had laid the other. Then I stood back.

Nothing happened. We waited nearly an hour and nothing happened.

"Maybe it was the moonlight and the knife," Dryser said.

"Maybe it was the silver and pearl handle," Marietta said.

"Maybe it was the timing," Bartell said.

Whatever it was, we couldn't duplicate it that night. Nor the next night, nor the next.

Then, on the third night, fire erupted in Felton Woods, burning the fairy circle and the surrounding trees. No one was injured, but when the smoke cleared, the rock was gone.

————

Of course, now we live in the realm of wackos. I tried to protect the team. I tried to let them fade into the woodwork, and claim that I was alone in the Felton Woods. But they had had an experience they wanted to discuss, and Harwell wanted to defend his photographs— decisions they would all live to regret.

We've been interviewed from everyone in the paranormal media from Art Bell to *Unsolved Mysteries*. We've signed with a studio that wants to make a film from our experience. We've made money. Marietta laughs at me. She says everything I touch turns to gold.

I wish that were true.

The price for all of this has been subtle. The Air Force no longer trusts our service, believing that we're searching for UFOs in the desert, not experimental aircraft. Bartell was quietly asked to leave Northwestern. Annapolis kept Dryser, partly because he was one of the most popular instructors on campus and partly because military folk are more accustomed to strange and unexplained experiences than they lead us to believe. The experience made Marietta a minor celebrity at NASA, something she never really wanted.

I'm the only one who is unchanged, at least professionally. Personally, I have spent more money than I care to think of, putting together a team of scientists to study the events in the Felton Woods. They're hampered by many things, including the anecdotal nature of much of the experience and the fact that the fairy circle is gone.

The night after the fire, the rains came and for the first time in forty years, the fairy circle turned to mud. In the spring, grass pushed its way to the top, and small seedlings sprouted into tiny trees. The radiation was gone as if it had never been.

The watches, the wallets, the wedding rings did indeed come from the missing people. All of the items were damaged in some way. Most authorities think they were frozen and then thawed out, but no one could prove that. The effect would be the same, they say, if some of these things were under the cold mountain run-off in Felton Creek for years.

Interviewers ask me if I have any theories and I tell them I don't. I'm lying. I have a theory. I just don't want to taint my scientists by saying it aloud.

The only person I've shared this idea with is Marietta. She listens sometimes, usually with a healthy skepticism. But on this one, she agrees with me.

I think the aliens—and I do believe they were aliens—had come to the Felton Woods forty years ago, and set up a blind. Jane Goodall from Mars, I guess. They used that blind to study human beings, and they thought they were perfectly safe. After all, except for moments at touchdown and takeoff, their ship existed in a slightly different dimension. No one could touch it. All it did was give off low levels of radiation, except of course for the door or the rock, as we called it, which had to remain in our dimension. The creatures could disguise themselves as mist, and walk among us, observing, studying, learning.

The problem they hadn't expected was the effect of the cold that emanated from their ship at odd moments. I don't know if that was exhaust, or waste being disposed of, or simply a combination of elements, but sometimes, humans, dogs, wolves, got caught in the cold and died—like my brother did. Exposure. Deep cold. Severe trauma to the skin tissue caused by natural elements. Only it masked time of death, and it would have revealed the position of the blind.

So they took the bodies and disposed of them, somehow, in their machine, maybe or in the creek. And they kept identification. Or perhaps the wallets and rings and collars served as souvenirs. I think they managed to dispose of Richard's tent and his things before someone stumbled on his body, just before dawn, but they hadn't taken him yet. They had screwed up, and that led us to them.

Richard and I had stumbled on an accidental way to open their ship. Only that first night, I had grabbed the knife before the entire procedure occurred. Perhaps I had felt fingers against my own as the knife dropped into my hand, or perhaps it was the first stages of the tissue damage that would have led to my death.

I will never know.

What I do know—what I believe and cannot prove—is that my team and I opened that ship. And when we did, the aliens saw us, knew that we had seen them, and knew their experiment was done. All those years of study ended when the creatures they were studying discovered the blind. The aliens could no longer watch in silence. They would have become the studied or, perhaps worse for them, they would have become part of the experiment.

Marietta disagrees with me on fundamentals. She believes they captured and killed the missing people, experimenting on the captives in a Whitley Strieber sort of way to gain a better understanding of human beings. That's why everyone who disappeared was unattached, or whose disappearance could be explained in other ways.

I think that last was merely a coincidence. She says there are no such thing as coincidences. We argue fruitlessly about this. Lack of proof is a serious problem.

The scientists don't even know where the aliens came from. Lately they've been suggesting that the aliens may live on Earth, only in that different dimension. I hate that explanation, and hope they find another. But I doubt we'll learn anything knew.

Of course, I've told all of this to Stacy, and Heather, and April. They don't care. Their mother has been under a psychiatrist's care now for the better portion of the year. Her mental state had been deteriorating when Richard was alive; his death had sent her over an edge that the doctors aren't sure she'll ever come back from.

I have bought a house in the new development near the golf course, and the girls live with me. Families are nothing like I had imagined they would be. From a distance they look completely different—easier, I think, and more orderly. April takes much of my time. She's anorexic, her response to her parents' obsessions. Heather challenges my authority at all times, and Stacy—well, Stacy has made Felton Woods the center of her life. Part of the reason I hired the scientists was so that I could reassure her that someone was working on her father's discovery, that he had not died in vain.

Although I am not sure of that. I think he and I were watching each other from opposite blinds, seeing only that little patch of woods available to our viewfinders. He believed that my life was better, and he tried to emulate it, in his own way, while, at the same time, believing that I had shut off the most important side of myself, the side that needed love and family and warmth.

From my blind, the view was just as narrow, and just as wrong. Richard's family wasn't perfect, and I really didn't know any of its members until he died. But he hadn't squandered his potential, as I had thought. And he faced each and every day with more courage than I had ever given him credit for.

I wonder sometimes what those aliens observed in that wood. The condoms and beer bottles give me some hint. But they must have seen other things, from frightened little boys approaching the circle on a dare to drug addicts shooting up and then acting crazy. Was the alien view of human existence as narrow and limiting as mine of Richard? Or were they savvy enough to know that all they had seen was one small corner of a very large and very complex world?

I don't know. I will never know, no matter how many scientists I buy, no matter how many hours they work in studying events in the Felton Woods.

For I am glimpsing the aliens from my own little blind, and my observation of them is even shorter than their observation of me and mine. And that is why I do not talk about them, except when I need to help out my friends, to support them as they go from talk show to talk show, from one well-paying but weird project to another.

Some of those shows say the greatest mystery of Felton Woods is what I think about the events. But that's not true. The greatest mystery of Felton Woods is why the aliens chose that spot, and stayed there for so long.

The next great mystery is why no one exposed them before we did.

I find myself thinking that we're like deer going about our business in the forest. We walk the same paths and do not look around us. And when we do look, we don't like what we see.

I know I don't like what I've seen. Not the aliens or Richard's family or the changes in my friends. I'm not referring to that. What I've seen is deeper, and more personal. My experiences in Felton Woods showed me the depth of my own ignorance.

And it astounds me.

FIT TO PRINT

KRISTINE KATHRYN RUSCH

FIT TO PRINT

First, let me give you the story as I reported it. From the Sunday edition of *The New York Times*, June 29, 1997:

Mysterious Fire Destroys Oregon Town
Frank Butler
Special Correspondent

PORTLAND, ORE., June 27, 1997. Fifteen people died as fire destroyed the sleepy hamlet of Bonner Bay on the Central Oregon Coast. The fire, which began in a hotel north of town just after midnight yesterday, quickly became an inferno that raced down the town's main road, leaping from roof to roof.

Residents sought shelter in caves on the town's north end. The caves, accessible only on the beach in low tide, provided a safe haven for nearly 3,500 people.

"We're lucky the tide was out," Mayor Ruth Anderson said. "We're lucky the fire burned out before the tide came in."

Experts believe Bonner Bay's location attributed to the fire's quick spread and its quick end. Bonner Bay was built on a four-mile-long rock ledge between two cliffs. With the ocean to the west, and the Coast Mountain Range to the east, Bonner Bay was isolated. Until 1950, Bonner Bay was inaccessible by land.

"By the time we learned of the fire, the entire bay was aflame," said Joe Roth of the Central Coast Fire District. "We couldn't get into the area, except by boat. I'm amazed anyone survived."

The fire burned out in a matter of hours, Roth said, "because it ran out of fuel."

The fifteen people who died were in the hotel where the fire started. Their names have not yet been released.

Four column inches. Four column inches to describe the experience of a lifetime.

———

My grandmother was born in Bonner Bay and she retained a home there until she died. The home then became my family's West Coast vacation house. We rented it out most of the year for the additional income, and used it ourselves two weeks every summer. When my parents died, they bequeathed the home to my two siblings and me, and we decided to maintain the arrangement: vacation rental much of the year, with six weeks carved out for individual family time. During my marriage, my wife and I only went to Bonner Bay once. She was a native New Yorker, and the isolation terrified her.

I returned every summer after the divorce.

My two weeks in Bonner Bay ran from June 16 to June 30. This year, conveniently, the two-week period began on a Monday. I have three weeks of vacation at the *Times* — I've been on staff since 1970 — and I usually used two of them in Bonner Bay.

A man could not get farther away from New York.

Bonner Bay was an old fishing community built around the turn of the last century. In the affluent '20s, Portland residents discovered it, and an enterprising businessman built a natatorium on the rock ledge overlooking the beach. Hundreds of homes were built in the small space, and almost all of them were abandoned in the 1930s. It wasn't until the fifties that the tourists rediscovered Bonner Bay.

I wrote it up in the mid-seventies for the *Times* travel section as a place that time forgot. And, indeed, it looked like a European fishing village. The nearby mountains had been deforested; the trees used to build the homes crammed side-by-side on the ledge. Because there was no main road, and no need of one, there were no streets. Only houses, packed together like an audience in a concert hall.

Television hadn't touched the community: no broadcast signals could come over the mountains. A local radio station tried to fill the gaps, but its performance barely rated above that of a community college station. Until the highway was carved through the cliffs, the food was either locally grown in the thin topsoil or brought in by ship. I remember childhood summers surviving only on the fish we caught because the local stores had run out of produce and basics before the weekly supply ships had come in.

The Bonner Bay of my adulthood had amenities courtesy of the highway: tiny shops that appealed to tourists; restaurants that specialized in seafood; and two grocery stores, one on either end of town. The town had cable and access to the more powerful coastal radio stations. The culture had finally invaded Bonner Bay.

Sort of.

Every time I drove in, I too noted the isolation. I spent my first nights in the upstairs bedroom still crammed with my great-grandparent's handmade furniture listening to the ocean and nothing else. I missed the sirens and the honks, the shouts and the bustle of the city that never sleeps. My Manhattan apartment with its constant noise comforted me, and it took days of adjusting before Bonner Bay's silence gave me the peace I craved.

On my first full day, to orient myself, I always walked to the caves.

But on June 17th, as I followed 101's curves through Bonner Bay, I noted the town no longer had the peace I remembered.

Everyone was worried — everyone was talking — about the strangers.

————

The first hint that something was different were the pictures taped to so many windows. The pictures were usually hand-drawn on 8 1/2" x 11" paper. I had to see the image several times before I realized what it was: a tiny person in a circle that appeared to be floating on the crest of a wave. Even though I figured out the image, I didn't know what it was for. I decided to go to the center of Bonner Bay's universe, to find out what was going on.

The hub of all local activity was the Bonner Bay Café. The café took up two lots in the exact center of town. The original café was a shack that still stood even though it had been remodeled several times. It reflected the locals' need to sit and converse in a public place, even in the days when maintaining a restaurant seemed to be a foolhardy idea. Since then, the restaurant had expanded several times, each time absorbing a building instead of adding on. The result was a labyrinthine maze that most tourists never figured out.

Mayor Ruth Anderson usually held court in the café, since Bonner Bay had never gotten around to building a town hall. The council met in the café on Tuesday nights, and most other local meetings were held there as well. In grand Bonner Bay tradition, each meeting had its own room of the restaurant, and none of the other meetings ventured into it. Mayor Anderson used the original shack which had no windows. That way, the town felt that her meetings were entirely private.

I went in the shack door, marveling, as I always did at the uneven wood flooring and the baked-in smell of coffee. The wood on the walls was so ancient that it was gray and flaking. The tables in this area were 1950s Formica, also gray. If it weren't for the plastic faux Tiffany lamps with Coke™ painted on them, the entire place would be dark and gloomy.

"Well, if it isn't the big shot," Ruth said when she saw me. She came and put her arms around me. She was a large woman who was probably in her eighties now. She had been mayor since the early seventies, and remembered my grandmother as well as my parents. Ever since I had gotten work at the *Times* I had been "the big shot." "How're you, son?"

No one had called me "son" since I turned fifty. "Fine, Ruthie," I said. "Mind if I have a cuppa?"

"Naw," she said. "Slow business day anyway. Not much happening in this town." And, as if to prove it, she went and poured me coffee herself. The shack truly was her domain. A waitress I didn't recognize stuck her head in the door, but Ruth waved her away.

I took the coffee and sat at Ruth's table. It had been the same one for years: the only wooden table in the place, pushed up against the back corner, a desk lamp on one side, and vinyl chairs on the others.

"What're all the signs, Ruthie?"

She laughed, a sound of great gusto that reverberated through the place. "Leave it to you, kiddo, to notice that right out. When'd you get here, last night?"

"Last night," I agreed, marveling at her prodigious memory. Bonner Bay may have been small, but it was Ruth's domain, the way that New York City had once been Fiorello La Guardia's.

"You were born to ask questions," she said, and for a moment I thought she wasn't going to answer me. "Guess I knew that when your father brought you in here with him after the war. 'How come is this place so dark?' you asked. 'Ain't they got money for lights?' And you just a little thing."

I'd heard that story so many times that I could ignore it with ease. "The pictures, Ruthie."

"You won't like this, Frank. And you won't print it in your rag."

"It's not mine, Ruth," I said, smiling. "And I usually don't print anything about Bonner Bay in the *Times*. I'm on vacation."

"Sure as spit," she said. "You'll go on vacation when you die. If a good story comes up in Bonner Bay, you'll write about it. You done that when we opened the new hotel. You wrote that whole travel article. And you wrote another thing when James bought the Sea Eagle."

"The travel article was nearly thirty years ago," I said, "And James buying the Sea Eagle was news to New Yorkers. He was one of Manhattan's premiere chefs."

"The whole summer we had people trying the helicopter in here to sample his cuisine." She pronounced it "qwe-zine."

"Ruthie, that was fifteen years ago. James is dead now."

"Still," she said.

"You're not getting off that easy," I said.

"You won't like this."

"Since when did you care about what I think?"

She grinned. "On this one, I care what everybody thinks. I'm getting old enough that folks might start considering me dotty."

"No one would consider you dotty."

"Not even if I told you we have a colony of space aliens living in the Sea Nest?"

I laughed. "Not even then." I sipped my coffee, and noticed she hadn't joined me in my mirth. "Ruthie? You can tell me."

"I just did," she said. "We have a colony of space aliens living in the Sea Nest."

I slowly set my cup down, not quite sure if her words were a test or not. I decided to treat her like any other difficult interview: I'd play along. "So then what are the signs?"

"Support."

"As in political support?" I asked, trying to imagine Bonner Bay divided enough to need rallying cries. The locals here kept their political opinions to themselves because they knew better than to start that kind of squabbling. The town was simply too small.

"Physical support," she said, not quite looking at me. "They're different from us."

"Didn't they bring their own life-support?"

"Sure," she said. "But they don't like to use it if they don't have to. So they use our homes as way stations."

"Way stations," I repeated. If she was testing me, this was a good one. "And they're staying at the Sea Nest?"

"Doris let 'em modify the ground floor."

"Does it still flood out?"

"Only in the rainy season," Ruth said. "Besides, it don't matter. They like mold."

"They sound like mighty accommodating aliens. What are they doing here, Ruthie?"

She sighed and sat down. Her chair groaned beneath her weight. "I knew you wouldn't believe me. Don't know why I even tried."

"I believe a lot of things, Ruthie. I haven't said I doubted you."

"Don't have to," she said. "You're playing them big city games on me. Humor the idiot."

"I would never consider you an idiot."

"Nope," she said. "But you might consider me a narrow-minded, small-town yokel."

"Only on a bad day," I said.

"I'm not sure I want to keep talking to you, Frank," she said.

"Sure you do," I said. "You've got my curiosity piqued. I'd like to meet those aliens."

"If you promise me you won't write about them."

"How can I promise that, Ruthie? If they're space aliens, they're news."

"That's why they're here, Frank. They don't want no media attention."

"Those sound like mighty savvy space aliens."

"You'd be surprised," she said.

———

The Sea Nest was a gorgeous five-story hotel built against one cliff face on the site of the old natatorium. In fact, the hotel had used the natatorium's floor plan and foundation. The result was a gothic building with real character: stonework, masonry, and gargoyles hanging off the roof. Its completion had sparked the now-infamous travel article. Ruthie never quite forgave me for that article because it had brought the first wave of out-of-state tourists into Bonner Bay. Once they discovered the quaint little hamlet they had told all their friends.

Bonner Bay had never been the same.

I didn't entirely regret that. I never took full responsibility for it either. I believed that the responsibility truly lay with the owners of the Sea Nest. They wouldn't have built such a large, inviting structure without wanting guests to inhabit it. Too many large hotels in out-of-the-way places went out of business in Oregon. The state had a (deserved) reputation for driving away outsiders.

I found that irony delicious as Ruth and I walked through the Sea Nest's parking lot.

Since it was summer, the lot was full of Lexus, Jaguars, BMWs, and the occasional Geo Metro. The hotel's four-star restaurant and its award-winning wine list had upgraded the clientele from the adventurous of the early days to the wealthy of today. I often thought — privately, because I didn't dare say anything to Ruthie — that the adventurous of those days had turned into the wealthy and that someday the clientele of the Sea Nest would simply die off.

I guess it doesn't matter now.

We bypassed the main entrance and went to one of the lower level doors. Ruthie stopped me before we entered.

"Okay," she said. "I'm going to prepare you for this, even though you'll think it strange."

"I think it's stranger that you worry about what I think."

She sighed. "Humor me," she said.

I nodded, waiting. Ruth glanced toward the sea. That morning it was a navy blue with patches of green. It was as calm as it gets which, by most standards, wasn't calm at all.

"I don't know the technical scientific terms for what they are. But they're like sea lions. They can be in the ocean and they can be on land.

Only they need to do both. They crave something in the salt water. If they don't get it, they shrivel up and start flaking."

"Flaking?"

"Frank," she said in that warning tone all women learn by the age of eighteen.

"All right," I said. "Keep going."

"The flaking's the reason for the signs. Those of us with signs have saltwater baths ready in our houses in case the aliens need it."

I think that was when I truly assumed she was batty. At this point, she was the only one I had talked to about the aliens. I hadn't seen them yet, and I couldn't quite comprehend houses with salt-water baths. Humans didn't do such nice things for each other. We didn't have cigarettes around in case someone needed a fix or additional oxygen in case someone went into arrest. Hell, most of us didn't even have extra soap, and I'll bet we all knew someone who needed that.

"I'm going to take you in," she said. "Remember your promise. No reporting."

"No reporting," I repeated.

She pulled open the door. It was a heavy metal door, rusted on the corners from exposure to the sea air. The Sea Nest never rented out its basement. The old foundation and the rough conditions had led to serious flooding in some stormy seasons, and the owners just felt it prudent to leave the basement alone. I had only been in there once, just after the building was finished. Even then the basement rooms had an old, musty air.

I stepped inside, expecting that musty smell. Instead, I nearly choked from the fetid odor of spoiled sea water and wet animal fur. It flashed across my mind that Ruthie was setting me up. Me and all the other reporters, the ones who had done travel articles on Bonner Bay and ruined its splendid isolation.

The lighting was thin and seventies: thick fixtures done in steel and dark wood that, no matter what the expense, still looked cheap. There was no carpet, only a gray concrete floor, with ancient white water marks. The walls had once been paneled. Some of the paneling remained, peeled and ragged, as if it had been broken off by high water.

The smell got worse the farther inside we went.

"What've you got in here?" I asked. "101 soggy Dalmatians?"

"You know, Frank, the one gift you never had was an effective sense of humor." Ruth led me through the wide corridor. It felt like night in there, even though it was the middle of the day.

Finally we reached the west side of the basement. Another door had been left open, letting in a thin trickle of sunlight. Through the door, I could see the edge of the rock ledge, and stone steps leading down to the boulder-strewn beach.

"I don't see any modifications," I said.

"Shush," Ruth said. She went to one of the side doors, and knocked.

There was some strange rustling and cooing inside. Then the door opened. I could see no one.

"I brought an old friend of mine," Ruth said to the empty air. "His name is Frank Butler. He owns a house here, and his grandmother was born here."

I heard some chittering, rather like a high-pitched voice speaking too fast to understand. Then Ruthie added, "Yes, I know he works for the *New York Times* but he's promised me he won't write about you."

"Folks," I said, wanting this charade over with, "if you're as real as Ruthie says, *The New York Times* will want nothing to do with you."

There was a bit more chittering. Ruthie stood with her hands clasped behind her back, waiting more patiently than I had ever seen her do. Then it ended, and she turned to me.

"They said it'll be okay."

I wasn't sure if I was relieved or annoyed. I usually did well with new things: I was a reporter who traveled endlessly, interviewed people I had never met about topics I had only recently heard of, and yet this new thing was filling me with a sort of silent dread. Maybe it was because I expected to revise my opinion of Ruth afterwards. Maybe it was because I was afraid I would discover I was gullible.

And maybe it was because I had never had an opinion about extra-terrestrials, and I didn't really want one.

I followed Ruthie inside the room.

The room had been modified. The windowpanes had been replaced with blue-green stained glass, and the light fixtures had blue-green bulbs. The effect was to make the room look as if it were part of a bad sixties movie — or if you squinted, an underwater dump.

The smell was stronger in here, wet fur and stagnant water, so strong that I had to fight to keep my hand from my face.

In the blue-green light, I could see dozens of small furry creatures. They looked like electric shoe polishers, the kind you could order from an elite catalogue. They were oblong, about a foot high, and covered with a thin layer of curly wool. Rather like a shrunken sheep without eyes, ears, or nose.

"Good heavens, Frank," Ruth said. "Look up."

"But —" I indicated the ground.

She snorted. "You've seen too many bad movies."

She had rounded a corner. I followed and ran into more than a dozen naked people. Then I paused and revised my first impression. They weren't people, at least, not completely. They all appeared young. They had two arms, two legs, a torso, a head and genitalia. They also had fins rising from their spine. Their eyes and mouths were completely round instead of oval-shaped, and they had little suckers on the ends of their fingers.

"What's in the other room?" I hissed.

"Their pelts," Ruth hissed back. Then she said in a normal tone: "This is Frank."

The strangers rose as a unit. Then I realized they had all been sitting in small tubs filled with half an inch of seawater. The water was particularly pungent. It was green with algae, like an overgrown, dying tidal pool that the sea hadn't reached in weeks.

One stranger came toward me. He was shorter than the rest, with hair the color of sea foam. He extended his hand, and I was about to take it when I heard a whoosh behind me. One of the shoe polishers zoomed through the air past me, connected with the stranger's hand, and covered him from his chin to his ankles. It looked like he was wearing an oddly sewn sweater that covered his entire body.

It also relieved me. I was too much a product of my culture to appreciate nakedness in anything vaguely human.

"You are the reporter," he said in a high squeaky voice. His lips moved like fish kisses as he spoke, and his eyes blinked in unison with the lip movement. I was amazed I could understand him.

"Well, I'm not just a reporter," I said. "I am also a person in my own right."

"Remains to be seen," he said. "Didn't think reporters were persons."

"What else would they be?" I asked.

"Unscrupulous money grubbers," he said with a primness that clashed with his kissing lips.

"Unscrupulous money grubbers are people too," I said, glancing at Ruth. She was watching me nervously, as if she had just introduced me to the Pope and was waiting for me to declare that I was an atheist.

"You will report us, no?"

I was confused and uncertain for the first time since I was a cub reporter. I hadn't felt this far over my head since I met John Gotti on his own turf.

"I promised Ruth I wouldn't," I said.

"And you will hold to such a promise?"

"Of course," I said.

"Then we have no more need of you." He waved his wool-covered hand. "Let us absorb in peace."

"All right." I backed out of the room and walked gingerly through the pelts until I reached the hallway. I had to blink to get my eyes used to the light again. When Ruth didn't follow me immediately, I went outside the open door and stood at the top of the stairs.

The air was brisk with a bit of mid-morning chill. The sea smell was strong and refreshing after the fetid odors of the inner rooms. I checked my feelings like an old man who'd tripped would check for broken bones:

Unsettled? Yes.

Frightened? No.

Curious? Yes.

Frightened? No.

Worried? Yes.

Frightened? *No!*

All right, I was frightened, and that worried me even more. I almost never got frightened any more. I had lived in New York City too long. I swore at potential muggers and shook hands with mobsters. I had insulted one of the biggest serial killers of the century once, and had shared a urinal with the President and a squadron of Secret Service guys. I'd been shot at, knifed, and my car'd been fire bombed.

Nothing should have bothered me. Especially nothing as mundane as a dirty hotel basement and a lot of creepy looking people.

"What did you do?" Ruth asked. She was behind me. I hadn't heard her coming.

"What did *I* do?"

"I'd never seen them so rude before."

"That wasn't a them. That was a him, and he didn't strike me as rude."

"He's their spokesman. I doubt the others can speak English."

"How did he learn it?" I asked.

"I don't know," she said. "Apparently they've been studying us for a long time."

"Or maybe they're just as human as we are."

"Frank." That tone again.

I sat on the top step and patted the space next to me so that she could join me. I wasn't really worried that the creatures would come outside, even though I wasn't sure why.

She went back, put a rock between the door and its jamb, then sat down beside me.

"Have you ever seen them outside that room?"

"Of course," she said. "I told you they wander through town. With their pelts on."

"How come they weren't wandering this morning?"

"It's too warm for them. Imagine how you'd feel under all that fur."

"That room was warm."

"They weren't wearing their pelts."

I sighed. The ocean spread before me, now half green and gold, an endless vista of water. "All right, Ruth," I said, "Suppose I grant that these are aliens. Suppose I give you that."

"Generous," she murmured.

"If they are, what are they doing here? If they know so much about us, how come they didn't appear at the White House or the Kremlin or something?"

"The White House isn't by the sea."

She said that so matter-of-factly that at first I wasn't sure if I had heard her correctly.

"What does the sea have to do with it?"

"They came out of the sea."

I turned to look at her. She was staring at the ocean, her nose and cheeks red with wind, her gray hair mussed.

"Their ships can't land on our ground," she said. "Something about pressure and movement and density and stuff I didn't understand. Their ships are like bubbles. They float on the sea's surface."

"And these guys swam ashore?"

She shook her head. "The bubbles dropped them off and then went out to sea. They'll call the ships when they need to go back."

"So they chose Bonner Bay specifically," I said. "Why?"

"I told you," she said. "Because it's isolated. They don't want coverage. They just want to learn about us."

"And you believe that?"

"Why shouldn't I?" she asked. "Why is it more normal to doubt them? Is mistrust so common in your life now that you can't accept a miracle when you see it?"

"You think they're miracles?" I asked.

"Hell," she said. "I think a sunset is a miracle. What do I know?"

"I don't know," I said. "It bothers me."

"Take them for what they are, Frank."

That surprised me more than anything. "What are they, Ruthie?"

"A gift," she said. "A gift from the sea."

"I hate anonymous gifts," I said. "They always have strings."

The next few days were weird. Beyond weird, really. Different and difficult for reasons hard to pinpoint.

I liked Bonner Bay for its clear blue summer skies, its cool breezes, and its lack of pretentiousness. In a way, my visits to the town were attempts to return to my boyhood — not my actual boyhood which was as confused and difficult as anyone else's — but those perfect boyhood moments when the air was warm, school was out, and the day felt full of possibilities. Possibilities and Tom Sawyer freedoms. Bonner Bay had that for me, with the ocean and the isolation, and those blissful moments when I would realize that the town would always remain the same, no matter how many personal computers people owned, or how many channels they could receive.

Bonner Bay would remain Bonner Bay.

Until this year. In those days, the aliens — which I took to calling them, like everyone else — appeared all over town. They walked every square inch of Bonner Bay, heads up, pelts on, greeting locals as they passed. Tourists stayed away from them, treating them like Bigfoot's cousins — something to cross the street to avoid. But the locals were intrigued and proud that these creatures had chosen Bonner Bay as a refuge, and they did all they could to accommodate the creatures' needs.

I ran into a number of the aliens. And, unlike the tourists, I didn't cross the street to avoid them. I went out of my way to say hello.

No alien ever answered me. They acted as if they couldn't see me.

And nothing I could do changed that.

They didn't spoil my vacation — Bonner Bay was still as calm and peaceful as ever — but they did ruin the possibilities of it: the Tom Sawyer/glimpse into my boyhood part. They constantly reminded me it was 1997, and that I was a man closer to dying than to his boyhood.

They also kept me from relaxing. The reporter part of my brain, the part that had enabled me to write several award-winning series on managed care, New York politics, and the mob's control of garbage service, wouldn't shut off. I couldn't believe these guys showed up to enjoy Bonner Bay's isolation. I was certain that there were more isolated places in the world. I knew of at least two in North America: one in the Idaho Mountains which, granted, had no ocean, and one in Alaska that had no roads. It bothered me that they didn't go to Seattle or San Francisco or Miami, some large city on the ocean, where they could be even more anonymous than they were here.

The fact that they could speak the language, even though they had just arrived, bothered me too. I had seen enough sf flicks to be suspicious of that. If they learned quickly, well, that frightened me. And if they had known it in advance, well, that frightened me too.

It also bothered me that I spent so much time thinking about them. After all, I couldn't write about them. **Aliens Arrive in Bonner Bay!** would never be a headline in *Times* no matter how accurate the story.

So I tried to ignore the aliens, as they ignored me.

And that worked.

For a while.

Until the night they woke me up.

————

My bedroom in my grandmother's house was at the top of the stairs, on the right, facing the ocean. The room was large by most standards and could fit two double beds and a cot easily. As children, my siblings and I shared that room. After my parents died, my siblings usually used the master bedroom on the first floor when they visited. I, however, could not break the old habit, and returned to my old room to sleep with the ghosts.

That room was alive. It creaked and moaned and moved ever so slightly in any wind. The constant roar of the ocean filled it, and always, on the first night of my arrival, I couldn't sleep, listening to the quiet sounds, letting them greet me after too many months away.

But by the middle of my visit, I would sleep sounder than I had in years. So when I awoke to a bright light and a chorus of voices, I at first thought it a dream.

The light had the intensity of a train's headlight on a moonless night. The voices were eerie, the whispered memories of an erased cassette. And the smell of wet fur was thick and pungent, a live thing that encased and enveloped me.

I never had odors in my dreams.

I sat up. A dozen aliens filled the room. One held the light — or seemed to hold the light — directly on me.

I held a hand over my face, blocking my eyes. "It's considered rude in our culture to invade a man's home and wake him up."

"You are Frank Butler?" The voice was androgynous and yet high-pitched.

"Last I checked."

"The reporter?"

"State your business," I said, bringing my arm down, "and get the hell out."

The speaker came toward me. Its pelt was dark black, so dark that it absorbed the light. "I am —" the name sounded like a sneeze "— and I too am a reporter. I wonder if we could 'let's make a deal'?"

"You learned our language through television transmissions," I said, finally realizing, with a bit of relief, how they had learned to speak English.

"Is that not what the transmissions were for?"

I shook my head. "Get the damn light out of my face. Then we'll negotiate."

I couldn't imagine them wanting to negotiate with me. They hadn't wanted to speak to me all week.

The light lowered. The full dozen wore pelts of different colors. They glistened in the brightness. This room hadn't seen so much light since the turn of the century. Cobwebs graced the corners, and the flowered wallpaper, which I had thought unchanged in all the decades I'd seen it, was peeling near the top of the window.

"We wish to 'let's make a deal,' Frank Butler."

"I got that. What kind of dealmaking do you want with me?"

The alien tilted its head and its entire pelt moved. "We too report. We believe information the center of all things. We will trade information with you."

This was a switch in attitude. But my reporter's instincts, never fully off, knew something was up. I wasn't going to give any information until I knew exactly what was going on.

"Trade information?"

The spokesalien nodded gravely. "We will let you be our contact to the earth. You will have our 'Breaking News Exclusive!' We will subject three of our number to your scientists. We will give interviews, meet your leaders, and allow you and people of your choice to visit our crafts."

Complete flip-flop. Despite the warmth in the room, I was cold. "What do I have to do in return?"

"Take us to the illegals."

I rubbed a hand over my face. It felt sleep grimy. I resisted the urge to pinch myself. "The 'illegals'?"

"Yes. You are the reporter. You will know where they are. We have located their crafts in your sea. Their beacons led us here. You are the reporter. You will know where they are."

My brain was slowly kicking in. "And that's what you base your assumption of knowledge on? My profession?"

"And your passion for knowledge. This story will earn you great — moneys — will it not?"

Maybe. If I fought it through the *Times* editorial staff. If I was willing to risk my reputation to do so. If I was willing to run to a less reputable news agency if the *Times* changed its mind.

"How come you can't find them?" I asked, stalling. "You found me."

"We have studied this town. Your presence here has been a comfort and a distraction. We did not know when we chose this pueblo that it would have an information gatherer in its midst, however irregularly."

"And that's bad?"

"It adds an element of living dangerous," the alien said.

"Oh." I frowned. "What are illegals?"

"You have met them," the spokesalien said. "You have seen them."

"How do you know?" I asked, not sure if that question gave me away or not.

"Because you are not shocked to see us."

Ooops. Had me there. I grinned. "It's the middle of the night. You're a dream. I expect anything in my dreams."

"You are awake," the spokesalien said.

"I'm not sure of that," I said. "How can you be?"

It turned and conferred with an alien near it. Their language sounded like sneezes, coughs and hiccups. Somehow, in the midst of all that hacking, I came to believe in them.

Aliens.

Weird creatures from outer space.

And I wanted nothing to do with them. I wanted them out of my grandmother's house.

The alien turned toward me. "Will you help us?" it asked, apparently deciding to ignore my dream discussion.

"What are illegals?" I asked. "Drugs?"

The alien tilted its head the other way. Its pelt shone blue. "You have them," it said. "We have heard on your new transmissions. Illegals. Those who cross the wrong border."

"Illegal aliens," I said. "But they're illegal in the country they *arrive* in, not in the country they have left."

"So, if our people land here, then they are illegals, no?"

I had never thought of that, but I suppose it was true. I had been culturally conditioned to think that any visitors from outer space would be treated differently than Mexicans trying to cross the Rio Grande. I suppose it depended on what numbers they arrived in, and whether or not the government believed they could be of use to the country.

"I thought you wanted them because they were outlaws in your country," I said.

"No." The creature sneezed and others sneezed as well. I hoped it was a gesture of disgust and not some alien virus. "We want them because they have broken the great taboo."

"The great taboo?"

"They have left the blind."

It took me a minute to realize that analogy came courtesy of the *Discovery* Channel. "You're observing us and they ruined the experiment?"

"Yes," the alien said. "They have decided to take the experiment a stage farther than mandated."

"Seems you have too," I said, not believing them. "Especially considering the offer you just made me."

The alien's pelt fur rose and fell. I guessed it to be an alien shrug. But I might have been wrong. It could have been annoyance. Or an itch.

"This experiment has already been contaminated," it said. "More will not hurt."

"Then I don't understand why you need them."

"We do not need them," the alien said. "We must charge them. Interfering with information is punishable by death."

"Serious charge," I said. "Here information is free, and anyone can tamper with it."

"So you believe," the alien said, sounding as if it did not.

I was a bit rattled. Not by its skepticism, although that surprised me too. But by the charge of death. We never took information that seriously here. In fact, as I got older, I found myself getting disgusted with my own business. No one cared about the facts, only the facts, ma'am. They cared about the scoop, only the scoop, sorry if it's wrong, folks. At the *Times* we tried not to fall into that, but we did, more and more, in a stuffy, snobby, elitist sort of way.

So if I gave those smelly pathetic creatures up to these smelly seemingly more powerful creatures, I would sign the first group's death warrant.

I'd be lying if I didn't say I considered it. After all, I was a practicing journalist. I had to make my money.

But I loved my job at the *Times*. And, as an editor there said to me just the week before as we casually discussed the possibility of reporting creatures from outer space: "Frank, aliens could bomb the White House, and we'd report it as 'Unidentified bomb destroys U.S. Capitol.' We can't publish anything that smacks of tabloids until we've got five years of documentation from national science centers and confirmation of the flight path from NASA. And maybe we couldn't publish it then."

These creatures would have been better off if Bonner Bay's resident reporter worked for the *Inquirer*.

"Sorry," I said. "I can't help you."

"Can't?" the alien asked. "Or won't?"

I fluffed my pillow, preparing to go back to sleep. "Can't," I said. "You're a dream, and I've never seen creatures like you before. If the aliens have taken over Bonner Bay, no one has told me about it. Better go invade someone else's sleep."

"You do not wish for the fame we offer?"

"Nope," I said. "I'm surprised I'm even dreaming of it."

"You are a fool, Frank Butler," the alien said. "You do not know what you have done."

———

Well, I know now.

Two nights later, I woke up to find myself in the sea caves, along with the rest of Bonner Bay. Some were nude, some weren't, but we were all wet, and we were, horror of horrors, smashing tide pools. The tide was out, and the caves were empty, and we were all confused. To add to the mess, all the house pets from town were in the caves as well. Dogs, cats, iguanas, houseplants, aquariums filled with fish. If it lived in a house, it was in the cave.

Unless it was an alien creature.

None of them were inside.

I hate thinking of this: The noise, the screams, the confusion. Waking up in the dark and the cold and the noise, not knowing how we got there, or why. Only Ruth seemed serene.

She said the aliens did it.

But she didn't know which ones.

She also organized us. Climbed onto a rock and shouted until she had our attention. She said there had to be a reason they hid us in here, and she said we would proceed slowly, in an orderly fashion, to the mouth of the cave.

It took five volunteer firefighters and a local bouncer to enforce orderly. But we went, lemming-like, to the mouth. I was with Ruthie at the head of the group. Fortunately, the two of us had chosen to wear pajamas that night. I'm not sure I wanted to see Ruthie nude.

When we got to the opening, we saw a bubblecraft, hovering low. It released several small bubbles of light, and when they landed, they turned into fireballs.

I cannot describe this in any more detail. I refuse to look any closer than this.

It was ugly.

The balls engulfed the city in a matter of moments. Ruthie and I, as well as several members of the volunteer fire department, had to restrain others who were trying to get to their homes. The entire town went up as if it were gasoline soaked kindling.

And the aliens went up with it.

Fifteen dead.

I had killed them anyway, along with the town.

And I didn't even get my story.

———

The last few months, I've been thinking about retiring. My editor says it's a grief reaction, triggered by losing my childhood home. But I think it's more than that.

I think I've lost my edge. I'm just not interested any more. That little spark, the one that made me investigate things, is completely gone. I could work a desk or even get promoted, assigning stories, making others do the running. But I don't want to.

Two ideas keep going through my mind:

One of them is the spokesalien's.

One of them is mine.

Information, in this society, is not free, no matter how much we like to pretend it is. It is paid for by corporate sponsors, from the ads on the TV News to the ads up front in the *Times*. It has rules and prejudices and traditions that defy the pure pursuit of knowledge.

And anyone can taint it.

Anyone.

Including a reporter, unwilling to stake his reputation on a difficult story.

I erred. I know I did. And the only reason I know it is because of the lost property as well as the lost lives. I didn't care about the lives. They were smelly, dirty, and alien. And, shameful as that is, it's my truth.

But I could have saved them. Or at least tried. If I had agreed to that Faustian bargain with the spokesalien, I could have gotten those pathetic creatures out of that basement, told the *Inquirer — The American Journal —* anyone who would listen that these creatures were about to be murdered.

It might not have saved them.

But it might have.

And it certainly would have saved Bonner Bay.

I cannot even return there now. No one can. Geologists have ruled the site unsafe for building. Too unstable. They claim to be glad the town is gone.

I'm not. A bit of heaven disappeared with it. Heaven I thought tainted by a few pelts, by a few signs. Heaven I hadn't realized I would miss.

Until now.

And with it went a bit of my soul. The part that like to reveal facts, to search for truth. My truth.

I found my truth.

And I hate what it revealed.

THE END OF THE WORLD

KRISTINE KATHRYN RUSCH

THEN

The air reeked of smoke.

The people ran, and the others chased them.

She kept tripping. Momma pulled her forward, but Momma's hand was slippery. Her hand slid out, and she fell, sprawling on the wooden sidewalk.

Momma reached for her, but the crowd swept Momma forward.

All she saw was Momma's face, panicked, her hands, grasping, and then Momma was gone.

Everyone ran around her, over her, on her. She put her hands over her head and cringed, curling herself into a little ball.

She made herself change color. Brown-gray like the sidewalk, with black lines running up and down.

Dress hems skimmed over her. Boots brushed her. Heels pinched the skin on her arms.

No spikes, Momma always said. *No spikes or they'll know.*

So she held her breath, hoping the spikes wouldn't break through her skin because she was so scared, and her side hurt where someone's boot hit it, and the wooden sidewalk bounced as more and more people ran past her.

Finally, she started squinching, like Daddy taught her before he left.

Slide, he said. *A little bit at a time. Slide. Squinch onto whatever surface you're on and cling.*

It was hard to squinch without spikes, but she did, her head tucked in her belly, her hair trailing to one side. More boots stomped on it, pulling it, but she bit her lower lip so that she wouldn't have to think about the pain.

She was almost to the bank door when the sidewalk stopped shaking. No one ran by her. She was alone.

She flattened herself against the brick and shuddered. Her skin smelled of chewing tobacco, spit and beer from the saloon next door.

She had shut down her ears, but she finally rotated them outward. Men were shouting, women yelling. There was pounding and screaming and a high-pitched noise she didn't like.

If they found her flattened against the brick, they'd know. If they saw the spikes rise from her body, they'd know. If they saw her squinching, they'd know.

But she couldn't move.

She was shivering, and she didn't know what to do.

NOW

The call didn't come through channels. It rang to Becca Keller's personal cell.

Chase Waterston hadn't even said hello.

"Got a problem at the End of the World," he'd said, his usually self-assured voice shaky. "Can you get here right away? Just you."

Normally, she would have told him to call the precinct or 911, but something stopped her. Probably that scared edge to his voice, a sound she'd never heard in all the years she'd known him.

She drove from the center of downtown Hope to the End of the World, a drive that, in the old days, would have taken five minutes. Now it took twenty, and the only thing that kept her from being annoyed at the traffic were the mountains, bleak and cold, rising up like goddesses at the edge of Hope.

Hope was a mountain city, but its terrain was high desert. Vast expanses of brown still marked the outskirts of town, although the interior had lost much of its desert feel. By the time she passed the latest ticky-tacky development, she hit the rolling dunes of her childhood. Even though she had on the air-conditioning, the smell of sagebrush blew in—full of promise.

If she kept going straight too much farther, she'd hit small windy roads filled with switchbacks that led to now-trendy ski resorts. If she turned right, she'd follow the old stage coach route over the edge of the mountains into the Willamette Valley where most of Oregon's population lived.

The End of the World was an ancient resort at the fork between the mountain roads and the old stagecoach route. At the turn of the previous century, some enterprising entrepreneur figured travelers who were taking the narrow road toward the Willamette Valley would welcome a place to rest and recover from the long dusty trip.

Now bumper-to-bumper traffic filled that wagon route, which had expanded to a four-lane highway. Hope actually had a real rush hour, thanks to ex-patriate Californians, retired baby boomers, and ridiculously cheap housing.

Chase was rebuilding the resort for those baby boomers and Californians. For some reason, he thought they'd want to stay in a hundred-year-old hotel, with a view of the mountains and the river, even in the heat of the summer and the deep cold of the desert winter.

Becca steered the squad with her left hand and fiddled with the air-conditioner with her right, wishing her own car was out of the shop. No matter what she did, she couldn't get the squad car cooled. Nothing seemed to be working properly. Or maybe that was the effect of the heat.

It was a hundred and three degrees, and the third week without rain. The radio's most recent weather report promised the temperature would reach one hundred and eight by the time the day was over.

Finally, she reached the construction site.

Chase had set up the site so that it only blocked part of the ever-present wind and as a consequence, the dust billowed across the highway with the gusts.

The city had cited Chase twice for the hazard, and he'd promised to fix it just after the Fourth of July holiday. It looked like he'd been keeping his word, too. A huge plastic construction fence leaned against the old building. Graders and post-diggers were parked on the side of the road.

Nothing moved. Not the cats Chase had been using to dig out the old parking lot, not the crane he'd rented the week before, and not the crew, most of whom sat on the backs of pick-up trucks, their faces blackened with dust and grime and too much sun. She could see their eyes, white against the darkness of their skins, watching her as she turned onto the dirt path that Chase had been using as an access road.

He was waiting for her in the doorway of what had once been a natatorium. Built over an old underground spring, the Natatorium had once boasted the largest swimming pool in Eastern Oregon. There was some kind of pipe system which pumped water into the pool, keeping it perpetually cold. In the Natatorium's heyday, the water had been replaced daily.

Behind the Natatorium was the old five-story brick hotel that still had the original fixtures. No vandals had ever attacked the place. Even the windows were intact.

Becca had gone inside more than once, first as an impressionable twelve-year-old, and ever since, part of her believed the rumors that the hotel was haunted.

She pulled up beside the Natatorium door, in a tiny patch of shade provided by the overhanging roof. She got out and the blast-furnace heat hit her, prickling sweat on her skin almost instantly. Apparently the air conditioner had been working in the piece-of-crap squad after all.

Chase watched her. His lips were chapped, his skin fried blackish red from the sun. He had weather-wrinkles around his eyes and narrow mouth. His hair was cropped short, and over it he wore a regulation hardhat. He clutched another one in his left hand, slapping it rhythmically against his thigh.

"Thanks for coming, Becca," he said, and he still sounded shaken.

The tone was unfamiliar, but the expression on his face wasn't. She'd seen it only once, after she'd told him she wanted out, that his values and hers were so different, she couldn't stomach a relationship any longer.

"What do you got, Chase?" she asked.

"Come with me." He handed her the hardhat he'd been holding.

She took it as a gust of wind caught her short hair and blew its clipped edges into her face. She slipped the hardhat on, and tucked her hair underneath it, then followed Chase inside the building.

It was hotter inside the Natatorium, and the air smelled of rot and mold. She usually thought of those as humidity smells, but the Natatorium's interior was so dry that it was crumbly.

The floor was shredded with age, the wood so brittle that she wondered if it would hold her weight. Most of the walls were gone, the remains of them piled in a corner. Chase had gutted the interior.

When she had been a girl, she had played in this place. Her parents had forbidden her to come, which made it all the more inviting. The rot and mold smells had been present even then. But the walls had still been up, and there had been some ancient furniture in here as well, made unusable by weather and critters chewing the interior.

She used to stand inside the entrance with the door open, the stream of sunlight carrying a spinning tunnel of dust motes. When she closed her eyes halfway, she could just imagine the people arriving here after a long day of travel, happy to be in a place of such elegance, such warmth.

But now even that sense of a long ago but lively past was gone, and all that remained was the shell of the building itself—a hazard, an eyesore, something to be torn down and replaced.

Chase's boots echoed on the wood floor. He led her along the edges, pointing at holes closer to the center. She wondered if any of his employees had caused the holes, walking imprudently across the floor, foot catching on the weak spot, and then slipping through.

He was taking her to the employees' staircase in the back. When they reached it, she saw why. It was made of metal. Rusted metal, but metal all the same. Someone had recently bolted the stairs into the wall, probably under Chase's orders. A metal hand railing had been reinforced as well.

Chase looked over his shoulder to make sure she was following. She caught a glimpse of something in his face—reluctance? Fear? She couldn't quite tell—and then, as suddenly as it appeared, it was gone.

He went down the steps two at a time. She followed. Even though the handrail had been rebolted, the metal still flaked under her hand. The bolts might hold if she suddenly fell through the stairs but she wasn't sure if the railing would.

The smell grew stronger here, as if the mold had somehow managed to survive the dry summers. The farther down she went, the cooler the air got. It was still hot, but no longer oppressive.

Chase stopped at the bottom of the stairs. He watched her come down the last few, his gaze holding hers. The intensity of his gaze startled her. It was vulnerable, in a way she hadn't seen since their first year together.

Then he stepped away so that she could stand on the floor below.

The smell was so strong that it overwhelmed her. Beneath the mold and rot, there was something else, something familiar, something foul. It made the hair rise on the back of her neck.

"That way," Chase said, and this time she wasn't mistaking it. His voice was shaking. "I'll wait here."

She frowned at him, and then kept going. The floor here was covered in ceramic tile, chipped and broken, but sturdy. She wondered what was beneath it. Ground? Old-fashioned concrete? Wood? She couldn't tell. But the floor didn't creak here, and it felt solid.

A long wall hid everything from view. A door stood open, sending in sunlight filled with dust motes, just like she remembered. Only there shouldn't be sunlight here. This was the basement, the miraculous swimming pool, the place that had helped make the End of the World famous.

She stepped through the door.

The light came from the back wall—or what had been the back. Chase's crew had destroyed this part of the building.

The basement of the End of the World was open to the air for the first time since it had been completed.

That strange feeling she'd had since she reached the bottom of the stairs grew. If the basement wasn't sealed, then the stench shouldn't have been so strong. The old air should have escaped, letting the freshness of the desert inside.

Some of the heat had trickled in, but not enough to dissipate the natural coolness. She stepped forward. The tile on the other side of the pool was hidden under mounds of dirt. The pool itself was half destroyed, but the cat which had done the damage wasn't anywhere near it. She could see the big tire tracks, scored deeply into the sandy earth, as if the cat itself had been stuck or if the operator had tried to escape in a hurry.

They had uncovered something. That much was clear. And she was beginning to get an idea as to what it was.

A body.

Given the smell, it had to have died here recently. Bodies didn't decay in the desert—not in the dry air and the sand. Inside a building like this, there might be standard decomposition, but considering how hot it had been, even that seemed unlikely.

She'd have to assume cause of death was suspicious because the body had been located here. And then she'd have to figure out a way to find out whose body it was.

She was already planning how she'd conduct her case when she stepped off the tile onto a mound of dirt, and peered into the gaping hole, and saw—

Bones. Piles of bones. Recognizable bones. Femurs, hip bones, pelvic bones, rib cages. Hundreds of human bones. And more skulls than she could count.

She rocked back on her heels, pressing her free hand to her face, the smell—the illogical and impossible smell—now turning her stomach.

A mass grave, of the kind she'd only seen in film or police academy photos.

A mass grave, anywhere from a hundred to seventy-five years old.

A mass grave, in Hope. She hadn't even heard rumors of it, and she had lived here all her life.

"Son of a bitch," she said.

"Yeah," Chase said from the stairs, "I couldn't agree more."

THEN

The screaming sent ripples through her. She couldn't complete the change. She couldn't even assume the color and texture of the brick.

Tears pricked her eyes. Tears, as big a giveaway as her hair, her fingers, her ears. Somehow, when she stopped the spikes, she stopped all her abilities.

Or maybe it was just the fear.

A door squeaked open, then boots hit the sidewalk. Polished boots with only a layer of black dust along the edge. Men's boots, not the dainty things Momma tried to wear.

She tried to will the shivering away, but she couldn't.

She couldn't move at all.

Not that she had anywhere to go.

She could only pray that he wouldn't look down, that he wouldn't see her, that she would be safe for just a little longer.

NOW

Becca stared at the hole. She couldn't even count all the skulls, rising like white stones out of the dirt. Not to mention the rib cages off to one side or the tiny bones lying in a corner, bones that probably belonged in a hand or a foot.

She couldn't do much on her own. But she could find out where that stink was coming from.

She turned around and headed for the stairs.

Chase tipped his hardhat back, revealing his dark eyes. "Where're you going?"

"To get some things from my evidence bag," Becca said.

"You're not going to call anyone, are you?" he asked.

She stopped in front of him. "I can't take care of this alone. You should know that."

He leaned against the railing, that assumed casual gesture which meant he was the most distressed. "This'll ruin me, Becca. Half my capital is in this place."

"You told me no good businessman ever invests his own money," she snapped, mostly because she was surprised.

He shrugged. "Guess I'm not a good businessman."

But he was. He had restored three of the downtown's oldest buildings, making them into expensive condominiums with views of the mountains. Single-handedly, he'd revitalized Hope's downtown, by adding trendy stores that the locals claimed would never succeed (yet somehow they did, thanks to the "foreigners," as the Californians were called) and restaurants so upscale that Becca would have to spend half a week's pay just to eat lunch.

"You knew I'd go by the book when you called me here," she said, more sharply than she intended. He'd gotten to her. That was the problem; he always did.

"I thought maybe we could talk. They're old bones. If we can get someone to recover them and keep it quiet—"

"How many workers saw this?" she asked. "Do you think they'll keep it quiet?"

"If I pay them enough," he said. "And if we move the bones to a proper cemetery."

"Is that what you think this is?" she asked. "A graveyard?"

"Isn't it?" He seemed genuinely surprised. "It was so far out in the desert when this place was built that it's possible—no, it's probable—that the memory of the graveyard got lost."

"I saw at least two ribcages with shattered bones, and several skulls looked crushed."

His lips trembled, and it was a moment before he spoke. "The equipment could have done that."

But he didn't sound convinced.

"It could have," she said. "But we need to know."

"Why?" he asked.

She looked over her shoulder. That patch of sunlight still glinted through the hole in the wall. The dust motes still floated. If she didn't look down, the place would seem just as beautiful and interesting as it always had.

"Because someone loved them once. Someone probably wants to know what happened to them."

"Someone?" He snorted. "Becca, the pool was put over a tennis court that was built at the turn of the 20th century. No one remembers these people. Only historians would care."

He paused, and she felt her breath catch.

Then he said, "This is my life."

He used a tone and inflection she used to find particularly mesmerizing. Once she told their couples therapist that with that tone, he could convince her to do anything, and that was when the therapist told her that she had to get out.

"It's a crime scene," Becca said, knowing that the argument was weak.

"You don't know that for sure, and even if it is, it's a hundred years old," he said.

"Then what's the smell?"

He frowned, clearly not understanding her.

"This is a desert, Chase. Bodies buried in dirt in a dry climate don't decay. They mummify."

He blinked. He obviously hadn't thought of that.

"And," she said, "even if they had decayed because of some strange environmental reason particular to this basement, they wouldn't smell after a hundred years."

That guarded expression had returned to his face. Only his eyes moved now.

"Maybe it's something small," he said. "A mouse, someone's lost cat."

She shook her head. "Smell's too strong, and over the entire building. If it were something small, the smell would have faded back when you broke open that wall."

"Not when it was dug up?" he asked, seeming surprised.

"No," she said. "Is that when you first smelled it?"

"That's when they called me."

They, meaning his crew. She frowned at him, wondering if he was going to blame them.

But for what? A smell?

She'd have to find the source before she made assumptions.
And that, she knew, was going to be hard.

THEN

A hand touched her shoulder. A human hand, warm and gentle. Another shivery ripple ran through her. She still had a shoulder; she hadn't gotten rid of that either. How silly she must look, plastered against the brick wall like a half formed younglin.

Screams still echoed. The shouts had died down, although sometimes they rose up altogether, like a group got excited about something.

"You're one of them, aren't you?"

Male voice, human, just as gentle as the hand. She couldn't stop shivering.

"I won't hurt you."

She resisted the urge to rotate an eye upwards, so that she could see more than the boot.

"But you better come with me before they find you."

That did startle her. Her eye moved before she could stop it. It formed above her shoulder. He jumped back slightly when her eye appeared, but his hand never left her skin, even though it was finally turning tannish-red like the brick.

She'd seen him before. Daddy had laughed with him in the good days. He had slicked-back hair and a narrow face and kind eyes.

He crouched beside her, and looked right at her eye, like it didn't bother him, even though she knew it did. He wouldn't've jumped like that if it didn't.

"Please," he said, "come with me. I don't know when they're coming back. And someone might see us. Please."

She had to form a mouth. Her nose remained, tucked against her stomach from when she'd formed a ball, but her mouth had disappeared when she had tried to take on the appearance of the wooden sidewalk.

It took all her strength to make the mouth come out near the eye, and from the look of disgust that passed over his face, she still didn't look right. Her hair was on the other side of her body, and her eye was just above her shoulder. The mouth had probably come out on what would have been her back if she put herself together right.

Right being human.

That's what Momma said.

Momma.

"Please," he said again, and this time, she heard panic in his voice.

"Stuck," she said.

"Oh, Christ." He looked up and down the street, then at the buildings across from it.

He seemed younger than she remembered, or maybe she was as bad at telling human ages as Momma was.

"How do we get you unstuck?" he asked.

She didn't know. She'd never been like this, not this scared, not all by herself.

She tried to shrug and felt her other shoulder form into the wood. A splinter dug into her skin, and her entire body turned red with pain.

"What a mess," he said, and she didn't know if he meant her or what was going on or how scared they both seemed to be.

She willed herself to let go, but she was attached to the brick, and she'd lost control of half her body functions. Daddy said fear would do that.

Whatever happens, baby, he'd say, *you have to trust us. You have to believe we'll get together again. Let that be your strength, so that you never, ever succumb to fear.*

But he'd been gone for a long time now. And Momma hadn't come back for her, even though people were screaming.

The man tried to pry a flat corner of her skin from the edge of the brick. She could feel the tug, saw his face scrunch up in disgust when he got to the sticky underneath part.

"How'd you get there?" he asked.

"Squinched," she said.

"Squinched." He didn't understand. And she spoke his language, she knew she did. She formed the right mouth, she'd been using the words for a long time now, and she knew how they felt inside her brain and out.

"Can you show me?" he asked. "Can you squinch onto my arm?"

She wasn't supposed to squinch to a human. Momma was strict about that. Like there was something bad about it, something awful would happen.

But something awful was happening now.

The screams...

"No," she said, even though that had to be a lie. Momma and Daddy wouldn't forbid something if she couldn't've done it in the first place.

"God," he said, then looked down the street where the screams had come from. Where the shouts had grown more and more angry every time they rose up.

Right now, it was quiet, and she hated that more.

She hated it all.

"Stay here," he said.

He stood up, letting go of her shoulder. The warm vanished, and the fear rose even worse. Her other shoulder disappeared, and she felt the spikes, threatening to appear.

She had to close both eyes and will the spikes away.

When she opened the eyes, he was gone.

She moved the eyes all over her skin, looking for him, and she didn't see him at all.

The street was still empty, and too quiet.

Then, faraway, someone laughed. A mean, nasty, brittle laugh.

She folded her ears inside her skin, and willed herself flat, hoping, this time, that it would work.

NOW

Becca climbed the stairs, clinging to the handrail, the rust flaking against her palms. She had to call for help. At most, she needed a coroner, and probably a few officers just to search for the source of that smell.

But she felt guilty about calling. Chase used to talk about restoring the End of the World when she'd met him. He had brought her out here on their first date, even though she'd told him that she had explored the property repeatedly when she was a child.

Maybe they'd be able to keep this out of the paper, particularly if it turned out to be a graveyard or a dumping ground. But even that probably wouldn't happen.

The newspapers seemed to love this kind of story.

If she reported this, she would condemn Chase's project to a kind of limbo. With so much capital invested, he probably couldn't afford to wait until the legal issues were solved.

She almost turned around to ask him how much time he could give them, but then she'd be compromising the investigation. For all she knew, there was a recently killed human beneath that dirt, and someone (Chase?) was using the old bones to hide it.

Then she shook her head. Not Chase. He was manipulative and difficult, moody and untrustworthy, but he wasn't—nor had he ever been—violent.

She sighed and continued up the stairs. Much as she wanted to help him, she couldn't. She had an obligation to the entire community.

She had an obligation to herself.

The wind hit her the moment she stepped outside. Bits of sand stung her skin, sticking to the sweat. Even with the sun, it now felt cooler out here because of that wind.

The construction workers watched her. She didn't know most of them; the town had grown too big for her to know everyone by sight like she had when she was a child. Many of these workers were Hispanic, some of them probably illegal.

Hispanics expected her to check their papers. She was supposed to do that too, although she never did. She didn't object to people who worked hard and tried to improve their lives.

With one hand, she tipped her hardhat back and nodded toward the workers. Then she opened the squad's driver's door, and winced at the heat which poured out at her. She leaned inside, unwilling to go into that heat voluntarily, and grabbed the radio's handset.

She paused before turning it on, knowing that even that momentary hesitation was a victory for Chase.

Then she clicked the handset and asked the dispatch to send Jillian Mills.

Jillian Mills was the head coroner for Hope and the surrounding counties. She actually worked the job full time, but her assistants were dentists and veterinarians, and one retired doctor.

"You want the crime scene unit?" the dispatch asked. It was standard procedure for a crime scene unit to come with the coroner.

"Not yet," Becca said. "I'm not sure what exactly we have here, except that it's dead."

Which was technically true, if she ignored all the crushed and broken bones.

"Tell her to hurry," Becca added. "It's hot as hell out here and there's a construction crew waiting."

That usually worked to get any city official moving. Lately, the "foreigners" had taken to suing the city if their emergency or official personnel delayed money-making operations, even for a day.

Chase would never do that—he knew that getting along with the city helped his permits go through and his iffy projects get approved—but Becca still used the excuse.

She didn't want to be here any longer than she had to.

She stood, lifted her hardhat, and wiped the sweat off her forehead. Then she closed the door and leaned on it for a moment.

The End of the World.

She wondered if Chase had ever thought that the name might have been prophetic.

THEN

She had shut down her ears, and didn't know he had come back until the sidewalk shook. She opened her eyes. He stood above her holding a long wooden box. His mouth was moving, but he kept looking down the street. A single bead of sweat ran down one side of his face.

She unfolded her ears, and said, "What?"

"This can hide you," he said, setting the box on the sidewalk. He glanced at her, then looked away. "Think maybe you can squinch into it?"

He set the box in front of her. It did cover her strangeness from anyone who didn't look too hard.

Her shivering stopped.

"Maybe," she said.

"Well," he said, wiping at that drop of sweat, "the sooner you squinch, the better chance I have of getting you out of here."

That brought a shiver. She looked at the box, saw it had some dirt inside. He had taken it from some kind of storage.

If she just thought about the box—not the screaming (which seemed to be gone? How come it was gone?)—not the way Momma's hand had slipped through hers, not the fall against the sidewalk, not the bruises that still radiated through her skin, maybe then she could squinch to it.

She'd have to stare at it like a younglin, think only of the box, only of the box and becoming part of it...

A long, drawn out scream sent ripples through her.

"Jesus," the man said and closed his eyes.

She squinched. She had to. The scream made her move. She squinched to the edge of the box, then cowered against the back, just a blob, as small as she could make herself.

"Mister?" she said and heard the terror in her voice. She wasn't sure why she was trusting him, but she didn't have a lot of choice.

That scream sounded like Momma.

He looked down, and his shoulders slumped.

"Thank God," he said, and picked up the box.

He tucked it under his arm like it weighed nothing, and hurried back through the door.

NOW

Jillian drove the white coroner's van. Becca's breath caught as she scanned the windshield, looking for an assistant.

There was none. Either none was available, or dispatch conveyed the message about the stalled work crew.

Either way, Becca was grateful.

She finished the last of her water and tossed the bottle in a nearby recycling can. She had waited up here, unwilling to go back inside without Jillian.

Or maybe she had just been unwilling to talk to Chase again.

He had come out of the basement after about ten minutes. He saw her near the squad, shook his head slightly, and sat against one of the cats, his face half-hidden by shade.

She didn't go to talk to him and he didn't talk to her. They both knew the futility of these kinds of arguments. Once again, she and Chase were on opposite paths, and trying to influence each other would only end in misery.

Jillian got out of the van. Her hair was already pulled back and tucked in a net. She was small and delicate, with skin so pale that it almost looked translucent. She seemed fragile at first glance, but Becca had seen her split a corpse's ribcage open with her bare hands.

"What've we got?" Jillian asked.

"I'm not sure," Becca said. She grabbed the flashlight and gloves from her own kit, as well as the portable radio, and led Jillian inside.

Chase didn't come with them. Instead, he watched them go with the same wariness that his crew had.

Becca was relieved. She half-hoped that Jillian hadn't noticed him, standing in the shade.

They were on the steps to the basement before Jillian said, "This is Chase Waterston's project, isn't it?"

"Unfortunately," Becca said.

Jillian knew Becca's troubles with Chase. It had been no-nonsense Jillian who had listened to Becca's difficulties extricating herself from Chase's world.

I'm a cop, she used to say, it seemed, during every conversation. *I shouldn't be so easily influenced.*

We all have a hook that'll draw us in, Jillian would respond. *He knows how to find yours.*

He did too. There should have been a full team here, along with a crime scene unit.

Jillian probably knew it just from the smell.

She stopped at the bottom of the stairs and looked around. "Where's the body?"

Becca had thought about how to answer that one the entire time she waited for Jillian.

"I don't know where the smell is coming from," Becca said. "But it's not our only problem."

Jillian glanced at her sideways. Becca sighed and led her to the hole.

The sun had moved away from the gap in the wall, no longer sending rays filled with dust motes into the basement. But the light was still strong enough that she didn't need a flashlight to lead Jillian to the dig itself.

"Chase thinks this is an old cemetery," Becca said as she approached.

"You don't," Jillian said, slipping on her gloves. "So you brought me here to be the bad guy."

Maybe she had. Or maybe she just needed someone between her and Chase, someone sensible.

She didn't say any more. Instead, she turned on the flashlight and turned it to the ribcages and skulls.

"Mother of God," Jillian said, touching the tiny cross she wore around her neck even though her Catholicism had lapsed decades ago. "This is going to take an entire team."

"I know," Becca said softly.

They stared for a long moment. Becca didn't move the flashlight beam. Finally, Jillian grabbed it from her and swept the entire large hole. The light caught more bits of bone, scattered throughout the dirt.

"How'd you even get me here?" Jillian asked. "Chase has to know this will ruin him."

"He does." Becca didn't look at Jillian.

"So he called you." Jillian shook her head. "Bastard."

"Jillian, it's bad enough."

"It's bad enough that he thought you'd cover for him."

"He didn't ask that," Becca said. But he had, hadn't he? He asked that this be handled quickly and discreetly and with a minimum of fuss.

Although he stopped arguing when she explained about the smell.

God, she was still making excuses for him, and she was no longer married to him.

"He knows I'm going to do this right."

"He knows," Becca said.

"That'll mean the media'll get wind."

"Let's try to prevent that as long as possible."

"So Chase can save his ass?"

"So that we don't have weirdos contaminating the crime scene."

"You didn't block it off. It could be contaminated now."

Becca pursed her lips. "I kept an eye on everyone."

"I hope so," Jillian said. "I'm going to call for backup."

Becca nodded.

Jillian didn't move, even though she said she was going to. "You think maybe you should take yourself off this investigation?"

Becca'd been thinking about it. "I'm the only qualified investigator we have. Everyone else has been promoted through the ranks and most haven't even completed the crime lab courses."

Because they were only offered in the Willamette Valley, and that was more than 2 hours from here. The department couldn't afford to lose personnel for days on end just so that they could have classes in criminal justice, classes that the chief—a good ole boy who had worked his way through the ranks without a damn class, thank you—didn't believe anyone needed, not even his detectives.

Jillian sighed. "You've got a conflict."

"No kidding."

"What if Chase is behind the smell?"

Becca almost said, *He isn't*, but she stopped herself in time. "I'll treat him like anyone else."

Even though she knew that was a lie the moment she spoke it.

"No matter what you do, everyone'll think you're soft on him."

"Then everyone'll be supervising me, won't they?" Becca snapped.

Jillian put a hand on her shoulder. "Rethink this, Becca."

Becca sighed. "If this starts leading to Chase, maybe I will."

THEN

He didn't take her very far. She managed to squinch part of herself to the edge of the box, away from his arm, and pop an eye forward.

They were inside the bank. No one else was. The afternoon sun filtered through the large windows, illuminating heavy wooden desks, the wide row of grills that people got money out of or put money into, the safe just behind the far door.

Momma and Daddy had brought her in here early, as part of her training in being "normal" and they explained how banks worked. She used to come with Daddy when he had money to deposit, but Momma didn't know how to get it when he went away.

Momma said maybe he got it, but she had that funny sound in her voice, the one that meant she really didn't believe it. She always sounded sad when she spoke of Daddy, and after a few weeks, she stopped speaking of him at all.

"We can't go far yet," the man said softly. "People'll wonder. They'll probably wonder why I was here, and not with them."

He said that last very very softly. She almost didn't hear him.

He hurried to one of the desks near the back and set the box underneath it with one edge sticking out.

"If you can, stay low," he said. "It's safer."

She wondered how he knew. Maybe he could tell her what was going on. Because she didn't know at all.

Momma had smelled the smoke—they were burning Shantytown, that's what Momma said. Then Momma grabbed her hand and pulled her to the safe place. She didn't know where that was either or what would happen there.

They had run to the middle of the town, right near the fanciest store where Momma liked to look through the windows sometimes, when people caught up to them. Running, just like they were, only the other people's running was different somehow.

Momma seemed really scared now. Some of the men smelled of kerosene, and one of them was laughing even though the edges of his hair were burned off.

Momma pulled and pulled and she was having trouble keeping up and people started looking at them and Momma tried to pick her up but didn't have the strength and she tried to keep running but she couldn't—she was getting so tired—and then she tripped and her hand slipped and she couldn't see Momma and she didn't know where Momma went or why she hadn't come back...

Except for the scream.

She closed her eyes and rolled up into a ball.

She wanted to forget the scream—and she couldn't, no matter how hard she tried.

NOW

Jillian started to work in one corner of the hole. Becca took the far end of the basement, using her nose first to see where the smell was the strongest.

Jillian had contacted the crime scene investigators, asking for everyone not just the folks on duty, and another detective as well as some officers to handle the interviews. Becca should have done that. But Jillian was covering for her, getting her off the hook with Chase.

Both of them knew that Chase was their key. He could set up a lot of roadblocks to the investigation, and he might have already done so. Becca would try to find out by remaining close to him, buddying him, if she could.

Jillian wasn't sure that Becca could manipulate him. Hence the request for the second detective.

Becca wasn't going to argue with that. She wasn't going to argue with any of it. Not yet.

But she did know Chase well enough that if he had committed a crime, he wouldn't have done it in a way that would jeopardize his entire fortune. He would have covered it up creatively, hidden the body in the desert or taken it to Waloon Lake or maybe all the way to the ocean.

He was too smart to kill someone and call her. He knew that he could manipulate her, but he also knew that the manipulation didn't always work.

She took a breath. Olfactory nerves grew used to smells, but this one—the smell of rot and decay—never completely vanished. You could live with that smell for weeks, and still recognize it, unlike most other odors. It just wouldn't seem as strong to you as it did to others.

It was still new to her at the moment. And it wasn't coming from this part of the basement.

She walked the perimeter, sniffing the whole way, knowing she would regret this part of the investigation. Strong smells like this remained in the nose and in the memory. She would be able to recall it whenever she wanted.

As if she would want to.

After she finished, she walked the perimeter again, careful to use the same tracks.

Finally, she said, "It's coming from the hole."

"Of course," Jillian said. She had started in one corner as well.

When Becca spoke, Jillian leaned back on her knees, resting on her heels. She brushed her hands together, then surveyed the mess before them.

"This is beyond me," she said. "I don't know how to proceed. We're not trained for a disaster this big. I'm going to have to call in experts."

"Experts?" Becca asked.

"There are people who specialize in dealing with mass graves."

"So this is a graveyard."

Jillian looked at her, as if Becca had deliberately misunderstood her.

"Mass graves. Like the ones they found in Iraq or Bosnia or Nazi Germany."

Becca let out a small breath. The air felt thicker than desert air usually did. The odors seemed to be getting worse, not better.

"That's what this is? Some kind of massacre?"

"I don't know for sure. That's why I want experts. You want to protect Chase—"

Becca started to deny it, but then that was silly. She did want to protect Chase.

"—but I want to protect Hope."

It took her a moment to understand what Jillian had said.

"Protect Hope?"

"How much history do you know, Becca?" Jillian asked.

"I know enough to know that no large group of people has ever died in Hope. We still have our Chinatown, and we were one of the havens for blacks, even when the State of Oregon constitutionally banned them. We had that in school, Jillian, remember?"

"You think people talk about massacres?"

"I think people remember," Becca said. "I think massacres don't stay buried forever."

Jillian looked at the dirt before her. A snapped femur was only a few inches from her knees.

"You're right," Jillian said. "Nothing stays buried forever."

THEN

"What's your name?" he asked after a little while.

The question startled her. The bank had been so quiet, even though she had kept one ear on top and an eye prepared. She could control the ears and the eyes and sometimes the mouth, she still hadn't got control over anything else. The shivers came less now, but they still came, rippling through her like water.

"It's okay," he said. "We're still alone."

Like that was the problem. Her family tried not to name anything. Names made items rigid.

Still, her parents had given her a human name, just so everyone had something to call her, and Momma said the name made it easier for her to keep her shape.

Maybe if she thought about it now...

He peered under the desk. "Are you all right?"

Another shiver ran through her and she couldn't find her mouth.

"They're not back yet."

If she had her human form, she'd nod. But she didn't. Then the mouth popped forward.

He moved away so fast, he hit his head on the underside of the desk.

"Sorry," he said. "You startled me."

"Sarah," she said.

"Hmm?" He frowned at her.

"I'm Sarah."

"Oh." He bit his upper lip, pulling it inward. "I'd thought maybe something more unusual...."

He stopped talking, wiped a hand over his mouth, then smiled.

"How about a last name?"

A second name. Momma had explained that too. The second name described your clan. The first name was just yours, special to you.

"Jones," she said.

"Jones," he repeated. "Earl Jones's daughter?"

Earl was what they decided to first-name Daddy.

"Yes," she said.

"Christ." He wiped his hand over his mouth again, then looked behind him. "I'm Jess Taylor. Your dad may have told you about me."

Daddy hadn't said anything about anybody, at least not to her.

"Have you seen him lately? Your dad? I have some things for him."

Tears filled her eye, then her face—her human face formed on top of her skin.

Jess Taylor's expression froze, then he smiled, even though the smile didn't look real.

She wanted to wipe the tear from her eye, but she didn't have hands. One started to form, and she willed it away. She had to stay small.

"You haven't seen him, have you?" Jess Taylor said.

"Not for a long time."

Jess nodded. Then he frowned. He slid out from under the desk, and sat up straight. She squinched to the edge of the box. He was looking at the windows, and now that he thought she couldn't see him, he looked scared.

"What's going on?" she asked.

"I think they're coming back," he said. "We have to move you. Can you stay quiet?"

She had stayed quiet until he asked questions. But she didn't say that. Instead, she said, "Yes."

"I'm going to cover the box. Don't do anything till I come for you. Okay?"

"Okay," she said, even though she was supposed to do two things. She was supposed to stay quiet, and she was supposed to hide.

Maybe when "they" came back, they would bring Momma. Maybe when "they" came back, she could finally go home.

NOW

Becca and Jillian used police tape to rope off the Natatorium. The crime scene squad could handle the upper floors. Becca saw no point. She knew that the body—the body that was freshly dead—was in that dug-out pool.

Jillian was in the basement of the Nat, laying out a grid to work the scene. She knew that some of the work would come from the local team. Even though she had been on the phone with the state crime lab, she had no idea when the experts would show up.

The sooner the better, she had told them, but both she and Becca knew that would make no difference. Oregon was a low tax state, and rather than fund important services, Oregon cut them. The lab was now working two years out on important cases, and had no extra people to spare for a mass grave deep in the desert.

The lab certainly didn't have the funds to hire an expert. Becca would have to take the money from the police budget or she would have to get the Hopewell County District Attorney to pay for the expert before any charges were filed.

Jillian's office certainly didn't have the money either. She barely had enough funds for an assistant.

Even though other officers showed up, as well as two more detectives, Becca handled most of the interviews herself. She didn't want her colleagues scaring off the illegals. She needed them for the investigation.

Using a mixture of English and her high school Spanish, she managed to interview the work crew. She also learned that several employees had vanished when Chase stopped work and called her, even though he had told them that they'd be safe.

Of course, no one would give her their names. The handful of employees who'd even mentioned their friends seemed frightened by the slip.

Even the legal citizens—the ones who had citizenship, and the ones who were born in the United States—insisted on showing her their papers. A number of the men slapped the documents with their hands, and said, "Test them. Go see. Everything is in order."

When she finished, she went to her car, got some more bottled water, and took a long drink. Yes, the heat had drained her, as had the bodies and the destruction below, but the fear she'd encountered had stressed her as well.

People shouldn't be afraid to answer simple questions. Not in America.

She sighed, then drank half a bottle. She set the bottle inside, shielded her eyes, and looked at the sun.

It seemed to have a long way to go before it disappeared behind the mountains. Usually she liked the long days of summer. Today she didn't.

"Can I send everyone home now?" Chase asked from behind her.

"Yeah." She didn't turn around. She hated his habit of standing so close that she would have to bump into him if she made any movement at all. "Unfortunately, they're not going to be able to work here tomorrow."

"Or the next day or the next. What's this about experts?"

"Jillian can't handle the site," Becca said. "She thinks it's historical, and if she does something wrong..."

He sighed. She knew he understood historical red tape. He had to deal with a lot of it just to get this project off the ground.

"What else do you need from me?" he asked.

I need you to back up a little, she thought. But she said, "I need to see the rest of the buildings. Are any of them locked?"

"A few," he said. "Mostly the theater, which is where I've been storing supplies, and of course, the hotel."

He had stepped into her line of sight, apparently annoyed at the way she had been ignoring him. Since he was no longer so close, she could turn.

"The hotel?" she asked. "Why the hotel? We all went in it as kids."

"And had no idea how much the front desk or the doorknobs were worth. I've got a lot of subcontractors here, and it's a different time." He ran a hand through his hair. Sweat glistened on some of the strands. "I'm going to lose it all, aren't I?"

She felt a pull of empathy. "I don't know. You will be able to work here again. I'm just not sure when."

He gave her a bitter smile. "Yeah."

She wanted to ask him if he regretted calling her. She wanted to ask if he was going to blame her for the loss of time.

But she didn't. The old Becca would have asked those questions.

The new Becca had to pretend she didn't care.

THEN

Jess Taylor picked up the box and carried it under his arm. It bumped as he walked. She lost her mouth and one of the eyes as more shivers ran through her.

She wondered: If she thought of herself as Sarah, would she change into a little human girl?

She wasn't willing to try it. Not yet.

He set her next to a filing cabinet. The grained wood reminded her of her father. He'd turned into an expensive filing cabinet once, just to show her how to change into common business objects.

For an emergency, he had said. *For an emergency*.

Like this one. If she had thought it through, she should have turned into something freestanding like the filing cabinet, not something long and seemingly never-ending, like the sidewalk or the bricks.

It was different to become a permanent non-breathing object. Then she had to cling to it, and somehow sleep. But younglins couldn't do that. It was a skill they got when they grew older.

At her age, only a parent could help her make a sleep-change.

Jess Taylor dropped a towel over the box. The towel smelled of soap and sweat. It filtered the light.

She closed her remaining eye, and listened as voices filled the bank. Excited voices, male—

"What the hell were you thinking staying here?"

"You missed it all."

"You should've seen it. They didn't even look human by the end."

The voices mingled and tumbled and twisted into jumbles of words. But *they didn't even look human* got repeated over and over again.

They didn't look human, her people. Not when they were filing cabinets or chairs or wooden sidewalk planks. But they breathed and fought and *thought*. Wasn't that enough?

Daddy had said it would be, that day so long ago:

We have no choice, he'd said to the assembled. *We're stuck here, and Hope is better than the other cities I've seen. We're isolated. If we can work our way into their minds as laborers, maybe they'll accept us. They can't see how we live—we'll have to live as they do. But after a while, they'll get used to us. They'll see how similar we are. We breathe like them, fight like them, think like them. They'll understand. They'll accept. Given time.*

Time passed. And nothing changed. They had their own part of town, near the Chinese who also refused to talk to them.

And when one of their own got attacked outside of town and couldn't hold her shape—

Well, Momma wouldn't talk about it. And everyone expected Daddy to do something, but he didn't know what to do. He told Momma that. He didn't know.

Then he left. Looking for someplace new, Momma said. But she didn't believe it any more. Daddy would have come back long before now. And he hadn't.

And Jess Taylor looked sad when he learned her human name. Because of Daddy.

The voices continued:

"They scream real pretty though."

"One of them even begged."

"You shoulda been there."

And then Jess Taylor said, "Someone had to watch the bank."

"If I didn't know better," said a deep male voice, "I'd check the vault. What a perfect time to take something for yourself."

"Please do, sir," Jess Taylor said. "You won't find anything awry."

He sounded funny. Like they'd hurt his feelings. Humans did that to each other sometimes. But they always made up. Never with her people, but with each other.

Only no one apologized to Jess Taylor. Instead, the conversations changed. Someone walked past her and she heard a dial spin, then something metal click. She swiveled her good eye, but she couldn't see through that towel Jess Taylor had thrown over her box.

"Looks fine to me, sir," said another voice.

"Double-check," said the deep voice.

"I don't receive credit for staying, do I?" Jess Taylor asked in that low tone he'd used when he called his own people names.

"What's that?" the deep voice asked.

"Nothing, sir."

More clicking. The sound of boots against marble. Low voices, counting and comparing.

Then deep voice—"Looks like you did well, Taylor."

"Thank you, sir."

"Just don't act on your own again, all right? Makes people suspicious. Especially in these times."

"Do you think I'm one of them, sir?"

"If you were, you'd be dumb to stay," deep voice said.

"Besides," said another voice, "we seen you hurt. You don't change like those demons do."

"I suppose," Jess Taylor said in that low tone again.

"You don't approve," said the other voice.

"Of what?" Jess Taylor asked, louder this time.

"What we done."

For a long moment, Jess Taylor didn't answer. She held her breath, hoping he wouldn't make a mistake. If he made a mistake, they would find her.

Finally, he said, "I don't know what you did."

"We could show you," one of the men said, and everyone laughed.

"Thank you," Jess Taylor said without any warmth, "but I think I can figure it out for myself."

NOW

The front door of the hotel was padlocked. The window shutters were closed and locked as well. When she was a child, this looked like an abandoned building, spooky but still alive. Now it seemed like an unloved place, a place that would fall apart if someone took the locks off.

Becca watched Chase remove the padlock and hook it onto his belt. Then he swung back the metal latch and pushed open the double mahogany doors.

Those Becca remembered. She remembered the way that the light filtered out through them, more dust motes than she thought possible dancing inside of it.

Small windows stood beside the door, but on the far side of the lobby, floor-to-ceiling windows opened onto the expanse of high desert and the mountains beyond. The glass was old and bubbled and clearly handmade. Such dramatic windows were rare a hundred years ago, and had been—in the hotel's heyday—one of its main drawing points.

She stepped inside, sneezed at the smells of mold and dust, and watched as more motes swirled because of her movements. Chase stood beside the door, watching her.

"We were going to revive it all," he said. The past tense saddened her. "Imagine that desk over there, polished, with employees behind it, computers on top, guests in front."

She looked at the registration desk, scratched and filthy, which wrapped around an entire corner of the room. Behind it were old-fashioned mail slots, some filled with stuffing from chairs—probably rats' or mice nests.

"People would look at the view, or go to the Natatorium for tennis or a swim. We were going to build a golf course alongside this, and build homes, just outside the line of sight for these windows." Chase stuck his hands in his back pockets. He stared at the view, still sending in light despite the dirty glass. "It would have been spectacular."

"It's not over yet, Chase," Becca said. It wasn't like him to give up so easily. In fact, this speech of his was making her suspicious. Had he run into financial difficulty? Had he put something recently dead among the bones as a way of notifying the authorities? Did he want the project to end for a reason she didn't understand yet?

"Half my crew probably ran away today."

"They aren't the people who will restore this building."

"Who's going to come once they find out there's a mass grave on the property?"

She didn't know the answer to that. "People go to battlefields all the time."

"Battlefields," he said, "are different."

"We went to Little Big Horn. They're still discovering bodies up there."

"From a hundred and forty years ago," he said.

"You have no idea how old these bodies are," she said.

He shrugged, then turned and gave her one of his "aw-what-the-hell" smiles. "You're right. I don't know anything yet. Except that this place was well named."

The End of the World. She sighed, and asked the question she'd suddenly started to dread. "Are you insured?"

"For what? Construction losses? Sure. Lost income and disability? Sure. Dead bodies on my construction site? Who the hell knows."

"Maybe you should find out," she said. "I'm sure this doesn't qualify as an act of God."

He inclined his head toward her, as if to say "Touché."

"I need to look," she said. "Alone."

He nodded, then walked to the door. "Find me when you're done."

"Yeah," she said, but he had already stepped outside. She sighed and looked at the floor. Dirt covered the old carpet. Footprints ran through it, some of them so old that they were buried under layers of sand. Broken chairs huddled in the corner, and the stairs to the second floor had rotted away.

But the hotel did have good bones. The brick on the outside had insulated it from harsh weather in the high desert—the hot, hot summers and the blisteringly cold winters. Even the floor-to-ceiling windows were double paned, something so unusual, she'd never seen it in a building this old.

The place didn't smell of death like the Natatorium. In fact, except for her prints and Chase's it didn't look like anyone had been here in a month or more.

She turned on her flashlight and aimed it at the dark corners. Something skittered away from the ornate gold leaf in front of the elevator. She scanned the steps—yep, rotted—and the scarred reception desk. A door was open behind it, leading to the offices. She'd been back there when she was a kid.

In fact, she'd been everywhere in this place as a child. The whole hotel had fascinated her, except for one part.

She steeled herself, then moved to the right, aiming the light at the far wall. When the beam hit it, the wallpaper shimmered like a heat mirage.

She swallowed. That, at least, hadn't changed. The shimmering wall and the building moans—probably from the way the wind whistled through it on dry desert days—gave rise to the stories of the hotel being haunted.

A shiver ran through her. She'd just seen a hole filled with long-dead bodies, her nose still carried the odor of decay (and her clothing probably did too), and it was the old hotel that scared her out of her wits.

Let someone else investigate it. Let the crime scene techs make sure nothing bad had happened here in the recent past. She'd done as much as she was going to.

She shut off her light, and tried not to listen to the rustling as she let herself out.

THEN

After a long long time, most of the voices stopped. A few continued. Deep Voice did. He gave orders and talked to some of the others.

Then he told Jess Taylor to leave.

She held her breath, wondering what would happen to her.

Then someone picked up the box. She bumped against the side.

"What've you got there?" Deep Voice asked.

"Just a box," Jess Taylor said. "I need to move a few things from my house. I thought I'd take this to pack them in. I'll bring it back in the morning."

"Check it, Dunnigan," Deep Voice said.

She shivered. She couldn't help herself. She squinched as far as she could into the corner of the box, turned her ear inward, and closed her remaining eye, hoping this Dunnigan couldn't see her—or if he did, he wouldn't know what he was looking at.

The box bounced, then the light changed. The towel must have come off. Tobacco and sweat filled the air. She held herself rigid, feeling a shiver start, and willing it away.

"It's empty, boss," said this Dunnigan, right above her.

The box bumped again, and the light dimmed.

"Satisfied?" Jess Taylor asked. His tone was bitter.

"You got to admit," Deep Voice said, "you've been acting odd today."

"I acted like a responsible employee," Jess Taylor said. "I stayed when everyone else left. No one thought to lock up in all the excitement. I made sure the drawers were closed and locked, the safe was closed, and the account registers were in the proper desks. I kept an eye on the place, and you treat me like a criminal."

"You'd do the same, Taylor," Deep Voice said.

"No, sir, I beg your pardon, but I wouldn't. I would acknowledge when an employee does well, not suspect him of thievery because he takes an initiative."

The silence went on forever. She was still holding her breath. She had to let it out, as quietly as she could. She could feel the box bounce with Jess Taylor's breathing—if he was the one holding it. She hoped he was.

He seemed like the only human—the only person—she could trust.

Finally, Deep Voice said, "You can keep the box."

"Thank you, sir." Such sarcasm in Jess Taylor's voice. She wondered if Deep Voice could hear it. "May I go now?"

"Of course," Deep Voice said.

The box bounced with each step. She heard a door screech open, then bang closed. The air grew warmer and the towel blew up ever so slightly.

"Stay still," Jess Taylor said in that undertone of his. "We're not out of this yet."

NOW

When she came out of the hotel, the sky was a deep grayish blue. Twilight had fallen fast, like it always did on the high desert. The moment the sun dipped behind the mountain peaks, the light changed and the air had a suggestion of coolness.

Now if only the wind would stop. It rose for a half-hour or so at real twilight, sending sand pellets against her skin like tiny knives.

Chase's employees had already left. So had the police, except for two officers who had been assigned to guard the crime scene. Apparently the crime scene techs weren't going to work at night, which made sense, given the location and the questions still lingering about how to handle the scene.

Chase leaned against his Ford Bronco, a cell phone pressed against his ear. His back was to her, but she could tell from the position of his shoulders how annoyed he was.

She walked toward him, then stopped when she heard what he was saying.

"...I'm not sure what they're going to find here, Lester, but that's not the point. The point is that this project probably won't go forward for months. I need you to check our liability. I also need you to examine the insurance policies, and to somehow, without tipping our hand, talk to the few investors who came on board early. I'd promised them the chance of a return within two years. This project came alive because I thought we could fast-track it."

He was talking to his lawyer. Usually such conversations had lawyer-client privilege, but she wasn't sure about that when he conducted it outside on a cell phone.

Still, she should let him know she was there.

She didn't move.

"That's not the point, Lester. The point is that I already have 1.2 million dollars in capital tied up in this place, and now everything's going to be on hold—."

One of the officers saw her. She nodded at him.

"That's why I want you to find out if we're insured for something like this. I'm not sure I can afford to have that much money tied up indefinitely."

She scraped her foot against the dirt as she walked forward again. He continued talking, so she coughed.

He turned, paused, and sighed. Then he said, "Listen, I'll call you in a few hours. Have some answers for me by then, will you?"

"How's Lester?" she asked.

"You heard that?"

"Enough to know who you were talking to." Lester had handled their divorce. He had been Chase's lawyer for more than two decades. She had no idea if he was any good, but Chase obviously had no complaints. He usually fired people who didn't perform their jobs well.

Chase stuck his phone into the front pocket of his shirt. Then he took the padlock off his belt. "I suppose this is the wrong time to ask you to dinner."

"It's always the wrong time, Chase," she said.

He shook his head ever so slightly. "What did I do, Becca? Was being married to me that bad?"

"I divorced you," she said. "That should be answer enough."

But it wasn't, because he asked her often. And he made it sound like she had been crazy to leave him. Which, her therapist said, was proof enough to her that she had done the right thing.

Becca waited until he'd padlocked the hotel before she walked to her squad. Even then, she stood with an arm resting on the open door as he walked back to his Bronco.

He looked defeated. Was Chase a good enough actor to play such a difficult emotion? She wasn't sure, but she doubted it.

And Jillian would say that she doubted it because she wanted to.

"Changed my mind," Becca said when he got close. "How's pizza sound to you?"

"Good if they had the real thing here."

He'd gone to school in Chicago; he thought the pizza out west was too mainstream or too California. Tasteless and low-fat, he'd once said.

She expected the response, just not the rote way he said it.

"Well, how about that thing we call pizza out here in the wild, wild west?"

He looked at her for the longest time as if he were sizing her up. She made sure her expression remained neutral.

"You going to interrogate me?" he asked.

"Should I?"

"I suppose you should." He opened the Bronco's door. "And you should know I'm ordering spaghetti."

"Spoilsport," she said, got into the squad, and followed Chase out of the lot.

THEN

The box bounced for what seemed like forever. She heard boots tapping on the wooden sidewalk, boots scraping on dirt, boots going silent as they hit the grass. She heard voices, conversations far from her. She heard a motorized engine, one of those new-fangled automobiles that made humans think they had entered a technological age.

Daddy had always said they were backwards. If they were just a bit farther along, if the Earth hadn't been so focused on oil and gas and coal, then maybe their people could have rebuilt the ship. But the materials hadn't been manufactured yet, and the energy sources were too heavy or too combustible. The people needed something more sophisticated, but didn't have the resources to make it themselves.

Nor did they have the ability to take what passed for technology in this place and modify it for their needs.

Occasionally one of the voices would greet Jess Taylor and ask him what he had in the box. He'd give the same reply—*Nothing*—and continue as if that were true.

He walked for a long time.

Then she heard boots on wood again, a few creaks, and the click of a doorknob. Another creak—this one different, like a door opening—and the light filtering through the towel seemed dimmer.

Finally, Jess Taylor set the box down.

"Just a minute," he said.

She heard a door close, then a swish that she recognized—curtains being closed. This place was hot. The windows should've been open instead of covered. The air smelled faintly of grease and unwashed sheets

Then the towel came off. She swiveled her eye upwards. Jess Taylor was looking down at her.

"This is my house," he said. "I live alone, so no one'll bother us. I don't have to be anywhere until tomorrow."

She wasn't sure why he was telling her all that.

He scooted a chair closer to the table, sat down, then asked, "Do you have any idea what we should do next?"

NOW

Becca didn't have to tell him where they were going because there was only one pizza parlor in all of Hope that he would step into. It was in a beat-up old building on the southeast side, about as far from the End of the World as they could go.

The pizza parlor—called Reuben's of all things—was actually owned by a displaced New York Italian who missed his grandmother's cooking. He made pizza because teenagers loved it and because it was a cheap, easy meal for families, but his heart was in the Italian dishes, from lasagna to a special homemade sausage marinara whose recipe he kept secret.

Chase came out of the bathroom as she went into the ladies room. When she came out, Chase was sitting toward the back, in a red vinyl booth, his hands folded on the checked tablecloth. The edges of his hair were wet as was one side of his face.

Washing up hadn't entirely gotten rid of the smell of rot that had permeated her nose, but it got knocked back a degree. The rich odor of garlic and baking bread helped.

By the time she got to the table, Chase was sipping a glass of wine. An iced tea waited for her. Irritation flooded through her—how did he know what she wanted? Had he asked? No, of course not—and then she shook it off.

He had always done this, and until she left him, she had let him. She hadn't told him in any way that he no longer had the right to make decisions for her, and now didn't seem the time.

"I ordered the family-sized spaghetti with the sausage marinara," he said.

She sighed. She was going to have to confront him after all.

But he held up his hand, as if to forestall anything she had to say.

"Then I realized I was being a jerk, so I ordered a small pepperoni pizza and a basket of garlic bread."

As he said that, the garlic bread arrived, looking crisp and greasy and delicious.

"Sorry. I know I should know better."

Becca wasn't sure if that was a real apology or not. She wasn't even sure she should be annoyed or not. Sometimes she wished her therapist was on speed-dial, so she could ask a simple question: What was the appropriate response to this particular Chase action? Should she be flattered or insulted? Should she set him in his place? Or should she do her breathing exercises while she reminded herself that they were no longer married?

"We could, I think, change the topping on the pizza." He actually sounded worried. "I don't think it went into the oven yet."

"No, that's fine," she said. "A hundred-thousand fat-filled calories actually sound good right now."

So she had opted onto a response, and it was passive/aggressive. Bully for her. How non-constructive.

Chase blinked, looking a little stunned, then shrugged. "Sounds like you're in the mood to interrogate me."

Becca grabbed a slice of garlic bread. The butter welled against her fingers, and she realized she was hungry.

"How much do you stand to lose if the End of the World folds?"

"Folds?" he asked. "Or gets put on hold?"

"It's the same thing, isn't it? Didn't you tell me you needed to finish this quick?"

He swirled his wine glass, then took a huge swig, something she'd never seen him do.

"Let me explain the End of the World, can I, before we get into the details you think important?"

She wasn't the only one capable of being passive/aggressive, but she let the comment slide. She had baited him, after all.

"Shoot," she said.

He flagged the waiter down, got them both water, and drank his so quickly that he looked like a man dying of thirst. Then he pushed his other glass toward the back of the table, as if saving the wine for later.

"The End of the World," he said, the words rolling off his tongue like a lover's. "Remember how much we loved it?"

How much he had loved it. But she didn't correct him. She nodded instead.

"Remember when I used to talk about restoring it, about making the End of the World *the* destination resort in Oregon, and you'd laugh, and you'd say who would want to come to Hope?"

"That was before the boom," she said, surprised that she wasn't feeling defensive.

"Before Hollywood discovered how cheap the land was, before they filmed half the Western films up here, before the Californians bought everything in sight."

And tried to change the town into a mini-California, with its strip malls and coffee bars and upscale shops that people like Becca couldn't set foot into unless there was a police emergency.

"Hollywood's left," she said. "They've gone to Canada."

"But they vacation here. They ski, they hunt, they fish. They look at the pretty views. They want to play golf and lacrosse and polo and soccer, if we could only accommodate them. The town doesn't have everything yet, and if we did, even more would come."

"Is this the speech you gave to prospective investors?" she asked. "Because I know the drill."

He'd practiced much of it on her over the years. She hadn't agreed with all of it, but she had encouraged some of it. She too wanted Hope to grow. When she'd been a girl, the town was dying, and the name seemed like the way the town planned for its future.

"Historic resorts are the next travel boom," he said. "People want to visit the past, so long as it has all the amenities of the present."

The waiter set down the pizza. The cheese was still popping because the tomato sauce was bubbling underneath.

Becca took a piece. To her surprise, Chase did too.

"So tell me," she said, "how come your money's in this instead of other people's?"

He sighed. "It costs more to refurbish the old hotel and the Natatorium than it would to tear the place down, and build comparable modern buildings from scratch."

"And your investors didn't like that?"

"They like everything else. They like the resort, the golf courses—

"Courses?" Becca asked.

"Four," he said, "along with residential housing, riding trails, and a possible dude ranch near the edge of the mountains."

"How much property did you buy?"

"Just the End of the World," he said. "Turns out that the property runs from the highway all the way to the mountains."

"My god," Becca said.

"It was all scrub and desert, not even good enough for ranching, although the End of the World's original owners did rent it out for that."

"Who did you buy it from?" she asked.

"The heirs. They don't live in Oregon any longer. They remembered it from their childhoods, figured the land wasn't worth much, and sold it for a song. The land wasn't the problem. The hotel and resort were."

"The investors wanted you to build new, and you refused." Her voice rose just a bit at the end of the statement, mostly because she was surprised. Chase did what he wanted within reason, but he never turned down money like this. "You really had your heart set on rebuilding the place."

"I had documents and itineraries and research and projections that showed just how much people would love it here. They go to historic lodges now. Hell, Timberline Resort is the number two destination in Oregon."

"Number one being?"

He looked down. "Spirit Mountain Casino."

Which had no historic hotel. Nothing except a rather cheap looking lodge and a large casino at the entrance to the Van Duzer Corridor in the coastal mountain range.

"But that land was considered worthless forty years ago," he said.

"Because it was tribal land in the middle of nowhere," she said.

"You don't have to side with them," he snapped.

The reaction shocked her. He never snapped. He got angry or frustrated and occasionally raised his voice, but usually he manipulated, twisting the conversation until she was surprised that she was agreeing with him, even when she knew she shouldn't.

"So I repeat," she said, "how deep are you into this?"

"Ninety percent of the resort funding is from me." He took another swig of the wine, leaving the glass nearly empty. How many times had he told her wine was meant to be sipped not guzzled? He probably hadn't even tasted this one.

"That's a lot of money."

"More than you realize."

"So you go bankrupt if this place never gets off the ground."

He finished the wine, then set the glass at the edge of the table, an obvious signal for more. "You're awful damn pessimistic."

"I'm not pessimistic, and I'm not here to judge you." Even though that was a lie. At this moment, it was her job to judge him. "I am trying to figure out what happened in that Natatorium."

"You think someone murdered a lot of people and buried them beneath the swimming pool. A long, long time ago. I think it shouldn't interfere with my project."

She sighed. "I'm not talking about the old bodies. I'm talking about the smell."

He froze. The waiter returned, grabbed the wine glass, and left without asking what he was supposed to do about Chase's beverage. Maybe the look on Chase's face scared him off.

"I told you," Chase said. "It was an animal."

"We haven't found it yet. We're operating on the assumption that the recent body is human."

"And you think I what? Sabotaged my own project? Why the hell would I do that?"

"I don't know." Becca raised her voice enough to drown his out. "Maybe you don't have enough funding. Maybe you want out now."

"And you think that destroying the project is the way to leave? If I want to lose several million dollars, I'd put it on the roulette table. If I want to shut down the project, I'll do that."

"So why didn't you?"

"I didn't want to." He grabbed the edge of the table. For a moment, she thought he was going to leverage himself out of it.

But he didn't. He ran a hand through his hair, took a deep breath, and forced himself to lean back.

"You don't want to?" she asked. "Or you see this as a win-win situation?"

He looked at her as if she was crazy. "Excuse me?"

"Once you found the bodies below the pool, you knew that might stall the project. But you wanted out without losing any money. So you found a way that the insurance might cover it. Something guaranteed, not an ancient burial ground like you thought, but a police investigation—"

"You think I planted a body there for the *insurance money?*"

"I don't know," she said. "Did you?"

His mouth was open. He stared at her like the day she told him she was leaving. If she had to, she would wager that he was telling the truth. But those kinds of experiences, that kind of hunch, didn't hold up in court.

Besides, she knew that her reactions to him weren't always the right ones.

"Do you really think that little of me?" he asked softly.

"What I think doesn't matter," she said. "This *is* a police investigation, and I have to—"

"Oh, bullshit," he said. "You don't have to explore every goddamn angle. You think I'm capable of killing someone and planting him in the Natatorium for the fucking insurance money."

The waiter hovered near the kitchen door. In his hand, he held another glass of wine. He watched them with a wary expression.

She had to get Chase to calm down. She needed him to think clearly.

"Do you want me to investigate this or someone from Portland? Because that's the way it's heading."

"Even if I turn out to be right and it's a goddamn coyote down there?"

"Even if," she said. "We have something big now, and there's no covering it up. Jillian called the state crime lab. We're going to have reporters. You want them to write about how we had a screaming fight in our favorite Italian restaurant?"

"Fuck you, Becca," he said. "You planned this."

"Your anger?'

"With a fucking audience. Do you hate me that much?"

She swallowed. She was getting angry now. "You ask me that a lot. So here's the answer, Chase. I don't hate you. If anything, I'm still in love with your sorry ass, and that's a problem for me. It's also a problem for this investigation, since I'm the only trained detective on Hope's police force. I'm holding off the Valley investigative team for the moment, but that won't last if we keep this up."

He slammed his hands on the booth so hard that the fake wood tabletop attached to the wall actually bounced. Then he stood up and stalked to the men's room.

Becca took a deep breath, let it out, and then took another. And another, and another, still wishing for the therapist on speed-dial.

Did she keep breathing until she was light-headed or did she just leave?

She was handling this all wrong, and pretty soon word would get out. The chief would relieve her, and the investigation would become a state thing instead of a local thing. And that kind of publicity would hurt the new Hope, the place that actually had a future.

The waiter came to the table. He was still cradling the wine glass. "You think he's gonna want this? Because—"

"Yeah," she said. "He'll want that and more. Bring the whole bottle."

She ate her piece of pizza slowly, drank the iced tea, and waited, keeping an eye on the men's room door. The three other tables, filled with young families, kept an eye on her, as if she had been the problem, not Chase.

The men's room door opened as she finished her third piece. The waiter had been back twice—once with the wine bottle and once with a heaping bowl of spaghetti in sausage marina sauce. As stressed as Becca was, she could probably eat the entire thing without Chase's help.

To her relief, he came back to the booth and slid in.

"Okay," he said, "since you're going all official on me, here's what you need to know. I have six million dollars into this thing. That's real money. I also have outstanding loans of ten million, and that's not nearly enough to get everything done. I'm hoping when the hotel and Nat are finished, the investors will pour in. If they don't, I'll be in debt until I die, even if the place is a success."

Becca set down the pizza crust she'd been clinging too. She resisted the urge to slide the plate of spaghetti toward her.

"Does my insurance cover this? How the hell would I know? I'm sure my agent doesn't know. I'm sure the insurance company has no real idea, and its legal department will be haggling over the policy language and the politics of the entire thing for months. That's what I was talking to Lester about. I'm hoping that he can find a few answers, or at least an argument, so that some of the back and forth gets forestalled if and when you people actually decide to shut me down."

"We already shut you down, Chase," she said. "The question now is for how long."

"I know." He picked up the glass and then set it down again. "But you know what I mean. This could be a two-day inconvenience or it could be a year-long nightmare. And since it's all one property, I'm pretty sure that you could tie me up for a long time."

"If those bodies are Native American, you could be right," she said.

He let out a long sigh. Then he moved the wine glass closer to her plate than his.

"So," he said, "do I have a motive to get insurance money? No. I'd be a fool to try this plan. If I wanted insurance money, I'd find another way to go about it. And I'd be smart, Becca. This is damn dumb. It jeopardizes everything without giving me any benefit at all. I'll be in the news forever, I won't be able to save face, and I'm going to go broke. Hell, I'd be better off disappearing and starting all over again than doing that. I'm not damn dumb, Becca."

"I know," she said.

"I have no reason to plant something there."

"Does anyone else?" she asked.

"Yeah," he said, reaching for the plate of spaghetti. "Yeah, I'm afraid a lot of people do."

THEN

Why would he ask her what to do next? Wasn't he the grown one, the one in charge? She was just a baby, really, younger than anyone else in their group.

But he wasn't part of their group. She wasn't even sure there was a group any more. Where had everyone gone?

When the shanties burned, the remaining people fled. Momma had grabbed her. They were just a little behind the group.

And she never knew what happened to any of them.

"What about my Momma?" she asked Jess Taylor.

He closed his eyes, turned his head, and wiped the sweat off his forehead. Then he glanced at the window, like he wanted to open it. He stood, and she thought he was going to, but all he did was get another towel and clean off his fingers.

When he sat back down, his face had a different look to it. His eyes were open, but sadder, if that was possible.

Sometimes she wondered how these humans could think themselves so different from the people. These humans changed too, just not as much. And sometimes these humans changed by force of will, just like the people did.

Just like Jess Taylor had done a moment ago.

"You're going to keep asking, aren't you?" he said.

She blinked at him. She didn't know how to answer, except maybe to say of course she would. She loved her momma and her momma left her on the sidewalk.

Bad things happened this afternoon, and she heard some of them. One of them sounded like Momma.

"I don't know what happened," he said. "I'll find out as best I can. I promise. But it might take days."

Days. She wanted to fold her ears in, close her eyes, and huddle into a little ball. What would happen to her for those days?

"I've seen this before," he said. "Not this, exactly, but the same kind of thing. Folks get riled up about the strangest things, and you have to admit, your people are strange."

She didn't think so. But she didn't answer that either, just kept watching him.

"I mean, I think I finally understand where this violence comes from, this impulse. Not because of you."

He held up a hand, as if to reassure her. She wasn't sure what he was reassuring her about.

"It comes about because of the differences. They're startling. And sometimes—I don't mean to offend you—but sometimes, they're revolting. Humans don't handle revulsion well. We...."

He shook his head and stood up, walking to the window, and peeking through the curtain. Sweat stained the back of his shirt, leaving a V-shaped wet spot in the fabric.

"I can't believe I'm defending them."

He shook his head again. Then he let the curtain drop close, and he came back to the chair.

"The chances are – I'm so sorry, but the chances are that your mother didn't make it. Just like your father. She probably—they probably—I mean, you heard it this afternoon. You're lucky to be here. And if your mother is alive—."

He stopped, wiped a hand over his mouth, then shook his head yet again.

He didn't say any more.

She was holding her breath. She finally let it out. Her other eye had appeared. Apparently she needed to see him. Her body was starting to make changes on its own.

"You think she's still alive?" she asked.

"No," he said.

"But you said—"

"I know what I said." He sighed. "Look, Sarah, if your mother is still alive, it probably won't be for long."

"Then we have to find her."

"That's not what I mean."

She felt her skin tighten. Another shiver ran through her. The spikes started to form and she willed them away. She didn't want him to know she suddenly felt threatened.

"What do you mean?" she asked.

"I mean they're probably not done."

"But I heard the men, they came into the bank, they said it was over, they said it was…fun…. They said—"

"I know what they said." He ran his fingers along his forehead. "I know. And I know a few of them will go back. Some probably haven't left. And they'll finish. Do you understand me? They'll finish."

"Can't we get her before they do?"

He stared at her, and that sadness returned to his eyes. His whole face looked sad, and she wondered for a minute if he even saw her, if he was looking at her or something else—someone else—like a memory, maybe, like those ghostly shapes that the people sometimes made when they thought of a relative long dead.

"If we try to get her," he said, "they'll kill us too."

"Not you," she said.

He let out half a laugh, like she'd startled the sound out of him.

"Sarah, honey," he said, "if your people hadn't come, they'd've gotten to me eventually. They always do."

NOW

"You know who doesn't like me." Chase used tongs to dish up his spaghetti. Somehow he managed to do so without getting sauce on his shirt. "You used to put up with the phone calls."

Becca remembered. The calls came in late at night. Sometimes they were just hang-ups. Sometimes they were more serious than that. A few even included threats.

In those days, Hope's telephone system was too unsophisticated to provide services like Caller I.D., so Becca had had to put a trace on the line. She had gone to every single one of the callers, warning them that their behavior was illegal and should Chase's businesses go under or should he get hurt, they would be the first suspects she went to.

Most seemed to listen. A few grumbled that Chase had only married her because he wanted police protection. Not even Becca was insecure enough to believe that.

She took a small portion of the spaghetti, barely enough to fill a corner of the plate provided, and then only because she loved the sauce. Mostly, she focused on the pizza, her iced tea, and Chase.

"What about this project?" she asked. "Anyone new surface?"

He used his spoon as a counterweight to keep the spaghetti he was winding from falling off his fork. He worked at it as if it were a particularly difficult puzzle.

"Obviously, you never went to the city council meetings."

"Not for this, no," she said. She avoided city business as much as possible.

"Half the town hated it. Some I didn't expect, folks who had supported me when I wanted to redo Beiker's Department Store downtown."

"The preservationists went against you?"

"Yeah." He ate the forkful, swallowed, and then drank some water. "They think the End of the World is a bad idea, a dangerous place, and the last straw in turning Hope into a replica of California."

"Wow," Becca said. "I'd've thought they would've loved it."

"Me, too," he said. "I was stunned. A few actually threatened me."

"You're kidding."

He shook his head. "Ray McGuillicuty, remember him? He told me I'd regret buying the End of the World."

"You think that was a threat, coming from a 90-year-old man?"

Chase shrugged. "I thought it was idle talk at the time. But he has money, connections, and a shady reputation. He made his money running illegal speakeasies in the late 30s, and gambling dens in the forties. Word around town was that if there was an illegal business—an abortionist, a fight ring, drug smuggling—McGuillicuty would rent space or manpower to that business for a cut, of course."

She had heard the rumors, but she also knew Old Man McGuillicuty had been an upstanding citizen since the 1960s.

"You think he's still got that kind of pull?"

"I think if anyone in Hope is smart enough to stop my project by burying a body on the property, it's Ray McGuillicuty."

"That's giving him a lot of power."

"If you're right," Chase said, "and someone is trying to shut me down, Ray's my first choice."

Becca tried not to laugh. She couldn't imagine that old man caring so much about the future of Hope. But she wasn't going to ignore this.

"Who else?" she asked as she finished her iced tea. She waved the glass at the waiter, and he nodded.

"Oh, Christ," Chase said. "Damn near the entire preservation society. All the matrons and their husbands too. Most of the old money in Hope—what there is of it—warned me away."

"Like Old Man McGuillicuty did?" Becca asked. The waiter showed up with a pitcher and set it on the table. He didn't even bother to pour. He still seemed a bit nervous about Chase's earlier outburst.

"Not that blatant," Chase said. "But they all took time to tell me that the End of the World is the most unlucky place in Hope and that everyone connected to it has been harmed by that connection."

"Lovely," Becca said. "Superstition still alive and well."

"And apparently they thought I should make business decisions based on it."

"You didn't, though," she said.

"I think some of my investors did," he said. "The preservation committee knew who my usual investors were. A number of them were contacted and a few backed out. One even told me that old properties that had bad luck rumors usually had a reason for them."

"Turns out he was right," Becca said.

"She," he said. "And I guess she was."

"Which means..." Becca tapped a finger against her chin. "...that someone knew about those bodies."

"How do you figure?" Chase asked.

She smiled at him. "Bad luck rumors have to start somewhere."

"You think that's tied to the smell?" he asked.

"Probably not, but right now, those old bodies are the only crime I have to investigate. I'll start there."

"After you finish harassing the local businessmen."

"After I finish dinner with my former husband, who has had a hell of a day."

THEN

She didn't know what Jess Taylor meant by the humans getting to him, and he wouldn't say. He paced around the front part of the cabin, poured some water from a pitcher into a glass, and drank.

Then he stared at her.

She wondered if he was sorry he'd helped her. Maybe he would turn her in.

Maybe she would scream.

She wanted to beg him to keep her, beg him to help her. But she didn't. Daddy used to say that people who begged didn't deserve help. They had to help themselves.

Only she couldn't do that, not without knowing what had happened. The answers weren't simple. Her home was gone—she knew that much. When the shanties burned, hers would've burned with it. Daddy always kept water near the candles. He used to say, *This place is so primitive and so badly built that we're going to die here in a stupid fire because we couldn't get to it in time.*

He'd been wrong about them dying. None of them had died in that cabin, although she wasn't sure about the others, the people who lived in the shanties where the fires started.

She wished Daddy were here now. She wished he would talk to Jess Taylor, grown one to grown one. They would understand each other. They would know what had happened and what would happen next.

"Do you eat?" Jess Taylor asked. He swished the water around in his glass. He was still looking at her that funny way.

She had to form a mouth. She had lost it while he'd been pacing. Her body wasn't sure what form to take so it was taking several at once, which made her dizzy.

"I eat," she said.

"I mean, do you eat what we eat?"

"When I look like you," she said. Her people's food had gone away when she was really, really little. They had to become like the humans just so that they could take in human nourishment.

"When you look like me," Jess Taylor repeated. "How about the way you look now?"

"I'm not anything now," she said. "I need to be something to take in food."

Something she understood. Something whose systems were somewhat compatible. Daddy and the other scientists had to work for a while to make their systems work like a human's. They still had to make changes—changes she didn't understand.

Daddy said she was lucky. She started changing into human form really young, so it would be ingrained. If she had to hide, she could hide as one of them forever because her body was used to their strangeness.

His never would be. Some of the older people got really sick in the first years.

Some of the older people died.

"How often do you have to eat?" Jess Taylor asked.

"I don't know," she said. "Whenever you do, I guess."

Because she always ate when Momma did. She was too young to pick her own times to eat. Eating had to be trained like everything else.

"Wonderful," he said in that low voice of his, the one no one else was supposed to hear. Then he raised it a little. "How about water? Do you need that too?"

"If I look like you," she said, "I act like you. My needs are like yours."

That's the beauty of it, Daddy said to Momma once. *And the curse. If we stay here too long, we lose our identity. We become someone else. Then they'll never find us.*

Why would they look for us? Momma asked. *For all they know, we missed our settlement location and made do.*

They trace new colonies. They have to, Daddy said. *We don't just move there because of population growth. These places are carefully chosen for raw material wealth as well.*

She wasn't sure what "raw material wealth" was, but Momma had known. Momma had looked at Daddy disapprovingly. Daddy had shrugged, because he wore his human all the time now, and then he had smiled at her.

They'll track us down, if only to see what kind of wealth we discovered here.

And if we don't find any? Momma said.

That's not the concern, Daddy said. *The concern is whether not they'll find us before we lose ourselves.*

"So you're going to have to pick a shape sometime tonight, aren't you?" Jess Taylor said. He had moved closer to her. She hadn't noticed before. Had she been so lost in her memories that she hadn't seen him walk?

"I guess," she said.

"Can you be something else for a while? A table, maybe or the box?"

"I'm too little," she said. "I can't do it by myself, not for long. That's why I couldn't be brick. I tried, but I'm not good yet. And I can't stay long anyway. I don't know the sleep-change. I need to move and breathe and feed myself like you."

He sighed. He sank into the chair next to the table. "I was afraid of that."

He took another sip of the water, studied his hand, then studied the small cabin. Then he got up and went to the window again, peering out the curtain.

"No one," he said. "We're okay for now."

"I know," she said, even though she didn't. She wanted him to figure out how to help her. She was becoming more and more afraid he would just throw her out now that he knew most of her secrets.

He put his hand in the box, near her skin but not touching it. "You turned the color of the brick this afternoon," he said. "Can you turn the same color as me?"

She looked at him as hard as he had looked at her. Then she let out a little sigh.

"Yes," she said.

"You sounded hesitant," he said.

"I can't do blue eyes," she said. "Yours aren't."

He smiled suddenly, as if he hadn't expected that. "You're right. Mine aren't. Anything else human you can't do?"

"I can't be a grown one," she said. "I have to 'roughly correspond.'"

She said those last two words carefully. They were Daddy's words. Before she had only known the concept, not how to express it. She used to point to things, things she wanted to be for more than an hour, more than a day.

He would shake his head. Sometimes he would laugh. She loved it when her Daddy laughed.

Younglin, he'd say, *they have to roughly correspond.*

Mostly she wanted to be a grown one. Humans, more than the people, treated their young ones very differently. But she didn't have enough years to be a grown one. She couldn't pretend it, couldn't even get the size right.

That problem translated to other living things as well. She could be a sapling, but not a tree. A kitten, but not a cat.

Someday, she would roughly correspond. But she wouldn't know when until she changed to human form, and that form was a grown one.

"You're a girl," Jess Taylor said, "or they wouldn't call you Sarah. What age do you roughly correspond to?"

"Ten," she said because that's what Momma said when she took her to the school two years before. Even though her learning had grown and her grades had advanced, she hadn't changed, not like her classmates.

So she'd asked Daddy about that, and he'd said, *Roughly, younglin. Roughly correspond. We age differently than they do. Slower, I think.*

But he didn't know. There was so much they didn't know. So much that they didn't understand.

Then he left and no one knew, and Momma hated the questions.

"Ten," Jess Taylor said, and nodded, almost pleased. "Ten might work."

"For what?" she asked, the words catching in her newly formed mouth.

"For keeping you alive, child," he said, and tapped the edge of the box as he stood. "For keeping you alive."

NOW

By the time Becca got home, she was too tired to chase rumors. She took a shower, which didn't get that smell out of her nose. Her tiny house was an oven, despite the heat pumped she'd wasted the last of her divorce settlement money on, and she actually had to turn on the good old fashioned swamp cooler she couldn't bring herself to get rid of.

Theoretically, the desert cooled at night, but lately the coolness had come without benefit of a breeze. She started with the air-conditioner, which was nearly as old as she was, and by midnight, shut it down, shoved a fan in the window, and hoped for the best.

She couldn't sleep. Worries about herself, about Chase, about the appropriateness of the investigation had her pacing. The mentions Chase had made over dinner about rumors concerning the End of the World had her worried as well.

Hope had once been called the Hope of the West. Founded just after the Civil War by philanthropists and political idealists, Hope was supposed to be a refuge for displaced former slaves as well as immigrants who weren't wanted in larger cities, and even Chinese families, so long as they remained in their own enclave at the edge of town.

The founders of Hope put ads in all the major newspapers,

promising land and jobs to people no one else wanted. Hope also promised full equality to blacks and immigrants, although "immigrants" did not include the Chinese, who wouldn't be allowed to vote or hold office. Hope was notable in its Chinese relations, though, for allowing entire families to live there, so long as they kept to themselves. Most states only tolerated Chinese males.

The experiment didn't last. The United States barred Chinese immigration in the early part of the 20th century, and then the State of Oregon itself started enforcing the discrimination built into its constitution, attempting to bodily throw Hope's blacks out of the state. The entire town prevented that, letting the blacks stay so long as the city (and county) promised not to let them hold elected office or take state jobs.

Still, Hope was something of a legend in the state, a place where people could be perceived as nothing more than a set of skills. Where, in the words of Martin Luther King Jr., people could be judged by the content of their character instead of the color of their skin.

That was Hope's legacy, and the reason for its name. Hope's children got spoon-fed this history from the moment they walked into Hope Elementary, and heard about it all the way to graduation from Hope High.

So the idea of a massacre, any massacre, particularly one that someone remembered and tried to hide, went against everything Hope stood for. People didn't die here, not in large groups. Hell, they didn't die in small ones.

Becca got out of bed, grabbed her lightest robe—which Chase had bought her for one of their anniversaries—and headed for the couch, the television, and late-night talk shows. Maybe some blathering would shut down her brain.

Because all this thinking about a possible massacre—even one nearly a hundred years old—upset her more than she wanted to admit.

THEN

They waited until it was full dark before she grew herself back to human. It took a long time.

Jess Taylor's cabin had three rooms and a windowless room he called a storage room. It scared her. It was like the box, only bigger, and it was in the middle of all three rooms—like it took a part off the corners of them and made its own little space.

She had never seen anything like that. He said he kept things in there, but there wasn't much, a few boxes pushed against a corner, and some jars filled with jam.

All three walls had hangers for lanterns. He hung one before he brought her into the room. He kept it on low, so it wouldn't burn too much kerosene and stink up the place—or start a fire. (At least, she hoped it wouldn't start a fire; she'd seen too much fire this day.)

He took the box off the table, talking to her the whole time, mostly nonsense stuff like humans did with babies, stuff about how it would be okay, and the room might be close, but it would do, no one could see in, they would be safe.

She wasn't sure about safe. She wasn't sure about trusting Jess

Taylor any more, but she had to. She didn't know what other choice she had.

He set her box on top of the other boxes, then propped the door partly open with one of the jars.

"I'll let you just change now," he said, like she was going to put on a dress. "Let me know when you're done."

"No!" she said, as loud as she could, which wasn't very loud, considering. She didn't have the body behind the sound, and she didn't know she needed it until just now.

That scared her too.

She finally realized how truly helpless she was.

"You have to stay," she said.

He sighed, keeping one hand on the door. "I'm sure it's private. We —folks like me—we let each other be private."

"I got to see you," she said.

"I'll be just outside the door," he said.

"To change," she said. "I got to see you to change. I can't do it without an example."

He frowned. "I can't...change...like you. I can't show you how."

She shook her head. "To look at. I need to see what I'm changing into."

And even then it might not work.

His head bowed, and his arm dropped. "I'm not sure I want to be here for that."

She wasn't sure she could do it without him. In the past, Momma or Daddy had always helped her. They had always found a way to get her through the difficult parts, like making the fingers different lengths or remembering to grow hair.

"How about I stand just outside the door with my back to you?" he asked. "Would that help?"

"Can you tell me if I get it wrong?" she asked.

He bowed his head even more, but he finally said, "I guess I could. Wait one moment, all right?"

She was scared. She knew that just as he left the room. If he hadn't propped open the door, she would've been even more scared. She couldn't see him at all.

Then he came back, carrying a sheet. "I don't have girl clothes. We'll have to find some for you. Can you put this on?"

Modesty, Daddy called it.

Silly, Momma called it, especially when it got really hot. But they learned how to wear things, and taught her about it too.

The clothes she'd been wearing when she was running probably got absorbed into her skin as fuel when she became the sidewalk. She'd been so scared, she hadn't noticed.

She'd most likely be sick later.

"If I put that on, how will you know if I get things right?" she asked.

"I'm sure no one'll notice and you'll do just fine," he said, running the words together like he couldn't breathe.

"I never got everything right before on the first try," she said.

"You'll do fine," he repeated and eased out the door, leaving the sheet on one of the shelves.

It took her a long time to squinch to the edge of the box. By then, she'd formed fingers (probably because she'd been thinking of them) and they were the wrong lengths. But they were good for grabbing onto stuff, especially when she was squinching, so she didn't pay attention to right or wrong.

When she reached the edge of the box, she either had to get all the way to the floor or she had to make legs. She couldn't quite remember the details of legs. The knees she knew and the ankles—they were the bendy parts—and the feet, but there was other stuff she'd forgotten about and she knew they'd look funny.

And she also knew if she hooked the legs up wrong, they'd be impossible to move. So she made hips too.

In fact, everything would be better if she did the bendy parts first. She just finished elbows when Jess Taylor leaned partway in the door, keeping his face averted.

"You all right?"

"Yeah," she said because she didn't know how else to answer.

"Will you be a lot longer?"

"I don't know." She didn't know how long she'd already been. She didn't really care. It took a lot of concentration to make herself all over again, and because she'd been so scared earlier, it was going to be harder.

Just him asking the question knocked her off for a little while. She put one of the elbows just above the hip, and she had to reform, trying to remember exactly how arms bend.

Finally, she had a guess at the human shape she used to wear—just that morning even though it seemed like forever ago—she grabbed the sheet and held it in front of her.

"Is this all right?" she asked.

Jess Taylor turned very slowly. And then he looked at her.

He was trying not to show how he felt, but she could see it in his eyes. Confused, sickened, surprised, all at the same time.

"Close," he said after a minute. "You're really close."

But it took most of the night just to get the general shape right—collarbones, she always forgot about collarbones—and somewhere along the way, he forgot about the sheet, telling her to make a belly button—which she'd never heard of—and explaining dimples in the knees.

By the time they got done, she had a hunch she was more human looking up close than any of her other people had ever been, and the thought made her sad.

But she didn't have long for sad. Because Jess Taylor gave her some bread and some water and an apple that he'd kept in the root cellar since last fall, and told her he needed just a little sleep before going to work.

"You're going to leave me?" she said.

"I have to," he said. "You'll be safe if you don't let anybody see you. They can't know you're here. I'll be back late afternoon. Maybe with some answers."

Maybe. She wanted him to promise her. But he couldn't promise her.

He couldn't promise her anything. Anything at all.

NOW

If this were a normal investigation regarding a murder that involved the town's history, Becca would go to the Blue Diamond Café. The Blue Diamond was in the exact center of town, in a building that had housed it since the 1930s. Tourists occasionally wandered into the Blue Diamond, saw the ripped booths and dirty windows, and wandered right out.

Becca looked at the Blue Diamond with longing as she walked past. Even though all the city old-timers would be long gone by now—it was the very late hour of 9 a.m.—she'd still find someone to welcome her and give her a free omelet that, in her private moments, she called a heart attack on a plate.

But she had to go two buildings down, to the Hope Historical Society, housed rent-free in one of Chase's renovations, the Hope Bankers Building and Trust.

The money people had long moved away from the Bankers Building, but they'd left behind one of the most solid brick buildings in all of Eastern Oregon. Chase had turned the lower floor into shops and restaurants, the second and third floors into offices, and the upper three floors into condos that sold for four times what Becca paid for her house just two years ago.

There was a diner in the Bankers Building, a 1950s wannabe called the Rock and Remember, and it was usually crammed with transplanted Californians or tourists or both. But the omelets, while large here, were made with egg-whites only, and the chefs—if you could call them that—used only "the good oils"—no butter or lard—which gave the food a cardboard aftertaste. Even the coffee wasn't coffee: it was a mochaccino or a cappuccino or an espresso, something that required a language all its own to order.

Still, she went inside, grabbed a double-tall latte with sprinkles and a "cuppa plain Joe," and then went to the elevator.

The only way she could get Gladys Conyers to talk to her, after that last disastrous interview, was to ply her with her favorite beverage, while making the bribe seem entirely accidental.

Gladys Conyers was forty-five and earnest, a California transplant herself who desperately wanted to convince the entire town of Hope that she was a local. She had some claim. Her grandparents were born here, her parents were raised here, and she spent every summer here from the day she was born.

Her grandfather, Jack Conyers, started the Hope Historical Society as a labor of love in the 1950s, after he came back from the war. He thought every small American town should have its history engraved on its downtown so Americans knew what a wonderful place they came from.

In addition to keeping all of Hope's newspapers, as well as any clippings that pertained to the city from any other periodical—even the flashy *New York Times* article forty years ago that put Hope's ski resorts on the map—, he also managed to acquire important items from Hope's history.

He used to run a small museum from the back of the Historical Society, but lately, he'd been involved in a fund-raising drive to give Hope its own historical museum.

Becca knew she wouldn't find Jack at the Historical Society. He had become understandably hard to reach these last few years, ever since his eighty-fifth birthday. He figured he only had a good ten years left, and he wanted to spend them preserving Hope's history, not talking to people who had questions they could easily answer on their own.

So Gladys had taken over the society. She had a lot of knowledge about Hope—more than most long-time residents, but nothing like her grandfather. Still, anyone who wanted to see Jack had to go through Gladys. If she could answer the questions, then she would and Jack wouldn't lose precious time talking about the past he supposedly loved.

The society had an office on the first floor because it sold items from various ski tournaments and rodeos as well as Hope memorabilia.

Becca tried to ignore the memorabilia, just as she tried to ignore the weird milky scent of the latte she carried in its cardboard holder. She headed to the back, past the teenager manning the sales desk, to the office where Gladys held court.

"Don't think a latte's gonna get me to do you any favors," Gladys said from behind the slatted door. The woman had to have a nose like a Great Dane.

Becca pushed the door open, set the latte on Gladys's specially made cup holder in the center of her desk, then grabbed her own cuppa plain Joe and sat in the easy chair.

"I'm not asking for a favor," Becca said.

"I hear you stopped the work at the Natatorium," Gladys was slender, tanned, and overdressed for Hope. She wore a designer suit—pastel, of course, since it was summer—sandal pumps, and too much makeup. "We have pictures down at the museum of the Nat being built, being used, and being abandoned. I have a computer list already prepared for you, not that I think it'll do any good."

"Why'd you think I'd be here?" Becca asked.

"You always come here, even when you have a current case. Besides, there's so much opposition to Chase's project, I figured you'd want to know if there's any historical reason for it."

Becca hid her smile behind her paper coffee cup. Gladys would be useful after all.

"Is there any historical reason?" Becca asked.

Gladys made a pfumph sound that she had to have learned from her curmudgeonly grandfather. "Besides the rumors of ghosts, of hauntings, of strange sounds in the night?"

"I know about those," Becca said.

"Wow," Gladys said, peeling the lid off her latte and adding even more sugar, "you actually admit you know something."

Becca sighed, and bit back her response. She knew she'd be in for some of this. Twice she had bypassed Gladys and gone to Jack directly, and neither of them let her forget it. For nearly a year, she had to send another officer to ask historical questions. Just recently, Becca had heard through the grapevine that she was welcome at the Historical Society again, so long as she respected its director.

She did respect its director, but she respected its director's grandfather more. Jack could answer her questions quickly and with a minimum of fuss. Gladys had to be babied, which Becca proceeded to do.

"I'm sorry about that," Becca said.

Gladys waved a beringed right hand. "Water under the bridge."

They continued that game until Gladys finished sugaring her latte and put the lid back on. Then she took a sip, eyed Becca, and said, "I hear there are some serious problems at the site."

Becca nodded. One more game, but a quick one. "You know I can't talk about the details, but there is a case."

"Murder?" Gladys asked.

"Sure looks that way," Becca said.

Gladys's eyes glinted. She loved crime and punishment so long as it didn't involve her family.

"Right now, I'm waiting for the crime lab," Becca said, "and while I'm stalled, I thought I'd ask you about a few other things I saw at the Nat."

Gladys tapped the lid of her latte. "Chase already had us run the history of the place. Aside from the usual drownings and accidental deaths that any long-running sports facility would have, we found nothing."

Becca nodded. She would take this one slow. "What about the ghost rumors?"

"Those are mostly from the hotel," Gladys said. "Apparently quite a few shady characters stayed there, as well as some famous folk. President Coolidge was the most famous, I would say. He loved the fishing up here. There are rumors that Hoover stayed there too, but I haven't been able to track them down. People weren't so proud of him, by the end."

Becca didn't need that kind of history lesson. "I'm more concerned with the Nat. Do you know what kind of laborers built it?"

"Of course I do." Gladys opened a drawer in her desk and pulled out a thick file. In it were computer reprints of the society's photos, articles on the construction of the End of the World, and the list that Gladys had mentioned right up front.

She put a lacquered nail on top of one of the photographs. A group of men stood on an empty patch of desert. Some leaned on shovels. Others held pickaxes. A few had rifles.

"These are the men who built the Nat," Gladys said. "We found all sorts of historical photographs for Chase. He loves the authenticity."

Gladys lingered over Chase's name. She'd had a crush on him for years, which bothered Chase a lot more than it bothered Becca.

"What're the rifles for?" Becca asked.

"Chase asked the same thing." Gladys spun the photograph so that she could look at it before spinning it back to Becca. "My grandfather says that the End of the World was so far out of town that the workers brought their guns, hoping that that night's dinner would lope past while they were working. This was jack rabbit country, back in the day, and from what I hear, you could find—and shoot—a rabbit as easily as a fly. The men got their paycheck and that night's supper."

"Was there labor trouble then?"

"In the 20s? In Oregon?" Gladys raised her voice just enough so that the teenager manning the sales desk could hear how stupid Becca was. "I'm sure in Portland, but not in Hope. And the End of the World was built around 1910, not the 20s. It became the premiere resort in this part of the country by 1918, with war vets bringing their brides here for a honeymoon. And I hear rumors that there was quite a speakeasy run out of the hotel's basement. The owners stocked up when it became clear that the dries were going to win."

Becca set the idea of the speakeasy aside for the moment. "What about among the crew? Troubles? Firings?"

"Do they look troubled?" Gladys tapped that nail on the photo again. "Take a close look. What do you see?"

Becca repressed a sigh and leaned forward. Gladys always made these visits seem like an oral exam. "A group of very rough-looking men."

"Well, they'd take any of our modern men and pound them into the ground, that's for sure," Gladys said, a trace of the Valley Girl she'd pretended to be still lingering in her speech. "But I mean their racial mix. Several black men standing side-by-side with several whites. Not even the Chinese are segregated in this photograph, and usually the old photographs kept all the minorities separate—or even more common, out of the picture altogether."

Becca peered at it. The men were touching shoulders, which wasn't something a racially mixed group did in those days.

"There are a few Native Americans as well," Gladys said. "I learned that from their names. These men are so grimy, it's hard to tell much else."

Becca nodded, then frowned. "So the building of the Nat went smoothly, then."

"And the building of the hotel. The rumors about the End of the World started after it opened for business," Gladys said.

"You mean the haunting."

"And the bad dreams. Those were the worst. People would stay at the End of the World, and wake up screaming. The interesting thing is that they all had the same complaint."

Becca swirled the coffee in her cup. She'd have to listen to this even though it wasn't what she had asked. She didn't care about the hauntings. All old hotels had ghost stories. She wanted to hear about the Nat.

"Which was?"

"That they'd had nightmares, and in the nightmares, they saw their long-dead relatives, begging for help." Gladys added a spooky tone to her voice, as if she actually believed this nonsense.

"Wow," Becca said, trying not to sound sarcastic. "Scary."

"No kidding. I've never heard of this kind of haunting."

"But nothing from the Nat?"

"Why do you ask? What did you find?"

"Evidence that something awful happened there as the place was being built," Becca said.

"What kind of awful?" Gladys asked.

"I was hoping you could tell me."

Gladys frowned at her, and Becca had to hide a smile again. For once Gladys had to be feeling as if she were taking a quiz.

"I've never heard a thing, and you'd think in this town, I would." She slid the picture back and studied it as if it held the answers. Then she put it in the file, and closed it.

For a moment, Becca thought the interview was over, and then Gladys said, "Here's what I know. I know the Natatorium was initially supposed to be an indoor tennis court which was, in its day, a revolutionary idea. That was about 1905 or so, when tennis was very popular, particularly out west."

"You're kidding," Becca said.

Gladys actually smiled at her. "Think of all those photographs of women in their long gowns, holding tennis rackets. These women played, and some played very well, despite the handicap."

Becca shook her head. "I thought it was an East Coast thing."

"Every small western town had courts, if they had respectable women. Most of the women were barred from the saloons and the clubs, so they had to have something to do or they might form a temperance society, or a ladies aide society or do something to take away the men's fun."

"Aren't we always that way?" Becca asked, and smiled.

Gladys smiled back. "It didn't work. They didn't build the tennis court for some reason, I never could find out why. The pool came later. It used the tennis court's foundation as the part of the pool itself, and then got built from there."

"Isn't that unusual?" Becca asked.

Gladys shrugged. "Construction in those days was haphazard. I don't know what was usual and what wasn't. I mean, a place could be as sturdy as the hotel or it could be some boards knocked together to be called a house. Really, though, they were just shanties."

"I thought Hope didn't have a shanty town."

"Oh, we did, but it burned," Gladys said. "No one bothered to rebuild it. Folks didn't like to talk about that day. The entire city could've gone up in flames. Somehow it didn't happen, though."

This was one of the things Becca hated about seeing either Conyers about Hope history—their tendency to digress.

"But nothing else about the Nat? Nothing unusual?"

"No, not even the Nat was unusual. They had Natatoriums all over Oregon. They started as playgrounds for the rich—mostly pools and tennis—and then as they fell apart, they became the community pools and playgrounds for the poorer kids. Most of them got shut down in the polio scares of the late 1940s and early 1950s. I think ours is the last one standing, which makes it eligible for historical preservation."

"Which Chase has begged you not to apply for until he's done with the work, right?"

Gladys nodded. "Nothing wrong with that. He doesn't want the extra inspectors. He does the work better than the national preservation standards ask for, so we have no objections here."

"We" being Gladys and her grandfather.

"I hesitate to ask this," Becca said, mostly because she was afraid of Gladys's reaction, "but could you ask your grandfather about the Nat? It's important."

"I'm sure he doesn't know more than I do. It predates him, you know."

"I know," Becca said. "I'm not looking for the official history. I'm looking for rumors or strange comments or stories that he gives no credence to."

"Grandfather ignores anything that can't be proven," Gladys said with something like pride. "If you want innuendo, go see Abigail Browning. She knows every old story about Hope—and most of them are just plain lies."

Becca had forgotten about Abigail Browning. She had been Jack Conyers' assistant—and first major resource—until they had some sort of falling out in the 1950s. For a while, she tried to run the "real" Hope Historical Society, but no one would give her funding, which she said was because she was a woman. Jack Conyers always claimed it was because she knew nothing about history.

She had become one of the town's characters until the transplanted Californian who started Hope's weekly "alternative" paper, printed a story about an affair Abigail Browning and Jack Conyers had. The story was supposed to be sympathetic to Abigail—see how poorly this married man treated this sad spinster lady—but it had the opposite effect. Abigail lost any support she had among the locals for trying to steal Jack Conyers from his still-living, still-popular wife.

Becca would talk to Abigail Browning. But Becca also wanted to talk to Jack Conyers.

She stood. "Please do ask him."

"Oh, I will," Gladys said. "But I'm sure he won't know more than I do."

And with that, Becca knew she had no hope of seeing the town's official historian. So she'd see the unofficial one, and hope for the best.

THEN

The cabin got really hot that day and she wanted to open a window, but she was scared to. Mostly she slept and she hoped Jess Taylor would come back for her. She had to keep reminding herself that it was his cabin, he'd be back, but he didn't seem to have many things there, and Daddy had run away from more, so maybe Jess Taylor would too.

Finally, Jess Taylor came back, looking tired and even more scared than when he'd left. His shirt was covered with sweat and some dirt ran along the side of his face. He had one of those overcoats—the short ones Daddy called a suit coat—and he hung it on a chair.

She stood beside the table, and waited for him to tell her to leave.

He looked at her, his big eyes sad. "I have bad news."

She held her breath. She wasn't sure what she'd do when he let her out of here. She hadn't eaten anything since that apple, and even though she took some water because she couldn't help herself—it was so hot inside—she would tell him and offer to repay him. Somehow. Maybe then he wouldn't turn her over to those people.

"Your mother," he said—and she let out a bit of that breath—"Your mother and the other people?...they're gone."

Her stomach clenched. "Gone?"

"That's what we say when we mean they died, honey."

Her cheeks heated. Everyone had told her Daddy was gone too.

"I thought it just meant they went away," she said.

"It's a euphemism."

She'd never heard the word.

He shook his head tiredly. "A word we use when we don't want to be blunt. There are a lot of euphemisms in our language."

She nodded, even though she wasn't sure she understood.

"You're sure she's...gone?" She asked.

"Oh, I'm sure," he said, and shuddered. "You wouldn't ask if you knew the day I had today."

"What did you do?" she asked.

"Work white men wouldn't do," he said. "They consider what I did the dirty work."

She frowned. "What did you do?"

"I'm supposed to sit in a bank," he said. "But they said, *If you want to keep your job, you'll—*"

He stopped. Studied her like he wasn't sure what to say.

Then sighed.

"I helped bury them, Sarah."

"Bury?" She knew what that was, at least. She'd seen it—the wooden boxes, the holes in the ground, the markers. "If they had the boxes and stuff, how did you know my mother was there?"

It seemed to take him a minute to understand her. Then he nodded, once. "There were no boxes, honey," he said gently. "They were just placed in the ground."

Barbaric, that's what it is, her daddy said. *How can they do that to their own?*

It's a religious custom, her mother said. *We used to have them too.*

"And they were dead?" she asked, her voice small.

"Oh, yeah," he said, and shuddered. "They were dead."

"Where are they?" she asked. "Where did you bury them?"

He studied her for a long time, as if he thought about whether or not to answer her.

Then he sighed again.

"It's a place they call the End of the World."

NOW

Abigail Browning lived in a fairytale cottage at the end of one of Hope's oldest streets. Large trees, which somehow thrived despite the desert air, surrounded the place, making it look even more like something out of Hansel and Gretel. Blooming plants lined the walk, plants which Becca knew took more water than summer water rationing allowed. She decided to ignore them as she stood on the brick steps and rapped on the solid oak door.

A latch slammed back and then the door pulled open, sending a wave of lavender scent outside. The woman who stood before Becca was short and hunched, not the tall powerhouse that Becca remembered from her childhood.

"Abigail Browning?" Becca asked.

"Don't you recognize me, Rebecca Keller? I practically raised you."

That wasn't quite true. Abigail Browning did baby-sit when Becca's parents couldn't find anyone else, but otherwise she had little to do with Becca's childhood.

"Sure I do, Mrs. Browning," Becca said, falling back on her childhood name for this woman, even though Abigail Browning had never married. "I was wondering if you could help me with a case."

Abigail Browning smiled and stepped away from the door. "Of course, my dear. Would you like some tea?"

"I'd love some," Becca said as she walked inside. The house smelled the same—lavender and baking bread with the faint undertone of cat.

Now Becca was old enough to appreciate the mahogany staircase, built Craftsman-style, and the matching bookcases that graced the living room. The entire house had mahogany trim as well as built-in shelving, a feature Becca knew that Chase would love—particularly since no one had painted over the original wood.

Mrs. Browning led her into the kitchen. A coffee cake sat in a glass case in the center of the table, almost as if Mrs. Browning had expected her. Mrs. Browning filled a kettle and put it on the stove, then climbed on a stool to remove large mugs from the shiny mahogany cupboards.

"I'm not as tall as I used to be," she said. "Time crushes all of us."

Becca nodded, uncertain what to say. "The kitchen looks just the same."

"Which negates the ten thousand dollar remodel I did two years ago," Mrs. Browning said.

Becca looked at her in surprise.

"I had to update everything. I had dry rot. Or the house did. Your husband helped me."

Becca opened her mouth to correct Mrs. Browning, then thought the better of it. Abigail Browning often made misstatements to see how other people stood on things.

"He's a good man," Mrs. Browning said. "Maybe the best in town, and you let him get away."

"I didn't let—"

"You confused him with your father, who was a horrid, manipulative man, and you forgot that men can be strong without being horrid."

Becca felt her cheeks heat. "Would you like to hear about the case?"

"More than you'd like to hear how you threw away a good man because a bad one raised you," Mrs. Browning said, taking down two plates.

Becca did not offer to help her. Instead, Becca stood near the table, hands crossed in front of her, feeling ten years old again.

"So tell me," Mrs. Browning said, putting the plates on the table. The kettle whistled, and she removed it from the heat. She grabbed a tea pot from a shelf that looked old, but had to be new because Becca didn't remember it.

"I was wondering what you know about the Natatorium."

"I can tell you how awful it smelled when I was a child, but that's not what you're asking, is it? Be specific, girl. Didn't I teach you anything?"

"What happened when it was built?"

"Which time?" Mrs. Browning set a beautiful wood trivet on the table, then placed the teapot on top of it.

"Which time?" Becca repeated. "Things are only built once, aren't they?"

Mrs. Browning stood near a chair near the teapot shelf, a chair that Becca remembered had always been Mrs. Browning's favorite. Becca had sat there once as a child, and had found it uncomfortable, molded to the elderly woman's body. Only then Mrs. Browning hadn't been elderly. She had only seemed that way.

"The foundation for the Natatorium was laid at the same time as the hotel, around 1908. It was abandoned that same year."

"Abandoned?" Becca asked. "I heard that the work stopped."

"Probably from that horrible Gladys Conyers. She really knows only the textbook history of this town which, I'm sorry to say, is wrong. People are never saints, you know. You always have to look for the darkness to balance the light."

Mrs. Browning peered at her. Mrs. Browning's eyes, buried under layers of wrinkles, were the same piercing blue they had always been.

Becca remembered Mrs. Browning trying to tell her that before. *You're the light, Rebecca. Remember that. Good things can come from dark places.*

She shook the memory away.

"Sit down, child, you're making me nervous."

Becca slid into her usual chair. Odd to think she had a usual chair, when she hadn't been to this house in more than twenty years.

"Do you still remember how to pour?"

Becca smiled. She did remember those lessons. Mrs. Browning had trained her in "company" manners, including how to set a table, how to dress for dinner, and how to pour for guests.

"I do," Becca said. She picked up the tea pot, handling it as if Mrs. Browning had pulled down her silver service instead of her every day.

Mrs. Browning watched her every move as if she were still being judged on perfection. Becca remembered everything, including when to ask if Mrs. Browning wanted sugar and cream, and to hold the top of the pot so that it wouldn't fall unceremoniously into Mrs. Browning's plate.

Mrs. Browning smiled, as if Becca's behavior was confirmation of the work she'd done bringing her up.

"So," Mrs. Browning said when Becca finished pouring, "which part of the Natatorium are you interested in? The first building or the second?"

"I'm interested in the pool, whenever it was laid."

"The pool." Mrs. Browning pursed her lips. "So your Chase finally found the bodies, did he?"

Becca felt her breath catch. Whatever she'd expected Mrs. Browning to say, it wasn't that.

"You knew?"

"Child, half the town knew. Why do you think that no one was allowed near that old wreck?"

"But you swam there as a child."

"All of us did," Mrs. Browning said. "And some of us brought our own children there, until the place shut down. It was just a rumor, after all. Except for the hotel."

Becca frowned. "We're talking about the Nat."

"We can't talk about the Nat without talking about the hotel. Have you ever been inside?"

"Just last night, as a matter of fact."

"Did you look at the walls?"

Becca's frown grew deeper. "Yes."

"Then you understand why I told your Chase not to tear them down."

"No," Becca said. "I don't."

Mrs. Browning touched her hand with dry fingers. "Rebecca, you've never been slow. Haven't you wondered why those walls move?"

"They don't move," Becca said. "They have heat shimmers. It piles up and—"

"Heat shimmers occur on pavement in sunlight," Mrs. Browning said. "Not in a dark dusty hotel in the middle of a summer evening."

Becca licked her lips. When she was fourteen, she'd run from that hotel. She'd gone there to neck with Zack Wheeler, and when he'd pressed her against one of the walls, it was squishy. She turned to look at the wood, saw it shimmer, change, and shimmer again, and she couldn't help it.

She screamed.

Zack saw it too, grabbed her hand, and pulled her out of there. They'd run all the way to his car, and even told his father, who had looked at them with contempt. That was the first time Becca had heard the heat shimmer idea, but it wasn't the last.

"So what causes it?" Becca asked.

"Aliens," Mrs. Browning said. "The aliens haunting the End of the World."

THEN

She couldn't go to the End of the World. She couldn't even leave the house. Jess Taylor didn't want her to. He was afraid for her. She was hot and sad and lonely, and she spent her days crying sometimes.

But she didn't practice changing. Instead, she worked on getting every detail right. Jess Taylor had to tell her sometimes that she was using masculine details—he'd actually laughed the time she put bits of hair on her own chin—but mostly, he said, she was looking solid.

Whatever that meant.

He wanted the town to think no one had survived. He didn't want them to question her or him.

It took him days and days to figure out how to do that.

Then one day he told her. She was going to take a train.

NOW

Aliens? Of all the things Becca had expected from Mrs. Browning, a popular crazy notion wasn't one of them. Hope had been the talk of the alien conspiracy community since 2001, when one of her colleagues had discovered some metal in Lake Waloon. The lake had receded during one of the driest years on record, leaving all sorts of artifacts in its cracked and much-abused bed.

The experts, called in by the Historical Society, claimed it was part of an experimental airplane or maybe even one of the early do-it-yourself models from the 1920s.

UFO groupies looked at the pictures on the internet, and descended *en masse* to Hope, believing they'd found another ship like the one the government supposedly hid in Roswell, New Mexico.

Ever since, Hope had to endure annual pilgrimages from the UFO faithful. Becca tried to ignore them, just like she used to ignore the Deadheads when they came through on their way to Eugene to see the Grateful Dead in its natural habitat.

"Aliens," Becca said. "Surely you don't believe that hype from a few years ago—"

"Yes," Mrs. Browning said as she cut Becca a piece of coffee cake.

"Of course I do. I grew up knowing that we'd been invaded. The fact that the ship was found simply confirmed it."

"The ship wasn't found," Becca said, and then caught herself. She'd learned in a few short months not to argue with the True Believers. Only she'd never taken Mrs. Browning to be one of them.

Mrs. Browning cut another piece of coffee cake and slid it onto her own plate. "If you do not believe that twisted hunk of metal was an alien spacecraft, then you won't believe anything I have to tell you about the Natatorium."

Becca sighed. "I saw the so-called ship. It's just a crumpled aircraft."

"No," Mrs. Browning said. "It was molded to look like an aircraft. It's a space ship."

Becca had heard this argument countless times as well. She took a deep breath, and then thought the better of all of it.

"All right," she said. "Let's pretend that you and I agree. Let's pretend that is a spaceship, and the squirming wall in the End of the World is made by alien ghosts. What else can you tell me?"

Mrs. Browning delicately cut her piece of coffee cake with her fork, her little finger extended. She had the same manners she always had. She seemed as sharp as she had thirty years ago.

But Becca knew that sometimes elderly people who lived alone developed "peculiarities." Now she was going to have to overlook Mrs. Browning's just to get to the heart of the story.

And maybe, just maybe, she was going to have to accept that she was wasting her time.

"Eat," Mrs. Browning said, "and I'll tell you what I know."

THEN

She hadn't been that frightened since Jess Taylor found her. She thought he was going to make her leave by train.

She didn't know where he'd send her or what she'd do or who she'd meet. But by now, she knew she could trust him. He brought her clothes. He fed her. He helped her.

They had long talks when he got home from the bank, and one night, he told her his family had died just like hers.

"In Hope?" she asked.

He shook his head. "Far away from Hope in a place called Mississippi."

"How come you didn't get killed?" she asked. She already knew he couldn't change, so she wanted to know how he got away.

"I was in the North," he said. "Ohio. Going to school in Antioch. Then the money stopped—my whole family was supporting me, giving me an education, and I sent letters to find out why, and someone sent me a postcard back. It was a drawing of the day—of the killings—like people were proud of it, and they said *Don't bother to come,* but I did anyway and..."

His voice trailed away. He didn't look at her. He was quiet a long time.

"What happened?" she asked because she couldn't take it anymore.

"I ran, and ended up in Hope."

NOW

Becca took a bite of her coffee cake. It was as good and rich as ever, a taste of her childhood.

Mrs. Browning watched her eat that bite, then leaned back in her own chair. Becca wondered if that position was even comfortable, given Mrs. Browning's pronounced dowager's hump.

"In the summer of Aught Eight, the shanty town just outside of Hope burned to the ground," Mrs. Browning began in her teacherly voice. "Most of the histories do not mention the shanty town. Those that do claim the fire threatened Hope itself. It didn't threaten the buildings that comprised Hope. It threatened the vision of Hope."

Very dramatic, Becca thought. She took another bite of cake, then followed it with a sip of tea, staining to keep her expression interested and credulous.

"The fire was as controlled a burn as the people of Hope could manage in those bygone days."

The ease with which Mrs. Browning told this story made Becca believe that Mrs. Browning used to recite it as part of the history project.

"The townspeople had gotten together and decided to rid themselves of the strangers once and for all."

Mrs. Browning shook her fork—still holding coffee cake—at Becca.

"If you look in the papers of the time, you'll see references to the strangers. They arrived in 1900, claiming to have lost their wagon several miles back. They had no luggage, few belongings, and they spoke a strange version of English. The locals thought they were ignorant immigrants who'd been tricked by their guide, and gave them some land just outside of town."

"Where the End of the World is?" Becca asked.

Mrs. Browning raised her eyebrows. "Am I telling this or are you?"

"Sorry," Becca said.

"Where that 1970s mall is. It's now near the center of town. But then, it was just outside, on land no one wanted. The strangers built their own little cabins—poorly. They looked like they didn't know what to do, and of course, no one was going to help them much more than provide a meal or some supplies. They got a bit of work too."

Becca nodded, wishing Mrs. Browning would get on with it.

"I don't know what happened. The reference in various letters I've seen is that the strangers confirmed their demonic qualities. I have no idea what that means or how they confirmed demonic qualities, but the upshot is that the town fathers asked them to leave. The strangers said they wouldn't. The fight went on for some months, when finally the shanty town burned."

"A controlled burn," Becca said. "Started by?"

"Anyone who's everyone," Mrs. Browning said. "I never asked. Besides, everyone would've told me they had nothing to do with it. But you'll notice—well, of course you won't, they're all dead—but I noticed when I was young just how many of the older generation carried some burn marks on their hands. Except for that controlled burn, and the loss of a building here and there, Hope was one of the few western communities that didn't have a serious fire. And not all of these men worked for the Hope Volunteer Fire Department."

Becca finished her coffee cake. Then she picked up her tea mug and cradled it. "So they burned the shanty town. What has that to do with the Natatorium?"

"It was being built. The hotel was just a shell—it wasn't nearly done yet—and the Nat was dug, but not poured. It was going to be a tennis court. In those days, I believe the courts were clay. Not that it matters. It never got finished."

"Because...?" Becca was trying to keep the frustration from her voice.

"Because the town hated the place. It reminded them that they hadn't lived up to that promise we all learned about."

Becca gripped the mug tightly. "I still don't see the connection."

Mrs. Browning sighed, as if Becca were a particularly slow student. "They used the fire to round up the strangers and herd them to the Nat. Do I need to spell it out for you?"

"You're saying the town killed these strangers?" Becca asked. "And buried them under the Nat?"

"Yes." Mrs. Browning sounded exasperated.

"How many?"

"I don't know. No one kept records. I heard that they tried to bury them under the hotel, and when that didn't work, they went to the Nat. That's why the ghosts haunt the hotel."

"You'd think they'd haunt the Nat," Becca said.

"Hauntings aren't logical," Mrs. Browning said.

None of this was, Becca thought. "How do you know that these strangers were aliens, not just a group of Eastern Europeans who ran into some people who didn't understand them?"

"Because of the stories," Mrs. Browning said. "They had glowing eyes. They talked gibberish. They could seem taller than they were. And they came from nowhere. There were no wagon tracks. There was no wagon. And these people had no idea how people behaved. Not how Americans behaved, but how human beings behaved. They had to learn it all."

Becca shook her head. "I'm sorry, Mrs. Browning. But humans differ greatly. And if this group had been from a very different culture, the residents of Hope could have made the same charge. Aliens is as farfetched as it came."

Mrs. Browning smiled sadly. "I believe it was aliens."

"Why?" Becca asked.

"Because I met one," Mrs. Browning said.

THEN

The train was big and dirty and smelly. Ash fell everywhere. It made an awful noise and she wanted to run away from it.

Jess Taylor stood beside her, holding her hand. He'd borrowed his neighbor's wagon, and they'd come to the small town of Brothers, which was two stops away from Hope.

"Remember," he said. "Tomorrow, you come here, and give the nice man this paper, and then you get on the train going that direction."

He pointed. He'd already shown her the engine, and how you could tell what direction a train was going in.

"I'll meet you at the station, and we'll pretend that we haven't seen each other in years. Okay?"

He'd told her all this before, and then it sounded easy, but now, it just sounded terrifying. She wanted to get back in the wagon, get back in his house, and hide there forever.

But he said, now that her people were gone, she needed to have a life.

Where will I have this life? She asked him.

In Hope, he said. *With me.*

Momma and Daddy said humans didn't do these things, they didn't

544

make that kind of commitment, they didn't understand permanence and obligation and responsibility, which made them dangerous.

But Jess Taylor wasn't dangerous. And he seemed to understand all those words. He seemed to live them.

Only they came back now that she was standing on the platform with him, staring at the train.

"It's only one night," he said. "I already paid for the room. You'll be safe."

She wanted to believe him. But she was scared. What if she changed by accident? What if she said something wrong? Would they make her scream? Would they bury her without a box?

Who would tell Jess Taylor?

How would he ever know?

NOW

"I was just a little girl," Mrs. Browning said, "and she was very old. Older than anyone I'd ever seen. She came to the Natatorium when I was swimming there. She cried."

"She cried?" Becca asked.

Mrs. Browning nodded. "She stood back from the pool, and she cried as she looked at it. My mother was there with me, and she just stared. Then she told me to get my towel. It was time to go."

"I don't understand," Becca said. "How do you know the old woman was an alien."

"There'd always been stories about her," Mrs. Browning said. "She came to town to see her uncle, and she never left. At least that was the story, and some people claimed they saw her get off the train. But a few said the luggage she carried was her uncle's, and that he'd brought her there that very afternoon."

"So?" Becca asked.

"So that was right after the massacre. It was strange that he had a niece no one had ever heard of."

Becca shrugged. "I'm so sorry to be skeptical, Mrs. Browning, but I still don't understand how that translates to alien."

"I saw her once, all by myself. She was sitting at a bus stop near the old bank, and she put her hand on the bench. Her hand slid right through it."

Becca sighed. "You're not going to convince me. Not without some kind of real proof."

"What about those bodies, young lady?" Mrs. Browning said, bringing herself up as close to her old height as she could. "Are those good enough for you? They're not human, are they?"

Becca flashed on the broken femurs, so recognizable. "Of course they are."

Mrs. Browning's cheeks flushed. "You're just saying that."

"Actually," Becca said. "I'm not."

THEN

That night, she slept on a single bed behind the kitchen of Mrs. Mother's Brothers Boarding House. Colored people—which was her and Jess Taylor, apparently—didn't get their own rooms. They couldn't even really stay at the boarding house, but Jess Taylor knew the cook, who volunteered to share her room. Mrs. Mother, the old lady who ran the place, had frowned in that mean way some humans had, but all she said was, "Make sure it doesn't get into the food."

She didn't understand for the longest time that the "it" Mrs. Mother referred to was her.

Maybe that's why Daddy said this was a dangerous place, why humans were scary people. She hadn't even known they cared about differences, and now she was finding out that the differences were everything.

No wonder they'd gone after her people. She hadn't noticed Jess Taylor's differences from the men at the bank and as time went on, she began to understand how badly her own people had mimicked the humans. No knee dimples, too smooth skin, eyes that didn't blink.

If the dark skin or the long braid of hair running down the back or the upswept eye angle scared them, they must've been really terrified by a whole group of people whose skin had no wrinkles, whose ankles didn't stick out, and whose expressions never changed.

No wonder.

Then she remembered Jess Taylor: *I can't believe I'm defending them* and she knew just how he felt.

The bed in the kitchen had bugs. They bit her during the night. Upstairs people laughed, and the place smelled like grease, and she wanted some water, just so she could wash the bugs off, but she didn't.

She picked them off and squished them between her fingers, and finally she got out of that bed and sat in a rocking chair, and watched out the window until the sun came up.

Then she picked up her little bag, and walked to the train station, just like Jess Taylor had told her to do, and she sat on the far edge of the platform so no one but the man who worked there saw her, and she waited for the train.

NOW

Becca was happy to leave. Mrs. Browning did tell her other stories about the Natatorium—stories about its first few days as a recreation center, stories about the celebrities who used it—but both Becca and Mrs. Browning knew that the stories were merely Mrs. Browning's way of saving face.

As Becca made her good-byes, holding a piece of that delicious coffee cake in a napkin, both she and Mrs. Browning knew that she would never really trust Mrs. Browning again.

All the way to her car, Becca tried not to let sadness overwhelm her. She had lost more than a source for Hope's history. She'd lost an icon of her youth.

She had always believed that Abigail Browning was a woman of unassailable intellect and integrity. Even through the Conyers' scandal, Becca's opinion did not change. She still nodded at Abigail Browning on the street when others hadn't, and she still revered the woman she had once known.

If anything, the scandal had clarified something for her: Becca finally understood why Mrs. Browning, who had always seemed more knowledgeable than Mr. Conyers, had stopped working at the Hope Historical Society.

Now Becca wasn't so sure. Now she wondered if Mrs. Browning was fired because she believed the strange stories—the ones that had always been part of Hope. Stories of ghosts and aliens and things that went bump in the night.

Becca got into the squad and turned the ignition. The crappy air conditioning felt worse than the heat in Mrs. Browning's garden. Maybe if Becca believed in fairy tales, she would actually believe that Mrs. Browning had some sort of magic that kept the heat and the desert at bay.

But Becca only believed in reality. And only the reality she could see, Chase used to say. She could never envision his projects, not even when she looked at the architectural renderings.

She always had to wait until he was done to understand how perfect his vision had been.

What had Mrs. Browning said about Chase? *You confused him with your father, who was a horrid, manipulative man, and you forgot that men can be strong without being horrid.*

That's what Becca should have asked about. She should have asked what Mrs. Browning meant by that statement—not about Chase: women who hadn't married Chase loved him. (Hell, *Becca* still loved him)—but about her father.

Tell me about your father, her therapist said once.

He was a good man, Becca said.

But he didn't like your job.

Becca had smiled. *He was old-fashioned. He believed women didn't belong outside the home.*

What about in a police car?

Becca had laughed. *Are you kidding? He stopped paying for my school when he heard what I wanted to do.*

Is Chase like him?

Of course not, Becca said.

But your father's action sounds manipulative. You say Chase is manipulative.

Not like that, Becca said. *He respects women.*

Does he respect you?

Becca sighed and leaned back against the seat of the squad. Did he respect her? Yesterday, she would have said no, and she would have said that his secretive call about the Nat proved it.

But couldn't it also be viewed the other way? Couldn't his call be a sign of trust, of faith in her abilities instead of faith in his own ability to control her?

Could Mrs. Browning be right?

Becca shook her head. A headache was forming between her eyes. She put the squad in gear just as her cell rang.

She unhooked it from her belt and looked at the display. Jillian Mills. Becca took the call.

"Can you come down here?" Jillian asked.

"Is this about the Nat?" Becca asked.

"Yeah," Jillian said. "I have the weirdest results."

THEN

They took her ticket just like Jess Taylor said they would, but they wouldn't let her sit in a chair like everybody else. They put her on one of the platforms in the back. The ash and the dirt and the stink were awful there, and as the train started to pull away, she could see the rails move.

She tried the door to get inside, but someone had locked it. She pounded on it, and the men in the nearby chairs—the men with white skin—laughed at her and pointed and she moved away from the blackened window so that they couldn't see her any more.

She was afraid they'd come out and hurt her.

Like they hurt her Momma.

Like they hurt Jess Taylor's family.

She was scared now, and she tried not to let that change her. Because if she changed, she'd lose this chance. She'd spend her life—what was left of it—as a railing or a board or a door knob. And then, because she couldn't sleep-change, she'd starve and fall off, all decayed, and they'd toss her aside—*what is that dried up thing?*—and she'd die, probably in the nearby sagebrush, all alone.

Just like her Daddy.

The whole trip, she stared straight ahead and clung to her bag and thought about Jess Taylor waiting for her. Thought about shoulders and backs and legs and human forms so that the spikes wouldn't come out of her spine or her eyes wouldn't shift to a different part of her head.

She thought and thought and was surprised when she realized she could hardly wait to get back to Hope.

NOW

Becca's stomach clenched the entire way to the coroner's office. She wished she hadn't eaten that coffee cake now. She wished she hadn't gone to Mrs. Browning's. She didn't want the thoughts that were crowding her brain. She didn't want to think the weird results were because some aliens were massacred in Hope.

And yet she was thinking just that.

The coroner's office was on a side street behind Hope's main police station. The office wasn't an office at all, more like a science lab, morgue, and training area rolled into one.

The college student who ran the front desk in exchange for rent in the studio apartment above was reading Dostoevsky. He barely looked up as Becca entered.

"She's expecting you," he said.

Becca nodded and continued to the small room that served as Jillian's office. The smell of decay and formaldehyde seemed less here than it did near the door, and wasn't nearly as strong as it was in the basement where the autopsies actually took place.

Jillian was standing behind her desk, sorting paper files. She wore a clean white smock over her clothes—a sure sign that she had just finished an autopsy—and had her hair pulled back with a copper barrette.

"Your life just got easier," Jillian said without preamble.

"How's that?" Becca asked.

"Close the door."

Becca did.

"I did some preliminary work before calling the state crime lab," Jillian said. "Those bodies down there, they're not human."

Becca felt a shiver run down her back.

"I'm not sure what they are. I'm not even sure they are bodies."

Becca gripped the back of the nearest chair. She didn't want Mrs. Browning to be right.

"What are they then? Aliens?"

Jillian laughed. "Of course not. Whatever gave you that idea?"

"Abigail Browning," Becca said.

"Oh, our local UFOlogist," Jillian said. "You know she's been making her living these last few years providing historical tours of Lake Waloon?"

How could Becca have missed that? So Abigail Browning had a stake in keeping the alien story alive. And what could be better than a tale of alien massacre?

Hell, that would even give her a measure of revenge against Jack Conyers, showing that the story of racial unity in Hope was really just a myth.

"Just wondering," Becca said, trying to make light of it.

"Well, we all are. From what I can tell, these are very old bones—if they are bones as we know them. The material is something else, and it's hollow."

"But they looked human."

"So do a lot of things. Mammalian bones tend to look alike. I've had new trainees mistake cat spines and ribcages for human babies."

Becca swallowed. "What about the smell?"

"Well, that's the odd part," Jillian said. "It's coming from the— whatever they are—bones."

"Huh?"

Jillian shrugged. "Let me show you."

She grabbed an evidence bag from a table beside her desk. Inside was what looked to Becca to be an adult human rib bone. It even had the proper curvature.

"Break it," Jillian said.

"Isn't this destroying evidence?"

"Of what? Alien massacre? Just break it."

Becca grabbed a pair of medical gloves from the box beside Jillian's desk, then opened the evidence bag. She took out the rib bone, and immediately felt a sense of wrongness. It was too squishy. Even bones that had been in damp ground for a long period of time never felt like this—almost like a rubber chew toy that had been well loved.

Becca turned it over in her fingers, feeling a gag reflex, and swallowing hard against it.

Jillian nodded. "Kinda gross, huh?"

Becca didn't answer. Instead, she grabbed both ends of the bone and bent.

If it had been made of rubber—even old rubber—the bone should've bent with her hands. But it didn't bend. It snapped, and a waft of rot filled Becca's nose, almost as if she had put her face in the middle of a decaying corpse.

"Jesus Christ," she said, dropping both pieces into the evidence bag. "You could've warned me."

The gag reflex had gotten worse. Her eyes watered and she resisted the urge to wipe at them. She'd learned that lesson long ago, when she'd been a rookie: *Don't touch your own skin after touching a corpse.*

But that wasn't a corpse. It wasn't even a real bone, at least not of a kind she was familiar with.

"C'mon." Jillian took the sealed evidence bag from her, and led Becca to the back room where cleaning solutions and the sharp-scented nostril-clearing substance that Jillian preferred waited.

Becca inhaled the substance, feeling her nose clear as if she'd sniffed smelling salts, and then she grabbed a clean washcloth, wiped her face, and leaned against a metal filing cabinet.

"So what the hell is it?" she asked.

"I wish I knew. I'm going to be calling not just the state, but some anthropologists to see if they've seen anything like it."

"Then why did you tell me my job got easier?"

"Because," Jillian said. "There's no recent body. There aren't even old bodies. There's a mystery, yes, but it's an archeological one. There's probably some plant or root or something that does this, and maybe it's extinct or something, which is why we're not familiar with it."

"You mean like that death plant?" Becca asked.

"The corpse flower?" Jillian nodded. "I forgot about that. I'll look it up on line. Maybe it used to grow around here."

Becca's fingers tingled. The bone—or whatever it was—had felt alive, but the way that plant roots did. She could believe that Chase had discovered the remains of a very old plant much easier than believing that an alien massacre happened in Hope.

"You want to tell Chase?" Jillian asked. "Or should I?"

Becca felt her breath catch. Chase's dream project was still on. It would still happen.

One day, the End of the World would become the premiere resort in Eastern Oregon.

"He's not going to be able to work for a while. If they think this thing is unusual, they'll do some excavation," Jillian said. "But it's not like a major dig, and it's not a crime scene. He should be thrilled."

Becca smiled in spite of her stinging nose. "Thrilled probably isn't the word I'd use. But he'll be relieved, once he's past the immediate inconvenience."

Jillian crossed her arms, looking amused. "So am I telling him?"

"No," Becca said. "I will."

THEN

The train passed it.

Jess Taylor hadn't warned her.

But there was a big hand-carved sign saying, *Future Home of the End of the World Resort.* And there was a finished building right at the edge, with the word *Hotel* on it. And a big brown patch where somebody had dug a hole and then covered it up.

Her mommy was in there.

She went to the edge of the platform and stared at it until it got tiny in the distance.

And then she remembered: Her daddy, days before he left, telling Momma—

If anything happens, we go to the End of the World. We burrow into the walls or slide against the frames. We become other. We hibernate until our own people return.

She never learned how. Grown ones could do it. And they could coax their children into it, but no child could do it on her own.

She'd only seen the shimmers a few times, back when she was really little, in the ship before it crashed. Lots and lots of her people,

people she didn't see until Daddy woke them, shimmered in the back compartment.

Sometimes they'd have dreams and you'd see their ghostly selves, wandering through the ship. She got scared by that, but Momma said it was normal. It was a way to check how time was passing, and when it was safe to wake up.

She didn't see any shimmers as she passed the End of the World.

She didn't see any one she knew. It was quiet and empty and lonely.

Her people were really and truly gone, and now she was the only one left to wait for the others. The ones who were supposed to rescue them.

If they ever came.

NOW

Becca and Chase stood at the End of the World, staring at the hole dug into the floor of the Natatorium. It was early evening, little more than twenty-four hours since Chase called Becca to the scene.

The area was quiet—as quiet as the desert got. A high-pitched whine that came from a bug Becca could not identify came from just outside the broken wall. The wind rustled a tarp that covered some of the wood Chase had bought, and not too far away, a bird peeped, probably as it hunted the whining bugs.

The sounds of workers waiting for instructions, the low buzz-growl of her radio unit, the crunch of vans on gravel were in the recent past. Right now, it was just her, Chase, and the plant-like bone-like things half buried in the ground.

The smell wasn't as bad as it had been the day before. The bone-like things weren't freshly broken. The scent was fading, just like the smell of a dead body faded to an annoyance when the body was removed from the scene.

She and Chase stood side-by-side in the patch of sunlight that filtered through the hole in the Natatorium wall. She had brought him down here to tell him the news, and when she finished, he didn't say a word.

He swallowed once, stared at the ground, and then closed his eyes. His entire body trembled. She thought he was going to cry.

Then he took a deep breath, pushed his hardhat back, and frowned. "No one died."

"That's right," Becca said.

"And these aren't bodies."

Not human ones anyway, she almost said, but then felt the joke was in poor taste. For all she knew, Chase could have talked to Mrs. Browning too. He might have heard the alien rumors as well.

"Jillian thinks they're the remains of plants."

"*Thinks?*" Chase asked.

Becca shrugged. "All she knows is that they're not bone, not from humans or from animals. And they're the source of the smell."

"Weird," Chase said.

"You won't be able to work in the Nat for a while," Becca said. "People are coming from U of O and OSU's science and archeological departments to see what they can learn. Jillian thinks they might contact the Smithsonian or someplace like that. She made a ballpark estimate of eight months, but it could be more than that. It could be less."

Chase nodded. He still wasn't looking at her. "I can finish the hotel, though."

"The hotel, the golf course, the houses, you can do all of it.'"

"Golf courses," he reminded her.

"Golf courses," she said.

They stood in silence for a moment longer. Chase had his head bowed, as if he were looking at a grave.

Then he asked, "They'll clear this away?"

"Probably," Becca said. "Or you might have to find a way to build over it. You certainly don't want one of those things to break while guests are using the pool."

He shuddered, then nodded. He took off his hardhat and twisted it between his hands.

"Mrs. Browning says you're keeping the walls of the hotel," Becca said.

He looked at her sideways. "You spoke to Abigail?"

Becca nodded. "You know she used to baby-sit me, way back when."

"That's what she said. She also said I should give you time."

Becca felt her cheeks flush. That old woman meddled. "For what?"

He shrugged and looked away. "I still love you, Becca."

She wondered if that was manipulation. Or if it was just truth. Had she always mistaken truth for manipulation, and manipulation for truth?

Had she thrown away the most important thing in her life because she hadn't recognized it, because she hadn't been prepared for it, because nothing in her life taught her how to understand it?

She had had set ideas on the way that men were, on the ways they treated their wives, on the way they lived their lives.

We all have prejudices, her therapist had once told her, early in their sessions. *The key is recognizing them, and going around them. Because if we don't, we never see what's in front of us.*

Becca looked at the plant-like things. She had initially seen bone because of the smell, but they weren't bone. They just looked like bone. They were harmless and old and a curiosity, but not evidence of a horrible past.

She had misunderstood. Chase had misunderstood. And the End of the World had nearly died once again.

"You really love this place, don't you?" she said to Chase.

"It's the first place I recognized Hope's potential," he said. "It just took me fifteen years to get enough money and clout to bring my dream to reality."

"And this almost ruined it. What would you have done if Mrs. Browning had been right? If this was the site of a massacre?"

He put his hardhat on, then gave her a rueful look. "She told you that? About the aliens? Is that why you asked about the walls?"

"If there are alien ghosts, then you'll have some troubles when the End of the World opens."

"If there are alien ghosts, I'll get a lot of free publicity from the *Sci-Fi Channel* and the *Travel Channel.*"

This time, she understood his tone. For all its lightness, it had some tension. He had thought about this. "It worried you, didn't it, when you dug this up?"

He nodded.

"Did you think she might be telling the truth?"

"Her version of it," he said. "Weren't you the one who told me that rumors hid real events? Maybe something bad had happened in Hope, and people made up the other story to cover it up."

"Not that anyone thought of aliens in 1908," Becca said.

He grinned, and slipped an arm around her. "Ever practical, aren't you, Becca?"

"Not ever," she said. Not during the drive from Mrs. Browning's to the coroner's office. Not when she remembered how that wall felt, squishy against her back.

"You never told me," she said. "Are you keeping the walls?"

"Why do you care?" he asked.

"They bother me," she said.

He looked at her. "You saw the alien ghosts."

She shook her head. "I didn't see anything. I just got scared as a teenager, is all."

He pulled her close. She didn't move away.

"Sometimes in old buildings," he said, "I feel like I can touch the past."

He wasn't looking at the ground any more. He was looking past the sunlight, into the desert itself.

"That's what you think that is?" Becca asked. "The past?"

"Or something," he said. "A bit of memory. A slice of time. Who knows? I always try to preserve that part of the old buildings, though."

"Why?" Becca asked.

"Because otherwise they're not worth saving. They're just wood or brick or marble. Ingredients. Buildings are living things, just like people."

She'd never heard mystical talk from him. Maybe she'd never listened.

"It's not about the money?" she asked.

"Becca, if it were about the money, I'd build cookie-cutter developments all over Hope and make millions." He shook his head. "It's about finding the surprises, whatever they might be. Good or bad."

"Or both," Becca said, moving some dirt at the edge of the hole.

"Or both," he said. "Sometimes I like both."

"Me too," she said. Then she studied him.

They were good together, but sometimes they were bad. She felt that longing for speed dial, then wondered if therapists were good and bad—good for some people, bad for others.

Maybe she should just trust herself.

She slid her hand into his.

He looked at her, surprised.

They stayed at the End of the World until the sun set—and waited for answers that might never ever come.

THEN

The train had stopped in Hope for a long time before Jess Taylor found her. Her hand had molded to the railing near the door, and she couldn't remember how to set it free.

Besides, no one had unlocked the door for her. Apparently they thought it would be funny for her to climb over the edge to get off the train.

When he saw her, stuck there, her arm ending not in a hand but in a railing that went around the back of the train, he didn't say anything. Instead, he came up beside her. He hugged her, and she leaned into him.

He'd never hugged her before.

Then he set his own arm right next to hers, placing his hand right next to the place hers should be. And he watched as she shifted, slowly —fingers were so hard—and his body shielded hers from the platform, and all those other people meeting their families.

When she finished, and her arm fell at her side—complete with perfectly formed hand—he said, very softly, "They locked you out here, huh?"

She nodded and felt tears for the second time that day.

"I'm sorry. I didn't think they'd do that to a child."

And she thought of the End of the World, and all the children—the older children who had been her friends—and how they hadn't been locked out, they'd been *killed* and he'd helped bury them to keep his job, and she wondered how he could say something like that.

But she kept quiet. She was learning it was best to keep quiet sometimes.

"From now on," he was saying softly—she almost couldn't hear him over the engine, clanging as it cooled, "everyone'll think you're my niece from Mississippi. Try to talk like I do, and don't answer a lot of questions about back home. All right?"

"All right." She already knew this anyway. He'd told her before they went to Brothers.

"If we do this right," he said, pulling her close, "no one will ever know."

She swallowed, just like he did when he was nervous. No one would ever know. About her, about her family, about her people. No one would understand that for a while, her people waited and hoped.

Maybe she'd live to see the rescue ship come.

She wondered if she would recognize it.

She wondered if she would care.

Jess Taylor took her little bag with one hand, and with the other, he took her newly made hand.

"Chin up, Sarah," he said using the name she would hear from now on. In time, it would become her, just like the two arms and two legs and the permanent form and the dark skin would become her. Her self. Her identity.

She straightened her shoulders like he had taught her. She held her head high.

And then, clinging to Jess Taylor for support, she took her final steps away from the world she'd always known.

She took her first real steps into Hope.

NEWSLETTER SIGN-UP

Be the first to know!

Please sign up for the Kristine Kathryn Rusch and Dean Wesley Smith newsletters, and receive exclusive content, keep up with the latest news, releases and so much more—even the occasional giveaway.

So, what are you waiting for?
To sign up for Kristine Kathryn Rusch's newsletter go to kristinekathrynrusch.com.
To sign up for Dean Wesley Smith's newsletter go to deanwesleysmith.com.

But wait! There's more. Sign up for the WMG Publishing newsletter, too, and get the latest news and releases from all of the WMG authors and lines, including Kristine Grayson, Kris Nelscott, Dean Wesley Smith, *Fiction River*, *Smith's Monthly*, *Pulphouse Fiction Magazine* and so much more.

To sign up go to wmgpublishing.com.

ABOUT THE AUTHOR

New York Times bestselling author Kristine Kathryn Rusch writes in almost every genre. Generally, she uses her real name (Rusch) for most of her writing. Under that name, she publishes bestselling science fiction and fantasy, award-winning mysteries, acclaimed mainstream fiction, controversial nonfiction, and the occasional romance. Her novels have made bestseller lists around the world and her short fiction has appeared in eighteen best of the year collections. She has won more than twenty-five awards for her fiction, including the Hugo, *Le Prix Imaginales*, the *Asimov's* Readers Choice award, and the *Ellery Queen Mystery Magazine* Readers Choice Award.

Publications from *The Chicago Tribune* to *Booklist* have included her Kris Nelscott mystery novels in their top-ten-best mystery novels of the year. The Nelscott books have received nominations for almost every award in the mystery field, including the best novel Edgar Award, and the Shamus Award.

She writes goofy romance novels as award-winner Kristine Grayson.

She also edits. Beginning with work at the innovative publishing company, Pulphouse, followed by her award-winning tenure at *The Magazine of Fantasy & Science Fiction*, she took fifteen years off before returning to editing with the original anthology series *Fiction River*, published by WMG Publishing. She acts as series editor with her husband, writer Dean Wesley Smith, and edits at least two anthologies in the series per year on her own.

To keep up with everything she does, go to kriswrites.com and sign up for her newsletter. To track her many pen names and series, see their individual websites (krisnelscott.com, kristinegrayson.com, retrievalartist.com, divingintothewreck.com, pulphouse.com).

kriswrites.com

ABOUT THE AUTHOR

Considered one of the most prolific writers working in modern fiction, *USA Today* bestselling writer Dean Wesley Smith published far more than a hundred novels in forty years, and hundreds of short stories across many genres.

At the moment he produces novels in several major series, including the time travel Thunder Mountain novels set in the Old West, the galaxy-spanning Seeders Universe series, the urban fantasy Ghost of a Chance series, a superhero series starring Poker Boy, and a mystery series featuring the retired detectives of the Cold Poker Gang.

His monthly magazine, *Smith's Monthly*, which consists of only his own fiction, premiered in October 2013 and offers readers more than 70,000 words per issue, including a new and original novel every month.

During his career, Dean also wrote a couple dozen *Star Trek* novels, the only two original *Men in Black* novels, Spider-Man and X-Men novels, plus novels set in gaming and television worlds. Writing with his wife Kristine Kathryn Rusch under the name Kathryn Wesley, he wrote the novel for the NBC miniseries The Tenth Kingdom and other books for *Hallmark Hall of Fame* movies.

He wrote novels under dozens of pen names in the worlds of comic books and movies, including novelizations of almost a dozen films, from *The Final Fantasy* to *Steel* to *Rundown*.

Dean also worked as a fiction editor off and on, starting at Pulphouse Publishing, then at *VB Tech Journal*, then Pocket Books, and now at WMG Publishing, where he and Kristine Kathryn Rusch serve as series editors for the acclaimed *Fiction River* anthology series.

For more information about Dean's books and ongoing projects, please visit his website at www.deanwesleysmith.com and sign up for his newsletter.

For more information:
www.deanwesleysmith.com

ALSO FROM WMG PUBLISHING

FICTION RIVER

Kristine Kathryn Rusch & Dean Wesley Smith, series
editors

Doorways to Enchantment
Edited by Dayle A. Dermatis

Stolen
Edited by Leah Cutter

Chances
Edited by Kristine Grayson

Passions
Edited by Kristine Kathryn Rusch

Broken Dreams
Edited by Kristine Kathryn Rusch

Missed a previously published volume? No problem. Buy individual
volumes anytime from your favorite bookseller.

Unnatural Worlds
Edited by Dean Wesley Smith & Kristine Kathryn Rusch

How to Save the World
Edited by John Helfers

Time Streams
Edited by Dean Wesley Smith

Christmas Ghosts
Edited by Kristine Grayson

Hex in the City
Edited by Kerrie L. Hughes

Moonscapes
Edited by Dean Wesley Smith

Special Edition: Crime
Edited by Kristine Kathryn Rusch

Fantasy Adrift
Edited by Kristine Kathryn Rusch

Universe Between
Edited by Dean Wesley Smith

Fantastic Detectives
Edited by Kristine Kathryn Rusch

Past Crime
Edited by Kristine Kathryn Rusch

Pulse Pounders
Edited by Kevin J. Anderson

Risk Takers
Edited by Dean Wesley Smith

FICTION RIVER PRESENTS

ALLYSON LONGUEIRA, SERIES EDITOR

Fiction River's line of reprint anthologies.

Fiction River has published more than 400 amazing stories by more than 100 talented authors since its inception, from *New York Times* bestsellers to debut authors. So, WMG Publishing decided to start bringing back some of the earlier stories in new compilations.

VOLUMES:
Debut Authors
The Unexpected
Darker Realms
Racing the Clock
Legacies
Readers' Choice
Writers Without Borders
Among the Stars
Sorcery & Steam
Cats!
Mysterious Women
Time Travelers

To learn more or to pick up your copy today, go to
www.FictionRiver.com.

PULPHOUSE FICTION MAGAZINE

Pulphouse Fiction Magazine, edited by Dean Wesley Smith, made its return in 2018, twenty years after its last issue. Each new issue contains about 70,000 words of short fiction. This reincarnation mixes some of the stories from the old *Pulphouse* days with brand-new fiction. The magazine has an attitude, as did the first run. No genre limitations, but high-quality writing and strangeness.

For more information or to subscribe, go to
www.pulphousemagazine.com.